D1593124

MORE HARDCORE

MORE HardCore

---

3 NOVELS

THE RIPOFF
ROUGHNECK
THE GOLDEN GIZMO

Jim Thompson

DONALD I. FINE, INC.
New York

THE
RIPOFF

I

I DIDN'T HEAR HER UNTIL SHE WAS ACTUALLY INSIDE THE ROOM, locking the door shut behind her. Because that kind of place, the better type of that kind of place—and this *was* the better type—has its taproot in quiet. Anonymity. So whatever is required for it is provided: thick walls, thick rugs, well-oiled hardware. Whatever is required, but no more. No bath, only a sink firmly anchored to the wall. No easy chairs, since you are not there to sit. No radio or television, since the most glorious of diversions is in yourself. Your two selves.

She was scowling agitatedly, literally dancing from foot to foot, as she flung off her clothes, tossing them onto the single wooden chair where mine were draped.

I laughed and sat up. "Have to pee?" I said. "Why do you always hold in until you're about to wet your pants?"

"I don't always! Just when I'm meeting you, and I don't want to take time to—*oops*! *Whoops*! Help me, darn it!" she said, trying to boost herself up on the sink. "*Hall-up!*"

I helped her, holding her on her porcelain perch until she had finished. Then I carried her to the bed, and lowered her to it. Looked wonderingly at the tiny immensity, the breathtaking miracle of her body.

She wasn't quite five feet tall. She weighed no more than ninety-five pounds, and I could almost encompass her waist with one hand. But somehow there was no skimpiness about her. Somehow her flesh flowed and curved and burgeoned. Extravagantly, deliciously lush.

"Manny," I said softly, marvelling. For as often as I had seen this miracle, it remained new to me. "Manuela Aloe."

"Present," she said. "Now, come to bed, you good-looking, darling son-of-a-bitch."

"You know something, Manny, my love? If I threw away your tits and your ass, God forbid, there wouldn't be anything left."

Her eyes flashed. Her hand darted and swung, slapping me smartly on the cheek.

"Don't you talk that way to me! Not ever!"

"What the hell?" I said. "You talk pretty rough yourself."

She didn't say anything. Simply stared at me, her eyes steady and unblinking. Telling me, without telling me, that how she talked had no bearing on how I should talk.

3

4 *Jim Thompson*

I lay down with her; kissed her, and held the kiss. And suddenly her arms tightened convulsively, and I was drawn onto and into her. And then there was a fierce muted sobbing, a delirious exulting, a frantic hysterical whispering . . .

"Oh, you dirty darling bastard! You sweet son-of-a-bitch! You dearest preciousest mother-loving sugar-pie . . ."

Manny.

Manuela Aloe.

I wondered how I could love her so deeply, and be so much afraid of her. So downright terrified.

And I damned well knew why.

After a while, and after we had rested awhile, she placed her hands against my chest and pushed me upward so that she could look into my face.

"That was good, Britt," she said. "Really wonderful. I've never enjoyed anything so much."

"Manny," I said. "You have just said the finest, the most exciting thing a woman can say to a man."

"I've never said it to anyone else. But, of course, there's never been anyone else."

"Except your husband, you mean."

"I never said it to him. You don't lie to people about things like this."

I shifted my gaze; afraid of the guilt she might read in my eyes. She laughed softly, on a submerged note of teasing.

"It bothers you, doesn't it, Britt? The fact that there was a man before you."

"Don't be silly. A girl like you would just about have to have other men in her life."

"Not *men*. Only the one man, my husband."

"Well, it doesn't bother me. He doesn't, I mean. Uh, just how did he die, anyway."

"Suddenly," she said. "Very suddenly. Let me up now, will you please?"

I helped her to use the sink, and then I used it. It couldn't have taken more than a minute or two, but when I turned around she had finished dressing. I was startled, although I shouldn't have been. She had the quick, sure movements characteristic of so many small women. Acting and reacting with lightning-like swiftness. Getting things done while I was still thinking about them.

"Running off mad?" I said; and then, comprehending, or thinking that I did, "Well, don't fall in, honey. I've got some plans for you."

She frowned at me reprovingly, and, still playing it light, I said she couldn't be going to take a bath. I'd swear she didn't need a bath; and who would know better than I?

That got me another frown, so I knocked off the kidding. "I like your dress, Manny. Paris job, is it?"

"Dallas. Nieman–Marcus."

"Tsk, tsk, such extravagance," I said. "And you were right there in Italy, anyway, to pick up your shoes."

She laughed, relenting. "Close, but no cigar," she said, pirouetting in the tiny spike-heeled pumps. "I. Pinna. You like?"

"Like. Come here, and I'll show you how much."

"Gotta go now, but just wait," she said, sliding me a sultry glance. "And leave the door unlocked. You'll have some company very soon."

I said I wondered who the company could be, and she said archly that I should just wait and see; I'd really be surprised. Then, she was gone, down the hall to the bathroom I supposed. And I stretched out on the bed, pulling the sheet up over me, and waited for her to return.

The door was not only unlocked, but ever-so-slightly ajar. But that was all right, no problem in a place like this. The lurking terror sank deeper and deeper into my mind, and disappeared. And I yawned luxuriously, and closed my eyes. Apparently, I dozed, for I suddenly sat up to glance at my wristwatch. Automatically obeying a whispered command which had penetrated my subconscious. *"Watch."*

I said I sat up.

That's wrong.

I only started to, had barely lifted my head from the pillows, when there was a short snarling-growl. A threat and a warning, as unmistakable as it was deadly. And slowly, ever so slowly, I sank back on the bed.

There was a softer growl, a kind of gruff whimper. Approval. I lay perfectly still for a time, scarcely breathing—and it is easy to stop breathing when one is scared stiff. Then, without moving my head, I slanted my eyes to the side. Directly into the unblinking stare of a huge German shepherd.

His massive snout was only inches from my face. The grayish-black lips were curled back from his teeth. And I remember thinking peevishly that he had too many, that no dog could possibly have this many teeth. Our eyes met and held for a moment. But dogs, members of the wolf family, regard such an encounter as a challenge. And a rising growl jerked my gaze back to the ceiling.

There was that gruff whimper again. Approval. Then, nothing.

Nothing but the wild beating of my heart. That, and the dog's warm breath on my face as he stood poised so close to me. Ready to move—decisively—if I should move.

"Watch!" He had been given an order. And until that order was revoked, he would stay where he was. Which would force me to stay where I was . . . lying very, very still. As, of course, I would not be able to do much longer.

Any moment now, I would start yawning. Accumulated tension would force me to. At almost any moment, my legs would jerk; an involuntary and uncontrollable reaction to prolonged inactivity. And when that happened . . .

The dog growled again. Differently from any of his previous growls. With the sound was another, the brief thud-thud of a tail against the carpet.

A friend—or perhaps an acquaintance—had come into the room. I was afraid to move my head, as the intruder was obviously aware, so she came around to the foot of the bed where I could see her without moving.

It was the mulatto slattern who sat behind the desk in the dimly lit lobby. The manager of the place, I had always assumed. The mock concern on her face didn't quite conceal her malicious grin; and there was spiteful laughter in her normally servile voice.

"Well, jus' looky heah, now! Mistah Britton Rainstar with a doggy in his room! How you doin', Mistah High-an'-mighty Rainstar?"

"G-Goddam you—!" I choked with fear and fury. "Get that dog out of here! Call him off!"

She said, Shuh, man. She wasn't tellin' *that* dog to do nothin'. "Ain't my houn'. Wouldn't pay no attention to me, 'ceptin' maybe to bite my fat ass."

"But goddam it—! I'm sorry," I said. "Please forgive me for being rude. If you'll get Manny—Miss Aloe, please. Tell her I'm very sorry, and I'm sure I can straighten everything out if she'll just—just—"

She broke in with another *"Shuh"* of disdain. "Where I get Miss Manny, anyways? Ain't seen Miss Manny since you-all come in t'day."

"I think she's in the bathroom, the one on this floor. She's got to be here somewhere. Now, please—!"

"Huh—*uh*! Sure ain't callin' her out of no bathroom. Not me, no, sir! Miss Manny wouldn't like that a-tall!"

"B—but—" I hesitated helplessly. "Call the police then. *Please!* And for God's sake, hurry!"

"Call the p'lice? *Here?* Not a chance, Mistah Rainstar. No, siree! Miss Manny sho' wouldn't like that!"

"To hell with what she likes! What's it to you, anyway? Why, goddam it to hell—"

"Jus' plenty t'me what she likes. Miss Manny my boss. That's right, Mistah Rainstar." She beamed at me falsely. "Miss Manny bought this place right after you-all started comin' here. Reckon she liked it real well."

She was lying. She had to be lying.

She wasn't lying.

She laughed softly, and turned to go. "You lookin' kinda peak-id, Mistah Rainstar. Reckon I better let you get some rest."

"Don't," I begged. "Don't do this to me. If you can't do anything else, at least stay with me. I can't move, and I can't lie still any longer, and—and that dog will kill me! He's trained to kill! S—So—so—please—" I gulped, swallowing an incipient sob, blinking the tears from my eyes. "Stay with me. Please stay until Miss Manny comes back."

My eyes cleared.

The woman was gone. Moved out of my line of vision. I started to turn my head, and the dog warned me to desist. Then, from somewhere near the door, the woman spoke again.

"Just stay until Miss Manny come back? That's what you said, Mistah Rainstar?"

"Yes, please. Just until then."

"But what if she don' come back? What about that, Mistah Rainstar?"

An ugly laugh, then. A laugh of mean merriment. And then she was gone. Closing the door firmly this time.

And locking it.

II

THE TERROR HAD BEGUN THREE MONTHS BEFORE.

It began at three o'clock in the morning with Mrs. Olmstead shaking me into wakefulness.

Mrs. Olmstead is my housekeeper, insofar as I have one. An old age pensioner, she occupies a downstairs bedroom in what, in better times, was called the Rainstar mansion. She does little else but occupy it, very little in the way of housekeeping. But, fortunately, I require little, and necessarily pay little. So one hand washes the other.

She wasn't a very bright woman at best, and she was far from her best at three in the morning. But I gathered from her gabbling and gesturing that there was an emergency somewhere below, so I pulled on some clothes over my pajamas and hurried downstairs.

A Mr. Jason was waiting for me, a stout apoplectic-looking man who was dressed pretty much as I was. He snapped out that he just couldn't have this sort of thing, y'know. It was a god damn imposition, and I had a hell of a lot of guts giving out his phone number. And so forth and so on.

"Now, look," I said, finally managing to break in on him. "Listen to me. I didn't give out your number to anyone. I don't know what the hell it is, for Christ's sake, and I don't want to know. And I don't know what you're talking about."

"Yeah? Y'don't, huh?" He seemed somewhat mollified. "Well. Better hurry up. Fellow said it was an emergency; matter of life and death."

He lived in an elaborate summer home about three miles from mine, in an area that was still very good. He stopped his car under the porte cochere, and preceded me into the entrance hall; then withdrew a few feet while I picked up the telephone.

I couldn't think who would be making a call to me under such circumstances. There just *wasn't* anyone. No one at the Foundation would do it. Except for the check which they sent me monthly, I had virtually no contact with the Hemisphere Foundation. As for Constance, my wife, now a resident, an apparently permanent one, at her father's home in the Midwest . . .

Constance had no reason to call. Except for being maimed and crippled, Constance was in quite good health. She would doubtless die in bed— thirty or forty years from now—sweetly smiling her forgiveness for the accident I had caused.

8

So she would not call, and her father would not. Conversation with me was something he did his best to avoid. Oh, he had been scrupulously fair, far more than I would have been in his place. He had publicly exonerated me of blame, stoutly maintaining to the authorities that there was no real evidence pointing to my culpability. But without saying so, he had let me know that he would be just as happy without my company or conversation.

So . . . ?

"Yes?" I spoke into the phone. "Britton Rainstar, here."

"Rainstar"—a husky semi-whisper, a disguised voice. "Get this, you deadbeat fuck-off. Pay up or you'll die cryin'. Pay up or else."

"Huh! Wh−aat?" I almost dropped the phone. "What—Who is this?"

"I kid you not, Rainstar. Decorate the deck, or you'll be trailing turds from here to Texas."

I was still sputtering when the wire went dead.

Jason glanced at me, and looked away. "Bet you could use a drink. Always helps at a time like this."

"Thanks, but I guess not," I said. "If you'll be kind enough to drive me home . . . "

He did so, mumbling vague words of sympathy (for just what, he didn't know). At my house, with its crumbling veranda and untended lawn, he pressed a fifty dollar bill into my hand.

"Get your phone reconnected, okay? No, I insist! And I'm sorry things are so bad for you. Damned shame."

I thanked him humbly, assuring him that I would do as he said.

By the time Mrs. Olmstead arose and began preparing breakfast, I had had two more callers, both crankily sympathetic as, like Jason, they brought word of a dire emergency.

I went with them, of course. How could I refuse? Or explain? And what if there actually *was* an emergency? There was always a chance, a million-to-one chance, that my caller might have a message of compelling importance. So it was simply impossible—impossible for me, at least—to ignore the summons.

The result was the same each time. An abusive demand to pay up or to suffer the ugly consequences.

I accepted some weak, lukewarm coffee from Mrs. Olmstead; I even ate a piece of her incredible toast and a bite or two of the scrambled eggs she prepared, which, preposterous as it seems, were half-raw but over-cooked.

Ignoring Mrs. Olmstead's inquiries about my "emergency" calls, I went up to my room and surrendered to a few hours of troubled rest. I came back downstairs shortly after noon, advised Mrs. Olmstead that I would fix my own lunch and that she should do as she pleased. She trudged down the road to the bus stop, going I knew not where nor cared. I cleaned myself up and dressed, not knowing what I was going to do either. And not caring much.

From the not too distant distance came a steady rumbling and clattering and rattling; the to-and-fro passage of an almost unbroken parade of trucks. Through the many gabled windows, their shutters opened to the spring breeze, came the sickly-pungent perfume of what the trucks were carrying.

I laughed. Softly, sadly, wonderingly. I jumped up, slamming a fist into my palm. I sat back down, and got up again. Aimlessly left the room to wander aimlessly through the house. Through the library with its threadbare carpet, and its long virtually empty bookshelves. Through the lofty drawing room, its faded tapestry peeling in tatters from the walls. The grand ballroom, its parquet floor inclining imperceptibly but ominously with the vast weight of its rust-ruined pipe organ.

I came out onto the rear veranda, where glass from shattered windows splattered over the few unsaleable items of furniture that remained. Expensively stained glass, bright with color.

I stood looking off into that previously mentioned not-too-distant distance. It was coming closer; it had come quite a bit closer since yesterday, it seemed to me. And why not, anyway, as rapidly as those trucks were dumping their burden?

At present, I was merely—*merely!*—in the environs of a garbage dump. But soon it would be right up to my back door. Soon, I would be right in the middle of the stinking, rat-infested horror.

And maybe that was as it should be, hmm? What better place for the unwanted, unneeded and worthless?

Jesus! I closed my eyes, shivering.

I went back through the house, and up to my bedroom. I glanced at myself in a floor-length mirror, and I doubt that I looked as bad as my warped and splotched reflection. But still I cursed and groaned out loud.

I flung off my clothes, and showered vigorously. I shaved again, doing it right instead of half-assed. And then I began rummaging through my closets, digging far back in them and uncovering items that I had forgotten.

An hour later, after some work with Mrs. Olmstead's steam iron, some shoe polish and a buffing brush, I again looked at myself. And warped as it was, the mirror told me my efforts were well-spent indeed!.

The handmade shoes were eternally new, ever-magnificent despite their chronological age. The cambric shirt from Sulka, and the watered-silk Countess Mara tie, *were* new—long-ago Christmas presents which I had only glanced at, and returned to their gift box. And a decade had been wonderfully kind to the Bond Street suit, swinging full circle through fads and freakishness, and bringing it back in style again.

I frowned, studying my hair.

The shagginess was not too bad, not unacceptable, but a trim was certainly in order. The gray temples, and the gray streak down the center, were also okay, a distinguished contrast for the jet blackness. However, that yellowish tinge which gray hair shittily acquires, was *not* all right. I needed to see a truly good hair man, a stylist, not the barber-college cruds that I customarily went to.

I examined my wallet—twelve dollars plus the fifty Jason had given me. So I *could* properly finish the job I had started, hair and all. And the wonders it would do for my frazzled morale to look decent again, the way Britton Rainstar had to look . . . having so little else but looks.

But if I did that, if I didn't make at least a token payment to Amicable Finance—!

The phone rang. It had not been disconnected, as Jason had assumed. Calling me at other numbers was simply part of the "treatment."

I picked up the phone, and identified myself.

A cheery man's voice said that he was Mr. Bradley, Amicable comptroller. "You have quite a large balance with us, Mr. Rainstar. I assume you'll be dropping in today to settle up?"

I started to say that I was sorry, that I simply couldn't pay the entire amount, as much as I desired to. *"But I'll pay something; that's a promise, Mr. Bradley. And I'll have the rest within a week—I swear I will! J—just don't do anything. D—don't hurt me. Please, Mr. Bradley."*

"Yes, Mr. Rainstar? What time can I expect you in today?"

"You can't," I said.

"How's that?" His voice cracked like a whip.

"Not today or any other day. You took my car. I repaid your loan in full, and you still took my car. Now—"

"Late charges, Rainstar. Interest penalties. Repossession costs. Nothing more than your contract called for."

I told him he could go fuck what the contract called for. He could blow it out his ass. "And if you bastards pull any more crap on me, any more of this calling me to the phone in the middle of the night . . . "

"Call you to the phone?" *He was laughing at me.* "Fake emergency calls? What makes you think we were responsible?"

I told him why I thought it; why I knew it. Because only Amicable Finance was lousy enough to pull such tricks. Others might screw their own mothers with syphilitic cocks, or pimp their sisters at a nickel a throw. But they weren't up to Amicable's stunts.

"So here's some advice for you, you liver-lipped asshole! You fuck with me any more, and it'll be shit in the fan! Before I'm through with you, you'll think lightning struck a crapper ... !"

I continued a minute or two longer, growing more elaborate in my cursing. And not surprisingly, I had quite a vocabulary of curses. Nothing is sacred to children, just as anything unusual is an affront to them, a challenge which cannot be ignored. And when you have a name like Britton Rainstar, you are accepted only after much fighting and cursing.

I slammed up the phone. Frightened stiff by what I had done, yet somehow pleased with myself. I had struck back for a change. For once, in a very long time, I had faced up to the ominous instead of ignoring or running from it.

I fixed the one drink I had in the house, a large drink of vodka. Sipping it, feeling the dullness go out of my heart, I decided that I *would* by God get the needful done with my hair. I would look like a man, by God, not the Jolly Green Giant, when Amicable Finance started giving me hell.

Before I could weaken and change my mind, I made an appointment with a hair stylist. Then, I finished my drink, dragging it out as long as I could, and stood up.

And the phone rang.

I almost didn't answer it; certain that it would get me nothing but a bad time. But few men are strong enough to ignore a ringing telephone, and I am not one of them.

A booming, infectiously good-natured voice blasted into my ear.

"Mr. Rainstar, Britt? How the hell are you, kid?"

I said I was fine, and how the hell was he? He said he was just as fine as I was, laughing uproariously. And I found myself smiling in spite of myself.

"This is Pat Aloe, Britt. Patrick Xavier Aloe, if you're going to be fussy." Another roar of laughter. "Look, kid. I'd come out there, but I'm tied up tighter than a popcorn fart. So's how about you dropping by my office in about an hour? Well, two hours, then."

"But—well, why?" I said. "Why do you want to see me, Mr. uh, Pat?"

"Because I owe you, Britt, baby. Want to make it up to you for those pissants at Amicable. Don't know what's the matter with the stupid bastards, anyway."

"But ... Amicable?" I hesitated. "You have something to do with them?"

A final roar of laughter. Apparently, I had said something hilariously funny. Then, good humor flooding his voice, he declared that he not only wanted to see me, but I also wanted to see him, even though I didn't know it yet. Thus, the vote for seeing each other was practically unanimous, by his account.

"So how about it, Britt, baby? See you in a couple of hours, okay?"

"Who am I to buck a majority vote?" I said. "I'll see you, Pat, uh, baby."

III

I GOT OUT TO THE CAB AT A DOWNTOWN OFFICE BUILDING. I entered its travertine—marble lobby, and studied the large office directory affixed to one wall. It was glassed-in, a long oblong of white plastic lettering against a black-felt background. The top line read:

PXA HOLDING CORPORATION

Beneath it, in substantially smaller letters, were the names of sixteen companies, including that of Amicable Finance. The final listing, in small red letters, read:

P. X. ALOE
— — P. H.
M. FRANCESCA ALOE

'allo, Aloe, I thought, stepping into the elevator. Patrick Xavier and M. Francesa, and Britt, baby, makes three. Or something. But whereof and why, for God's sake?

I punched the button marked P.H., and was zoomed forty floors upward to the penthouse floor. As I debarked into its richly furnished reception area, a muscular young man with gleaming black hair stepped in front of me. He looked sharply into my face, then smiled and stepped back.

"How are you, Mr. Rainstar? Nice day."

"How are you?" I said, for I am nothing if not polite. "A nice day so far, at least."

A truly beautiful, beautifully dressed woman came forward, and urgently squeezed my hand.

"Such a pleasure to meet you, Mr. Rainstar! Do come with me, please."

I followed her across a hundred feet or so of carpet (a foot deep, or so) to an unmarked door. She started to knock, then jerked her hand back. Turned to me still smiling, but rather whitishly.

"If you'll wait just a moment, please . . . "

She started to shoo me away, then froze at the sound from within the room. A sound that could only be made by a palm swung against a face. Swung hard, again, again. Like the stuttering, staccato crackling of an automatic rifle.

It went on for all of a minute, a very long time to get slapped. Abruptly, as though a gag had been removed, a woman screamed.

"N—No! D—don't, please! I'll never do—!"

The scream ended with the suddenness of its beginning. The slapping also. The beautiful, beautifully dressed young woman waited about ten seconds. (I counted them off silently.) Then, she knocked on the door and ushered me inside.

"Miss Manuela Aloe," she said. "Mr. Britton Rainstar."

A young woman came toward me smiling; rubbing her hand, her *right* hand, against her dress before extending it to me. "Thank you, Sydney," she said, dismissing the receptionist with a nod. "Mr. Rainstar, let's just sit here on the lounge."

We sat down on the long velour lounge. She crossed one leg over the other, rested an elbow on her knee, and looked at me smiling, her chin propped in the palm of her hand. I looked at her—the silver-blonde hair, the startlingly black eyes and lashes, the flawlessly creamy complexion. I looked and found it impossible to believe that such a delicious bon bon of a girl would do harm to anyone.

Couldn't I have heard a recording? And if there had been another woman, where was she? The only door in the room was the one I had entered by, and no one had passed me on the way out.

"You look just like him," Manuela was saying. "We-ell, almost just. You don't have your hair in braids."

I said, What? And then I said, Oh, for several questions in my mind had been answered. "You mean Chief Britton Rainstar," I said. "The Remington portrait of him in the Metropolitan."

She said, No, she'd missed that one, darn it. "I was talking about the one in the Royal Museum by James McNeill Whistler. But tell me. Isn't Britton a kind of funny name for an Indian chief?"

"Hilarious," I said. "I guess we got it from the nutty whites the Rainstars intermarried with, early and often. Now, if you want a real honest to Hannah, jumpin' by Jesus Indian name—well, how does George strike you?"

"George?" she laughed. "*George?*"

"George Creekmore. Inventor of the Cherokee alphabet, and publisher of the first newspaper west of the Mississippi."

"And I guess that'll teach me," she smiled, coloring slightly. "But, anyway, you certainly bear a strong resemblance to the Chief. Of course,

I'd heard that all the Rainstar men did, but—"

"We're hard to tell apart," I agreed. "The only significant difference is in the pockets of later generations."

"The pockets?"

"They're empty," I said, and tapped myself on the chest. "Meet Lo, the poor Indian."

"Hi, Lo," she said, laughing. And I said, Hi, and then we were silent for a time.

But it was not an uncomfortable silence. We smiled and looked at each other without self-consciousness, both of us liking what we saw. When she spoke it was to ask more questions about the Rainstar family; and while I didn't mind talking about it, having little else to be proud of, there were things I wanted to know, too. So, after rambling on awhile, I got down to them.

"Like when and why the heck," I said, "am I seeing P. X. Aloe?"

"I don't think you'll be able to see Uncle Pat today," she said. "Some last minute business came up. But there's nothing sinister afoot"—she gave me a reassuring little pat on the arm. "Now, unless you're in a hurry . . . "

"Well, I *am* due in Washington to address the cabinet," I said. "I thought it was already addressed, but I guess some one left off the zone number."

"You dear!" she laughed delightedly. "You absolute dear! Let's go have some drinks and dinner, and talk and talk and talk. . . ."

She got her hat and purse from a mahogany cabinet. The hat was a sailor with a turned-up brim, and she cocked it over one eye, giving me an impish look. Then, she grinned and righted it, and the last faint traces of apprehension washed out of my mind.

Give another woman a vicious slapping? This darling, diminutive child? Rainstar, you are nuts!

We took the elevator down to PXA's executive dining room, in a sub-basement of the building. A smiling maitre d', with a large menu under his arm, came out of the shadows and bowed to us graciously.

"A pleasure to see you, Miss Aloe. And you, too, sir, needless to say."

"Not at all," I said. "*My* pleasure."

He looked at me a little startled. I am inclined to gag it up and talk too much when I am uneasy or unsure of myself, which means that I am almost always gagging it up and talking too much.

"This is Mr. Britton Rainstar, Albert (Albehr)," Manuela Aloe said. "I hope you'll be seeing him often."

"My own hope. Will you have a drink at the bar, while your table is being readied?"

She said we would, and we did. In fact, we had a couple, since the night employees were just arriving at this early hour, and there was some delay in preparing our table.

"Very nice," I said, taking an icy sip of martini. "A very nice place, Miss Aloe. Or is it Mrs.?"

She said it was Miss—she had taken her own name after her husband died—and I could call her Manny if I liked. "But yes"—she glanced around casually. "It is nice, isn't it? Not that it shouldn't be, considering."

"Uh-huh," I said. "Or should I say ah-ha? I'm afraid I'm going to have to rush right off to Geneva, Manny."

"Wha—aat?"

"Just as soon as I pay for these drinks. Unless you insist on going dutch on them."

"Silly!" She wriggled deliciously. "You're with me, and everything's complimentary."

"But you said considering," I pointed out. "A word hinting at the dread unknown, in my case at least. To wit, money."

"Oh, well," she shrugged, dismissing the subject. "Money isn't everything."

IV

WITH AN OPERATION AS LARGE AND MULTIFACETED AS PXA, one with so many employees and interests, it was impossible to maintain supervision and surveillance in every place it might be required. It would have been impossible, even if PXA's activities were all utterly legitimate instead of borderline, with personnel which figuratively cried out to be spied upon. Pat Aloe had handed the problem to his niece Manny, a graduate student in psychology. After months of consultation with behaviorists and recording experts, she had come up with the bugging system used throughout the PXA complex.

It was activated by *tones*, and was uncannily accurate in deciding when a person's voice tone was not what it should be. Thus, Bradley, the man who had called me this morning, had been revealed as a "switcher," one who diverted business to competitors. So all of his calls were completely recorded, instead of receiving a sporadic spot check.

"I see," I nodded to Manny, as we dawdled over coffee and liqueurs, "about as clearly as I see through mud. Everything is completely opaque to me."

"Oh, now, why do you say that?" she said. "I'd seen that portrait when I was a little girl, and I'd never gotten it out of my mind. So when I found out that the last of the Rainstars was right here in town . . . !"

"Recalling part of the conversation," I said, "you must have felt that the last of the Rainstars needed his mouth washed out with soap."

She laughed and said, Nope, cursing out Bradley had been a plus. "That was just about the clincher for you with Pat. Someone of impeccable background and breeding, who could still get tough if he had to."

"Manny," I said, "exactly what is this all about, anyway? Why PXA's interest in me?"

"Well . . . "

"Before you answer, maybe I'd better set you straight on something. I've never been mixed up in anything shady, and PXA seems to be mixed up in nothing else but. Oh, I know you're not doing anything illegal, nothing you can go to prison for. But, still, well—"

"PXA is right out in the open," Manny said firmly. "Anyone that wants to try, can take a crack at us. We don't rewrite any laws, and we don't ask any to be written for us. We don't own any big politicians. I'd say that for every dollar we make with our so-called shady operations, there's a thousand being stolen by some highly respectable cartel."

"Well," I nodded uncomfortably, "there's no disputing that, of course. But I don't feel that one wrong justifies another, if you'll pardon an unpardonable cliché."

"Pardoned"—she grinned at me openly. "We don't try to justify it. No justifications, no apologies."

"And this bugging business." I shook my head. "It seems like something right out of *Nineteen Eighty-four*. It's sneaky and Big Brotherish, and it scares the hell out of me."

Manny shrugged, remarking that it was probably everything I said. But bugging wasn't an invention of PXA, and it didn't and wouldn't affect me. "We're on your side, Britt. We're against the people who've been against your people."

"My people?" I said, and I grimaced a little wryly. "I doubt that any of us can be bracketed so neatly any more. We may be more of one race than we are another, but I suspect we're all a little of everything. White, yellow, black and red."

"Oh, well"—she glanced at her wristwatch. "You're saying that there are no minorities?"

I said that I wasn't sure what I was saying, or, rather, what the point to it was. "But I don't believe that a man who's being pushed around has a right to push anyone but the person pushing him . . . if you can untangle that. His license to push is particular, not general. If he starts lashing out at everyone and anyone, he's asking for it and he ought to get it."

It was all very high-sounding and noble, and it also had the virtue, fortunately or otherwise, of being what I believed. What I had been bred to believe. And now I was sorry I had said it. For I seemed to be hopelessly out of step with the only world I had, and again I was about to be left alone and afraid in that world, which I had had no hand in making. This lovely child, Manny, the one person to be kind to me or show interest in me for so very long, was getting ready to leave.

She was looking at me, brows raised quizzically. She was patting her mouth with her napkin, then crumpling it to the table. She was glancing at herself in the mirror in her purse. Then, snapping the purse shut, and starting to rise.

And then, praise be, glory to the Great Mixedblood Father, she sat back down.

"All right," she said crisply. "Let's say that PXA is interested in using the Rainstar name. Let's say that. It would be pretty stupid of us to dirty up that name, now, wouldn't it?"

"Well, yes, I suppose it would," I said. "And look. I'm sorry if I said anything to offend you. I always kid around and talk a lot whenever I'm—"

"Forget it. How old are you?"

"Thirty-six."

"You're forty. Or so you stated on your loan-application blank. What do you do for a living, if you can call it that?"

I said, why ask me something she already knew? "That information's also on the application. Along with practically everything else about me, except the number and location of my dimples."

"You mean you have some I can't see?" She smiled, her voice friendlier, almost tender. "But what I meant to ask was, what do you write for this Hemisphere Foundation?"

"Studies. In-depth monographs on this region from various aspects: ecological, etiological, ethological, ethnological. That sort of thing. Sometimes one of them is published in Hemisphere's *Quarterly Reports*. But they usually go in the file-and-forget department."

"Mmm-hmm," she said thoughtfully, musingly. "Very interesting. I think something could be worked out there. Something satisfactory to both of us."

"If you could tell me just what you have in mind . . . "

"Well, I'll have to clear it with Pat, of course, but . . . Thirty-five thousand a year?"

"That's not what I meant. I—*What*?" I gasped. "Did you say *thirty-five thousand*?"

"Plus expenses, and certain fringe benefits."

"Thirty-five thousand," I said, running a finger around my collar. "Uh, how much change do you want back?"

She threw back her head and laughed, hugging herself ecstatically. "Ah, Britt, Britt," she said, brushing mirth tears from her eyes. "Everything's going to be wonderful for you. I'll make it wonderful, you funny-sweet man. Now, do me a small favor, hmm?"

"Practically anything," I said, "if you'll laugh like that again."

"Please don't worry about silly things, like our bugging system. Everyone knows we have it. We're out in the open on that as we are with everything else. If someone thinks he can beat it, well, it isn't as if he hadn't been warned, is it?"

"I see what you mean," I said, although I actually didn't. I was just being agreeable. "What happens when someone is caught pulling a fast one?"

"Well, naturally," she said, "we have to remove him from the payroll."

"I see," I said again. Lying again when I said it. Because, of course, there are many ways to remove a man from the payroll. (Horizontal was one that occurred to me.) My immediate concern, however, as it so often is, was me. Specifically the details of my employment. But I was not allowed to inquire into them.

Before I could frame another question, she had moved with a kind of unhurried haste, with the quick little movements which typified her. Rising from her chair, tucking her purse under her arm, gesturing me back when I also started to rise; all in one swift-smooth uninterrupted action.

"Stay where you are, Britt," she smiled. "Have a drink or something. I'll have someone pick you up and drive you home."

"Well . . . " I settled back into my chair. "Shall I call you tomorrow?"

"I'll call you. Pat or I will. Good-night, now."

She left the table, her tinily full figure with its crown of thick blonde hair quickly losing itself in the dining room's dimness.

I waited. I had another liqueur and more coffee. And continued to wait. An hour passed. A waiter brushed by the table, and when he had gone, I saw a check lying in front of me.

I picked it up, a nervous lump clotting in my stomach. My eyes blurred, and I rubbed them, at last managing to read the total.

Sixty-three dollars and thirty cents.

Sixty-three dollars and—!

I don't know how you are in such situations, but I always feel guilty. The mere need to explain, that such and such is a mistake, et cetera, stiffens my smile exaggeratedly and sets me to sweating profusely, and causes my voice to go tremulous and shaky. So that I not only feel guilty as hell, but also look it.

It is really pretty terrible.

It is no wonder that I was suspected of the attempted murder of my wife. The wonder is that I wasn't lynched.

Albert, the maitre d', approached. As I always do, I over-explained, apologizing when I should have demanded apologies. Sweating and shaking and squeakily stammering, and acting like nine kinds of a damned fool.

When I was completely self-demolished, Albert cut me off with a knifing gesture of his hand.

"No," he said coldly, "Miss Aloe did not introduce you to me. If she had, I would have remembered it." And he said, "No, she made no arrangement about the check. Obviously, the check is to be paid by you."

Then, he leaned down and forward, resting his hands on the table, so that his face was only inches from mine. And I remember thinking that I had known this was going to happen, not exactly this, perhaps, but something that would clearly expose the vicious potential of PXA. A taste of what could happen if I incurred the Aloe displeasure.

For she had said—remember?—that they did not pretend or apologize. You were warned, you knew exactly what to expect *if*.

"You deadbeat bastard," Albert said. "Pay your check or we'll drag you back in the kitchen, and beat the shit out of you."

V

I WAS ON AN AIMLESS TOUR OF THE COUNTRY WHEN I MET MY WIFE-TO-BE, Connie. I'd gotten together some money through borrowing and peddling the few remaining Rainstar valuables, so I'd bought a car and taken off. No particular, no clear objective in mind. I simply didn't like it where I was, and I wanted to find a place where I would like it. Which, of course was impossible. Because the reason I disliked places I was in—and the disheartening knowledge was growing on me—was my being in them. I disliked *me*, me, myself and I, as kids used to say, and far and fast as I ran I could not escape the bastardly trio.

Late one afternoon, I strayed off the highway and wound up in a homey little town, nestled among rolling green hills. I also wound up with a broken spring, from a plunge into a deep rut, and a broken cylinder and corollary damage from getting out of the rut.

The town's only garage was the blacksmith shop. Or, to put it another way, the blacksmith did auto repairs . . . except for those who could drive a hundred-plus miles to the nearest city. The blacksmith-mechanic quoted a very reasonable price for repairing my car, but he would have to send away for parts, and what with one thing and another, he couldn't promise to have the work done in less than a week.

There was one small restaurant in the town, sharing space with the post office. But there was no hotel, motel or boarding house. The blacksmith-mechanic suggested that I check with the real estate dealer to see if some private family would take me in for a few days. Without much hope, I did so.

The sign on the window read LUTHER BANNERMAN—REAL ESTATE & INSURANCE. Inside, a young woman was disinterestedly pecking away at an ancient typewriter with a three-row keyboard. She was a little on the scrawny side, with mouse-colored hair. But she laughed wildly when I asked if she was Luther Bannerman, and otherwise endeared herself to me by childish eagerness to be of help, smiling and bobbing her head sympathetically as I explained my situation. When I had finished, however, she seemed to draw back a bit, becoming cautiously reserved.

"Well, I just don't know, Mr. . . . . Britton, is it?"

"Rainstar. Britt, for Britton, Rainstar."

"I was going to say, Mr.—oh, I'll make it Britt, okay? I was just going to say, Britt. We're kind of out of the mainstream here, and and I'm afraid you'd find it hard to keep in touch and carry on your business affairs, and"—she bared her teeth in a smile—"and so forth and so on."

I explained that I had no pressing business affairs, not a single so forth let alone a so on. I was just travelling, seeing the country and gathering material for a book. I also explained, when she raised the question of accommodations for my wife and family, that I had none with me or elsewhere and that my needs were solely for myself.

At this, she insisted on pouring me coffee from the pot on a one-burner heater. Then, having made me "comfy"—also nauseous: the coffee was lousy—she hurried back to a small partitioned-off private office. After several minutes of closed-door conversation, she returned with her father, Luther Bannerman.

Of course, he and she collectively insisted that I stay at their house. (It would be no trouble at all, but I could pay a little something if I wanted to.)

Of course, I accepted their invitation. And, of course, I was in her pants the very first night. Or, rather, I was in what was in her pants. Or, to be absolutely accurate, she was in my pants. She charged into my room as soon as the light went out. And I did not resist her, despite her considerable resistibility.

I felt that it was the very least I could do for her, although quite a few others had obviously done as much. I doubt that they had fought for it either, since it simply wasn't the sort of thing for which men do battle. Frankly, if it had been tendered as inspiration for the launching of a thousand ships (or even a toy canoe), not a one would have hoisted anchor.

Ah, well. Who am I to kid around about poor Connie and her over-stretched snatch? Or to kid about anyone, for that matter. It is one of fate's saddest pranks to imbue the least sexually appetizing of us with the hugest sexual appetites. To atone for that joke, I feel, is the obligation of all who are better endowed. And in keeping that obligation, I have had many sorrier screws than Connie. I have received little gratitude for my efforts. On the contrary, I invariably wind up with a worse fucking than the fucking I got. For it is also one of fate's jokes to dower superiority complexes on girls with the worst fornicating furniture. And they seem to feel justified in figuratively giving you something as bad as they have given you literally.

Of course, Connie's father discovered us in coitus before the week was out. And, of course, I agreed to do the "right thing" by his little girl. Which characteristically was the easiest thing for me to do. Or so it seemed at the time. I may struggle a little bit, but I almost always do the easiest thing. Or what seems to be and never is.

At the time I was born, promising was the word for Rainstar prospects. Thus, I was placed on the path of least resistance early in life, and I remained on it despite my growing awareness that promise was not synonymous with delivery. I had gathered too much speed to get off, and I could find no better path to be on anyway. I'm sure you've seen people like me.

If I stumbled over an occasional rock, I might curse and kick out at it. But only briefly, and not very often at all. I was so unused to having my course unimpeded, that, normally, I figuratively fell apart when it was. It was the only recourse for a man made defenseless by breeding and habit.

Both Connie and her father were provoked to find that my prosperousness was exactly one hundred per cent more apparent than real. They whined that I had deceived them, maintaining that since I was nothing but a well-dressed personable bum, I should have said so. Which, to me, seemed unreasonable. After all, why do your utmost *not* to look like a bum if you are going to announce that you are one?

Obviously, there were basic philosophical differences between me and the Bannermans. But they finally seemed resigned to me, if not to my way of thinking. In fact, I was given their rather grim assurance that I would come around to their viewpoint eventually, and be much the better man for it. Meanwhile, Mr. Bannerman would not only provide me with a job, but would give Connie and me $100,000 life insurance policies as a wedding present.

I felt that it was money wasted, since Connie, like all noxious growths, had a built-in resistance to scourge, and I had grown skilled in the art of self-preservation, having devoted a lifetime to it. However, it was Mr. Bannerman's money, and I doubted that it would amount to much, since he was in the insurance business as well as real estate.

So he wrote the policies on Connie and me, with each of us the beneficiary of the other. Connie's policy was approved. Mine was rejected. Not on grounds of health, my father-in-law advised me. My health was excellent for a man wholly unaddicted to healthful hard work.

The reason for my rejection was not spelled out to Mr. Bannerman, but he had a pretty good idea as to its nature, and so did I. It was a matter of character. A man with a decidedly truncated work history—me, that is—who played around whenever he had the money for playing around—again me—was apt to come to an early end, and possibly a bad one. Or so statistics indicated. And the insurance company was not betting a potential $100,000—200,000, double indemnity—on my longevity when their own statistics branded me a no-no.

With unusual generosity, Mr. Bannerman conceded that there were probably a great many decadent bums in the world, and that I was no worse than the worst of them. The best course for me was to re-apply for the policy, after I had "proved myself" with a few years of steady and diligent employment.

To this end, he hired me as a commission salesman. It proved nothing except what I already knew—that I was no more qualified to sell than I apparently was for any other gainful occupation.

I continued to be nagged by Papa and Daughter Bannerman, but I was given up on after a few weeks. Grimly allowed to "play around" with my typewriter while they—"other people"—*worked* for a living. Neither would hear of a divorce, or the suggestion that I get the hell out of their lives. I was to "come to my senses" and "be a man"—or do *something!* Surely, I could do *something!*

Well, though, the fact was that I couldn't do something. The something that I could do did not count as something with them. And they were keeping the score.

Thus matters stood at the time of the accident which left me unscathed but almost killed Connie. I, an unemployed bum living on my father-in-law's bounty, was driving the car when the accident happened. And while I carried no insurance, my wife was heavily insured in my favor.

"Dig this character." Albert, the maitre d', jerked a thumb at me, addressing the circle of onlooking diners. *"These bums are getting fancier every day, but this one takes the brass ring. What did you say your name was, bum?"*

"Rainstar." A reassuring hand dropped on my shoulder. *"He said it was, and I say it is. Any other questions?"*

"Oh, well, certainly not, sir! A stupid mistake on my part, sir, and I'm sure that—"

"Come on, Britt. Let's get out of here."

VI

WE STOOD WAITING FOR THE ELEVATOR, Albert and I and my friend, whoever he was. Albert was begging, seemingly almost on the point of tears.

" . . . a terrible mistake, believe me, gentlemen! I can't think how I could have been guilty of it. I recall Mr. Rainstar perfectly now. Everything was exactly as he says, but—"

"But it slipped your mind. You completely forgot."

"Exactly!"

"So you treated me like any other deadbeat. You were just following orders."

"Then you do understand, sir?"

"I understand," I said.

We took the elevator up to the street, my friend and I. I accompanied him to his car, trying to remember who he was, knowing that I had had far more than a passing acquaintance with him at one time. At last, as we passed under a streetlight, it came to me.

"Mr. Claggett, Jeff Claggett!" I wrung his hand. "How could I ever have forgotten?"

"Oh, well, it's been a long time." He grinned deprecatingly. "You're looking good, Britt."

"Not exactly a barometer of my true condition," I said. "But how about you? Still with the university."

"Police Department, Detective Sergeant." He nodded toward the lighted window of a nearby restaurant. "Let's have some coffee, and a talk."

He was in his early sixties, a graying square-shouldered man with startlingly blue eyes. He had been chief of campus security when my father was on the university faculty. "I left shortly after your dad did," he said. "The coldblooded way they dumped him was a little more than I could stomach."

"It wasn't very nice," I admitted. "But what else could they do, Jeff? You know how he was drinking there at the last. You were always having to bring him home."

"I wish I could have done more. I would have drunk more than he did, if I'd had his problems."

"But he brought them all on himself," I pointed out. "He was slandered, sure. But if he'd just ignored it, instead of trying to get the

26

UnAmerican Activities Committee abolished, it would all have been forgotten. As it was, well, what's the use talking?"

"Not much," Claggett said. "Not any more."

I said, Oh, for God's sake. It sounded like I was knocking the old man; and, of course, I didn't mean to. "I didn't mind his drinking, per se. It was just that it left him vulnerable to being kicked around by people who weren't fit to wipe his ass."

Jeff Claggett nodded, saying that a lot of nominally good people seemed to have a crappy streak in them. "Give them any sort of excuse, and they trot it out. Yeah, and they're virtuous as all hell about it. So-and-so drinks, so that cleans the slate. They don't even owe him common decency."

He put down his coffee cup with a bang, and signaled for a refill. He sipped from it, sighed and grimaced tiredly.

"Well, no use hashing over the past, I guess. How come you were in that place I got you out of tonight, Britt?"

"Through a misunderstanding," I said firmly. "A mistake that isn't going to be repeated."

"Yeah?" He waited a moment. "Well, you're smart to steer clear of 'em. We haven't been able to hang anything on them, but, by God, we will."

"With my blessings," I said. "You were on official business tonight?"

"Sort of. Just letting them know we were on the job. Well"—he glanced at his watch, and started to rise. "Guess I better run. Can I drop you some place?"

I declined with thanks, saying that I had a little business to take care of. He said, Well, in that case. . . .

"By the way, I drove past the old Rainstar place a while back, Britt. Looks like someone is still living there."

"Yes," I said. "I guess someone is."

"In a *dump*? The city garbage dump? But—" His voice trailed away, comprehension slowly dawning in his eyes. Finally, he said, "Hang around a minute, Britt. I've got to make a few phone calls, and then we'll have a good talk."

We sat in Claggett's car, in the driveway of the Rainstar mansion, and he frowned in the darkness, looking at me curiously. "I don't see how they can do this to you, Britt. Grab your property while you're out of the state."

"Well, they paid me for it," I said. "Around three thousand dollars after the bank loan was paid. And they gave me the privilege of staying in the house as long I want to."

"Oh, shit!" Claggett snorted angrily. "How long is that going to be? You've been swindled, Britt, but you sure as hell don't have to hold still for it!"

"I don't know," I said. "I don't see that there's much I can do about it."

"Of course, there's something you can do! This place was deeded tax-free to the Rainstars in perpetuity, in recognition of the thousands of acres the family had given to the state. It's not subject to mortgage or the laws of eminent domain. Why, I'll tell you, Britt, you go into court with this deal, and ... "

I listened to him, without really listening. There was nothing he could tell me that I hadn't told myself. I'd argued it all out with myself, visualizing the newspaper stories, the courtroom scenes, the courtroom scenes, the endless questions. And I'd said to hell with it. I knew myself, and I knew I couldn't do it for any amount of money.

"I can't do it, Jeff ... " I cut in on him, at last. "I don't want to go into the details, but I have a wife in another state. An invalided wife. I was suspected of trying to kill her. I didn't, of course, but—"

"Of course, you didn't!" Jeff said warmly. "Murder just isn't in you. Anyway, you wouldn't be here if there was any real case against you."

"The case is still open," I said. "I'm not so sure I'm in the clear yet. At any rate, the story would be bound to come out if I made waves over this condemnation deal, so I'm not making any. I, the family and I, have had nothing but trouble as far back as I remember. I don't want any more."

"No one wants trouble, dammit," Claggett scowled. "But you don't avoid it by turning your back on it. The more you run from, the more you have chasing you."

"I'm sure you're right," I said. "But just the same—"

"Your father would fight, Britt. He *did* fight! They didn't get away with piling garbage on him!"

They didn't?" I said. "Well, well."

We said good-night.

He drove off, gravel spinning angrily from the wheels of his car.

I entered the house, catching up the phone on its first ring. I said, Hello, putting a lot of ice into the word. I started to say a lot more, believing that the caller was Manuela Aloe, but fortunately I didn't. Fortunately, since the call was from Connie, my wife.

"Britt? Where have you been?"

"Out trying to make some money," I said. "I wasn't successful, but I'm still trying."

She said that she certainly hoped so. All her terrible expenses were awfully hard on her daddy; and it did seem like a grown, healthy man like me, with a good education, should be able to do a little something. "If you could just send me a *little* money, Britt. Just a teensy-weensy bit—"

"Goddammit!" I yelled. "What's with this teensy-weensy crap? I send you practically everything I get from the Foundation, and you know I do because you wrote them and found out how much they pay me! You had to embarrass me, like a goddamned two-bit shyster!"

She began to cry. She said it wasn't her fault that she was crippled, and that she was worried out of her mind about money. I should just be in the fix she was in for a while, and see how I liked it. And so forth and so on, ad finitum, ad nauseum.

And I apologized and apologized and apologized. And I swore that I would somehow someway get more money to her than I had been sending. And then I apologized three or four hundred additional times, and, at last, when I was hoarse from apologies and promises, she wished me sweet dreams, and hung up.

Sweet dreams!

I was so soaked with sweat that you would have thought I'd had a wet dream.

Which was not the kind of dream one had about Connie.

VII

MRS. OLMSTEAD SET BREAKFAST BEFORE ME THE NEXT MORNING, re-marking—doubtless by way of whetting my appetite—that we would probably have rat dew in the food before long.

"I seen some chasin' around the backyard yesterday, so they'll be in the house next. Can't be this close to a garbage dump without havin' rats."

"I see," I said absently. "Well, we'll face the problem when it comes."

"Time t'face it is now," she asserted. "Be too late when the rats is facin' us."

I closed my ears to her gabbling, finishing what little breakfast I was able to eat. As I left the table, Mrs. Olmstead handed me a letter to mail when I went to town, if I didn't mind, o' course.

"But I was going to work at home today," I said. "I hadn't really planned on going to town."

"How come you're all fixed up, then?" she demanded. "You don't never fix yourself up unless you're going somewheres."

I promised to mail the letter, if and when. I tucked it into my pocket as I went into the living room, noting that it was addressed to the old-age pension bureau. More than a year ago her monthly check had been three dollars short—by her calculations, that is. She had been writing them ever since, sometimes three times a week, demanding reimbursement. I had pointed out that she had spent far more than three dollars in postage, but she still stubbornly persisted.

Without any notion of actually working, I went into the small room, at one time a serving pantry, which does duty as my study. I sat down at my typewriter, wrote a few exercise sentences, and various versions of my name. After about thirty minutes of such fiddling around, I jumped up and fled to my bedroom. Fretfully examined myself in the warped full-length mirror.

And I thought, All dressed up and no place to go.

There would be no call from PXA. If there was one, I couldn't respond to it. Not after the ordeal I had been put through last night. No one who was serious about giving me worthwhile employment would have done such a thing to me. And it had to have been done deliberately. An outfit as cruelly efficient as PXA didn't allow things like that to come about accidentally.

I closed my eyes, clenched my mind to the incident, unable to live through it again even in memory. Wondering why it was that I seemed constantly called upon to face things that I couldn't. I went back down to my study, but not to my typewriter. For what was there to write? Who would want anything written by me?

I sat down on a small loveseat. A spiny tuft of horsehair burst through the upholstery, and stabbed me in the butt. Something that seemed to typify the hysterically hilarious tragedy of my life. I was pining away of a broken heart or something. But instead of being allowed a little dignity and gravity, I got my ass tickled.

Determinedly, I stayed where I was and as I was. Bent forward with my head in my sands. Sourly resisting the urge to squirm or snicker.

Poor Lo ...

"Poor Lo ... "

I chuckled wryly, poking fun at myself.

"Well, screw it," I said. "They may kill me, but they can't eat me."

There was a light patter of applause. Hand clapping.

I sat up startled, and Manuela Aloe laughed and sat down at my side.

"I'm sorry," she said. "I spoke to you a couple of times, but you didn't hear me."

"B—but—but—" I began to get hold of myself. "What are you doing here?"

"Your housekeeper showed me in. I came out here, because I was afraid you wouldn't come to the office after the terrible time you must have had last night."

"You were right," I said. "I wouldn't have gone down to your office. And there really wasn't much point to your coming out here."

"I did send a car to pick you up last night, Britt. I don't blame you for being angry, but I did do it."

"Whatever you say," I said.

"I don't know what happened to the driver. No one's seen him since. Our people aren't ordinarily so irresponsible, but it's not unheard of. But, anyway, I am sorry."

"So much for the driver," I said. "Now what about Albert?"

"Albert," she grimaced. "I don't know whether it was booze or dope or just plain stupidity that made him do what he did. I don't care, either. But he's out of a job as of this morning, and he'll be a long time in getting another one."

She nodded to me earnestly, the dark eyes warm with concern. I hesitated, wanting to swallow my pride—how could I afford pride? Remembering Connie's demands for money.

"There was something else," I said. "Something that came to me when I was outside your office yesterday."

"Yes?" She smiled encouragingly. "What was that, Britt?"

I hesitated again, trying to find some amiable euphemism for what was virtually an accusation. And finding excuses instead. After all, her office *would* logically have sound equipment in it; devices for auditing the tapes. And why, when I was so strongly drawn to this girl, and when I needed money so badly, should I continue to squeeze her for apologies and explanations.

"Yes, Britt?

"Nothing," I said. "No, I mean it. Thinking it over, I seem to have found the answer to my own question."

That wasn't true. Aside from the woman's being slapped, there was something else. The fact that PXA had milked me for all kinds of personal information as a condition for granting my loan. My likes and dislikes, my habits and weaknesses. Information that could be used to drive me up a figurative wall, should they take the notion.

But I meant to give them no cause to take such a notion. And I am an incurable optimist, always hoping for the best despite the many times I have gotten the worst.

Manny was studying me, her dark eyes boring into mine. Seemingly boring into my mind. And a sudden shadow blighted the room, and I was chilled with a sickening sense of premonition.

Then she laughed gaily, gave herself a little shake, and assumed a businesslike manner.

"Well, now," she said briskly. "I've had a long talk with Uncle Pat, and he's left everything to me. So how about a series of pamphlets on the kind of subjects you deal with for the Foundation?"

"It sounds fine," I said. "Just, well, fine."

"The pamphlets will be distributed free to schools, libraries and other institutions. They won't carry any advertising. Just a line to the effect that they are sponsored by PXA, as a public service."

I said that was fine, too. Just fine. She opened her blonde leather purse, took out a check and handed it to me. A check for thirty-five hundred dollars. Approximately twenty-nine hundred for the first month's work, with the rest for expenses.

"Well?" She looked at me pertly. "All right? Any questions?"

I let out a deep breath. "My God!" I breathed fervently. "Of course, it's all right! And no, no questions."

She smiled and stood up, a lushly diminutive figure in her fawn-colored pantsuit. Her breasts and her bottom bulged deliciously against the material, seemed to strain for release. And I thought thoughts that brought a flush to my face.

"Come on." She wiggled her fingers. "Show me around, hmm? I've heard so much about this place I'm dying to see it."

"I'm afraid it's not much to see any more," I said. "But if you're really interested in ruins . . . "

I showed her through the house, or much of it. She murmured appreciatively over the decaying evidence of past grandeur, and regretfully at the ravages of time.

We finished our tour of the house, and Manny again became businesslike. "We'll have a lot of conferring to do to get this project operating, Britt. Do you want an office, or will you work here?"

"Here, if it's agreeable to you," I said. "I have a great deal of research material here, and I'm used to the place. Of course, if it's inconvenient for you . . . "

"Oh, we'll work it out," she promised. "Now, if you'll drive me back to town . . . "

The car she had driven out in was mine, she explained, pointing to the gleaming new vehicle which stood in the driveway. Obviously, I would need a car, and PXA owed me one. And she did hope I wouldn't be stuffy about it.

I said I never got stuffy over girls of single cars. Only fleets of them, and not always then. Manny laughed, and gave me a playful punch on the arm.

"Silly! Now, come on, will you? We have a lot to do today."

We did have a lot to do, as it turned out. At least we did a lot—far more than I anticipated. But that's getting ahead of the story. To take events in their proper order:

I drove into town, Manny sitting carelessly close to me. I deposited the check in my bank, drew some cash and returned to the car—*my* car. It was lunchtime by then, so we lunched and talked. I talked mostly, since I have a knack for talk, if little else, and Manny seemed to enjoy listening to me.

We came out of the restaurant into mid-afternoon, and, talking, I drove around until sunset. By which time, needless to say, it was time for a drink. We had it, rather we had *them*, and eventually we had dinner. When twilight fell, we were far out on the outskirts of town; parked by the lake which formed the bulwark of the city's water system.

Manny's legs were tucked up in the seat. Her head rested on my shoulder, and my arm was around her. It was really a very nice way to be.

"Britt . . . " she murmured, breaking the drowsy, comfortable silence. "I've enjoyed myself so much, today. I think it's been the very best day in my life."

"You're a thief, Manuela Aloe," I said. "You've stolen the very speech I was going to make."

"Tell me something, Britt. How does anyone as nice as you are, as attractive and intelligent and bubbling over with charm—how does he, why does he ... ?"

"Wind up as I have?" I said. "Because I never found a seller's market for those things until I met you."

It was a pretty blunt thing to say. She sat up with a start, glaring at me coldly. But I smiled at her determinedly, and said I meant no offense.

"But let's face it, Manny. The Rainstar name isn't worth much any more, and my talent never was. So the good looks and the charm et cetera is what I've sold, isn't it?"

"No, it isn't!" she snapped; and then, hesitating, biting her lip. "Well, not entirely. You wouldn't have got the job if you hadn't been like you are, but neither would you have got it if you hadn't been qualified."

"So it was half one, half the other," I said. "And what's wrong with fifty-fifty?"

"Nothing. And don't you act like there is either!"

"Not even a little bit?"

"No!"

"All right, I won't," I said. "Providing you smile real pretty for me, and then lie down with your head in my lap."

She did so, although the smile was just a trifle weak. I bent down and kissed her gently, and was kissed in return. I put a hand on her breast, gave it a gentle squeeze. She shivered delicately, eyes clouding.

"I'm not an easy lay, Britt. I don't sleep around."

"What am I to do with you, Manny?" I said. "You are now twice a thief."

"I guess I've been waiting for you. It had to be someone like you, and there wasn't anyone like that but you."

"I know," I said. "I also have been waiting."

You can see why I said it, why I just about *had* to say it. She was my munificent benefactor and she was gorgeous beyond my wildest dreams, and she obviously wanted to and needed to be screwed. So what the hell else could I do?

"Britt ... " She wiggled restlessly. "I have a live-in maid at my apartment."

"Unfortunate," I said. "My housekeeper also lives in."

"Well? Well, Britt, dear?"

"Well, I know of a place ... " I broke off, carefully amended the statement. "I mean, I've *heard* of one. It's nothing fancy, I understand. No private baths or similar niceties. But it's clean and comfortable and safe ... or so I'm reliably told."

"Well?" she said.

"Well?" I said.

She didn't say anything. Simply reached out and turned on the ignition.

VIII

MORE THAN A MONTH WENT BY BEFORE I MET PATRICK XAVIER ALOE. It was at a party at his house, and Manny and I went to it together.

Judging by his voice, the one telephone conversation I had had with him, I supposed him to be a towering giant of a man. But while he was broad shouldered and powerful-looking, he was little taller than Manny.

"Glad to finally meet up with you, Britt, baby." He beamed at me out of his broad darkly Irish face. "What have you got under your arm there, one of Manny's pizzas?"

"He has the complete manuscript of a pamphlet," Manny said proudly. "And it's darned good, too!"

"It is, huh? What d'ya say, Britt? Is she telling the truth or not?"

"Well . . . " I hesitated modestly. "I'm sure there's room for improvement, but—"

"We'll see, we'll see," he broke in laughing. "You two grab a drink, and come on."

We followed him through the small crowd of guests, all polite and respectable-appearing, but perhaps a little on the watchful side. We went into the library, and Pat Aloe waved us to chairs, then sat down behind the desk, carefully removed my manuscript from its envelope and began to read.

He read rapidly but intently, with no skimming or skipping. I could tell that by his occasional questions. In fact, he was so long in reading that Manny asked crossly if he was trying to memorize the script, adding that we didn't have the whole goddamned evening to spend at his stupid house. Pat Aloe told her mildly to shut her goddamned mouth, and went back to his reading.

I had long since become used to Manny's occasionally salty talk, and learned that I was not privileged to respond in kind. But Pat clearly was not taking orders from her. Despite his air of easygoing geniality, he was very much in command of Aloe activities. And, I was to find, he tolerated no violation of his authority.

When he had finished the last page of my manuscript, he put it with the others and returned them all to their envelope. Then, he removed his reading glasses, thoughtfully massaged the bridge of his nose, and at last turned to me with a sober nod.

"You're a good man, Britt. It's a good job."

"Thank you," I said. "Thank you, very much."

Manny said words were cheap. How about a bonus for me? But Pat winked at her, and waved her to silence.

"Y'know, Britt, I thought this deal would turn out the same kind of frammis that Manny's husband pulled. Banging the b'Jesus out of her, and pissing off on the work. But I'm glad to admit I was wrong. You're A—OK, baby, and I'll swear to it on a stack of Bibles!"

Fortunately, I didn't have to acknowledge the compliment—such as it was—since Manny had begun cursing him luridly with his overripe appraisal of her late husband. Pat's booming laugh drowned out her protest.

"Ain't she a terror, though, Britt? Just like the rest of her family, when she had a family. Her folks didn't speak to mine for years, just because my pop married an Irisher."

"Just don't you forget that bonus," Manny said. "You do and it'll be your big red ass."

"Hell, take care of it yourself," Pat said. "Make her come across heavy, Britt, baby. Hear me?"

I mumbled that I would do it. Grinning stiffly, feeling awkward and embarrassed to a degree I had never known before. He walked out of the library between the two of us, a hand on each of our shoulders. Then, when we were at the door and had said our good-night, he laughingly roared that he expected me to collect heavy loot from Manny.

"Make her mind, Britt. 'S' only kind of wife to have. Tell her you won't marry her until she comes through with your bonus!"

Marry her?

Marry her!

Well, what did I expect?

I tottered out of the house, with Manny clinging possessively to my arm. And there was a coldish lump in my throat, a numbing chill in my spine.

We got in the car, and I drove away. Manny looked at me speculatively and asked why I was so quiet. And I said I wasn't being quiet, and then I said, What was wrong with being quiet. Did I have to talk every damned minute to keep her happy?

Ordinarily, popping-off to her like that would have gotten me a chewing out or maybe a sharp slap. But tonight she said soothingly that of course I could be silent whenever I chose, because whatever I chose was also her choice.

"After all we're a team, darling. Not two people, but a *couple*. Maybe we have our little spats, but there can't be any serious division between us."

I groaned. I said, "Oh, my God, Manny! Oh, Mary and Jesus, and his brother, James!"

"What's the matter, Britt? Isn't that the way you feel?"

What I felt was that I was about to do something wholly irrelevant and unconstructive. Like soiling my clothes. For I was being edged closer and closer to the impossible. I mumbled something indistinguishable— something noncomittally agreeable. Because I knew now that I had to keep talking. Only in talk, light talk, lay safety.

Luckily, Manny indirectly threw me a cue by pushing the stole back from her shoulders, and stretching her legs out in front of her. An action which tantalizingly exhibited her gold lamé evening gown; very short, very low cut, very tight-seeming on her small, ultra-full body.

"It looks like it was painted on you," I said. "How in the world did you get into it?"

"Maybe you'll find out"—giving me a look. "After all, you have to take it off of me."

"We shall see," I said, desperate for words. For any kind of light talk. "We shall certainly see about this."

"Well, hurry up, for gosh sake! I've got to pee."

"Oh, my God," I said. "Why didn't you go before we left the house?"

"Because I needed help with my dress, darn it!"

I got her to the place. The place that had become *our* place.

I got her up to the room and out of her clothes, and onto the sink.

With no time to spare, either.

She cut loose, and continued to let go at length. Sighing happily with the simple pleasure of relieving herself. She was such an earthy little thing, and I suppose few things are as good as a good leak when one has held in to the bursting point.

When she had finished, she reached a towel from the rack, and handed it to me. "Wipe, please."

"Wipe what?" I said.

"You know what—and where it is, too!"

"I will. If you'll promise to give me a tip ... "

Talking, talking. Even after we were in bed, and she was pressed tightly against me in epigrammiatic surgings.

" ... what kind of tip are you giving me?"

"Guess."

"Something very soft and very firm?"

"Mmm."

"Possessing an elastic quality?"

"Mmm."

"Almost painfully but wonderfully tight?"
"Mmm."
"Self-lubricating?"
"Mmm."
"Mmm. Now, what in the world could it be?"

IX

I WAS PHYSICALLY ILL BY THE TIME I GOT HOME THAT NIGHT. Sick with fear that the subject of marriage would be raised again, that it would be tossed to me like a ball and that I would not be allowed to bat it aside or let it drop.

Repeatedly staggered out of my bed and went to the bathroom. Over and over, I went down on my knees and vomited into the bowl. Gagging up the bile of fear, as I shivered and sweated with its burning chill. I tried to blame it on an overactive imagination, but I couldn't lie to myself. I'd lied once too often when I lied to Manny—about the one thing I should never have lied about. And the fact that the lie was one of omission, rather than commission, and that lying was more or less a way of life with me, would not lift me off the hook a fraction of an inch. Not with Manuela Aloe. She would regard my lie as inexcusable, as, of course, it was.

In saying that I was unmarried on my PXA loan application, I hadn't meant to harm anyone. (I have never meant to harm anyone with what I did and didn't do.) It was just a way of avoiding troublesome questions re the status of my marriage: were my wife and I living together; and if not, why not, and so on.

But I knew that Manny depended on that application for her information about me. And I could have and should have set her straight. For I knew—must have known—that I was not being treated with such extravagant generosity to buy Manny a passing relationship. She wanted a husband. One with good looks, good breeding and a good name—the kind not easily found in her world or any world. Then she had found me, and oh-so-clearly demonstrated the advantages of marriage to her, and I, tacitly, had agreed to the marriage. She had been completely honest with me, and I had been just as completely dishonest with her. And, now, by God—!

Now . . . ?

But a man can be afraid just so much. (I say that as an expert on being afraid.) When he reaches that limit, he can fear no more. And so, at last, my pajamas wet with cold sweat, I returned to bed and fell into restless sleep.

In the morning, Mrs. Olmstead brought me toast and coffee and asked suspiciously if I had mailed a letter she had given me yesterday. I said that I had, for she was always giving me letters to mail, and I always remembered to mail. Or almost always. She nagged me, with increasing vehemence, about the imminent peril of rats. And I swore I would do something about them, too; and mumbling and grumbling, she at last left me alone.

I lay back down and closed my eyes ... *and Manny came into my room*, a deceptive smile on her lovely face. For naturally, although she had learned that I was married, she showed no sign of displeasure.

"But it's all right, darling, and I understand perfectly. You needed the money and you were dying to sleep with me. And—here, have a drink of this nice coffee I fixed for you."

"No! It's poisoned, and—yahh!"

"Oh, I'm so sorry, dear! I wouldn't have spilled it on you for the world. Let me just wipe it off—"

"Yeeow! You're scratching my eyes out! Get away, go away. ..."

My eyes snapped open.

I sat up with a start.

Mrs. Olmstead was bent over me. "My goodness, goodness me!" she exclaimed. "What's the matter, Mr. Rainstar?"

"Nothing; must've been having a nightmare," I said sheepishly. "Was I making a lot of racket?"

"Were you ever! Sounded like you was scared to death." Shaking her head grumpily, she turned toward the door. "Oh, yeah, your girlfriend wants you."

"What?" I said.

"Reckon she's your girlfriend, the way you're always pawing at each other."

"But—you mean, Miss Aloe?" I stammered. "She's here?"

"'Course, she's not here. Don't see her, do you?" She gestured exasperatedly. "Answer the phone, a—fore she hangs up!"

I threw on a robe, and ran downstairs.

I grabbed up the phone, and said hello.

"Boo, you pretty man!" Manny laughed teasingly. "What's the matter with you anyway?"

"Matter?" I said. "Uh, what makes you think anything's the matter?"

"I thought you sounded rather gruff and strained. But never mind. I want to see you. Be at our place in about an hour, okay?"

I swallowed heavily. Had she decided that something was wrong? That I was hiding something?

"Britt ... ?"

"Why?" I said. "What did you want to see me about?"

"What?" I could almost see her frown. "What did I want to see you *about?*"

I apologized hastily. I said I'd just gone to sleep after tossing and turning all night, and I seemed to be coming down with the flu. "I'd love to see you, Manny, child, but I think it would be bad for you. The way I'm feeling, the farther you keep away from me the better."

She said, Oh, disappointedly, but agreed that it was probably best not to see me. She was leaving town for a couple of weeks—some business for Uncle Pat. Naturally, she would have liked a session with me before departing. But since I seemed to coming down with something, and it wouldn't do for her to catch it . . .

"You just take care of yourself, Britt. Get to feeling hale and hearty again, because you'll have to be when I get back."

"I'll look forward to it," I said. "have a good trip, baby."

"And, Britt. I put a two-thousand dollar bonus check in the mail to you."

"Oh, that's too much," I said. "I'm really overpaid as it is, and—"

"You just shut up!" she said sternly, then laughed. "'Bye, now, darling. I gotta run."

"'Bye to you," I said. And we hung up.

I had sent Connie three thousand dollars out of my first PXA check, and another three out of the second. Explaining that I'd gotten on to something good, though probably temporary, and that I'd send her all I could as long as it lasted. After all, I hadn't sent much before, lacking much to send, and it was sort of a conscience salve for my affair with Manny.

When my bonus arrived, I mailed Connie a check for the full two thousand. Then, after waiting a few days, until I was sure she had got it, I called her.

Britt Rainstar, stupe de luxe, figured that getting so much scratch—seven grand in less than two months—would put her in a fine mood. Bonehead Britt, sometimes known as the Peabrain Pollyanna, reasoned that all that loot would buy reasonableness and tolerance from Connie. Which just goes to show you. Yessir, that shows you, and it shows something about him, too. (*And please stop laughing, dammit!*)

For she was verbally leaping all over me, almost before I had asked her how she was feeling.

"I want to know where you got that money, Britt. I want to know how much more you got—a full and complete accounting, as Daddy says. And don't tell me that you got it from Hemisphere, because we've already talked to them and they said that you didn't. They said that you had severed your association with them. So you tell me where you're getting the money, and exactly how much you're getting. Or, by golly, you'll wish you had."

"I see," I said numbly; surprised, though God knows I should not have been. I was always surprised, when being stupid, that people thought I was stupid. "I think I really see for the first time, namely that you and your daddy are a couple of miserable piles of shit."

"Who from and how much? I either find out from you, Mister Britton Rainstar, or—*What?* What did you say to me?"

"Never mind," I said. "I tell you the source of the money, and you check to see if I'm telling the truth—as to the quantity, that is. That's your plan, isn't it?"

"Well . . . " She hesitated. "But I have a right to know! I'm your wife."

"Do you and are you?" I said. "A wife usually trusts her husband, when he treats her as generously as I've been treating you."

That made her hesitate again, brought her to a still longer pause.

"Well, *all right*," she said at last, grudgingly defensive. "I certainly don't want to make you lose your job, and—and—well, Hemisphere had no right to get huffy about it! Anyway, just look at what you did to me!"

"I didn't do anything to you, Connie. It was an accident."

"Well, anyway," she said. "Just the same!"

I didn't say anything. Simply waited. After a long silence, I heard her take a deep breath, and she spoke with an incipient sob.

"I s—suppose you want a divorce, now. You wouldn't talk to me this way, if you didn't."

"Divorce makes sense, Connie. You'll get just as much money, as if we were married, and I know you can't feel any great love for me."

"Then *you* do want a divorce?"

"Yes. It's the best thing for both of us, and—"

"WELL, YOU JUST TRY AND GET ONE!" she yelled. "I'll have you in jail for attempted murder so fast, it'll make your head swim! You arranged that accident that almost killed me, and the case isn't closed yet! They're ready to reopen it any time Daddy and I say the word. And, golly, you try and get a divorce, and, by gosh—!"

"Connie," I said. "You surely can't mean that!"

"You'll see! You'll see if I don't. Just let me hear one more word out of you about a divorce, and—and—*I'll show you who's a pile of shit!*"

She slammed up the phone, completing any damage to my eardrum that had not been accomplished by her banshee scream. Of course, I'd hardly expected her to bedeck me with a crown of olive leaves, or to release a covey of white doves to flutter about my head. But a threat to have me prosecuted for attempted murder was considerably much more than I *had* expected.

At any rate, a divorce was impossible unless she agreed to it. Which meant that it was impossible period. Which meant that I could not marry Manny.

Which meant . . . ?

X

SHE, Manny, was back in town two weeks later, and she called me immediately upon her arrival. She suggested that I pick her up at the airport, and go immediately to our place. I suggested that we have dinner and a talk before we did anything else. So, a little puzzled and reluctant, she agreed to that.

The restaurant was near the lake I have mentioned earlier. The city waterworks lake. There was only a handful of patrons in it, this early evening hour, and they gradually drifted out as I talked to Manny, apologizing and explaining. Explaining the inexplicable and apologizing for the inexcusable.

Manny said not a word throughout my recital. Merely stared at me expressionlessly over her untouched dinner.

At last, I had nothing more to say, if I had ever had anything to say. And, then, finally, she spoke, pulling a fringed-silk shawl around her shoulders and rising to her feet.

"Pay the check, and get out of here."

"What? Oh, well, sure," I said, dropping bills on the table as I also stood up. "And, Manny, I want you to know that—"

"Get! March yourself out to the car!"

We got out of the restaurant, with Manny clinging to my arm, virtually propelling me by it. She helped *me* into the car, instead of vice versa. Then, she got in, into the rear, sitting immediately behind me.

I heard her purse snap open. She said, "I've got a gun on you, Britt. So you get out of line just a little bit, and you won't like what happens to you."

"M-Manny," I quavered. "P-please don't—"

"Do you know where I went while I was out of town?"

"N-no."

"Do you want to know what I did?"

"Uh, n-no," I said. "I don't think I do."

"Start driving. You know where."

"But—You mean, our place? W-why do you want to—"

"*Drive!*"

I drove.

We reached the place. She made me walk ahead of her, inside and up the stairs and into our room.

I heard the click of the door lock. And then Manny asked if I'd heard a woman being slapped on the first day I went to her office.

I said that I had—or, rather, a recording of same; I had grown calmer by now, with a sense of fatalism.

"You heard *her*, Britt. She left the office by my private elevator."

I nodded, without turning around. "You wanted me to hear her. It was arranged, like the scene with Albert after you'd left that night. I was being warned that I'd better fly straight or else."

"You admit you *were* warned, then?"

"Yes. I tried to kid myself that it was all an unfortunate accident. But I knew better."

"But you went right ahead and deceived and cheated me. Did you really think I'd let you get away with it?"

I shook my head miserably, said I wanted to make things right insofar as I could. I'd give the car back, and what little money I had left. And I'd sell everything I owned—clothes, typewriter, books, everything—to raise the rest. Anything she or PXA had given me, I'd give back, and—and—

"What about all the screwing I gave you? I suppose you'll give that back, too!"

"No," I said. "I'm afraid I can't do anything about that."

"Oh, sure you can," she said. "You can give me a good one right now."

And I whirled around, and she collapsed in my arms, laughing.

"Ahhh, Britt, darling! If you could have seen your face! You were really frightened, weren't you? You really thought I was angry with you, didn't you?"

"Of course, I thought it!" I said, and, hugging her, kissing her, I swatted her bottom. "My God! The way you were talking, and waving that gun around—!"

"Gun? Look, no gun!" She held her purse open for examination. "I couldn't be angry with you, Britt. What reason would I have? You were married, and you couldn't get unmarried. But you just about had to have the job, and you wanted me. So you did the only thing you could. I understand perfectly, and don't you give it another thought, because nothing is changed. We'll go on just like we were; and everything's all right."

It was hard to believe that things would be all right. Knowing her as well as I did, I didn't see how they could be. As the weeks passed, however, my suspicions were lulled—almost, *almost* leaving me—for there was nothing whatsoever to justify them. I even found the courage to criticize her about her language, pointing out that it was hardly suitable to one with two college degrees. I can't say that it changed anything, but she acknowledged the criticism with seeming humility, and solemnly promised to mend her ways.

So everything *was* all right—ostensibly. The work went on, and went well. Ditto for my relationship with Manny. No one could have been more loving or understanding. Certainly, no one, no other woman, had ever been as exciting. Over and over, I told myself how lucky I was to have such a woman. A wildly sensuous, highly intelligent woman who also had money and was generous with it, thus freeing me from the niggling and nagging and guilt feelings which had heretofore hindered and inhibited me.

It is a fallacy that people who do not obtain the finer things in life have no appreciation for them. Actually, no one likes good things more than a bum—and I say this knowing whereof I speak. I truly appreciated Manny after all the sorry b-axes which had previously been my lot. I truly appreciated everything she gave me, all the creature comforts she made possible for me, in addition to herself.

Everything wasn't just all right, as she had promised. Hell, everything was beautiful.

Until today.

The Day of the Dog . . .

. . . I lay on my back, bracing myself against any movement which would cause him to attack.

I ached hideously, then grew numb from lack of movement; and shadows fell on the blinded windows. It was late lafternoon. The sun was going down, and now—*my legs jerked convulsively*. They jerked again, even as I was trying to brace them. And now I heard a faint rustling sound: The dog tensing himself, getting ready to spring.

"*D-don't! Please don't!*"

Laughter. Vicious, maliciously amused laughter.

I rubbed my eyes with a trembling hand. Brushed the blinding sweat from them.

The dog was gone. The manager of the place, the mulatto woman, stood at the foot of the bed. She jerked a thumb over her shoulder in a contemptuous gesture of dismissal.

"All right, prick. Beat it!"

"W-what?" I sat up shakily. "What did you say?"

"Get out. Grab your rags, and drag ass!"

"Now, listen, you—you can't—"

"I can't what?"

"Nothing," I said. "If you'll just leave, so that I can get dressed . . . "

She said I'd get dressed while she was there, by God, because she wanted to look at the bed before I left. She figured a yellow bastard like me had probably shit in it. (*And where had I heard such talk before—the unnerving, ego-smashing talk of terror?*)

"Jus' so damned scared," she jeered. "Prob'ly shit the bed like a fucking baby. You did, I'm gonna make you clean it up."

I got dressed, with her watching.

I waited, head hanging like a whipped animal, while she jerked the sheets back, examined them, and then sniffed them.

"Okay," she said, at last. "Reckon you got all your shit in you. Still full of it, like always."

I turned, and started for the door.

"Don't you never come back, hear? I see your skinny ass again, I lays a belt on it!"

I got out of the place. So fast that I fell, rather than walked down the stairs; almost crashed throught the street door, in attempting to open it the wrong way.

After the dog, I had thought nothing more could be done to me, that I was as demoralized as a man could get. But I was wrong. The vicious abuse of the mulatto woman had shaken me in a way that fear could not. Or perhaps it was the fear and the abuse together.

I drove blindly for several minutes, oblivious to the hysterical horn-blasts of other cars. The outraged shouts of their drivers, and the squealing of brakes. Finally, however, when I barely escaped a head-on collision with a truck, I managed to pull myself together sufficiently to turn in to the curb and park.

I was on an unfamiliar street, one that I could not remember. I was stopped in front of a small cocktail lounge. Wiping my face and hand dry of sweat, I combed my hair and went inside.

"Yes, sir?" The bartender beamed in greeting, pushing a bowl of pretzels toward me. "What'll it be, sir?"

"I think I'll have a—"

I broke off at the sudden insistent jangling from a rear telephone booth. The bartender nodded toward it apologetically, and said, "If you'll excuse me, sir—?" And I told him to go ahead.

He hurried from behind the bar, and back to the booth. He entered, and closed the door. He remained inside for some two or three minutes. Then he came back, again stood in front of me.

"Yes, sir?"

"A martini," I said. "Very dry. Twist instead of olive."

He mixed the drink, poured it with a flourish. He punched numbers on the tabulating cash register, extended a check as he placed the glass before me.

"One-fifty, sir. You pay now."
"Well—" I hesitated; shrugged. "Why not?"
I handed him two dollar bills. He said, "Exact change, sir."
And he picked up the drink, and threw it in my face.

XI

HE WAS A LUCKY MAN. As I have said, my general easygoing attitude, an ah-to-hell-with-it attitude, is marred by an occasional brief but violent flare-up. And if I had not been so completely beaten down by the dog and the mulatto woman, he would have gotten a broken arm.

But, of course, he had known I had nothing to strike back with. Manny, or the person who had made the call for her, had convinced him of the fact. Convinced him that he could pick up a nice piece of change without the slightest danger to himself.

I ran a sleeve across my face. I got up from my stool, turned and started to leave. Then, I stopped and turned back around, gave the bartender a long, hard stare. I wasn't capable of punching him, but there was something that I could do. I could make sure that there was a connection between the thrown drink, and the afternoon's other unpleasantries—that, briefly, his action was motivated and not mere coincidence.

"Well?" His eyes flickered nervously. "What somethin'?"

"People shouldn't tell you to do things," I said, "that they're afraid to do themselves."

"Huh? What're you drivin' at?"

"You mean, that was your own idea? You weren't paid to do it?"

"Do what? I don't know what you're talkin' about."

"All right," I said. "I'll tell some friends of mine what a nice guy you are."

I nodded coldly, again turned toward the door.

"Wait!" he said. "Wait a munute—uh—sir?

"It was a joke, see? Just a joke. I wasn't s'posed t'tell ya, an'—I can't tell ya nothin' else! I just *can't!* But—but—"

"It's all right," I said. "You don't need to."

I left the bar.

I drove home.

I parked in the driveway near the porch. Another car wheeled up behind mine, and Manny got out. Smiling gaily as she came trotting up to me, and hooked an arm through mine.

"Guess what I've got for you, darling. Give you three guesses!"

"A cobra," I said, "and two stink bombs."

"Silly! Let's go inside and I'll show you."

48

"Let's," I said grimly, "and I'll show *you*."

We went up the steps, and across the porch, Manny hugging my arm, smiling up into my face. The very picture of a woman with her love. Mrs. Olmstead heard us enter the house, and hurried in from the kitchen.

"My, my!" she chortled, beaming at Manny. "I swear you get prettier every day, Miss Aloe."

"Oh, now," Manny laughed. "I couldn't look half as nice as your dinner smells. Were you inviting me to stay—I hope?"

"'Course, I'm inviting you! You betcha!" Mrs. Olmstead nodded vigorously. "You an' Mr. Rainstar just set yourselves right down, an'—"

"I'm not sure I'll be here for dinner," I said. "I suspect that Miss Aloe won't be either. Please come upstairs, Manuela."

"But, looky here, now!" Mrs. Olmstead protested. "How come you ain't eatin' dinner? How come you let me go to all the trouble o' fixin' it if you wasn't going to eat."

"I'll explain later. Kindly get up those stairs, Manuela."

I pointed sternly. Manny preceded me up the stairs, and I stood aside, waving her into my bedroom ahead of me. Then I closed and locked the door.

I was trembling a little. Shaking with the day's pent-up fear and frustration, its fury and worry. Inwardly, I screamed to strike out at something, the most tempting target being Manny's plump little bottom.

So I wheeled around, my palm literally itching to connect with her flesh. But, instead, Manny's soft mouth connected with mine. She had been waiting on tiptoe, waiting for me to turn. And, now, having kissed me soundly, she urged me down on the bed and sat down at my side.

"I don't blame you for being miffed with me, honey. But I really couldn't help it. I honestly couldn't, Britt!"

"You couldn't, hmm?" I said. "You own the place, and that orange-colored bitch works for you, but you couldn't—"

"*Wh-aat?*" She stared at me incredulously. "Own it—our place, you mean? Why, that's crazy! Of course, I don't own it, and that woman certainly does not work for me!"

"But, dammit to hell—! Wait a minute," I said. "What did you mean when you said you didn't blame me for being miffed with you?"

"Well . . . I thought that was why you were angry. Because I didn't come back from the bathroom."

"Oh," I said. "Oh, yeah. Why didn't you, anyway?"

"Because I couldn't, that's why. I had a little problem, one of those girl things, and it had to be taken care of in a hurry . . . " So she'd hailed a cab, and headed for the nearest drugstore. But it didn't have what she needed and she'd had to visit two other stores before she found one that did. And by the time she'd returned to our place, and taken care of the problem . . .

"You might have waited, Britt. If you'd only waited, and given me a chance to explain—but never mind." She took a three thousand dollar check from her purse, and handed it to me. "Another bonus for you, dear"—she smiled placatingly. "Isn't that nice?"

"Very," I said, folding it and tucking it in my pocket. "I'm going to keep it."

"Keep it? Why, of course, you are. I—"

"I'm keeping the car, too," I said.

"Why not? It's your car."

"But my employment with PXA is finished as of right now. And if you want to know why—as if you didn't already know!—I'll tell you," I said. "And if I catch any more crap like I caught today, I'll tell you what I'll do about that, too!"

I told her in detail—the why and the what—with suitable embellishments and flourishes. I told her in more detail than I had planned, and with considerable ornamentation. For a while she heard me out in silence and without change of expression. I had a strong hunch that she was laughing at me.

When I had at last finished, out of breath and vituperation, she looked at me silently for several moments. Then she shrugged, and stood up.

"I'll run along now. Good-bye and good luck."

I hadn't expected that. I don't know what I had expected, but not that.

"Well, look," I said. "Aren't you going to say anything?"

"I said good-bye and good luck. I see no point in saying anything else."

"But, dammit—! Well, all right!" I said. "Good-bye and good luck to you. And take your stinking bonus check with you!"

I thrust it on her, shoved it into her hand and folded her fingers around it. She left the room, and I hesitated, feeling foolish and helpless, that I had made a botch of everything. Then I started after her, stopping short as I heard her talking with Mrs. Olmstead.

" . . . *loved to have dinner with you, Mrs. Olmstead. But in view of Mr. Rainstar's attitude . . .*"

" . . . *just mean, he is! Accused me of bein' sloppy. Says I'm always sprinklin' rat poison on everything. O' course, I don't do nothin' of the kind . . .*"

"*He should be grateful to you! Most women would leave at the sight of a rat.*"

"*Well . . . Just a minute, Miss Aloe. I'll walk you to your car.*"

It was several minutes before Mrs. Olmstead came back into the house. I waited until I heard her banging around in the kitchen, then went cautiously down the stairs and moved on tiptoe toward the front door.

"Uh-hah!" Her voice arrested me. "Whatcha sneakin' out for? Ashamed because you was so nasty to Miss Aloe?"

She had been lurking at the side of the staircase, out of sight from the upstairs. Apparently she had rushed in and hidden here, after making the racket in the kitchen.

"Well?" She grinned at me with mocking accusation, hands on her skinny old hips. "Whatcha got to say for yourself?"

"What am I sneaking out for?" I said. "What have I got to say for myself? Why, goddammit—!" I stormed toward the door, cursing and fuming. More shamed and furious at myself than I was with her. "And another thing!" I yelled. "Another thing, Mrs. Olmstead! You'd better remember what your position is in this house, if you want to keep it!"

"Now you're threatenin' me." She began to sob noisily. "Threatenin' a poor old woman! Just as mean as you can be, that's what you are!"

"I'm not either mean!" I said. "I don't know how to be mean, and I wouldn't be, if I did know how. I don't like mean people, and— Goddammit, will you stop that goddam bawling?"

"If you wasn't mean, you wouldn't always forget to mail my letters! I found another one this mornin' when I was sending your clothes to the cleaners! I told you it was real important, an'—!"

"Oh, God, I *am* sorry," I said. "Please forgive me, Mrs. Olmstead."

I ran out the door and down the steps. But she was calling to me before I could get out of earshot.

"Your dinner, Mr. Rainstar. It's all ready and waiting."

"Thank you very much," I said. "I'm hungry now, but I'll eat some later."

"It'll be all cold. You better eat now."

"I'm not hungry now. I've had a bad day, and I want to take a walk before I eat."

There was more argument, much more, but she finally slammed the door.

Not that I ever felt much like eating Mrs. Olmstead's cooking, but I certainly had no appetite for it tonight. And, of course, I felt guilty for not wanting to eat, and having to tell her that I didn't. Regardless of whether something is my fault—and why should I have to eat if I didn't want to?—I always feel that I am in the wrong.

Along with feeling guilty, I was worried. About what Manny had done or had arranged to have done, its implications of shrewdness and power. And the fact that I had figuratively flung three thousand dollars in her face, as well as cutting myself off from all further income. At the time, I had felt that I had to do it. But what about the other categorical imperative which faced me? What about the absolute necessity to send money to Connie—to do it or else?

Well, balls to it, I thought, mentally throwing up my hands. I had told Mrs. Olmstead that I wanted to take a walk, so I had better be doing it.

I took a stroll up and down the road, a matter of a hundred yards or so. Then I walked around to the rear of the house, and the weed-grown disarray of the backyard.

A couple of uprights of the gazebo had rotted away, allowing the roof to topple until it was standing almost on edge. The striped awning of the lawn swing hung in faded tatters, and the seats of the swing lay splintered in the weeds where the wind had tossed them. The statuary—the little that hadn't been sold—was now merely fragmented trash, gleaming whitely in the night.

The fountain, at the extreme rear of the yard, had long since ceased to spout. But in the days when water poured from it, the ever-thirsting weeds and other rank growths had flourished into a minuscule jungle. And the jungle still endured, all but obscuring the elaborate masonry and piping of the fountain.

I walked toward it absently, somehow reminded of Goldsmith's *The Deserted Village*.

Reaching the periphery of the ugly overgrowth, I thought I heard the gurgling trickle of water. And, curiously, I parted the dank and dying tangle with my hands, and peered through the opening.

Inches from my face, eyeless eyes peered back at me. The bleached skull of skeleton.

We stared at each other, each seemingly frozen in shock.

Then the skeleton raised a bony hand, and levelled a gun at me.

XII

I SUDDENLY CAME ALIVE. I let out a yell, and flung myself to one side.

The overgrowth closed in front of the skeleton, with my letting go of it. And as he pawed throught it, I scrambled around to the rear of the fountain. There was cover that way, a shield from my frightful pursuer. But that way was also a trap.

The skeleton was between me and the house. Looming behind me, in the moonlit dimness, was the labyrinthine mass, the twisting hills and valleys, of the garbage dump.

I raced toward it, knowing that it was a bad move, that I was running away from possible help. But I continued to run. Running—fleeing—was a way of life with me. Buying temporary safety, regardless of its long-term cost.

Nearing the immediate environs of the garbage mounds, I began to trip and stumble over discarded bottles and cans and other refuse. Once my foot came down hard on a huge rat. And he leaped at me, screaming with pain and rage. Once, when I fell, a rat scampered inside of my coat, clawing and scratching as he raced over my chest and back. And I screamed and beat at myself, long after I was rid of him.

There was a deafening roar in my ears: the thunder of my over-exerted heart and lungs. I began to weep and sob wildly in fear-crazed hysteria, but the sound of it was lost to me.

I crawled-clawed-climbed up a small mountain of refuse, and fell tumbling and stumbling down the other side. Broken bottles and rotting newspapers and stinking globs of food came down on top of me, along with the hideously bloated body of a dead rat. And I swarmed up out of the mess, and continued my staggering, wobble-legged run.

I ran down the littered lanes between the garbage hillocks. I ran back up the lanes. Up, down, down, up. Zigzagging, repeatedly falling and getting to my feet. And going on and on and on. Fleeing through this lonely stinking planet, this lost world of garbage.

I dared not stop. For I was pursued, and my pursuer was gaining on me. Getting closer and closer with every passing moment.

Thoroughly in the thrall of hysteria, I couldn't actually see or hear him. Not in the literal meaning of the words. It was more a matter of being made aware of certain things, of having them thrust upon my consciousness: a discarded bottle, rolling down a garbage heap. Or a heavy shadow falling over my own. Or hurrying footsteps splashing up a spray of filth.

At last, I tottered to the top of a long hummock, and down the other side.

And there, He—It—was. Grabbing me from behind. Wrapping strong arms around me, and holding me helpless.

I screamed, screams that I could not hear.

I struggled violently, fear giving me superhuman strength. And I managed to break free.

But for only a split second.

Then, an arm went around my head, holding it motionless—a target. And then a heavy fist came up, swung in a short, swift arc. And collided numbingly with my chin.

And I went down, down, down.

Into darkness.

XIII

AT THE TIME OF THE ACCIDENT, Connie and I had been married about six months. I had been at work all day on an article for a teacher's magazine, and I came down into the kitchen that evening, tired and hungry, to find Connie clearing away the dirty dishes.

She said she and her father had already eaten, and he'd gone back to his office. She said there were some people in this world who had to work for a living, even if I didn't know it.

"I've been working," I said. "I've almost finished my article."

"Never mind," she said. "Do you want some pancakes or something? There isn't any of the stew left."

"I'm sorry I didn't hear you call me for dinner. I would have been glad to join you."

"Will you kindly tell me whether you want something to eat?" she yelled. "I'm worn out, and I don't feel like arguing. It's just been work, work, work from the time I got up this morning. Cooking and sewing and cleaning, and—and I even washed the car on top of everything else!"

I said that she should never wash a car on top of anything, let alone everything. Then, I said, "Sorry, I would have washed the car. I told you I would."

She said, Oh, sure, a lot I would do. "Just look at you! You can't even shine your shoes. You don't see my daddy going around without his shoes shined, and he *works*."

I looked at her. The spitefully glaring eyes, the shrewish thrust of her chin. And I thought, What the hell gives here, anyway? She and her papa had been increasingly nasty to me almost from the day we were married. But tonight's performance beat anything I had previously been subjected to.

"You and your daddy," I said, "are very, very lovely people. Strange as it may seem, however, your unfailing courtesy and consideration have not made a diet of pancakes and table scraps palatable to me. So I'll go into town and get something to eat, and you and your daddy can go burp in your bibs!"

I was heading for the door as I spoke, for Connie had a vile temper and was not above throwing things at me or striking me with them.

I flung the door open, and—and there was a sickening *thud* and a pained scream from Connie, a scream that ended almost as soon as it began. I turned around, suddenly numb with fear.

Connie lay crumpled on the floor. A deep crease, oozing slow drops of blackish blood, stretched jaggedly across her forehead.

She had been hit by the sharp edge of the door when I threw it open. She was very still, as pale as death.

I grabbed her up and raced out to the car with her. I placed her on the back seat, and slid under the wheel. And I sent the car roaring down the lane from the house, and into the road that ran in front of it. Or, rather, *across* the road. For I was going too fast to make the turn.

The turn was sharp, one that was dangerous even at relatively low speeds. I knew it was, as did everyone else in the area. And I could never satisfactorily explain why I was travelling as fast as I was.

I was unnerved, of course. And, of course, I had lost my head, as I habitually did when confronted with an emergency. But, still . . .

Kind of strange for a man to do something when he danged well knew he shouldn't. Kind of suspicious.

The road skirted a steep cliff. It was almost three hundred feet from the top of the cliff to the bottom. The car went over it, and down it.

I don't know why I didn't go over with it . . . as Connie did.

I couldn't explain, no more than I could explain why I was speeding when I hit the turn. Nor could I prove that I had hit Connie with the door accidentally instead of deliberately.

I was an outsider in a clannish little community, and it was known that I constantly bickered with my wife. And I was the beneficiary of her $100,000 life insurance policy—$200,000 double indemnity.

If Connie's father hadn't stoutly proclaimed me innocent—Connie also defending me as soon as she was able—I suspect that I would have been convicted of attempted murder.

As I still might be . . . unless I myself was murdered.

XIV

THE NIGHT OF THE SKELETON, of my chase through the garbage dump . . .

I was kept under sedation for the rest of that night, and much of the next day and night. I had to be, so great was the damage to my nervous system. Early the following afternoon, after I had gotten some thirty-six hours of rest and treatment, Detective Sergeant Jeff Claggett was admitted to my hospital room.

It was Jeff who had followed me into the garbage dump, subsequently knocking me out when I could not be reasoned with. He had taken up the chase after hearing my yell, and seeing my flight away from the house. But he had seen no one pursuing me.

"I suppose no one was," I admitted, a little sheepishly. "I know he started around the fountain after me. But I was so damned sure that he was right on my tail that I didn't turn around to see if he was."

"Can't say that I blame you," Claggett nodded. "Must've given you a hell of shock to come up against something like that pointing a gun at you. Any idea who it was?"

"No way of telling." I shook my head. "Just someone in a skeleton costume. You've probably seen them—a luminous skeleton painted on black cloth."

"Not much of a lead. Could've been picked up anywhere in the country," Claggett said. "Tell me, Britt. Do you walk around in your backyard as a regular thing. I mean, could the guy have known you'd be there at about such and such a time?"

"No way," I said. "I haven't been in the backyard in the last five years."

"Then he was just hiding there in the weeds, don't you suppose? Keeping out of sight, say, until he could safely come into the house."

"Come into the house?" I laughed shakily. "Why would he want to do that?"

"Well . . . " Jeff Claggett gave me a deadpan look. "Possibly he was after your money and valuables. After all, everyone knows you're a very wealthy man."

"You're kidding!" I said. "Anyone who knows anything about me knows that I don't have a pot to—"

"Right." He cut me off. "So what the guy was after was you. He'd have you pinned down in the house. You'd probably wake up—he'd wake you, of course—to find him bending over your bed. A skeleton grinning

57

at you in the dark. You couldn't get away from him, and—yes? Something wrong, Britt?"

"Something *wrong!*" I shuddered. "What are you trying to do to me, Jeff?"

"Who hates you that much, Britt? And don't tell me you don't know!"

"But—but I don't," I stammered. "I've probably rubbed a lot of people the wrong way, but . . . "

I broke off, for he was holding something in front of me, then dropping it on the bed with a grimace. A pamphlet bylined by me, with a line attributing sponsorship to PXA.

"That's why I came out to see you the other night, Britt. I ran across it in the library, and I was sure the use of your name was unauthorized. But I guess I was wrong, wasn't I?"

I hesitated, unable to meet his straightforward blue eyes, their uncompromising honesty. I took a sip of water through a glass straw, mumbled a kind of defiant apology for my employment with PXA.

"It's nothing to be ashamed of, Jeff. It was a public service thing. Nothing to do with the company's other activities."

"No?" Claggett said wryly. "Those activities paid for your work, didn't they? A lot more than it was worth, too, unless my information is all wrong. Three thousand dollars a month, plus bonuses, plus a car, plus an expense account, plus—Let's see. What else was included in the deal? A very juicy—and willing—young widow?"

"Look," I said, red-faced. "What's this got to do with what happened to me?"

"Don't kid me, Britt. I've talked to her—her and her uncle both. It's normal procedure to inform a man's employers when he's had a mishap. So I had a nice little chat with them, and you know what I think?"

"I think you're going to tell me what you think."

"I think that Patrick Xavier Aloe had been expecting Manuela to visit some unpleasantness upon you, and is now sure that she did. I think he gave her plenty of hell, as soon as I left the office."

I thought the same, although I didn't say so. Claggett went on to reveal that he had talked with Mrs. Olmstead. Learning, of course, that we were much more than employer and employee.

"She put out a lot of money for you, my friend. Or arranged to have it put out. She also put out something far more important to a girl like that. I imagine she only did it in the belief that you were going to marry her . . . "

He waited, studying me. I nodded reluctantly.

"I should have known what was expected of me," I said. "Hell, maybe I did know, but wouldn't admit it. At any rate, it was a lousy thing to do, and I probably deserve whatever she hands out."

"Oh, well," Claggett shrugged. "You weren't very nice to your wife either."

"Probably not, but she's an entirely different case. Manny was good to me. I never got anything from Connie and her old man but a hard time."

"You say so, and I believe you," said Claggett warmly. "Any damage you do, I imagine, is the result of *not* doing; just letting things slide. You don't have the initiative to deliberately hurt anyone."

"Thanks," I said. "I guess."

He chuckled good-naturedly. "Tell me about Connie and her father. Tell me how you happened to marry her, since it obviously wasn't a love match."

I gave him a brief history of my meeting and association with the Bannermans. Then, since he seemed genuinely interested, I gave him a quick rundown on Britton Rainstar, after fortune had ceased to smile upon him and he had become Lo, the Poor Indian.

Jeff Claggett listened attentively. Laughing, frowning, exclaiming, wincing and shaking his head, by turns. When I had finished, he said that I was obviously much tougher than he had supposed. I must be to survive the many messes I had got myself into.

"Just one damned thing after another!" he swore. "I don't know how the hell you could do it!"

"Join the crowd," I said. "Nobody has ever known how I did it. Including me."

"Well, getting back to the present. Miss Aloe expected you to marry her. How did she take the news that you couldn't?"

"A lot better than I had any right to expect," I said. "She was just too good about it to be true, if you know what I mean. Everything was beautiful for around six weeks, just as nice as it had been from the beginning. Then a couple of days ago, the day of the evening I jumped this character in the skeleton suit—"

"Hold it a minute. I want to write this down."

He took a notebook and pencil from his pocket, then nodded for me to proceed. I did so, telling him of the dog and the mulatto woman, and the bartender who had thrown the drink in my face.

Jeff made a few notations to his notes when I had finished, then returned the book and pencil to his coat. Leaning back in his chair, he stared up at the ceiling meditatively, hands locked behind his head.

"Three separate acts," he said, musingly. "Four counting the skeleton routine. But there's a connection between them. The tie-in is in the result of those acts. To give you a hard jolt when you least expect it."

"Yes," I said uneasily. "They certainly did that all right."

"I wonder. I just wonder if that's how her husband died."

"You know about him?" An icy rill tingled down my spine. "She told me he died very suddenly, but I just assumed it was from a heart attack."

Claggett said that all deaths were ultimately attributable to heart failure, adding that he had no very sound grounds for regarding the death of Manny's husband as murder.

"They were at this little seacoast when it was hit by a hurricane. Wiped out almost half the town. Her husband was one of the dead. Wait, now"—he held up his hand, as I started to speak. "Naturally, she couldn't have arranged the hurricane, but she could have used it to cover his murder. I'd say she had plenty of reason to want him out of the way."

"I gather that he wasn't much good," I said. "But—"

"She dropped out of sight right after the funeral. Disappeared without a trace, and she didn't show up again for about a year."

"Well?" I said. "I still don't see . . . "

"Well, neither do I," Claggett said easily, his manner suddenly changing. "What are you going to do now, Britt, that you've quit the pamphlet writing?"

I said that I wished to God I knew. I wouldn't have any money to live on, and none to send Connie, which would surely cause all hell to pop. I was beginning to regret that I'd quit the job, even though I'd had no choice in the matter.

Claggett said I didn't have one now either. I had to go back on the job. "You'll be safer than if you didn't, Britt. So far Miss Aloe's only given you a bad shaking up. But she might try for a knockout if she thinks you're getting away from her."

"We don't actually *know* that she's done anything," I said. "We think she's responsible, but we're certainly not sure."

"Right. And we never will be if you break completely with her. Not until it's too late."

"But I've already quit! And I made it pretty damned clear that I meant it!"

"But she didn't tell her uncle apparently. Probably afraid of catching more hell than he's already given her." He stood up, dusting at his trousers. "I'll be having a little chat with both of them today, and I'll tip her off privately first—let her know that you're keeping the job. You can bet she'll be tickled pink to hear it."

The door opened and a bright-faced young nurse came in. She gave me a quick smile, then said something to Jeff that was too low for me to hear.

He nodded, dismissing her, and turned back to me. "Have to run, I guess," he said. "Okay? Everything all right?"

"Absolutely perfect," I said bitterly. "How else could it be for a guy with a schizoid wife, and a paranoid girlfriend? If one of them can't send me to prison or the electric chair, the other will put me in the nuthouse or the morgue! Well, screw it"—I plopped back on the pillows. "What are you chatting with the Aloes about?"

"Oh, this and that," he shrugged. "About you mainly, I suppose. They're very concerned about you and anxious to see you, of course . . . "

"Of course!

"So, if it's all right with you, I'll have them drop in around five."

XV

THERE IS SOMETHING UTTERLY UNNERVING ABOUT AN ABSOLUTELY HONEST MAN, a man like Sergeant Jeff Claggett. You rationalize and lie to him until your supply of deceit is exhausted; and his questions and comments are never brutal or blunt. He simply persists, when you have already had your say, looking at you when you can no longer look at him. And, finally, though nothing has been admitted, you know you have been in the fight of your life.

So I don't know what Jeff said that afternoon to Manuela and Patrick Xavier Aloe. It is likely that he was quite offhand and casual, that he said nothing at all of intrinsic significance. But they came into my room, a tinge of strain to their expressions, and Manny's lips seemed a little stiff as she stooped to kiss me.

I shook hands with Pat and stated that I was fine, just fine. They stated that that was fine, just fine, and that I was looking fine, just fine.

There was an awkward moment of silence after that, while I smiled at them and was smiled back at. Manny shattered the tension by bursting into giggles. They made her very nice to look at, shaking and shivering her in all her shakable, shivery parts.

Pulse pounding, I tentatively joined in her laughter. But Pat saw no cause for amusement.

"What's with you?" He glared at her. "We got a sick man here. He gets a damned stupid joke pulled on him, and it puts him in the hospital. You think that's funny?"

"Now, Uncle Pat ... " Manny gestured placatingly.

"Britt lands in the hospital, and we get cops nosing all around! Maybe you like that, huh? You think cops are funny?"

"There was only one, Pat. Just Sergeant Claggett, and he's a family friend, isn't he, Britt?"

"A very old friend," I said. "Jeff—Sergeant Claggett, that is—would be concerned, regardless of why I was in the hospital."

"Well—" Pat Aloe was somewhat reassured. "Anything else happen to you recently, Britt? I mean, any little jokes like this last one?"

I hesitated, feeling Manny's eyes on me. Wondering what Jeff would consider the best answer. Pat's gaze moved from me to Manny, and she smiled at him sunnily.

"Of course, nothing else has happened to him, Pat. This is his first time in the hospital, isn't it?"

"That's right," I said; and gave him the qualified truth. "There's been nothing like this before."

He relaxed at that, his map-of-Ireland face creasing in a grin. He said he was damned glad to hear it, because they'd been getting A-OK reactions to the pamphlets, and he'd hate to see them loused up.

"And we'd hate to lose the tax write-off," Manny said. "Don't forget that, Uncle Pat."

"Shut up," Pat said, and to me: "Then everything's copacetic, right, Britt? You're gonna go right on working for us?"

"I'd like to," I said. "I understand that I'll be under medical supervision for a while, have to take things kind of easy. But if that's all right with you . . . "

He boomed that, of course, it was all right. "And don't you worry about the hospital and doctor bills. We got kind of a private insurance plan that takes care of everything in the medical line."

"That's great," I said. "I'm obliged to you."

"Forget it. Whatever makes you happy makes us happy, right, Manny? Anything that's jake with Britt—Britt and his friend, Sergeant Claggett—"

"—is jake with us," Manny said emphatically. "Right, Uncle Pat! Right on!"

And Pat shot her a warning look. "One more thing, Britt, baby. I was way out of line saying anything about you and Manny getting married. What the hell? That's your business not mine."

"*Right!*" said Manny.

"You want a bat in the chops?" He half-raised his hand. "Keep askin', and you're gonna get it."

I broke in to say quite truthfully that I would have been glad to marry Manny, if I had been free to do so. Pat said, sure, sure, so who was kicking? "It's okay with me, and it's okay with her. She don't like it, she can shove it up her ass."

"Right back at you, you sawed-off son-of-a-bitch," said Manny, and she made an upward jabbing motion with one finger.

Pat leaped. He grabbed her by the shoulders; shook her so vigorously that her head seemed to oscillate, her hair flying out from it in a golden blur. He released her with a shove that slammed her into the wall. And the noise of his angry breathing almost filled the room.

I felt a litle sick. Savagery like this was something I had never seen before. As for Manny . . .

Something undefinable happened to her face. A flickering of expressions that wiped it free of expression, then caused it to crinkle joyously, to wreathe itself in a cherubic smile.

Pat looked away, gruffly abashed. "Let's go"—he jerked a thumb over his shoulder. "Get out of here, and let Britt get some rest."

"You go ahead," she said. "I want to kiss Britt good-night."

"Who's stopping you? You kissed him in front of me before."

"Huh-uh. Not this way I didn't."

He gave me an embarrassed glance, then shrugged and said he could stand it if I could. He told me to take it easy, and left. And Manny crossed to the door, locked it and came back to the bed. She looked down, then bent down so close that her breasts brushed against me.

"Go ahead," she whispered. "Grab a handful."

"Now, dammit, Manny . . . !" I tried to sit up. "Listen to me, Manny!"

"Look"—edging her blouse down. "Look how nice they are."

"I said, *listen to me!*"

"Oh, all right," she said poutingly. "I'm listening."

"You've got to stop it," I said. "We'll forget what's already happened. Just say I had it coming, and call it quits. But there can't be any more, understand? And don't ask me any more what!"

"Any more what?"

"Please," I said. "I'm trying to help you. If you'll just stop now . . . "

"But I really don't know what you mean, darling. If you'll just tell me what you want me to stop, what else I shouldn't do . . . "

"All right," I said. "I've done my best."

She studied me a moment, the tip of her finger in her mouth. Then, she nodded, became pseudo-businesslike. Declared that she knew just what I needed, and it so happened that she had brought a supply with her.

As I have noted previously, she moved very, very quickly when she chose. So she was on the bed, on top of me, before I knew what was happening. Smothering me with softness, moving against me sensuously.

There was an abrupt metallic squeal from the bed. Then a grating and a scraping, and a *crash*. Instinctively, I jerked my head up, so it did not smash against the hard hospital floor. But my neck snapped, painfully, and Manny helped me to my feet, murmuring apologies.

Someone was pounding on the door, noisily working at the lock. It opened suddenly and the nurse came in, almost at a run. It was the nurse I had seen earlier, the bright-faced young woman. None-too-gently she brushed Manny aside, and seated me comfortably in a chair. She felt my pulse and forehead, gave me a few fussy little pats. Then, she turned on Manny, who was casually adjusting her clothes.

"Just what happened here, miss? Why was that door locked?"

Manny grinned at her impudently. "A broken down bed and a locked door, and you ask me what *happened?* How long have you been a woman, dear?"

The nurse turned brick red. Her arm shot out, the finger at its end pointing sternly toward the door. "I want you out of here, miss! Right this minute!"

"Oh, all right," Manny said. "Unless I can do something else for Britt . . . "

"No," I said. "Please do as the nurse says, Manny."

She did so, lushly compact hips swinging provocatively. The nurse looked after her, a little downcast, I thought, as though doing some comparative weighing and finding herself sadly wanting.

An orderly removed the collapsed bed, and wheeled in another. I was put into it, and a doctor examined me and pronounced me indestructible.

"Just the same," he said, winking at me lewdly, "you lay off the double-sacking with types like that pocket Venus that was in here. I'd say she could spot you a tailwind, and still beat you into port."

"Oh, she could not," the nurse said, reddening gloriously the moment the words were out of her mouth. "How would you know, anyway?"

"We-ll . . . " He gave her a wisely laconic grin. "How would *you?*"

He slapped unsuccessfully at her bottom on the way out. She jerked away, greatly flustered, and darted a glance at me. And, of course, found nothing in my expression but earnest goodwill.

She was much prettier than I had thought at first glance. She had superb bone structure, and her hair, too austerely coiffed beneath her nurse's cap, was deep auburn.

"I don't believe I've seen you before today," I said. "Are you new on this floor?"

"Well . . . " She hesitated. "I guess I'm new on all of them. I mean, I'm a substitute nurse."

"I see," I said. "Well, I think you're a fine nurse, and I'm sure you'll have regular duty before long."

She twitched pleasurably, like a petted puppy. Then, her scrubbed-clean face fell, and she sighed heavily.

"I thought I was going to have steady work starting tomorrow," she said. "Steady for a while, anyway. But after what happened today—Well, I'll be held responsible. The bed wouldn't have been broken down, if I hadn't allowed the door to be locked. You could have been seriously injured, and it's all my fault and—"

"Wait." I held up a hand. "Hold it a minute. It wasn't your fault, it was mine, and I won't allow the hospital to blame you for it. You just have your supervisor talk to me, and I'll straighten her out fast."

· "Thank you, Mr. Rainstar, but the supervisor has already reported the matter to Sergeant Claggett. She had to, you know. Her orders were to report anything unusual that happened to you. So . . . "

I was the regular duty the nurse had hoped to have. The doctors felt that for a time at least, when I returned home, I should have a full-time nurse available. and she had seemed a likely candidate for the job. But Jeff Claggett would never approve of her now.

"I really blew it," she said, with unconscious humor. "I'll bet the sergeant is really disgusted with me."

I said loftily that she was to forget the sergeant. After all, *I* was the one who had to be satisfied, and she satisfied me in every respect, so she could consider herself hired.

"Oh, that's wonderful, just wonderful!" She wriggled delightedly. "You're sure Sergeant Claggett will approve?"

"If he doesn't, he'll have me to deal with," I said. "But I'm sure it'll be fine with him."

But I wasn't sure, of course. And, of course, it wasn't fine with him.

XVI

HE RETURNED TO THE HOSPITAL SHORTLY AFTER I HAD FINISHED MY DINNER THAT EVENING. He had been busy since leaving me, checking at the cocktail lounge where I had gotten a drink in my face, and with the mulatto woman who managed the quiet little hotel. In neither case had his investigation come to aught but naught.

The bartender had quit his job, and departed town for parts unknown to the lounge owner. Or so, at least, the latter said. The hotel had the same owners it had always had—a large eastern realty company, which was the absentee landlord for literally hundreds of properties. The manageress owned no dog, denied any knowledge of one, also denying that she had done anything but rent me and "my wife" a room.

"So that's that," Claggett said. "If you like, I can put out a John Doe warrant on the bartender, but I don't think it's worth the trouble. Assuming we could run him down, which I doubt, throwing a drink on you wouldn't add up to more than a misdemeanor."

"By itself," I nodded. "But when you add it onto the business with the dog, and—"

"How are you going to add it on? You're a married man, but you register into this hotel with another woman as Mr. and Mrs. Phoneyname. And you tied your hands right there. The manageress was lying, sure. But try to prove it, and you'll look like a jerk."

He seemed rather cross and out of sorts. I suggested as much, adding that I hoped I wasn't the cause of same.

He gave me a look, seemed on the point of saying something intemperate. Then he sighed wearily, and shook his head.

"I guess you just can't help it," he said tiredly. "You seem incapable of learning from experience. You know, or should know, that Miss Aloe is out to harm you. You don't know how far she intends to go, which makes her all the more dangerous to you. But you let her get rid of Pat, you let her lock the door, you let her come back to the bed and make certain adjustments to it—"

"Look," I protested. "She didn't do all those things separately with a time lapse between them. She's a very quick-moving little girl, and she did everything in a matter of seconds. Before I knew what was happening, she—" I broke off. "Uh, what do you mean, certain adjustments?" I said.

"The bed goes up and down, right? Depending on whether you want to sit up or sleep or whatever. And here, right here where I'm pointing"—he pointed. "Do you see it, that little lever?"

"I see it," I said.

"Well, that's the safety. It locks the bed into the position you put it in."

"I know," I said. "They explained that to me the first day I was here."

"That's good," Claggett said grimly. "That's real good. Well, if Miss Aloe was out to fracture your skull, she couldn't have had a more cooperative subject. You let her flip the safety, and use her weight to give you an extra-hard bang against the the floor. You didn't let her tie a rocket to you, but I imagine you would if she'd asked you."

My mouth was suddenly very dry. I took a sip or two of water, then raised the glass and drained it.

"I thought it was just a silly accident," I said. "It never occurred to me that she'd try anything here in the hospital."

"Well, watch yourself from now on," Claggett said. "You're going to be thrown together a lot, I understand, in the course of doing these pamphlets. Or am I correct about that?"

"Well"—I shrugged. "That depends largely on Manny. She's calling the turns. The amount of time we spend together depends on her."

"Better count on more time with her than less, then," he said. "This little stunt she pulled today—well, I doubt that it was really a try for a knockout. Whenever she's ready for that, if she ever is ready, I think she'll stay in the background and have someone else do it."

I said, Yes, I supposed he was right. He made an impatient little gesture, as though I had said something annoying.

"But we can't be sure, Britt! We can't say what she might do since she probably doesn't know herself. Look at what's happened to you so far. She couldn't have planned those things. They've just been spur-of-the-moment—pulled out of her hat as she went along."

I made no comment this time. He went on to say that he'd done some heavy thinking about Manny's vanishing for a year after her husband's death. And there was only one logical answer as to where she had been, and why.

"A private sanitarium, Britt, a place where she could get psychiatric help. Her mind started bending with the trouble her husband gave her, and it finally broke when he died—or when she killed him. I'd say that your telling her you were married was more than she could take, and it's started her on another mental breakdown."

"Well," I laughed nervously. "That's not a very comforting thought."

"You'll be all right as long as you're careful. Just watch yourself—and her. Think now. Everything that's happened to you so far has been at least partly your own fault. In a sense, you've set yourself up."

I gave that a moment's thought, and then I said, All right, he was right. I would be very, very careful from now on. Since I had but one life to live, I would do everything in my power to go on living it.

"You have my solemn promise, Jeff. *I* shall do everything in *my* power to keep *myself* alive and unmaimed. Now, just what are you doing along that line?"

"I've done certain things inside your house," he said. "If there's ever any trouble just let out a yell, and you'll have help within a minute."

"How?" I said. "You mean you have the place bugged?"

"Don't try to find out," he said. "If you don't know, Miss Aloe won't, and if you did she would. You're really pretty transparent, Britt."

"Oh, now, I don't know about that," I said. "I—"

"Well, I *do* know. You're not only just about incapable of deceiving anyone for any length of time, but you're also very easy to deceive. So take my word for it that you'll be all right. Just yell and you'll have help."

"I don't like it," I said. "Suppose I couldn't yell? That I didn't have time, or I wasn't allowed to?"

Claggett laughed, shook his head chidingly. "Now, Britt, be reasonable. You'll have a full-time nurse right in the house with you, and she'll be checking on you periodically. It's inconceivable that you could need help and be unable to get it."

It wasn't inconceivable to me. I could think of any number of situations in which I would need help and be unable to cry out for it. And, for the record, one of those situations *did* come about. It *did* happen, the spine-chilling, hair-raising occurrence I had most feared. And just when I was feeling safest, and most secure. And I could see no way of hollering for help without hastening my already imminent demise.

All I could do was lie quiet, as I was ordered to, and listen to my hair turn grayer still. Wondering, foolishly, if I could ever get an acceptable tint job on it, assuming that I lived long enough to need one.

But that is getting ahead of the story. It is something that was yet to happen. Tonight, the night of which I am writing, Claggett pointed out that he was only a detective sergeant and that as such there was a limit to what he could do for my protection.

"And I'm sure the arrangements I've made are enough, Britt. With you staying on the alert, and with a good reliable nurse on hand, I'm confident that—" He broke off, giving me a sudden sharp look. "Yes?" he said. "Something on your mind?"

"Well, uh, yes," I said uncomfortably. "About the nurse. I'd like to have the one who's on duty tonight. That kind of pretty reddish-haired one. I—I, uh—I mean, she needs the job, and—"

"Not a chance," Claggett said flatly. "Not in a thousand years. I've got another nurse in mind, an older woman. Used to be a matron at the jail a few years back. I'll have her come in right now, and you can be getting acquainted tonight."

He got up and started toward the door. I said, Wait a minute, and he paused and turned around.

"Well?"

"Well, I'd kind of like to have the reddish-haired girl. She wants the job, and I'm sure she'd be just fine."

"Fine for what?" Claggett said. "No, don't tell me. You just take care of golden-haired Miss Aloe, and forget about your pretty little redhead."

I said I didn't have anything like that in mind at all. Whatever it was he thought I had in mind. My God, with Connie and Manny to contend with, I'd be crazy to start anything up with another girl.

"So?" said Claggett, then cut me off with a knifing gesture of his hand as I began another protest. "I don't care if you did promise her the job. You had no right to make such a promise, and she knows it as well as you do."

He turned, and stalked out of the room.

I expected him to be back almost immediately, bringing the ex-police matron with him. But he was gone for almost a half an hour, and he came back looking wearily resigned.

"You win," he said, dropping heavily into a chair. "You get your redhaired nurse."

"I do?" I said. "I mean, why?"

"Because she spread it all around that she had the job. She was so positive about it that even the nurse I had in mind was convinced and she got sore and quit."

"I'm sorry," I said. "I really didn't mean to upset your plans, Jeff."

"I know." He shrugged. "I just wish I could feel better about the redhead."

"I'm sure she'll work out fine," I said. "She got off to a bad start today by letting Manny lock the door and pull the bed trick. But—"

"What?" said Claggett. "Oh, well, that didn't bother me. That could have happened, regardless of who was on duty. The thing that bothers me about Miss Redhead Scrubbed-Clean is that I can't check her out."

I said, Oh—not knowing quite why I said it. Or why the hair on the back of my neck had gone through the motions of attempting to rise.

" . . . raised on a farm," Jeff Claggett was saying. "No neighbors for miles around. No friends. Her parents were ex-teachers, and they gave her her schooling. They did a first-class job of it, too, judging by her entrance exams at nursing school. She scored an academic rating of high-school graduate plus two years of college. She was an honors graduate in nursing, and I can't turn up anything but good about her since she made RN. Still"—he shook his head troubledly. "I don't actually *know* anything about her for the first eighteen years of her life. There's nothing I can check on, not even a birth certificate, from the time she was born until she entered nurses' training."

A linen creaked noisily down the hallway. From somewhere came the crash of a dinner tray. (*Probably the redhead pounding on a patient.*)

"Look, Jeff," I said. "In view of what you've told me, and after much deliberation, I think I'd better have a different nurse."

"Not possible." Jeff shook his head firmly. "You promised her the job. I went along with your decision, when I found that my matron friend wasn't and wouldn't be available. Try to back down on the deal now, and we'd have the union on us."

"I'll tell you something," I said. "I find that I've undergone a very dramatic recovery. My condition has improved at least a thousand percent, and I'm not going to need a nurse at all."

Claggett complained that I hadn't been listening to him. I'd already engaged a nurse, the redhead, and the doctors said I *did* need one.

"I've probably got the wind up over nothing, anyway, Britt. After all, the fact that I can't check on her doesn't mean that she's hiding anything, now does it?"

"Yes," I said. "I think it's proof positive that she was up to no good during those lost years of her nonage, and that she is planning more of the same for me."

Claggett chuckled that I was kidding, that I was always kidding. I said, Not so, that I only kidded when I was nervous or in mortal fear for my life, as in the present instance.

"It's kind of a defense mechanism," I explained. "I reason that I can't be murdered or maimed while would-be evildoers are laughing."

Claggett said brusquely to knock off the nonsense. He was confident that the nurse would work out fine. If he'd had any serious doubts about her, he'd've acted upon them.

"I'll have to go now, Britt. Have a good night, and I'll talk to you tomorrow."

"Wait!" I said. "What if I'm murdered in my sleep?"

"Then I won't talk to you," he said, irritably.

And he left the room before I could say anything else.

I got up and went to the bathroom. The constant dryness of my mouth had caused me to drink an overabundance of water.

I came out of the bathroom, and climbed back into bed.

The hall door opened silently, and the reddish-haired nurse came in.

XVII

SHE WAS WHEELING A MEDICINE CART IN FRONT OF HER, a cart covered with a chaos of bottles and vials and hypodermic needles. Having gotten the job as my regular full-time nurse seemed to have given her self-confidence. And she smiled at me brilliantly, and introduced herself.

"I'm Miss Nolton, Mr. Rainstar. Full name, Kate Nolton, but I prefer to be called Kay."

"Well, all right, Kay," I said, smiling stiffly (and doubtless foolishly). "It seems like a logical preference."

"What?" she frowned curiously. "I don't understand."

"I mean, it's reasonable to call you Kay since your name is Kate. But it wouldn't seem right to call you Kate if your name was Kay. I mean—Oh, forget it," I groaned. "My God! Do you play tennis, Kay?"

"I love tennis! How about you?"

"Yeah, how about me?" I said.

"Well?"

"Not very," I said.

"I mean, do you play tennis?"

No," I said.

She sort of smile-frowned at me. She picked up my wrist, and tested my pulse. "Very fast. I thought so," she said. "Turn over on your side, please."

She took a hypodermic needle from the sterilizer, and began to draw liquid into it from a vial. Then she glanced at me, and gestured with light impatience.

"I said to turn on your side, Mr. Rainstar."

"I am on my side."

"I mean, the other side! Turn your back to me."

"But that wouldn't be polite."

"Mr. Rainstar!" She almost stamped her foot. "If you don't turn your back to me, right this minute—!"

I turned, as requested. She jerked the string on my pajamas, and started to lower them.

"Wait a minute!" I said. "What are you doing, anyway?"

She told me what she was doing, adding that I was the silliest man she had ever seen in her life. I told her I couldn't allow it. It was the complete reversal of the normal order of things.

"A girl doesn't take a *man's* pants down," I said. "Everyone knows that. The correct procedure is for the man to take the *girl's—Ooowtch!* WHAT THE GODDAM HELL ARE YOU TRYING TO DO, WOMAN?"

"Shh, hush! The very idea making all that fuss over a teensy little hypo! Sergeant Claggett told me you were just a big old baby."

"That's why he's only a sergeant," I said. "An upper echelon officer would have instructed you in the proper treatment of wounds, namely to kiss them and make them well."

That got her. Her face turned as red as her hair. "Why, you—you—! Are you suggesting that I kiss your *a* double *s?*"

I yawned prodigiously. "That's exactly what I'm suggesting," I said, and yawned again. "I might add that it's probably the best *o* double *f* offer you'll ever get in your career as an assassin."

"All right," she said. "I think I'll just take you up on it. Just push it up here where I can get at it good, and—"

"Get away from me, goddammit!" I said. "Go scrub out a bedpan or something."

"Let's see now. Ahh, there it is! *Kitchy-coo!*"

"Get! Go away, you crazy broad!"

"*Kitchy-kitchy-coo. . . .*"

"Dammit, if you don't get away from me, I'm going to . . . going to . . . going—"

My eyes snapped shut. I drifted into sleep. Or, rather, half-sleep.

I was asleep, but aware that she had dropped into a chair. That she was shaking silently, hugging herself; then rocking back and forth helplessly and shrieking with laughter. I was aware when other people came into the room to investigate. Other nurses, and some orderlies and a couple of doctors.

The silly bastards were practically packed into my room. A couple of them even sat down on my bed, jouncing me up and down on it as they laughed.

I thought, *Now, dammit—*

My thought ended there.

I lost all awareness.

And I fell into deep unknowing sleep.

I slept so soundly that I felt hung over and somewhat grouchy the next morning when Kay Nolton awakened me. She looked positively asceptic, all bright-eyed and clean-scrubbed. It depressed me to see anyone look that good in the early morning, and it was particularly depressing in view of the way I looked, which, I'm sure, was ghastly. Or shitty, to use the polite term.

Kay secured the usual matchbook size bar of hospital soap—one wholly adequate for lathering the ass of a sick gnat. She secured a tiny wedge of threadbare washcloth, suitable for scrubbing the aforementioned. She dumped soap and washcloth into one of those shiny hospital basins—which, I suspect, are used for puking in as well as sponge-bathing—and she carried it into the bathroom to fill with water.

I jumped out of bed, and flattened myself against the wall at one side of the bathroom door. When she came out, eyes fixed on the basin, I slipped into the bathroom and into the shower.

I heard her say, "Mr. Rainstar. *Mr. Rainstar!* Where in the world—"

Then, I turned on the shower full, and I heard no more.

I came back into my room with a towel wrapped around me. Kay popped a thermometer into my mouth.

"Now why did you do that anyway? I had everything all ready to—*Don't talk! You'll drop the thermometer!*—give you a sponge bath! You knew I did! So why in the world did you—*I said, Don't talk, Mr. Rainstar!* I know you probably don't feel well, and I appreciate your giving me a job. But is that any reason to—*Mr. Rainstar!*"

She relieved me of the thermometer at last. Frowned slightly as she examined it, then shrugged, apparently finding its verdict acceptable. She checked my pulse, and ditto, ditto. She asked if I needed any help in dressing, and I said I didn't. She said I should just go ahead then, and she would bring in my breakfast. And I said I would and I did and she did.

Since she was now officially my employee, rather than the hospital's, she brought coffee for herself on the breakfast tray. Sat sipping it, chatting companionably, as I ate.

"You know what I'm going to do for you today, Mr. Rainstar? I mean, I will if you want me to."

"All I want you to do," I said, "is shoot me with a silver bullet. Only thus will my tortured heart be at rest."

"Oh?" she said blankly. "I was going to say that I'd wash and tint your hair for you. If you wanted me to, that is."

I grinned, then laughed out loud. Not at her, but myself. Because how could anyone have behaved as idiotically as I had? And with no real reason whatsoever. I had stepped on Jeff Claggett's toes, making a commitment without first consulting him. He hadn't liked that naturally enough; I had already stretched his patience to the breaking point. So he had punished me—warned me against any further intrusions upon his authority—by expressing serious doubts about Kay Nolton. When I over-reacted to this he had hastily backed-water, pointing out that he would not be leaving me in her care, if he had had any reservations about her. But I was off and running by then. Popping off every which way, carrying on like a damned nut, and getting wilder and wilder by the minute.

Kay was looking at me uncertainly, a lovely blush spreading over her face and neck and down into her cleavage. So I stopped laughing and said she must pay no attention to me, since I, sad to say, was a complete jackass.

"I'm sorry as hell about last night. I don't know why I get that way, but if I do it again, give me an enema in the ear of something. Okay?"

"Now, you were perfectly all right, Mr. Rainstar," she said stoutly. "I was pretty far out of line myself. I knew you were a highly nervous type, but I teased you and made jokes when I should have—"

"—when you should have given me that enema," I said. "How are you at ear enemas, anyway? The technique is practically the same as if you were doing it you-know-where. Just remember to start at the top instead of the bottom, and you'll have it made."

She had started giggling; rosy face glowing, eyes bright with mirth. I said I was giving her life tenure at the task of futzing with my hair. I said I would also give her a beating with a wet rope if she didn't start calling me Britt instead of Mr. Rainstar.

"Now that we have that settled," I said, "I want you to get up, back up and bend over."

"B-bend over—*ah, ha, ha*—W-why, Britt?"

"So that I can climb on your shoulders, of course. I assume you are carrying me out of this joint piggyback?"

She said, "Ooops!" and jumped up. "Be back in just a minute, Britt!"

She hurried out of the room, promptly hurrying back with a wheelchair. It was a rule, it seemed, that all patients, ambulatory or not, had to be wheeled out of the hospital. So I climbed into the conveyance, and Kay fastened the crossbar across my lap, locking me into it. Then she wheeled me down to and into the elevator, and, subsequently, out of the elevator and into the lobby.

She parked me there at a point near the admitting desk, Admitting also being the place where departing patients were checked out. While she crossed to the desk and conferred with the registrar—or *un*-registrar—I sat gazing out through the building's main entrance, musing that the hospital's bills could be reduced to a level the average patient could pay if so much money had not been spent on inexcusable nonsense.

A particularly execrable example of such nonsense was this so-called main entrance of the hospital, which was not so much an entrance—main or otherwise—as it was a purely decorative and downright silly integrant of the structure's facade.

Interiorly, it consisted of four double doors, electronically activated. The exterior approach was via some thirty steep steps, each some forty feet in length, mounting to a gin-mill Gothic quadruple archway. (It looked like a series of half-horseshoes doing a daisy chain.)

Hardly anyone used this multimillion-dollar monstrosity for entrance or egress. How the hell could they? People came and went by the completely plain, but absolutely utilitarian, side entrance, which was flush with the abutting pavement, and required neither stepping down from nor up to.

It was actually the only one the hospital needed. The other was not only extravagantly impractical, it also had a kind of vertigo-ish, acrophobic quality.

Staring out on its stupidly expensive expanse, one became a little dizzy, struck with the notion that he was being swept forward at a smoothly imperceptible but swiftly increasing speed. Even I, a level-headed, unflappable guy like me, was beginning to feel that way.

I rubbed my eyes, looked away from the entrance toward Kay. But neither she nor the admitting desk were where I had left them. The desk was far, far behind me and so was Kay. She was sprinting toward me as fast as her lovely, long legs could carry her, and yet she was receding, like a character in one of those old-timey silent movies.

I waved to her, exaggeratedly mouthing the words, "What gives?"

She responded with a wild waving and flapping of both her arms, simultaneously jumping up and down as though taken by a fit of hysterics.

Ah-ha! I thought shrewdly. Something exceeding strange is going on here!

There was a loud *SWOOSH* as one of the double doors launched open.

There was a loud *"YIKE!"* as I shot through it.

There were mingled moans and groans, yells and screams (also from me), as I sped across the terrazzo esplanade to the dizzying brink of those steep, seemingly endless stone steps.

I had the feeling that those steps were much harder than they looked, and that they were even harder than they looked.

I had the feeling that I had no feeling.

Then, I shot over the brink, and went down the steps with the sound of a stuttering, off-key cannon—or a very large frog with laryngitis: *BONK-BLONK-BRONK*. And I rode the chair and the chair rode me, by turns.

About halfway down, one of the steps reared up, turned its sharp edge up and whacked me unconscious. So only God knows whether I or the chair did the riding from then on.

XVIII

I WAS BACK IN MY HOSPITAL ROOM.

Except for being dead, I felt quite well. Oh, I was riddled with aches and twinges and bruises, but it is scientific fact that the dead cannot become so without having *some* pain. All things are relative, you know. And I knew I was dead, since no man could live—or want to live—with a nose the size of an eggplant.

I could barely see around it, but I got a glimpse of Kay sitting at the side of the door. Her attention was focused on the doctor and Claggett, who stood in the doorway talking quietly. So I focused on them also, relatively speaking, that is.

" . . . a hell of a kickback on the sedatives, Sergeant. A kind of cumulative kickback, I'd say, reoccurring over the last several days. You may have noticed a rambling, seriocomic speech pattern, a tendency to express alarm and worry through preposterous philosophizing?"

"Hmmm. He normally does a lot of that, Doctor."

"Yes. An inability to cope, I suspect. But the sedatives seem to have carried the thing full circle. Defense became offense, possibly in response to this morning's crisis. It could have kept him from being killed by the accident."

My head suddenly cleared. The gauzy fogginess which had hung over everyone and everything was ripped away. And despite the enormous burden of my nose, I sat up.

Kay, Claggett and the doctor immediately converged upon my bed.

I held up my hand and said, "Please, gentlemen and lady. Please do not ask me how I feel."

"You might tell us?" the doctor chuckled. "And you don't want to see us cry."

"Second please," I said, and I again held up my hand. "Please don't joke with me. It might destroy the little sense of humor I have left. Also, and believe you me, I'm in no damned mood for jokes or kidding. I've had my moments of that, but that's passed. And I contemplate no more of it for the forseeable future."

"I imagine you're in quite a bit of pain," the doctor said quietly. "Nurse, will you—"

"No," I said. "I can survive the pain. What I want right now is a large pot of coffee."

"Have it after you've rested. You really should rest, Mr. Rainstar."

I said I was sure he was right. But I'd prefer rest that wasn't drug induced, and I felt well enough to wait for it. "I want to talk to Sergeant Claggett, too," I said, " and I can't do it if I'm doped."

The doctor glanced at Claggett, and Jeff nodded. "I won't let him overdo it, Doc."

"Good enough, then," the doctor said. "If he can make it on his own, I'm all for it."

He left, and Kay got the coffee for me. It did a little more for me than I needed doing, making my over-alerted nerves cry out for something to calm them. But I fought the desire down, indicating to Claggett that I was ready to talk.

"I don't think I can tell you anything, though," I said. "I didn't realize it at the time, but I think I was in a kind of dream state. I mean, everything seemed to be out of kilter, but not in a way that I couldn't accept."

"It didn't jar you when you were shoved forward? That seemed okay to you?"

"I wasn't aware that I had been shoved forward. My feeling was that things had been shoved away from me, not me from them. I didn't begin to straighten out until I shot through those doors, and I wasn't completely unfogged when I went down the steps."

"Damn!" Claggett frowned at me. "But people were passing all around you. You must—"

"No," I said, "they weren't. Almost no one comes and goes through that front entrance, and I'm sure that no one did during the time I was there ... "

Kay said quickly, a little anxiously, that my recollection was right. I was out of the way of passersby, which was why she had left me there in the entrance area.

Claggett looked at her, and his look was extremely cold.

Kay seemed to wilt under it, and Claggett turned back to me. "Yes, Britt? Something else?"

"Nothing helpful, I'm afraid. I know that people passed behind me. I could hear them and occasionally see their shadows. But I never saw any of them."

Claggett grimaced, said that he apparently didn't live right. Or something.

"Everything points to the fact that someone tried to kill you, or made a damned good stab at it. But since no one saw anyone, maybe there wasn't anyone. Maybe it was just an evil spirit or a malignant force or something of the kind. Isn't that what you think, Nolton?"

"No, sir." Kay bit her lip. "What I think—I *know*—is that I should have taken Mr. Rainstar with me when I went to the admitting desk. You warned me not to leave him untended, and I shouldn't have done it, and I'm very sorry that I did."

"Did you see anyone go near, Mr. Rainstar?"

"No, sir. Well, yes, I may have. That's a pretty busy place, the lobby and desk area, and people would just about have to pass in Mr. Rainstar's vicinity."

"But they made no impression on you? You wouldn't remember what they looked like?"

"No, I wouldn't," Kay said, just a wee bit snappishly. "How could I, anyway? They were just a lot of people like you see anywhere."

"One of 'em wasn't," said Claggett. "But let it go. I believe I told you—but I'll tell you again since you seem pretty forgetful—that Mr. Rainstar has been seriously harassed, and that an attempt might be made on his life. I also told you—but I'll tell you again—that Miss Aloe is not above suspicion in the matter. We do not believe she would be directly responsible, although she could be, but rather as an employer of others. Do you think you can remember that, Miss Nolton."

"Yes, sir." Kay bobbed her head meekly. "I'll remember."

"I should hope so. I certainly hope so." Claggett allowed a little warmth to come into his frosty blue eyes. "Now, you do understand, Nolton, that you could get hurt on this job. You'd represent a danger or an obstacle to the people who are out to get him, and you could get hurt bad. You might even get killed."

"Yes, sir," said Kay. "I understand that."

"And you still want the job?"

"Yes, sir."

"Why?"

"Sir?"

"You heard me, Nolton!" Claggett leaned forward, his eyes stabbing into her like blue icicles. "Jobs aren't that hard to get for a registered nurse. They aren't hard to get period. So why are you so damned anxious to have this one? A first-class chance to screw yourself up? Well, what's the answer? Why—"

"I'm trying to tell you, Sergeant! If you'll just—"

"You some kind of a bum or something? A nut? Too dumb or shiftless to make out on a regular job? Or maybe you're working an angle, hmmm. You're a plant. You're going to do a job on Britt yourself."

Kay was trembling all over. Her face had turned from white to red to a mixture of the two, and now it was a beautiful combination flushed cream and reddish-streaked pastels.

Her mouth opened, and I braced myself for a yell. But she spoke very quietly, with only a slight shakiness hinting at the anger which she must have felt.

"I want the job, Sergeant Claggett, for two reasons. One is that I like Mr. Rainstar. I like him very much, and I want to help him."

"Thank you, Kay," I mumbled—I had to say something, didn't I?—stealing a glance at Claggett. "I, uh, like you, too."

"Thank you, Mr. Rainstar. The second reason I want the job, Sergeant Claggett, is because I'm not sure I belong in nursing. I want to find out whether I do or not before it's too late to change to another field. So . . . "

So she wanted to take what would probably be the toughest job she would ever encounter as a nurse. If she could measure up to it, fine. If not, well, that was also all right. She would either make or break quickly. Her mind would be made up for her, and without any prolonged wavering, any mental seesawing.

"Those are my reasons for wanting the job, Sergeant Claggett. I hope they're enough, because I can't give you any others."

Kay finished speaking, sat very straight and dignified in her chair, hands folded primly in her lap. I wanted to take her in my arms and kiss her. But I had felt that way before, with results that were not always happy for me. Except for that pleasant weakness, I would not be where I was now, with a nose which I could barely see around.

Claggett scrubbed his jaw thoughtfully, then cocked a brow at me. I cocked one at him, making it tit for tat. He grinned at me narrowly, acknowledging my studiously equivocal position.

"Well, now, young woman," he said, "a fine speech like that must have taken a lot out of you. Suppose you take a relief or have lunch, and come back in about an hour?"

"Well"—Kay stood hesitantly. "I really don't mind waiting, Sergeant. In fact—"

"I want to talk to Mr. Rainstar privately. Some other business. We'll settle this job matter when you get back."

"I see. Well, whatever you say, sir."

Kay nodded to us, and left.

Claggett stretched his legs in front of him, and said he was glad to get that out of the way. "Now, to pick up on your accident—"

"Just a minute, Jeff," I said. "You said we had that out of the way. You're referring to Nurse Nolton's employment?"

"Let it ride, will you?" He gestured impatiently. "I was going to tell you that I dropped in on PXA this morning. Just a routine visit, you know, to tell them about the accident to their favorite employee?"

"Well?" I said.

"Pat was pretty shook up about it. Reacted about the same as he did on my first visit. Kind of worried and angry, you know, like he might get hurt by a mess he wasn't responsible for. Then he turned sort of foxy and clammed up. Because—as I read him—he knew we'd have a hell of time proving anything against his niece, even though she had ordered the hit."

"Yes?" I frowned. "How do you mean?"

"She's in the hospital, Britt. Saint Christopher's. She's been there since just before midnight last night. Two highly reputable doctors in attendance, and they're not giving out any information nor allowing any visitors."

I gulped, blinked at him stupidly. I moved my nose out of the way, and had a small drink of water.

"Quite a coincidence, wouldn't you say, Britt." He winked at me narrowly. "Kind of an unusual alibi, but she's kind of an unusual girl."

"Maybe she really is sick," I said. "She could be."

"So she could," Claggett shrugged. "It's practically a cinch that she is, in that hospital with those doctors. But that doesn't keep it from being a very convenient time to be sick. She could set the deal up, then put herself well out of the way of it with a nice, legitimate sickness."

"Oh, well, yeah." I nodded slowly. "A fake attempt at suicide. Or an appendicitis attack—acute but simulated."

"Possibly but not necessarily," Claggett said, and he pointed out that Manny had been under a great deal of nervous stress. She had concealed it, but this itself had added to the tension. Finally, after doing that which only she could do, she had collapsed with exhaustion.

"It's my guess that she did pretty much the same thing, after her husband's death. About the only difference is that she needed more time to recuperate then, and she went into seclusion."

I said that killing her husband would certainly have put a lot of strain on her. But where was the evidence that she had killed him? He was only one of many who had died during the hurricane.

"Right," said Claggett, "but the other deaths were all from drowning or being buried under the wreckage. Her husband apparently was killed by flying timbers; in other words, he was out in the open at the time the hurricane struck. Of course, he could have been, and might have been. But . . . "

He broke off, spread his hands expressively. I wet my lips nervously, then brushed a hand against them.

"I see what you mean," I said. "She could have battered the hell out of him, beaten him to death. Then, dragged his body outside."

"That's what I mean," said Claggett.

From the hallway, there came the muted clatter of dishes, the faint aromas of the noon meal. They were not exactly appetite-stimulating; and

I had to swallow down nausea as Claggett and I continued our conversation.

"Jeff," I said at last. "I just don't see how I can go through with this. How the hell can I, under the circumstances?"

"You mean, seeing Miss Aloe?"

"Of course, that's what I mean! I can't do the pamphlets without seeing her. I'll have to confer with her more or less regularly."

"Well . . . " Claggett sighed, then shrugged. "If you can't, you can't."

"Oh, hell," I said miserably. "Naturally, I'll go through with it. I've got no choice."

"Good! Good," he said. "Let's hope you can get out of here within the next few days. The doctors tell me that aside from your nose, and your nerves, and—"

"There's nothing they can do for me here that can't be done at home," I said. "And I want to get out of here. No later than tomorrow morning. This place is dangerous. It makes me nervous. A lot of people die in hospitals."

Claggett chuckled knowingly. "Here we go again, hmm? You just take it easy, my friend. Calm down, and pull yourself together."

I said I wasn't being nutty, dammit. The hospital *was* dangerous, which had damn well been proved in my case. There were too many people around, and it was simply impossible to ward them off or to check on all of them.

"At home, I won't have more than two visitors at most. Manny and possibly, Pat Aloe. Only those two—only one of them, actually—will be all that have to be watched. I say that's a hell of a lot better than the way it is here."

Claggett deliberated briefly, and agreed with me. "If it's all right with the doctors, it's all right with me," he said, getting to his feet. "I'll be going now, but I'll be in touch."

"Wait a minute," I said. "What about the nurse?"

"What? Oh, yes, she almost slipped my mind. Hadn't decided about her yet, had I?"

"No, you hadn't. You were going to talk to her when she came back from lunch."

"Uh-huh. Well"—he glanced at his watch. "I'm going to have to go now. I'll talk to her on the way out."

He left before I could ask what he was going to say to her. But when she came in a few minutes later, I learned that he had okayed her for the job—but not very pleasantly.

"The very idea!" she said indignantly. "Saying he'd go after my hide if anything happened to you! I'd just like to see him try, darn him!"

"Don't say that," I said. "Bite your tongue, Kay."

She looked blank, then caught my meaning and laughed. "I didn't think how that sounded, Britt. Naturally, he isn't going to try because nothing *is* going to happen to you."

My lunch tray was brought in. Consommé with toast, vanilla custard and tea. It looked reasonably good to me, but I ate almost none of it. I couldn't. After a couple of sips of tea, I suddenly went to sleep.

Claggett called me that night to say that I would be checking out of the hospital in the morning. He told me the conditions under which I would be checking out, and going from the hospital to my home. I listened stunned, then sputtered profane objections.

He laughed uproariously. "But you just think about it, Britt. Think it over, and it doesn't sound so crazy, does it? Sure, it's his own idea, and I say it's a good one. You couldn't be any safer in your mother's arms."

I said that wasn't very safe. My mother, the first woman judge of the State Circuit Court, had taken to the sauce harder than Dad.

"The poor old biddy dropped me on my head more times than she was overturned, and, believe me, they didn't call her Reverse-Decision Rainstar for nothing."

"Aaah, she wasn't that bad," Claggett chuckled. "but what do you think about this other? It's the safest way, right?"

"Right," I said.

XIX

KAY NOLTON AND I LEFT THE HOSPITAL NEXT MORNING IN THE COMPANY OF PAT ALOE, and two very tough-looking guards. I don't know whether Pat was armed or not, but the guards carried shotguns.

A very large black limousine with a uniformed chauffeur was waiting at the side entrance for us. I got into the back seat between the two guards. Kay rode in front between Pat and the chauffeur. Pat jabbed a finger at him, and nodded to me.

"This is the character that was supposed to have picked you up at the restaurant that night two—three months ago, Britt. Too damned stupid to do what he's told, but who the hell ain't these days?"

The man grinned sheepishly. Pat scowled at him for a moment, then turned his gaze on Kay. Looked at her long and thoughtfully.

She jerked her head around suddenly, and looked at him.

"Yes?" she said. "Something wrong?"

"I've seen you before," he said. "Where was it?"

"Nowhere. You're mistaken."

"You guys back there! Where have I seen her."

The guards leaned forward, examined Kay meticulously. They made a big business out of squinting at her, stroking their chins with pseudo shrewdness, and the like—a pantomime of great minds at work. Pat put an end to the charade with a rude order to knock it off for Nellie's sake.

"What about you, Johnnie?"—to the chauffeur; and then, disgustedly, "Ahh, why do I ask? You're as stupid as these guys."

"*Mis-ter Aloe!*" Kay heaved a sigh of exaggerated exasperation. "We have *not* met before! I would certainly remember it if we had!"

I murmured for her to take it easy, also quietly suggesting to Pat that the subject was hardly worth pursuing. He glanced at me absently, not seeming to hear what I had said.

"I never forget a face, Britt, baby. Ask anyone that knows me."

"*You sure don't, Mr. Aloe! Not never ever!*"

"I don't know where or when it was. But I've seen her, and I'll remember."

He let it go at that, facing back around in the seat. Kay gave me a smile of thanks for my support in the rearview. I smiled back at her, then shifted my gaze. What difference did it make, whether he had or hadn't seen her? And why should I be again starting to feel that creeping uneasiness in my stomach?

Pat took an envelope from his pocket, and handed it to me. It was the bonus check I had so foolishly given back to Manny, and I accepted it gratefully. The money would keep Connie off my back indefinitely, relieving me of at least one of my major worries.

We arrived at the house. The guards and the chauffeur remained with the car while Pat accompanied Kay and me inside. As she preceded us up the steps, he told me sotto voce that I should have a salary check coming pretty soon, and that he would see to it and anything else that needed taking care of, in case Manny wasn't available.

I said that was very nice of him, and how was Manny getting along? "I hope she's not seriously ill?"

"Naah, nothing like it," he grunted. "Just been working too hard, I guess. Got herself run down, and picked up a touch of flu."

"Well, give her my best," I said. "And thanks very much for seeing me safely home."

I held out my hand tentatively. He said he'd go in the house with me if I didn't mind. "Reckon you'll want to check in with the sergeant, and let him know you got here all right."

"I'll do that," I said, "and you can let him know that you got here all right."

He gave me a puzzled look, and said, Huh? And I said, Never mind, to forget it; and rang the doorbell.

I rang it several times, but there was no response from Mrs. Olmstead. So, finally, I unlocked the door and we went in.

She was in the kitchen talking on the telephone. Hearing us enter the house, she hurriedly concluded her call and came into the living room, carrying the phone with her and almost becoming entangled in its long extension cord.

I took it from her, introducing her to Kay and Pat as I dialed Claggett's number. They grimaced briefly at one another, mumbling inconsequentialities, and I reported in to Jeff and then passed the phone to Pat. He did as I did, and hung up the receiver.

I walked Pat to the door. As we stood there for a moment, shaking hands and exchanging the usual polite pleasantries customary to departures and arrivals, he looked past me to Kay, eyes narrowing reflectively. He was obviously trying to remember where he had seen her before, and was, just as obviously, disturbed at his inability to do so. Fortunately, however, he left without giving voice to his thoughts; and I started back to the living room. I stopped short of it, in the entrance foyer, listening to the repartee between Kay Nolton and Mrs. Olmstead.

"Now, Mrs. Olmstead. All I said was that the house needs a good airing out, and it most certainly does!"

"Doesn't neither! Who're you to be giving me orders, anyway?"

"You know very well who I am—I've told you several times. My job is to help Mr. Rainstar recover his health, which means that he must have fresh air to breathe—"

"HE'S GOT FRESH AIR!"

"—clean, wholesome, well-prepared meals—"

"THAT'S THE ONLY KIND I FIX!"

"—and plenty of peace and quiet."

"WHY DON'T YOU BUTT OUT, THEN?"

I turned quietly away, and went silently up the stairs. I went into my room, stretched out on the bed and closed my eyes. I kept them closed, too, breathing gently and otherwise simulating sleep, when they came noisily up the steps to secure my services as arbitrator.

They left grudgingly, without disturbing me, each noisily shushing the other. I got up, visited the bathroom to dab cold water on my nose, then stretched out on the bed again.

I suppose I shoud have known that there would be friction between any woman as stubbornly sloppy as Mrs. Olmstead and one who was not only red-haired but as patently hygienic as scrubbed-looking Kay Nolton. I suppose that I should also have known that I would be caught in the middle of the dispute, since, like the legendary hapless Pierre, unpleasantness was always catching me in the middle of it. What I should *not* have supposed, I suppose, was that I would have known what the crud to do about it. Because about all I ever had known to do about something inevitably turned out to be the wrong thing.

So there you were, and here I was, and the air did smell pretty foul, but then it never did smell very good. And I was rather worn out from too much exercise, following no exercise at all, so I went to sleep.

XX

I WENT TO WORK ON A PAMPHLET THE NEXT MORNING. I kept at it, at first turning out nothing but pointless drivel. But, then, inspiration came to me, and my interest rose higher and higher, and the pages flowed from my typewriter.

It was a day over two weeks before I saw Manny. It was a Friday, her first day out of the hospital, and she came out to the house as soon as she had gone to mass. She had lost weight, and it had been taken from her face. But she had a good color, having sunned frequently in the hospital's solarium, and the thinning of her face gave a quality of spirituality to her beauty it had lacked before.

She—

But hold it! Hold it right there! I have gone way ahead of myself, skimming over events which should certainly deserve telling.

To take things in reasonably proper order (or as much as their frequent impropriety will allow):

I worked. I badly wanted to work, and I am a very hard guy to distract when I am that way. When I was distracted, as, of course, I soon was, I dealt with the distraction—Kay and Mrs. Olmstead—with exceptional shrewdness and diplomacy, thus keeping my time-waste minimal.

I explained to Mrs. Olmstead that it was only fair that Kay should take over the cooking and certain other chores since she, Mrs. Olmstead, was terribly overworked, and certain changes in household routine were necessary due to my illness.

"The doctors have forbidden me to leave the house, and Miss Nolton is required to stay in the house with me at all times. She can't order up a taxi, as you can, and go shopping and buy ice cream sodas and, oh, a lot of things, like you'll be doing for me. I doubt if she *could* do it, even if she was allowed to leave the house. But I trust *you*, Mrs. Olmstead. I know you'll do the job *right*. So I'm putting a supply of money in the telephone-stand drawer, and you can help yourself to whatever you need. And if any problems do arise I know you'll know how to handle them, without any advice from me."

That disposed of Mrs. Olmstead—almost. She could not quite accept what was a very good thing for her without a grumbled recital of complaints against me—principally, my occasional failure to mail her letters, or to "do something" about a possible invasion by rats. Still, I was sure she would cooperate, since she had no good reason to do otherwise, and I said as much to Kay.

She said flatly that I didn't know what I was talking about, then hastily apologized for the statement.

"I'm here to help you, Britt. To make things as easy for you as possible. And I'm afraid I've added to the strain you've been under by letting Mrs. Olmstead provoke me into quarreling with her. I—no, wait now, please!" She held up a hand as I started to interrupt. "I've been at least partly at fault, and I'm sorry, and I'll try to do better from now on. I'll humor Mrs. Olmstead. I'll consult her. I'll do what has to be done without being obtrusive about it—making it seem like a rebuke to her. But I don't think it'll do any good. I've seen too many other people like her. They have a very keen sense of their privileges and rights, but they're blind to their obligations. They're constantly criticizing others, but they never do anything wrong themselves. Not to hear *them* tell it. I think she spells trouble, Britt, regardless of what you do or I do. For your own good, I think you should fire her."

"But I need her," I said. "She has to do the shopping for us."

"You can order whatever we need. Have it delivered."

"Well, uh, there are other things besides shopping. Anyway—anyway—"

"Yes?"

"Well, it wouldn't seem quite right for us to be alone in the house. Just the two of us, I mean. It just wouldn't be right, now, would it?"

"Why not?" said Kay; and as I hesitated, fumbling for words, she said quietly, "All right, Britt. You're too softhearted to get rid of her, and I probably wouldn't like you as much as I do if you weren't that way. So I'll say no more about it. Mrs. Olmstead stays, and I just hope you're not sorry."

She left my office, leaving me greatly relieved as I returned to my work. Glad that I had not had to explain why I did not want to live alone in the house with her. I had no concrete reason to suspect her, or, rather, to be afraid of her. Nothing at all but the uneasy doubts planted in my mind by Claggett and Pat Aloe. Still, I knew I would be more comfortable with a third person present. And I was very happy to have managed it without a lot of fussing and fuming.

The pamphlet I was doing was on soil erosion, a subject I had shied away from in the past. I was afraid I would be inadequate to such an important topic, with so many facets, i.e., flood, drought, wind and irresponsible agricultural practices. Somehow, however, I had found the courage to plunge into the job and persist at it, meeting its challenges instead of veering or backing away—my customary reaction when confronted with the difficult. And I had advanced to its approximate halfway point when I looked up one afternoon to find Kay smiling at me from the doorway.

I stood up automatically, and started to unbuckle my belt. But she laughed and said we could dispense with the vitamin shot today.

"Just let me get your pulse and your temperature," she said, and proceeded to get them. "You're doing very well, Britt. Working hard and apparently enjoying it."

I agreed that I was doing both, adding that I was going to be very irritated if I was finished off before the job was finished.

"Well, then, I do solemnly swear to keep you alive," she said piously. "Not that I know why it's so important, but . . . "

I told her to sit down, and I would give her a hint of its importance. Which she did, and I did.

It was as important as life itself, I said. In fact it *was* life. Yet we sat around on our butts, uncaring, while it was slowly being stolen from us.

"Do you know that three-fourths of this state's topsoil has been washed away, blown away, or just by-God pooped away? Do you know that an immeasurable but dangerously tragic amount of its subsoil has gone the same route? Given a millenium and enough million-millions you can replace the topsoil, but once the subsoil's gone it's gone forever. In other words, you've got nothing to grow crops on, and nothing"—I broke off; paused a moment. "In other words," I said, "it stinks. Thanks for being so graphic."

She looked at me absently, nose crinkled with distaste. Then, she suddenly came alive, stammering embarrassed apologies.

"Please forgive me, Britt. It sounds terribly interesting, and you must tell me more. But what *is* that awful smell? It stinks like, well I don't know what! It's worse than anything I've smelled before in this house, and that's really saying something!"

I said I had noticed nothing much worse than usual. I also said I had a lot of work to do, and that I was anxious to get back to it.

"Now, Britt—" She got to her feet. "I'm sorry, and I'll run right along. Can I do anything for you before I go?"

Mollified, I said that, as a matter of fact, she could do something. There were some USDA brochures in the top drawer of my topmost filing cabinet, and if she would hold a chair while I climbed up on it, I would dance at her wedding or render any other small favor to her.

"You just stay right where you are," she said firmly. "I'll do any climbing that's done around here!"

She dragged a chair over to the stack of files, hiked her skirt and stepped up on it. Standing on tiptoe, she edged out the top file drawer and reached inside. She fumbled blindly inside, trying to grasp the documents inside. And, then, suddenly, she gasped and her face went livid.

For a moment I thought she was going to topple from the chair, and I jumped up and started toward her. But she motioned me back with a grim jerk of her head, then jumped down from the chair, white-faced with anger.

She was holding a large dead rat by the tail. Without a word she marched out of the room, and, by the sound of things, disposed of it in the rear porch garbage can. She returned to my office, stopping on the way to scrub her hands at the kitchen sink.

"All right, Britt"—she confronted me again. "I hope you're going to do something now!"

"Yes, I am," I said. "I'm going to go up to my room, and lie down."

"*Britt!* What are you going to do about that awful woman?"

"Now, Kay," I said. "That rat could have crawled in there and died. You know it could ! Why—"

Kay said she knew it could *not*. The rat's head had been smashed. It had been killed, then put in the file.

"The shock of finding it could have killed you, Britt. Or if you were standing on a chair, you could have fallen and broken your neck! I just can't allow this kind of thing to go on, Britt. I'm responsible, and—you've got to fire her!"

I pointed out that I couldn't fire Mrs. Olmstead. Not, at least, until she returned from shopping. I pointed out—rather piteously—that I was not at all well. This in the opinion of medical experts.

"Now, please help me up to my bed. I implore you, Kay Nolton."

She did so, though irritably. Then, looking up at her from the counterpane, I smiled at her and took one of her hands in mine. I said that perhaps she would not mind discussing Mrs. Olmstead when I was feeling better—say, tomorrow or the next day or, perhaps, the day after that. And I gave her a small pinch on the thigh.

She drew back skittishly, but not without a certain coyness. Which was all right with me. I wanted only to avoid a problem—Mrs. Olmstead—not to walk into another one. But Kay had her wants as well as I. And to get one must give. So when she said that she had to go to her room for a moment but would be right back, I told her I would count on it.

"I'll hold your place for you," I promised. "I'll also move over on the bed, in case you want to sit down, in case you cannot think of a more comfortable position than sitting."

Well.

When we heard Mrs. Olmstead return an hour later, we were locked together as the blissful beast-with-two-heads. We sprang apart, and she trotted into the bathroom ahead of me, her white uniform drawn high upon her sweet nakedness. I used the sink, while she sat on the toilet, tinkling pleasantly. And then I went over to her and hugged her red head against my stomach, and she nuzzled and kissed its environs in unashamed womanliness.

I congratulated myself.

For once, Britton Rainstar, I thought, you bridged a puddle without putting your foot down in stinky stuff. You've closed the door to debates on Mrs. Olmstead. Without compromising yourself, you've had a nice time and given same to a very nice young lady.

That's what I thought—and why not?

I nourished that thought, while I returned to bed and Kay went downstairs to prepare my dinner. It began to glimmer away, due to a kind of bashful shyness of manner as she served said dinner to me. And at bedtime, when she came into my room in an old-fashioned, unrevealing flannel, lips trembling, eyes downcast, a pastel symphony of embarrassment—*bingo*. The sound was the sound of my comforting thought leaping out the window.

But I didn't think of that then. All I could think of was drawing her down into my arms and holding her tight and trying to pet away her sadness.

"You won't like me any more, now," she sobbed brokenheartedly. "You think I'm awful, now. You think I'm not a nice girl, now . . . " And so on, until I thought my heart was breaking, too.

"Please, please don't cry, darling," I pleaded. "Please don't, baby girl. Of course, I like you. Of course, I think you're a nice girl. Of course, I think—I *don't* think you're awful."

But she continued to weep and sob. Oh, she didn't blame me. Not for a moment! She knew I was married, so it was all her fault. But men never did like you *afterwards*. There was this intern and she'd liked him a lot and he'd kept after her, and finally she'd done it with him. And he'd told everyone in this hospital that she did it, and they'd all laughed and thought she was awful. Then there was this obstetrician she'd worked for, a wonderfully sweet, considerate man—but after she did it with him awhile, he must have thought she was awful (and not very nice, either) because he decided not to get a divorce after all. Then there was this—

"Well, pee on all of them!" I broke in. "Doing it is one of the very nicest things girls do, and any guy who wouldn't treat her nice afterwards would doubtless eat dog-hockey in Hammacher-Schlemmer's side window."

She giggled, then sniffled and giggled simultaneously. She asked if she could ask me something, and then she asked it.

"Would you—I know you can't, because you're already married—but would you, if you weren't? I mean, you wouldn't think I was too awful to marry, just because I did it?"

"You asked me something, my precious love-pot," I said, "so let me tell you something. If I was not married—and please note that I use the verb *was*, not *were*, since *were* connotes the wildly impractical or impossible, as in 'If I were you,' and no one but a pretentious damned fool would say, 'If I were not married' because that's not only possible but, in my case, a lousy actuality. But, uh, what was the question?"

"Would you marry me if you were not—I mean, *was* not—already married."

"The answer is *absotively*, and, look, dear. *Were* is proper when prefixed by the pronoun *you*. That's one of those exceptions—"

"You really would, Britt? Honestly? You wouldn't think I was too awful to marry."

"Let me put it this way, my dearest dear," I said. "I would not only marry you, and consider myself the luckiest and most honored of men, but after God's blessing had been called down upon our union and the minister had given me permission to raise your bridal veil, I would raise your bridal gown instead, and I would shower kisses of gratitude all over your cute little butt."

She heaved a great shuddery sigh. Then, her head resting cozily against my chest, she asked if I had really meant what I had said.

"My God," I said indignantly, "would I make such a statement if I didn't mean it?"

"I mean, honest and truly."

"Oh," I said. "So *that's* what you mean."

"Uh-huh."

"I cannot tell a lie," I said. "Thus, my answer must be, yes: honest and truly, and a pail of wild honey with brown sugar on it."

She fell asleep in my arms, the untroubled sleep of an innocent child; and flights of angels must have guided her into it, for her smile was the smile of heaven's own.

I brushed my lips against her hair, thinking that everyone should know such peace and happiness. Wondering why they didn't when it was so easily managed. The ingredients were to be found in everyone's cupboard, or the cupboard which everyone is, and you could put them together as easily as you could button your britches. All that was necessary was to combine any good brand of kindness and any standard type of goodwill, plus a generous dab of love; then, shake well and serve. There you had peace and happiness—beautifully personified by this sleeping angel in my arms.

Without disturbing her, I shifted my position ever-so-slightly, and I took another look at her.

And I thought, *I have seen Manny sleep like this, too. Manny, who thus far has done everything but kill me, and doubtless plans to do just that.*

Then, I thought, *Connie looked thus also, for God's sake! The homeliest, scrawniest broad in the world has at least a moment of surpassing beauty, else a majority of the world's female population would go unscrewed and unmarried. And I thought that Connie would probably like to kill me, and quite likely would do so if she knew how to safely wangle it.*

And I thought, *And how about Kay, this lovely child? For all I know about her—or DON'T know about her—she, too, could have my murder on her mind. Yeah, verily, even while screwing me, she could be plotting my slaughter. Perhaps she would see my death as atonement for her misuse by guys who had used her. Guys who thought she was awful and not a nice girl just because she did it.*

Finally, in that prescient moment preceding sleep, I thought, *Congratulations, Rainstar. You have done it again. A very small puddle was in your path, one that you could have walked through without dampening your shoe soles. Yet you shrank—you chronic shrinker!—from even that small hazard. You must spring over the literal wet spot in your walkway, and that mess you came down in on the other side was definitely not a beehive.*

XXI

MANNY CAME OUT TO THE HOUSE THE NEXT DAY.

She looked very beautiful. Her illness had left her even lovelier than she had been, and . . . but I believe we've already covered that. So let us move on.

I was naturally pretty wary, and she also was on guard. We exchanged greetings stiffly, and moved on to a stilted exchange of conversational banalities. With that behind us, I think we were on the point of breaking the ice when Kay popped in with the coffee service. She declared brightly that she just knew that we two convalescents would feel better after a good cup of coffee, and she poured and passed a cup to each of us.

Manny barely tasted hers, and said it was very good.

I tasted mine, and also lied about it.

Kay said she would just wait until we finished it, by which time doubtless, since I was not feeling very well, Miss Aloe would want to leave. Manny promptly put her cup down, and stood up.

"I'll leave right now, Britt. It was thoughtless of me to come out so soon, so—"

"Sit down," I said. "I am quite well, and I'm sure that neither of us wants any more of this coffee. So please remove it, Miss Nolton, and leave Miss Aloe and me to conduct our business in private."

Manny said timidly that she would be glad to come back another time. But I told her again to sit down, and she sat. Kay snatched up the coffee things and clumped to the door. She turned around there, addressing me with sorrowful reproach.

"I was just doing my job, Mr. Rainstar. I'm responsible for your health, you know."

"I know," I said, "and I'm grateful."

"It would be easier for me if I *wasn't* so conscientious. My salary would be the same, and it would be a lot easier for me, if I didn't do—"

"I'd better leave," said Manny, picking up her purse.

"And I think you'd better not!" I said. "I think Miss Nolton had better leave—right this minute!"

Kay left, slamming the door behind her. I smiled apologetically at Manny.

"I'm sorry," I said. "She's a very nice young woman, and she's very good at her job. But sometimes . . . "

"Mmm. I'll just bet she is!" Manny said, and then, with a small diffident gesture, "I want to tell you something, and it's, well, not easy for me. Could you come a little closer, please?"

"Of course," I said, and I moved over to her side on the love seat. I waited, and her lips parted, then closed again. And she looked at me helplessly, apparently unable to find the words for what she wanted to say.

I told her gently to take her time, we had all the time in the world; and then, by way of easing her tenseness, I asked her if she remembered the last time we had been in this room together.

"It was months ago, and I thought I'd lost the pamphlet-writing job before I even had it. So I was sitting here with my head in my hands, feeling sorry as hell for myself. And I wasn't aware that you'd come into the room until—"

"Of course, I remember!" She clapped her hands delightedly. "You looked like this"—she puffed her cheeks out and rolled her eyes inward in a hilarious caricature of despair. "That's just the way you looked, darling. And then I said:

"Lo, the Poor Indian)
                              we said in unison.
"Lo, the Poor Indian)

We laughed, and smiled at each other. She took my month's retainer from her purse and gave it to me, and we went on smiling at one another. And she spoke to me in a voice as soft and tender as her smile.

"Poor Lo. How are you, my dearest darling?"

"Well, you know"—I shrugged. "For a guy who's been shot out of the saddle a few times, not bad, not bad at all."

"I'm sorry, Britt. Terribly, terribly sorry. That's what I was trying to tell you. I haven't been myself. At least, I hope the self I've been showing wasn't the real Manuela Aloe, but I'm going to be all right now. I—I—"

"Of course, you're going to be all right," I said. "I pulled a lousy trick on you, and you paid me off for it. So now we're all even-steven."

"Nothing more will happen to you, Britt! I swear it won't!"

"Didn't I just say so?" I said. "Now, be a nice girl and say no more about it, and start reading these beautiful words I've written for you."

She said, All right, Britt, swallowing heavily, eyes shining too brightly. Then the tears brimmed over, and she began to weep silently and I hastily looked away. Because I'd never known what to do when a woman started crying, and I particularly didn't know what to do when the woman was Manny.

"Aah, Britt," she said tremulously. "How could I ever have been mean to anyone as nice as you?"

"Doggone it, everyone keeps asking me that!" I said. "And what the heck can I tell them?"

She laughed tearily. She said, "Britt, oh, Britt, my darling!" and then she broke down completely, great sobs tearing through her body.

I held her and patted her head, and that sort of thing. I took out my breast-pocket handkerchief and dabbed her eyes, and honked her nose in it. Conscious that there was something a little nutty about performing such chores for a girl who had almost killed me, even though she hadn't meant to. Conscious that I again might be playing the chump, and, at the moment, not really caring if I was.

I crossed to my desk, and began putting the pages I had written into an envelope. I took my time about it, giving her time to pull herself together. Rattling on with some backhanded kidding to brighten things up.

"Now, hear me," I said. "I don't want you looking at this bawling and honking your schnozzle, and being so disgustingly messy. Us Noble Redmen don't put up with such white-eye tricks, get me, you silly squaw?"

"G-gotcha ... " A small and shaky snicker. "Silly squaw always gets Noble Redman."

"Well, I just hope you're not speaking with a forked tongue," I said. "These are very precious words, lovingly typed on top grade erasable-bond paper, and God pity you if you louse them up."

"All right, Britt ... "

She did sound like she was, so I turned back around. I helped her up from the love seat, gave her a small pat on the bottom and pressed the envelope into her hands. As I walked her to the front door, I told her a little about the manuscript and said that I would look forward to hearing from her about it. She said that I would, no later than the day after the morrow.

"No, wait a minute," she said. "Today's Friday, isn't it?"

"All day, I believe."

"Let's make it Monday, then. I'll see you Monday."

"No one should ever see anyone on Monday," I said. "Let's make it Tuesday."

We settled on a Tuesday P.M. meeting. Pausing at the front door, she glanced out to where her own car stood in the driveway and asked what had happened to mine. "I hope the company hasn't pulled another booboo and come out and gotten it, Britt. After all the stupid mix-ups we've had in the past, that would be a little too much."

"No, no," I said. "Everything is as it should be. I believe that exposure to the elements is good for a car, helps it to grow strong and tough, you know. But since I haven't been using it these several weeks, I locked it up in the garage."

"Yes?" She looked up at me curiously. "But you get out a little bit, don't you? You don't stay in the house all the time?"

"That's what I do," I said. "Doctor's orders. I think it's pretty extreme, but ... " I shrugged, leaving the sentence unfinished.

Again, she gave me a curious frown. "Very strange," she murmured, a slight chill coming into her voice. "I was certain that the doctors would want you to get a little fresh air and sunshine."

I said that, Oh, well, she knew how doctors were, knowing that it sounded pretty feeble. Actually, of course, it was not the doctors but Claggett who had absolutely forbidden me to leave the house.

Manny said, Yes, she did know how doctors were. "I'll say good-bye here, then. I wouldn't want you to go against orders by walking to my car with me."

"Oh, now, wait a minute," I said, taking a quick look over my shoulder. "Of course, I'll walk to the car with you."

I tucked her arm through mine, and we crossed the porch and started down the steps.

We descended to the driveway and sauntered the few steps to her car. I helped her into it, and closed the door quietly.

Mrs. Olmstead was out shopping per usual, so she could not reveal my sneaking out of the house. But I was fearful that Kay might spot me, and come storming out to yank me back inside again.

"Well, good-bye, darling," I said, and I stooped and hastily kissed Manny. "Take care, and I'll see you Tuesday."

"Wait, Britt. Please!"

"Yes?" I threw another quick glance over my shoulder. "I love being with you, dear, but I really shouldn't be standing out here."

"It's just me, isn't it? You're afraid of being here with me."

"Dammit, no," I said. "That isn't it at all. It's just that, I—"

"I told you nothing more would happen to you, Britt. I'm all right now, and there'll never be anything like that again, and—Don't you believe me?"

Her voice broke and she turned her head quickly, looking at the scantily populated countryside across the road. There were a few houses scattered over a wide area, and land had been graded for a number of others. But everything had come to a halt with the advent of the garbage dump on former Rainstar property.

"Manny," I said. "Listen to me. Please listen to me, Manny."

"Well?" She faced me again, but slowly, her gaze still lingering on the near-empty expanse beyond the road, seeming to search for something there. "Yes, Britt?"

"I'm not afraid of being here with you at all. You said that nothing more would happen to me, and I believe you. It's just that I'm supposed to stay in the house—not to come outside at all. And I'm afraid there'll be a hell of a brouhaha if—"

"But you've been going out." Manny smiled at me thinly. "You've been going out and staying out for hours."

"What?" I said. "Why do you say that?"

"Why?" she said. "Yes, why do I? I've certainly no right to make an issue of it."

And before I could say anything more, she nodded coldly and drove away.

I looked after her, as her car sped down the driveway and turned into the road, became lost in the dust of the ubiquitous dump trucks wending their way toward the garbage hummocks.

I turned away, vaguely troubled, and moved absently toward the porch.

I went up the steps, still discomfited and puzzled by Manny's attitude, but grateful that Kay had not discovered me in my fracture of a strict order. One of the few unhappy aspects of sex is that it places you much too close physically while you are still mentally poles apart. So that a categorical imperative is apt to be juxtaposed with a constitutional impossibility, for how can one kick someone—or part of someone—that he has laved with love.

I couldn't face up to the consequences of Kay Nolton's throwing her weight around with me again. No sadist I, I could not slug the provably and delightfully screwable.

I reached the top step, and—

There was a sudden angry sound at my ear, the *buzz* of a maddened hornet. The hornet zoomed in and stung me painfully on the forehead, the sting burning like acid.

I slapped at it, then rubbed the tortured flesh with my fingers. As a boy, growing up on the old place, I had been "hit" by hornets many times. But I could remember none having the effect of this one.

It was numbing, almost as if I had been hit by an instrument that was at once edged and blunt. I felt a little dizzy and faint, and—

I took my hand away from my head.

I stared at it stupidly.

It was red and wet, dripping with blood, and more blood was dripping down onto the age-faded wood of the porch.

My knees buckled slowly, and I sank down to them. My eyes closed, and I slowly toppled over and lay prone.

My last thought, before I lost consciousness, was of Manny. Her indirect insistence that I accompany her to her car. The hurt in her voice and her eyes when I had hesitated about leaving the safety of the house— hurt which I could only expunge by doing what I had been sternly ordered not to do.

So I had done as she wanted, because I loved her and believed in her.

And then, loving and trusting her, I had remained out in the open exposed to the danger which is always latent in loving and trusting.

I had lingered at the side of her car, pleading with her. And she had sat with her back turned to me, her gaze searching the landscape, apparently searching it for . . . ? A signal? A rifle, say, with a telescopic sight.

I heard myself laugh, even as the very last of my consciousness glimmered away. Because, you see, it was really terribly funny. Almost as funny as it was sad.

I had always shunned guns, always maintaining that guns had been known to kill people and even defenseless animals, and that those who fooled around with guns had holes in their heads. And now, I . . . I . . . I had been . . . and I had a hole in my . . .

XXII

WHEN I CAME BACK INTO MY CONSCIOUSNESS, I was lying on my own bed, and Kay was hunkered down at the bedside, staring anxiously into my face.

I started to rear up, but she pressed me back upon the pillows. I stammered nonsensically, "What why where how . . . " and then the jumble in my mind cleared, and I said, "How did I get up here? Who brought me up?"

"Shhh," said Kay. "I—we made it together, remember? With me steering you, and hanging onto you for dear life."

"Mrs. Olmstead helped you. I wouldn't have thought the old gal had it in her."

"Mrs. Olmstead isn't back yet. She's never around when you need her for anything. Now, will you just shut up for goodness sake, and tell me how—Doggone it, anyway!" Kay scowled, her voice rising angrily. "It's just too darned much! I have to follow that woman around, do everything over after she's done it! I have to watch you every minute, to keep you from doing something silly, and all I get is bawled out for it! I have to—"

"Oh, come on now," I said, "it really isn't that bad, is it?"

"Yes, it is! And now you've made me lose control of myself, and act as crazy as you are! Now, you listen to me, Britt Rainstar! Are you listening?"

She was trembling with fury, her face an unrelieved white against the contrasting red of her hair. I tried to take her hand, and she knocked it away. Then, she quickly recovered it and squeezed it, smiling at me determinedly through gritted teeth.

"I asked you if you were—oh, the heck with it," she said. "How are you feeling, honey?"

"Tol'able, ma'am," I said. "Tolerable. How are you?"

She said she was darned mad, that's how she was. Then she told me to hold still, darn it, and she tested the strip of adhesive bandage on my forehead. And then she leaned down and gently kissed it.

"Does it hurt very much, Britt?"

"You wouldn't ask that, if you were really a nurse."

"What? What do you mean by that?"

"Anyone with the slightest smattering of medical knowledge knows that when you kiss something you make it well."

100

"Ha!" She brushed her lips against mine. "You were told not to leave this house, Britt. Not under any circumstances. Why did you do it?"

"It wasn't really going out," I said. "I just saw Miss Aloe to her car."

"And you got shot."

"But there was no connection between the two events. She'd been gone for, oh, a couple of minutes when it happened."

"What does that prove?"

"I'm sure she had nothing to do with it," I said stubbornly. "She told me she was sorry for what she'd done, and she swore that there'd be no more trouble. And she was telling the truth! I know she was, Kay."

"And *I* know you got shot," Kay said. "I also know that I'll get blamed for it. It's not my fault. You practically threw me out of your office, and told me to leave you alone. I was only t-trying to look after you, b-but you—"

I cut in on her, telling her to listen to me and listen good. And when she persisted, obviously working herself up to a tear storm, I took her by the shoulders and shook her.

"Don't you pull that on me!" I said. "Don't pretend that that little stunt you pulled down in my office was an attempt to protect me. You were just being nosy. Acting like a jealous wife. Miss Aloe and I were discussing business, and—"

"Ha! I know her kind of business. She's got her business right in her—well, never mind. I won't say it."

She dropped her eyes, blushing. I stared at her grimly, and finally she looked up and asked me what I was looking at.

"At you," I said. "What's with this blushing bit? I think it's just about impossible for you to be embarrassed. I don't think you'd be embarrassed if you rode naked through Coventry on a Kiddy-Kar with a bull's-eye on each titty and a feather duster up your arse! You've repeatedly proved that you're shameless, goddammit, yet you go around kicking shit, and turning red as a billy goat's butt every time you see the letter *p*. You—"

"*Oops!*" said Kay. "*Whoops!*" And she lost her balance and went over backwards, sitting down on the floor with a thud. She sat thus, shaking and trembling, her hands covering her face; making rather strange and fearful sounds.

"What's the matter?" I said. "Are you throwing a fit? That's all I need, by God, a blushing fit-thrower!"

And her hands came away from her face, they were literally exploded, as she burst into wild peals of laughter. The force of it made me wince, but it was somehow contagious. I started laughing, too, laughing harder at each new blast from her. And the harder I laughed the harder she laughed.

That kind of laughter does something to some people, and it did it to her. She staggered to her feet, trying to get to the bathroom, but she just couldn't make it. Instead, she fell down across me, now crying from laughing so much, and I took her by her wet seat, and hauled her over to my other side.

"You dirty girl," I said. "Why don't you carry a cork with you?"

"D-don't," she begged. "Please d-don't . . . "

I didn't; that is, I didn't say anything more. For practically anything will start a person up again when he has passed a certain point in laughing.

We lay quiet together, with the only sound the sound of our breathing.

After a long time, she sighed luxuriously and asked if I really minded her blushing, and I said I supposed there were worse things.

"I don't know why I do it, Britt, but I always have. I've tried not to, but it just makes it worse."

"I used to know a girl who was that way," I said. "But an old gypsy cured her of it."

I told her how it was done. Following the old gypsy's instructions, she sprinkled salt on a sparrow's tail when it was looking the other way. When the sparrow flew off, it took her blushes with her.

"Just like that?" Kay said. "She didn't blush any more?"

"No, but it started a blushing epidemic among the sparrows. For years, before they lost their shame by do-doing on people, the midnight sky was brilliant with their blushes, and—"

"*Darn you!*" An incipient trembling of the bed. "You shut up!"

I said quickly that we should both think of something unpleasant. Something that definitely was not a laughing matter. And it was no trouble at all to think of such a something.

"I'm gonna catch holy heck," Kay said solemnly. "Boy, oh, boy, am I gonna catch it."

"You mean, I'm going to catch it," I said. "I was the one that got shot."

"But I let you. I didn't stop you from going outside."

"Stop me? How the hell could you stop me? I'm a grown man, and if I wanted to go outside I'd go, regardless of what you said or did."

"You'll see," Kay said. "Sergeant Claggett will hold me responsible. He's already said he would."

I couldn't talk her out of her qualms, nor did I try to very hard. I was the one who had goofed—and I would hear from Claggett about that!—but she would be held responsible. He would have her yanked off the job, possibly even fired.

"Look, Kay," I said. "We don't know that I was actually shot. We don't *know* anything of the kind, now, do we?"

Kay said that of course, we knew it. At least, she did. That crease across my temple had been put there by a bullet.

"Now, we *don't* know," she added thoughtfully, "that anyone was actually trying to hit you. That it was a professional, say, which it would just about have to be, wouldn't it, if the shooting was intentional?"

"Why, that's right!" I said. "And a pro wouldn't have just creased me. He'd have put one through my head. I'll bet it was an accident, Kay. Some character hunting rabbits across the road, or—or else—" I broke off, remembering the other things that had happened to me.

"Or else what, Britt?"

"He wasn't trying to kill me or seriously injure me. Just to give me a bad jolt."

"Oh," said Kay, slowly. "Oh, yes. I guess you're probably right, all right. I guess your darling little Miss Aloe was lying when she promised not to give you any more trouble."

I snapped that Manny hadn't been lying—something that I was by no means sure of, much as I wanted to be. Kay shrugged that, of course, I knew more about my business than she did. So who was responsible for the shooting, if Manny was not?

"I thought she was the only one you and Sergeant Claggett suspected. Of giving you such a bad time, I mean. I guess you did say that her uncle *might* be involved, but you really didn't seem to believe it."

"Didn't and don't," I said curtly. "That was just a far-out possibility."

"Well, just don't you worry your sweet tinted-gray head about it," said Kay. "I imagine that Miss Aloe just forgot that she'd ordered someone to take a shot at you. I'll bet that now that she remembers doing it, she's just as sorry as she can be."

I said something that sounded like ship but wasn't. Kay said brightly that she'd just thought of another explanation for the shooting. Manny had ordered it, and then ordered it cancelled. But the gunman had forgotten the cancellation.

"That's probably what happened, Britt, don't you think so? Of course, you'd think a professional gunman would be a little more careful, but, oh, well, that's life."

"That's life," I said, "and this is my hand. And if you don't stop needling me, dammit . . . !"

"I'm sorry, darling. It just about had to be an accident, didn't it? A stray bullet from a hunter's gun."

"Well . . . " I hesitated.

"Right," said Kay. "So there's no reason to tell Sergeant Claggett that you were ever outside the house. He'd just get all upset and mad, and maybe take me away from you, and, oh, boy," sighed Kay. "Am I glad to get that settled! Let's go to the bathroom, shall we?"

We went to the bathroom.

We got out of our clothes and washed, and helped each other wash, and Kay carefully removed the adhesive strip and examined my head wound.

"Mmm-hmm. It doesn't look so bad, Britt. How does it feel?"

"No problem. A very slight itching and stinging occasionally."

"Well, we'll leave it unbandaged for the time being. Let the air get to it. Have you felt any more faintness?"

"Nope. Not the faintest."

She lowered the toilet seat, and told me to sit down on it. I did, and she took my pulse while resting a palm on my forehead. Then—

The bathroom suddenly began to shake. There was a sudden ominous creaking and cracking, slowly mounting in volume.

Kay pitched sideways, and her mouth opened to scream. I laughed, grabbed her and pulled her down on my lap.

"It's all right," I said, "don't be afraid. I've been through the same thing a dozen times. There's a lot of shaking and trembling, and some of the damnedest racket you ever heard, but . . . "

I tightened my grip on her, for the shaking was already pretty violent. And the noise was so bad that I was virtually yelling in her ear.

The house was "settling," I explained. Something it had done sporadically for decades. The phenomenon was due to aging and exceptionally heavy building materials, and, possibly, to deep subterranean springs which lay beneath the structure. But frightening as it was to anyone unaccustomed to it, there was absolutely no danger. In a few minutes it would all be over.

The few minutes were actually more than ten. Kay sat with her arms wound around my neck, hanging on so tightly at times that I was almost strangled. It was not a bad way to go, though, if one had to, being hugged to death by a girl who was not only very pretty but also very naked. And I held her nakedness to mine, as enthusiastically as she held mine to hers.

It was so pleasant, in fact, that neither of us was in any hurry to let go even after the noise and the trembling had ceased.

I patted her on the flank, and said she wiggled very good. She whispered naughtily in my ear—something which I shall not repeat—and then she blushed violently. And I even blushed a little myself.

I was trying to think of some suitable, or rather, unsuitable reply, when she let out a startled gasp.

"Oh, my God, Britt"—she pointed a trembling finger. "L-look!"

I looked. And laughed. "It's all right," I said, giving her another flank spank. "It always does that."

"B-but the doorknob turned! It's still turning."

"I know. I imagine every other doorknob in the place is doing the same thing. As I understand it, the house undergoes a kind of winding-up during the settling process. Then when the tension is relieved, there's a general relaxing or unwinding, and you see such thing as doors flying open or their knobs turning."

Kay said, *Whew*, brushing imaginary perspiration from her brow.

"It scared me to death, Britt! Really!"

"No, it didn't, Kay," I said. "Really!"

"Well, I sure wouldn't want to be alone when it happened. You see the knob turn, and—how do you know someone's not there?"

"Very simply," I said. "If someone's there, he just opens the door."

The door opened, and Sergeant Claggett came in.

He stood frozen in his tracks for a moment, blinking at us incredulously. Then he said "Excuse *me*!", retreating across the threshold with a hasty back step.

"Excuse me for not getting up," I said.

"I want to see you downstairs, Britt!" He spoke with his head turned. "Immediately, understand?"

"Of course," I said. "Just as soon as I get something in—order."

"And you, too." He addressed Kay without looking at her. "I want to see you, too, *Officer Nolton!*"

XXIII

I SUPPOSE I SHOULD HAVE SEEN THE TRUTH FROM THE START. Almost any fool would have, I am sure, so that should have qualified me for seeing it. I hadn't because I am a plain, garden-variety sort of fool, not the devious kind. I am a worshipper at the shrine of laissez faire, a devotee of the status quo. I accept things as they are, *for* what they are, without proof or documentation. I ask no more than a quid pro quo. And failing to get a fair exchange, I will normally accept the less that is offered. In a word, I am about as un-devious as one can be. And having no talent nor liking for deception, I am easily deceived. As per, the present instance.

Claggett wanted me to have round-the-clock protection. Which is not easily managed by a mere detective sergeant in an undermanned, tightly budgeted police department. He didn't want me to know that I had such protection, believing that I would inadvertently reveal it where it was best not revealed. So the cop he planted on me was also a nurse, someone whose presence in the house would be taken for granted. And since she *was* a nurse, he could have her wages paid by PXA's insurers, thus quieting any objections from the P.D.

Naive as I was I would still ask myself why a nurse would take such a potentially dangerous job. Claggett had provided the answer by making it appear that there was something wrong with her, or that there *could* be something wrong with her. That not only satisfied my curiosity as to why she was taking the job, but it would also—he hoped—make me wary of her. I would shy away from any personal involvement with her, and she would not be distracted from her duties as a cop.

Well, the deception had worked fine, up to a point. A cop had been planted on me, and I had no idea that she was a cop. Doubts about her good intentions had been planted in my mind, and I did my damnedest to hold her at a distance. Why then had I wound up in bed with her? How could she have been so outrageously derelict in her duty?

Claggett swore savagely that it was too damned much for him.

I said, somewhat uncomfortably, that he seemed to be making too much of a much over the matter. "After all, it's Friday afternoon, Jeff. Everyone relaxes and lets down a bit on Friday afternoon."

"Everyone doesn't have a nut after him," snapped Claggett. "A screwed-up broad who's been snatching his scalp by bits and pieces, and just may decide she wants his life along with it!"

"Now, Jeff," I said. "I'm practically convinced that Manny—"

"Shut up," Claggett said, and turned coldly to Kay. "I don't believe you were wearing a gun when I arrived today. What do regulations say about that?"

"I'm sorry, sir. I—"

"You're a disgrace!" said Claggett, cutting me off again before I was able to say anything effective. "I found the door unlocked, and standing wide open! And you naked and unarmed with the man you were supposedly protecting!"

"Y-yes, sir. I'm thoroughly ashamed, sir, and I swear it won't happen again!"

"No, it won't. You're suspended from duty, as of this moment, and you'll be up before the disciplinary board just as soon as I can arrange it!"

Kay wasn't blushing any more. She was apparently fresh out of blushes, and she was very pale as she got to her feet. "Whatever you say, Sergeant. I'll start getting my things together."

Claggett brought her back to her chair with a roar. "You, Officer Nolton, will remain in this room until you are told to do otherwise. As for you, Britt"—he gave me a look of weary distaste, "I've been trying to help you, and I've gone to considerable lengths to do it. Much further than I should have, in fact. Do you think this was the right way to repay me?"

"Of course, I don't, since you obviously consider it wrong and it's caused problems for Miss Nolton. I myself don't feel that it was wrong per se but there's a variable factor involved. I mean, something is good only so long as it doesn't make others unhappy."

"Hmmm," he said, his blue eyes brooding. "Well! I do feel that you've let me down, but that doesn't excuse Officer Nolton. If—"

"It should. Let's face it, Jeff," I said. "I'm quite a bit older than Miss Nolton—also a lot more experienced. And I'm afraid I was persistent with her to a shameful degree. Please don't blame her, Jeff. It really was all my fault."

Claggett's brows went up.

He grimaced, lips pursed, then turned an enigmatic gaze on Kay. "How about it, Nolton? Is that the way it was?"

"Well, I *am* much younger than—" She broke off, sat very erect and dignified. "I wouldn't care to say, sir!"

Claggett ran a hand over his mouth. He looked at Kay a moment or two longer, apparently seeing something in her of great interest, then faced back around to me. "You started to say something about Miss Aloe. Anything important?"

"I think so. She was out here to the house today, and she apologized for what she'd done. Implied that she hadn't been rational or responsible for her actions."

"And?"

"She promised not to make any more trouble—got pretty emotional about it. I'm convinced that she meant it, Jeff."

"Well, I'm *not*," said Kay; and here came that pretty blush again. "I'm sorry, Sergeant. I didn't mean to butt in, but I've observed Miss Aloe very carefully and I thought you'd want my opinion as a police officer."

"I do," said Claggett. "In detail, please."

"She's just a snippy, snotty little wop, that's what! I'm sure there are a great many good people of her race, but she's not one of them."

Claggett's interest in her seemed to increase tremendously. He would shift his fascinated gaze away from her; then, as though against his will, it would slowly move back and fasten on her again. Meanwhile, he was saying that he had undergone a complete change of mind, and that she should by all means remain on her present duty.

"Oh, thank you, Sergeant!" She smiled on him brilliantly. "I know you were kind of disappointed about . . . but it won't happen again, sir!"

"Ah, well," said Claggett, easily. "A pretty young girl and a handsome, sophisticated older man—how could I blame you for succumbing? And what's to blame, anyway? Just don't forget you've got business here, too."

"Yes, sir! I won't get caught with my—I'll remember, sir!"

"Good," Claggett beamed. "I'm sure you mean that, and it wouldn't be practical to pull you off the job, anyway. Not with so short a time to go."

"Uh, sir?"

"I mean, we should know how things stand with Miss Aloe very soon. If she's going to pull anything, she'll do it within the next week or so, don't you think?"

"Well . . . " Kay hesitated doubtfully. "Why do you say that, sir."

"Because she's a very pretty girl, too," Claggett said, "and pretty girls have a way of being jealous of other pretty girls. If she still cares enough for Mr. Rainstar to be mad at him, she'll try to stop him having fun with you. And she won't waste time about it."

Kay said, "Well, yes, sir. Maybe." But rather doubtfully. Not exactly sure that she had been complimented.

Claggett said he was glad she agreed with him. And he was glad to be glad, he said, because he was really pretty sad when he thought of her imminent resignation from the police department.

"Just as soon as you've finished this assignment. Of course," he went on, "I realize it's the smart thing for you to do, a girl who's shown an aptitude for so many things in such a short span of time. Let's see. You've been a nurse, a secretary, an airline stewardess, a—yes, Officer Nolton?"

"I said, you can have my resignation right now if you want it! And you know what you can do with it, too!"

"Well, sure, sure," Claggett said heartily. "For that matter, I could have you kicked out on your ass. For stated reasons that would make it hard for you to get a job washing towels in a whorehouse. Well?" He paused. "Do you want me to do that?"

Kay muttered something under her breath.

Claggett leaned forward. "I didn't hear you! Speak up!"

"I . . . " Kay wet her lips. "No, sir. I don't want you to."

"Don't want me to do what?"

"Don't!" I said. "For God's sake, drop it, Jeff."

He gestured curtly, ordering me to butt out. To mind my own business and let him mind his. I said I couldn't do that.

"You've made your point, Jeff. So let it go at that. You don't need to watch her bleed." I crossed over to Kay, spoke to her gently. "Want to go up to your room. It'll be all right with the sergeant, won't it, Jeff?"

"Yeah, hell, dammit!" he said sourly.

"Kay." I touched her on the shoulder. "Want me to help you?"

She shook off my hand.

She buried her face in her hands, and began to shake with silent weeping.

Claggett and I exchanged a glance. He stood up, jerked his head toward the door and went out. I took another glance at Kay, saw that her trembling had stopped and followed him.

We shook hands at the front door, and he apologized for coming down hard on Kay. But he seemed considerably less than overwhelmed with regret. The little lady had been under official scrutiny for a long time, he said, and her conduct today had simply triggered an already loaded gun.

"I'm not referring to catching her in the raw with you. I had to bawl her out for it, but that's as far as it would have gone—if there'd been nothing more than that. It was her attitude about it, her attitude in general, the things she said. If you know what I mean." He sighed, shook his head. "And if you don't know, to hell with you."

"I know," I said. "But she was pretty upset, Jeff. If you'll look at things from her viewpoint—"

"I won't," said Jeff. "You can be fair without seeing the other fellow's side of things, Britt. Keep doing that and you stop having a side of your own. You get so damned broad-minded that you don't know right from wrong."

I said that I didn't always know now, and he said I should ask him whenever I was in doubt. "Incidentally, I spoke to a lawyer about the way you'd been gypped out of your property for that city dump, and he thinks you've got a hell of a good case. In fact, he's willing to take it on a contingency for a third of what he can recover."

"But I've told you," I said, "I just can't do it, Jeff. I'm simply not up to a courtroom battle."

"My lawyer friend thinks they'd go for an out-of-court settlement."

"Well, maybe," I said. "But Connie would be sure to find out about it, and I'd still be up the creek. She'd grab any money I got, and give me a good smearing besides."

"I don't see that." Claggett frowned. "You've been sending her quite a bit of money, haven't you?"

"Better than four thousand since I got out of the hospital."

"Then why should she want to give you a bad time? Why should she throw a wrench in a money machine? She hurts you, she hurts herself."

I nodded, said he was probably right. But still . . .

"I'm just afraid to do it, Jeff. I don't know why I am but I am."

He looked at me exasperatedly, and seemed on the point of saying something pointed. Instead, however, he sighed heavily and said he guessed I just couldn't help it.

"But think it over, anyway, won't you? You don't need to commit yourself, but you can at least think about it, can't you?"

"Oh, well, sure," I said. "Sure, I'll think about it."

"That's a promise?"

"Of course," I said.

He left. I returned to Kay who was well-prepared to receive me.

"I could simply kill you!" she exploded. "You made me lose my job, you stupid old boob you!"

"I'm sorry," I said. "But I'm sure you were much too good for it."

"I was not! I mean—why didn't you speak up for me? It was all your fault, anyway, but you didn't say a word to defend me!"

"I thought I did, but possibly I didn't say enough," I said. "I really don't think it would have changed anything, however, regardless of what I'd said."

"Oh, *you*! What do you know, you silly old fool?"

"Very little," I said. "And at the rate I'm aging, I'm afraid I won't be able to add much to my store of knowledge."

She glared at me, her face blotched and ugly like a soiled picture. She said angrily that I hadn't needed to act like a fool, had I? Well, *had* I?

"You didn't even give him time to open his mouth before you were cracking your silly jokes! Saying that I couldn't wear my gun because it didn't match my birthday suit, and a lot of other stupid silly stuff. Well, you weren't funny, not a doggone bit! Just a plain darned fool, that's all you were!"

"I know," I said.

"You *know?*"

"It's a protective device." I nodded. "The I-ain't-nothin'-but-a-hound-dawg syndrome. When a dog can't cope, he flops over on his back, thumps his tail, wiggles his paws and exposes his balls. Briefly, he demonstrates that he is a harmless and amusing fellow, so why the hell should anyone hurt him? And it works pretty well with other dogs, literal and figurative. The meanest mastiff has never masticated me, but I've taken some plumb awful stompings from pussycats."

"*Huh!* You think you're so smart, don't you?"

"Meow, sppftt," I said.

XXIV

IT WAS A PRETTY GRIM WEEKEND.

Mrs. Olmstead decided to replace her usual grumbling and mumbling with silence—the kind in which conversation is omitted but not the clashing and crashing of pans, the smashing of dishes and the like.

Kay performed her nurse's duties with a vengeance, taking my pulse and temperature every hour on the hour or so it seemed to me, and generally interrupting me so often in doing her job that doing my own was virtually impossible.

Sunday night, after dinner, there was a respite in the turmoil. Kay had retired to her room for a time, and Mrs. Olmstead was apparently doing something that could not be done noisily. At any rate, it seemed to be a good time to do some writing, and I dragged a chair up to my typewriter and went to work. Or, rather, I tried to. The weekend's incessant clatter and interruptions had gotten me so keyed up that I couldn't write a word.

I got up and paced around my office, then went back to my typewriter. I squirmed and fidgeted, and stared helplessly at the paper. And, finally, I went out into the kitchen for a cup of coffee.

I shook the pot, discovering that there was still some in it. I put it on the stove to warm, and got a cup and saucer from the cupboard. Moving very quiety, to be sure. Keeping an eye on the door to Mrs. Olmstead's quarters, and listening for any sounds that might signal a resumption of her racket.

I poured my coffee and sipped it standing by the stove, then quietly washed and dried the cup and saucer and returned them to the cupboard. And suddenly I found myself grimacing with irritation at the preposterousness of my situation.

This was *my* house. Kay and Mrs. Olmstead were working for *me*. Yet they had made nothing but trouble for me throughout the weekend, and they had certainly not refrained from throwing their weight around before then—forcing *me* to cater to *them*. And just why the hell should things be this way?

Why had most of my life been like this, a constant giving-in and knuckling-under to people who didn't give a damn about my welfare, regardless of what they professed or pretended?

I was brooding over the matter, silently swearing that there were going to be some changes made, when I became aware of a very muted buzzing. So muted that I almost failed to hear it.

I looked around, listening, trying to locate the source of the sound. I looked down at the floor, saw the faint outline of the telephone cord extending along the baseboard of the cabinetwork. And I yanked open the door of the lower cupboard and snatched out the telephone.

Just as Manny was about to give up and hang up.

She asked me where in the world I'd been, and I said I'd been right there, and I'd explain the delay in answering when I saw her. "But I'm sorry I kept you waiting. I wasn't expecting any calls tonight."

"I know, but I just had to call you, Britt. I've been reading the manuscript you gave me on erosion, and I think it's wonderful, darling! Absolutely beautiful! The parallel you draw between the decline of the soil and the deterioration of the people—the lowering of life expectancy and the incidence of serious disease. Britt, I can't tell you when I've been so excited about something!"

"Well, thank you," I said, grinning from ear to ear. "I'm very pleased that you like it."

"Oh, I do! In its own way, I think it's every bit as good as *Deserts on the March*."

I mumbled, pleased, saying nothing that made any sense, I'm sure. Even to be mentioned in the same breath with Dr. Paul Sears' classic work was overwhelming. And I knew that Manny wasn't simply buttering me up to make me feel good.

"There's only one thing wrong with what you've done," she went on. "It's far too good for us. You've got to make it into a full-length book that will reach the kind of audience it deserves."

"But PXA is paying for it. Paying very well, too."

"I know. But I'm sure something can be worked out with Pat. I'll talk to him after I talk to you, let's see, the day after tomorrow, is it?"

"That's right," I said.

"Well, I haven't read all you've done, and I want to read back through the whole manuscript before our meeting. So ... " She hesitated. "I'm not sure I can make it on Tuesday. Suppose I call you Wednesday, and see what we can set up?"

I said that was fine with me; I was glad to have the additional time to work. We talked a few minutes more, largely about the work and how well she liked it. Then we hung up, and I started to leave the kitchen. And Mrs. Olmstead's surly voice brought me to a halt.

"What's going on here, anyways? Wakin' folks up at this time o'night!"

Her face was sleep-puffed, her eyes streaked with threads of yellowish matter. She rubbed them with a grayish-looking fist, meanwhile surveying me sourly.

"Well," she grunted, "I ast you a question, Mis-ter Rainstar."

"Hold out your hands," I said.

"Huh?" She blinked stupidly. "What for?"

"Hold them out! *Now!*"

She held them out. I put the phone in them, took her by the elbow and hustled her out to the hallway writing desk. I took the phone out of her hands and placed it on the desk.

"Now that is where it belongs," I said, "and that is where I want it. Can you remember that, Mrs. Olmstead?"

She said surlily that she could. She could remember things a heck a lot better than people who couldn't even remember to mail a letter.

"I tell you one thing, though. That phone's out here an' I'm back in the kitchen, I ain't sure I'm gonna hear it."

"All right," I said. "When you're actually in the kitchen working, you can keep the phone with you. But never put it away in a cupboard where I found it just now."

She shrugged, started to turn away without answering.

"One thing more," I said. "I've noticed that we're always running out of shopping money. No matter how much I leave for you, you use it. It's going to have to stop, Mrs. Olmstead?"

"Now you listen to me," she said, shaking a belligerent finger at me. "I can't help it that groceries is high! I don't spend a nickel more for 'em than I have to."

I said I knew groceries were high. I also knew that Jack Daniels was high, and I'd noticed several bottles of it stowed in the bottom cupboard.

"You'll have to start drinking something cheaper," I said. "You apparently do a great deal of drinking in bars when you're supposedly out shopping, so I can't supply you with Jack Daniels for your home consumption."

She looked pretty woebegone at that, so I told her not to worry about it, for God's sake, and to go to bed and get a good night's sleep. And watching her trudge away, shoulders slumped, in her dirty old robe, I felt like nine kinds of a heel. Because, really, why fuss about a little booze if it made her feel good? At her age, with all passion spent and the capacity for all other good things gone, she surely was entitled to good booze. Drinking was probably all that made life-become-existence tolerable for her as it probably is for all who drink.

I went to bed and to sleep. Thinking that the reason I hated getting tough with people was that it was too tough on me.

The next day went fairly well for me. There was practically no trouble from Mrs. Olmstead. I avoided any with Kay by simply submitting to her ministrations.

I got in a good day's work, and continued to work until after nine that night.

Around ten, while I was toweling myself off after a shower, Kay came into the bathroom bearing a thermometer.

I took her by the shoulders, pushed her outside and locked the door.

When I had finished drying myself, I put on my pajamas, came out of the bathroom and climbed into bed. Nodding at Kay who stood waiting for me, prim-faced.

"Does that mean," she said icily, "that I now have your permission to take your temperature?"

"If you like," I said.

"Well, thank you so much!" she said.

She took my temperature. I held up my wrist, and she took my pulse, almost hurling my hand away from her when she had finished.

She left then, turning the light off and closing the door very gently. Some twenty minutes later, she tapped on the door with her fingernails, pushed it open and came in. Through slitted eyes I watched her approach my bed. A soft, sweet-smelling shadow in the dim glow of the hall light.

She stood looking down at me. Then her hands came out from behind her, and went up over her head. And they were holding a long sharp knife.

I let out a wild yell, but the knife was already plunging downward.

It stabbed against my chest, then folded over as cardboard will. And Kay fell across me, shaking with laughter.

After a time, she crawled over into bed next to me, shedding her shorty nightgown en route. She nuzzled me and whispered naughtily in my ear. I told her she wasn't funny, dammit; she'd damned near scared me to death. She said she was terribly sorry, but she'd just had to snap me out of my stiffishness some way. And, I said, Oh, well.

We were about to take it from there when I remembered something, and sat up abruptly.

"My God!" I said. "You've got to get out of here! This place is going to be full of cops in about a minute!"

"*What*? What the heck are you talking about?"

"The walls are bugged! Any loud cry for help will bring the police."

"Britt, darling," she said soothingly, "you just lie right back down here by mama. You just shut your mouth so mama can kiss it."

"But you don't understand, dammit! Jeff Claggett couldn't stake the place out, but I was afraid to come back here without plenty of protection. So—"

"So he told you that story," said Kay, and determinedly pulled me back down at her side. "And he gave you me. It's all the protection he could give you, and it's all you need. Take it from Officer Nolton, Britt. Soon-to-be-resigned Officer Nolton, thanks to your dear friend, the sergeant."

"Knock it off," I said crossly. "I had an idea all along that I was being kidded."

"Why, of course, you did," Kay said smoothly. "And, now, you're sure."

And now, of course, I was, since my yell for help had brought no response. Jeff had deceived me about the house being bugged, just as he had about Kay's status. He had done it in my own best interests, and I was hardly inclined to chide or reproach him.

Still, I couldn't help feeling that uneasiness which comes to one whose welfare is almost totally dependent upon another person, no matter how well-intentioned that person may be. Nor could I help wondering whether there were other deceptions I didn't yet know about. Or whether something meant for my own good might turn out just the opposite.

XXV

MY SENSE OF UNEASINESS INCREASED RATHER THAN DIMINISHED. It became so aggravated under Kay's incessant inquiries as to what was bothering me that I blew up and told her she was.

"Everything about you is getting to me," I said. "That blushing trick, the prudish-sweet manner, the cute-kiddy way you talk, like you wouldn't say crap if you were up to your collar in it, the—Oh, crud to it!" I said. "You've got me so bollixed up I don't know what I'm saying any more."

We were in my bedroom at the time—where else—and I was fully prepared to go to bed—*by myself.*

Kay said she was sorry she got on my nerves, but I'd feel a lot better after I had something she had for me. She started to climb into bed with me. I put a leg up in the air, warding her off. She tried to come by the other way, and I stuck up an arm.

She frowned at me, hands on her hips. "Now, you see here, I have as much right to that bed as you have."

"Right to it?" I said. "You talk like a girl in a wooden hat, baby."

"You said you didn't think I was awful. Because I did it, I mean. You said you'd marry me if you weren't already married."

"Which I am," I said. "Don't forget that."

Kay said that part didn't matter. What was important was that I wanted to marry her, and that kind of made her my wife, and this was a community property state so half of the bed was hers. And while I was unravelling that one she hopped over me and into bed.

I let her stay. For one thing, it is very hard to push a beautiful, well-built girl out of your bed. For another, while I knew she had skunked me again, that I had fallen for her act, it *was* a very good act. And what did one more fall matter to an incurable fall guy?

By the following day, Wednesday, my feelings of uneasiness had blossomed into a sense of foreboding. The feeling grew in me that things had gotten completely out of hand and were about to become worse, and that there was nothing I could do about it.

It wasn't helped much by the bitter look Mrs. Olmstead gave me, as she departed to do her shopping or drinking or whatever she did with my money. Nor was I cheered by a brief bit of sharpness which I had with Manny when she called to make an appointment with me. We finally made one for that afternoon, but I was still feeling quite down and more than a little irritated when Kay showed her into my office around four o'clock.

As it turned out, she also was not feeling her best, a fact she admitted as soon as our opening pleasantries were over.

"I don't want to argue with you, Britt," she said. "But you look quite well. I think you're probably in a lot better condition than I am. And as long as you've been going out, anyway—it isn't as if you were bedridden—I don't see why you couldn't have come to the office."

"Wait a minute," I said. "Hold it right there. Regardless of how well I look or don't look, I'm under strict orders not to leave the house."

"But I called here several times when you were out. At least Mrs. Olmstead told me you were. Of course ..." Manny paused, frowning. "Of course, that could have been her way of saying that you just didn't want to talk to me ... "

"There'd never be a time when I didn't want to talk to you. You should know that."

"I know. But ... " she hesitated again. "Perhaps it wasn't Mrs. Olmstead. I thought it was, and she said it was but—Do you suppose it could have been what's-her-name, your nurse?"

"I'll find out," I said. "I know they've been feuding, and they just might have—one of them might have—tried to drag me into the quarrel." I pondered the matter a moment, then sighed and threw up my hands. "Hell, I'll never find out. Both of them are entirely capable of lying."

"Poor Britt." Manny laughed softly. "Well, it doesn't matter, dear. It doesn't bother me now that I know you haven't been going out at all."

"I haven't been. That's the truth, Manny."

"I believe you."

"The only time I've left the house was when I walked to your car with you last Friday."

"Well ... " She smiled at me, her golden head tilted to one side. "Since it's been so long, maybe you should walk to my car with me again today."

"Well ... "

"Well?" Her smile faded, began to draw in around the edges. "You're afraid to, is that it? You still don't trust me."

"I haven't said that," I said. "You gave me your word that I had nothing more to fear from you, and I'm more than anxious to believe you. I could probably say something more positive if I wasn't a little bewildered."

"Yes? About what?"

"About your visit here this afternoon. I thought you were here to discuss my manuscript. But we've talked about practically nothing except my mishandled telephone calls and my walking to your car with you."

Manny's expression cleared, and she apologized hastily. "I'm sorry, dear. You have every right to be puzzled. But I like the manuscript better than ever, and Pat thinks it's a fine job, too. He agrees that you should make a book out of it, and there won't be any problem about the money. We'll call it square for the right to do a digest."

"That's very generous of you," I said, "and I'm very grateful."

"We consider it a privilege to be associated with the project. I just wish I could be here to see it through to the end—not that you need my help, of course. But I can't be. Th-that's w-why?"—she averted her head suddenly. "That's why I made such a bit thing of being outside the house with you. Even for a little while."

"I don't understand," I said. "What do you mean you can't be here until the work is finished?"

"I mean, this is the last time I'll see you. I'm leaving the company, and going back east."

"B-but—" I stared at her, stunned. "But, why?"

"I'm getting married."

I continued to stare at her. I shook my head incredulously, unable to believe what I had heard.

"You're the only person I've told, so please keep it to yourself. I don't want anyone else to know just yet."

Married! My Manny getting married!

"But you can't!" I suddenly exploded. "I won't let you!"

"Oh?" She smiled at me sadly. "Why not, Britt?"

"Well, all right," I said doggedly. "I can't marry you. Not now, anyway. Maybe never. But why the big hurry? We'd got everything straightened out between us, and I thought that—that—"

"That we could pick up where we left off? I'd've been willing to settle for that, at least until something better could be worked out. But it just isn't possible." She stood up and held out her hand. "Good-bye and good luck, Britt."

"Wait a minute." I also stood up, and I took her hand and held onto it. "Who is this guy anyway?"

"You wouldn't know him. I knew him in the east a long time ago."

"But why are you suddenly rushing into marriage with him?"

"Why do you think I'm rushing? But never mind. It's settled, Britt, so please let go of my hand."

I let go of it.

She turned toward the door, and I started to accompany her. But she gestured for me to remain where I was.

"I'm afraid I'm pretty stupid, darling. It's the police who've ordered you to stay in the house, isn't it? And your nurse is one of them?"

"Yes," I said. "To both questions."

"That's what Pat figured. He remembered her from somewhere, and it finally dawned on him that he'd seen her in uniform."

"All right," I said. "She's a cop, and I'm under orders not to leave the house. But I did it once, and since this is a pretty special occasion—the last time we'll see each other—"

"No!" she said sharply. "You'll stay inside as you've been told to!"

I said I'd at least walk to the front door with her, and I did. She held out her hand to me again, a firm little smile on her face, and I took it and pulled her into my arms. There was the briefest moment of resistance, then she came to me almost violently, as though swept on a wave of emotion. She embraced me, kissed me over and over, ran her soft, small hands through my hair.

And Kay Nolton cleared her throat noisily, and said, "Well, excuse me!"

Manny drew away from me, giving Kay an icy look. "How long were you watching us?" she demanded. "Or did you lose track of the time?"

"Never you mind, toots. I'm paid to watch people!"

"You should be paying," said Manny. "You get so much fun out of it."

And before Kay could come up with a retort, she was out of the house and slamming the door of the car. Kay said something obscene, then turned angrily on me. She said it was a darned good thing that Manny wasn't coming back to the house, and that she, Kay, would snatch her bald-headed if she ever did.

I accused her of snooping, listening outside the door while Manny and I were talking. She said, I was doggone right she'd been listening, and if I didn't like it I could do the next best thing. I went into my office and closed the door, and at dinnertime she brought a tray in to me, also bringing a cup of coffee for herself.

She sat down across me, sipping from it, as I ate. I complimented her on the dinner, and made other small talk. In the midst of it, she broke in with a curt question.

"Why isn't Miss Aloe coming here to the house any more, Britt? I know she isn't, but I don't know why."

"You mean you missed part of our conversation?" I said.

"Answer me! I've got a right to know."

I lifted the tray from my lap, and set it on a chair. I shook out my napkin, and dropped it on top of the tray. Then I leaned back in my chair, and looked thoughtfully out the window.

"Well?" she said sullenly.

"I was just mulling over your remark," I said, "about your having a right to know. I don't feel that you have a right to know anything about my personal affairs. But I can see how you might, and I suppose it's my fault that you do. So, to answer your question: Miss Aloe is giving up her position here, and going back east. That's why I won't be seeing her again."

Kay said, Oh, in a rather timid tone. She said that she was sorry if she'd said or done anything that she shouldn't have.

I shook my head, brushing off her statement. Not trusting myself to speak. I was suddenly overwhelmed by my sense of loss, the knowledge of how much Manny had meant to me. And I jumped up and went over to the window. Stood there staring out into the gathering dusk.

Behind me, I heard Kay getting up quietly. I heard her pick up the dinner tray and leave the room, softly clicking the door shut behind her.

Several minutes passed. Then, she knocked and came in again, carrying the phone on its long extension cord. She handed it to me and started to leave, but I motioned for her to remain. She did so, taking the chair she had occupied before.

"Britt?" It was Jeff Claggett. "How was your visit with Miss Aloe?"

"All right," I said. "At least partly all right. She's leaving town, and going back east. Yes, within the next day or so, I believe."

"The hell!" He grunted with surprise. "Just like that, huh? She give you any reason?"

"Well"—I hesitated. "I don't need to consult with her any more. I'm going ahead with the work on my own."

"Yes? Nothing else?"

"I couldn't say," I said carefully. "What else could there be, and what does it matter, anyway? I am sure that I have nothing more to fear from her. I'm positive of it, Jeff. And that's all I'm concerned about."

"So who said no?" He sounded amused. "Why so emphatic?"

"Let it go," I said. "The point is that there's no longer any reason to continue our present arrangement. If you'd like to make it official, Miss Nolton is right here and—"

"Hold it! Hold it, Britt!" Claggett snapped. "I think we can close things out there very soon. But you leave it to me to say when, okay?"

"Well, all right," I said. "I think it would be better to—"

"Why guess about something when you can be sure? Why not wait until Miss Aloe actually leaves town?" He paused, then lowered his voice. "Nolton throwing her weight around? Is that it, Britt?"

"Well"—I sidled a glance at Kay. "I imagine it would be difficult to make a change, wouldn't it?"

"It would."

"All right, then," I said. "I'll manage."

We hung up, and I passed the phone back to Kay. She took it silently, but at the door she turned and gave me a stricken look.

I faced around to my typewriter, and began pounding on the keys. And I kept at it until I was sure she had gone.

I had had about enough of Kay Nolton. What had started out as a pleasant giving, something that we could both enjoy, had wound up as an attempt to take me over.

I wasn't ready to be taken over, and I never would be. Nor would I ever want to take anyone else over. Love isn't tantamount to ownership. Love is being part of someone else, while still remaining yourself.

That was the way it had been with me and Manny. And now that she was gone from my life . . . ·

Well. Kay could not fill the space Manny had left. It was too great for any other to fill.

Kay left me alone that night. Which was just as well for her. I had discovered that confronting people when they insisted on it was not nearly so fearful as I had thought, and I was all ready to do it again.

The mood was with me the next day, and when Mrs. Olmstead appeared in my office doorway and announced that she needed more money to go shopping, I flatly refused to give her any.

"You've had far too much already," I told her coldly. "You've constantly emptied that cash box in the telephone desk, and then come grumbling to me for more. You must have had over six hundred dollars in less than two weeks' time. The best thing you can do now is to pack up your belongings and clear out."

"That don't make me mad none!" She glared at me defiantly. "You just pay me my wages, an' I'll be out of here faster'n you can say scat!"

"I don't have to pay you," I said. "You've already paid yourself several times over."

If she had given me any kind of argument, I probably would have relented. But surprisingly she didn't argue at all. Oh, she did a little under-the-breath cursing on her way out of my office. In no more than ten minutes, however, she was packed and gone from the house.

Kay, who had been standing by during the proceedings, declared that I had done exactly the right thing. "You should have done it long ago, Britt. You were far too patient with that woman."

"I've been that way with a lot of people," I said. "But it's a fault I'm going to correct."

She dropped her eyes, toeing-in with one white-shod foot. A slow blush spreading up her cheeks to blend with the auburn of her hair. It was all beautifully calculated. I have never seen such control. She was saying, as clearly as if she had spoken, that she had been a naughty-naughty girl and she was truly sorry for it.

"Will you forgive your naughty girl, Britt?" She spoke in a cute-child's voice. "She's awfully sorry, and she promises never to be naughty again."

"It doesn't matter," I said. "Forget it."

"Why, of course, it matters. But I'll be good from now on, honey. I swear I'll—"

"I don't care whether you are or not," I said. "I can hang by my thumbs a few days if I have to. If it takes any longer than that to wrap things up here, and if I still need a cop-nurse, you won't be her."

She gave me no more argument than Mrs. Olmstead had. I was amazed at how easy it was to tell people off—without being very proud of it—although, admittedly, my experience was pretty limited.

I didn't feel much like working; the thought of Manny, *my Manny*, being married to another was too much on my mind. But I worked, anyway, and I was still at it when Claggett arrived in mid-afternoon.

Manny was back in the hospital, he informed me. The same reputable hospital she had been in before with the same reputable doctors in attendance.

And, as before, she was in absolute seclusion, and no information about her condition or the nature of her illness was being given out.

XXVI

"I COULD PROBABLY GET A COURT ORDER AND FIND OUT," Claggett said. "If I could show any reason why it was necessary for me to know. But I can't think what the hell it would be."

"Probably there isn't any," I said. "Nothing sinister, I mean. She told me yesterday that she wasn't feeling well. Possibly she got to feeling worse, and had to go to the hospital."

"Possibly. But why so secretive about it?"

"Well . . . "

"Tell you something," Claggett said. "Maybe I'm a little cynical, but I've never known anyone to pull a cover-up yet unless there was something to cover up."

"That's probably true. But this could hardly be called a cover-up, could it?"

"It's close enough. And the one thing I've found that's usually covered up with doctors is mental illness. It's my guess," said Claggett thoughtfully, "that Miss Aloe has had a nervous breakdown or something of the kind. The second one in less than a month. Either that or she's pretending to. So that leaves us with a couple of questions."

"Yes?" I said. "I mean, it does?"

"To take the last one first. If she's pretending, why is she? And, secondly, if she's actually had a nervous collapse, what brought it on?"

"I just hope she's all right," I said. "In any case, I don't see what her being in the hospital has to do with me."

"Well, it could be just a coincidence, but the last time she was hospitalized you had a pretty bad accident."

"It *was* a coincidence," I said, and wondered why I suddenly felt so uncomfortable and uneasy. "I'm positive that she's levelling with me, Jeff. I knew it when she wasn't, and I know it now that she is."

Claggett shrugged, and said that was good. He, himself, would never trust his own judgment where someone he loved was concerned. Because you could love someone who was completely no good and untrustworthy.

"But we'll see," he said, and stood up. "I have no basis for believing that she's not on the level with you, but we shouldn't be long in finding out."

I walked to the door with him, wondering whether I should tell him about Manny's impending marriage. But I had promised not to, and I could think of no reason why I should.

We shook hands, and he promised to keep me in touch. Then, just as he was leaving, he abruptly pulled me back from the door and moved back into the shadows himself.

I started to ask what was the matter, and he gestured me to silence. So we stood there tensely in silence, waiting. And then there was the sound of footsteps mounting to the porch and crossing to the door.

My view was obscured by Jeff Claggett, and the heavy shadows of the porch. But I could see a little, see that a man was standing with his face pressed against the screen to peer inside.

Apparently he also was having a problem in seeing, for he reached down to the door handle, pulled it open and stepped uncertainly across the threshold.

Claggett grabbed him in a bone-crushing bear hug, pinning his arms to his sides. The man let out a startled gasp.

"W-what's going on here?"

"You tell me, you son-of-a-bitch!" rasped Claggett. "Let's see how fast you can talk."

"It's all right, Jeff," I said. "He's my father-in-law."

XXVII

CONNIE'S LETTERS TO ME HAD GONE UNANSWERED. When she telephoned, Mrs. Olmstead told her I had moved, and that she had no idea where I was. And for the last ten days or so, the phone had simply gone unanswered. Luther Bannerman had determined to find out just what was what (to borrow his expression). And he'd driven all the way here from the Midwest to do it.

He was in the dining room now with Kay, stuffing himself with the impromptu meal she had prepared for him at my request. Rambling and rumbling on endlessly about my general worthlessness.

"... me an' daughter just couldn't support him any longer, so he comes back down here. An' he sent her a little money, but it was like pulling teeth to get it out of him. And this last month, more than a month, I guess, he didn't send nothing! No, sir, not one red cent! So I just up and decided—Pass me that coffee pot, will you, miss? Yes, and I believe I'll have some more of them beans an' potato salad, and a few of them ... "

In the kitchen, Jeff Claggett unwrapped the strip of black tape from around the telephone cord, and held the two ends apart.

"A real sweet old lady," he laughed sourly. "Well, that takes care of any calls since she left today, if you had any since then. But I'm damned if I understand how she could head off the others."

I said it was easy, as easy as it was for her to see that I got no mail that would reveal what she was up to. "She kept the phone out in the kitchen when she was in the house, and when she was away she hid it where it couldn't be heard."

"And you never caught on?" Claggett frowned. "She pulls this for almost a month, and you never tipped?"

"Why should I?" I said. "If someone like you called, of course, she'd see that you got through to me. Anyone else would be inclined to take her at her word. She had a little luck, I'll admit. But it wasn't all that hard to pull off with someone who gets and makes as few calls as I do."

"Yeah, well, let's get on with the rest of it," Claggett sighed. "I hate to ask, but ... ?"

"The answer is yes to both questions," I said. "Mrs. Olmstead mailed the checks I sent to my wife—or rather she didn't mail them. And she made my bank deposits for me—or didn't make them."

Claggett asked me if I hadn't gotten deposit slips, and I said, no, but the amounts were noted in my bankbook. Claggett said he'd just bet they were, and he'd bet I hadn't written "for deposit only" on the back of the checks. I said I hadn't and couldn't.

"I needed some cash for household expenses," I explained, "and I'd run out of personal checks. I had some on order, but they never arrived."

"I wonder why." Claggett laughed shortly. "Well, I guess there's no way of knowing how much she's taken you for offhand, or how much if any we can recover—when and if we catch up with her. But Mr. Blabber-mouth or Bannerman shapes up to me like a guy who means to get money out of you right now."

"I'm sure of it," I said. "I should have at least a few hundred left in the bank, but it wouldn't be enough to get him off my back."

"No," he said. "With a guy like him there's never enough. Well—he drew a glass of water from the sink, drank it down thoughtfully. "Want me to handle him for you?"

"Well ... " I hesitated. "How are you going to do it?"

"Yes or no, Britt."

I said, Yes. He said, All right, then. *He* would do it, and there was to be no interference from me.

We went into the dining room, and sat down across from Bannerman. He had stuffed his mouth so full that a slimy trickle streaked down from the corner of it. Claggett told him disgustedly to use his napkin, for God's sake. My father-in-law did so, but with a pious word of rebuke.

"Good men got good appetites, Mister Detective. Surest sign there is of a clean conscience. Like I was telling the young lady—"

"We heard what you told her," Claggett said coldly. "The kind of crap I'd expect from a peabrain loudmouth. No, stick around, Nolton"—he nodded to Kay, who resumed her chair. "I'd like to know what you think of this character."

"He already knows," Kay said. "I told him when he tried to give me a feel."

Bannerman spluttered red-faced that he'd done nothing of the kind. He'd just been tryin' to show his appreciation for all the trouble she'd gone to for him. But Kay had taken her cue from Claggett—that here was a guy who should have his ears pinned back. And she was more than ready to do the job.

"Are you calling me a liar, buster?" She gave him a pugnacious glare. "Well, are you?"

He said, "N-no, ma'am, 'course not. I was just—"

"Aaah, shut up!" she said.

And Claggett said, Yes, shut up, Bannerman. "You've been talking ever since you stepped through the door today, and now it's time you did some listening. You want to, or do you want trouble?"

"He wants trouble," Kay said.

"I don't neither!" Bannerman waved his hands a little wildly. "Britt, make these people stop—"

"All right, listen and listen good," Claggett said. "Mr. Rainstar has already given your daughter a great deal of money. I imagine he'll probably provide her with a little more when he's able to, which he isn't at present. Meanwhile, you can pack up that rattletrap heap you drove down here in, and get the hell back where you came from."

Anger stained Luther Bannerman's face the color of eggplant. "I know what I can do all right!" he said hoarsely. "An' it's just what I'm gonna do! I'm gonna have Mr. Britton Rainstar in jail for the attempted murder of my daughter!"

"How are you going to do that?" Claggett asked. "You and your daughter are going to be in jail for the attempted murder of Mr. Rainstar."

"*W-what?*" Bannerman's mouth dropped open. "Why that's crazy!"

"You hated his guts," Claggett continued evenly. "You'd convinced yourselves that he was a very bad man. By being different than you were, by being poor instead of rich. So you tried to kill him, and here's how you went about it ... "

He proceeded to explain, despite Bannerman's repeated attempts to interrupt. Increasingly fearful and frantic attempts. And his explanation was so cool and persuasive that it was as though he was reciting an actual chronicle of events.

The steering apparatus of my car had been tampered with; also, probably, the accelerator. Evidence of the tampering would be destroyed, of course, when my car went over the cliff. All that was necessary then was for me to be literally driven out of the house. So angered that I would jump into the car, and head for town.

But Connie had overdone the business of making me angry. She had pursued me to the kitchen door—and been knocked unconscious when I flung it open. And when I headed for town, she was in the car with me ...

"That's the way it was, wasn't it?" Claggett concluded. "You and your daughter tried to kill Mr. Rainstar, and your little plan backfired on you."

My father-in-law looked at Claggett helplessly. He looked at me, eyes welling piteously.

"Tell him, Britt. Tell him that Connie and me w-wouldn't, that we just ain't the kind of p-people to—to—"

He broke off, obviously—*very* obviously—overcome with emotion.

I wet my lips hesitantly. In spite of myself, I felt sorry for him. This man who had done so much to humiliate me, to make me feel small and worthless, now seemed very much that way himself. And I think I might have spoken up for him, despite a stern glance from Jeff Claggett. But my father-in-law compensated in blind doggedness for his considerable short-comings in cerebral talents, and he was talking again before I had a chance to speak.

"I'll tell you what happened!" he said surlily. "That fella right there, that half-breed Injun, Britt Rainstar, tried to kill my daughter for her insurance! He stood to collect a couple of hundred thousand dollars, and that was just plenty of motive for a no-account loafer like him!"

Claggett appeared astonished. "You mean to tell me that Mr. Rainstar was your daughter's beneficiary?"

"Yes, he was! I'm in the insurance business, and I wrote the policy myself!"

"Well, I'll be damned!" Claggett said in a shocked voice. "Did you know about this, Britt?"

"I told you about it," I said, a little puzzled. "Don't you remember? Mr. Bannerman wrote up a similar policy on me with my wife as benefici-ary, at the same time."

He nodded, and said, Oh, yes; it all came back to him now. "But the company rejected you, didn't they? They wouldn't approve of your policy."

"That's right. I don't know why exactly, but apparently I wasn't con-sidered a very stable character or something of the kind."

"You were a danged poor risk, that's what!" Bannerman said grimly. "Just the kind of fella that would get himself in a fix with the law. Which is just what you went and done! Why, if I hadn't spoken up to the sheriff, after you tried to kill poor, little Connie—"

He chopped the sentence off suddenly. He gulped painfully, as though swallowing something which had turned out to be much larger than he had thought.

Kay gave him a cold, narrow-eyed grin. There was a snap to Claggett's voice like a trap being sprung.

"So Mr. Rainstar was a pretty disreputable character, was he? *Was he, Bannerman?*"

"I—I—I didn't say that! I didn't say nothin' like that, a-tall, an' don't you—"

"Sure, you did. And you told everyone in town what a no-goodnik he was. A blabbermouth like you would be bound to tell 'em, and don't think I won't dig up the witnesses who'll swear that you did!"

"But I didn't mean nothin' by it. I was just talkin'," Bannerman whined. "You know how it is, Britt. You say you wish someone was dead, or you'd like to kill 'em, but—"

"No," I said. "I've never said anything like that in my life."

"You didn't trust your son-in-law, Bannerman," Claggett persisted. "And you sure as hell didn't like him. But you allowed the policy on your daughter to stand—a policy that made him her beneficiary? Why didn't you cancel it?"

"I—Never you mind!" Bannerman said peevishly. "None of your doggoned business, that's why!"

Claggett asked me if I had ever seen the policy, and I said I hadn't. He turned back to Bannerman, his eyes like blue ice.

"There isn't any policy, is there? There never was. It was just a gimmick to squeeze Mr. Rainstar. Something to threaten him with when he tried to get a divorce."

"That ain't so! There is too a policy!"

"All right. What's the name of the insurance company?"

"I—I disremember, offhand," Bannerman stammered, and then blurted out, "I don't have to tell you, anyway!"

"Now, look you!" Claggett leaned forward, jaw jutting. "Maybe you can throw your weight around with your friendly hometown sheriff. Maybe he thinks the sun rises and sets in your ass. But with me, you're just a pimple on the ass of progress. So you tell me: what's the name of the insurance company?"

"But I—I really don't—"

"All right." Claggett made motions of rising. "Don't tell me. I'll just check it out with the Underwriters' Bureau."

And, at that, Bannerman gave up.

He admitted weakly that there was no policy, and that there never had been. But he brazenly denied that he and Connie had done wrong by lying about it.

Ol' Britt was tryin' to get a divorce, and she had a right to keep him from it, any way she could. And never mind why she was so dead set against a divorce. A woman didn't have to explain a thing like that. The fact that she didn't want one was reason enough.

"Anyways, Connie hasn't been at all well since the accident. Taken all kinds of money to pervide for her. If she hadn't had some way of scarin' money out o' Britt—"

"Apparently, she's able to take care of herself now," Claggett said. "Or do you have round-the-clock nurses. And just remember I'll check up on your story!"

"Well—" Bannerman hesitated. "Yeah, Connie's coming along pretty good right now. 'Course, she's all jammed up inside, an' she's always gonna be an invalid—"

"What doctor told you that? What doctors? What hospital did her X-rays?"

"Well . . . " Bannerman said weakly. "Well . . . " And said no more.

"Jeff," I said. "Can't we wind this up? Just get this—this *thing* the hell out of here? If I have to look at him another minute, I'm going to throw up!"

Claggett said he felt the same way, and he jerked a thumb at Bannerman and told him to beat it. The latter said he'd like to, there was nothing he'd like to do more. But he just didn't see how he could do it.

"I used practically every cent I had comin' down here. And that ol' car of mine ain't gonna go much further, without some work bein' done on it. I *want* t'get back home, these here big cities ain't for me. But—"

"Save it," Claggett said curtly. "You've probably got half of the first nickle you ever made, but I'll give you a stake to get rid of you. Nolton"— he gestured to Kay—"Get him in his car, and see that he stays in it till I come out."

"Yes, sir! Come on, you!"

She hustled my father-in-law out of the room, and the front door opened then closed behind them.

I gave Claggett my heartfelt thanks for the way he had handled things, and promised to pay back whatever money he gave my father-in-law.

"No problem"—he dismissed the matter. "But tell me, Britt. I was just bluffing, of course, trying to shake him up, but do you suppose he and your wife did try to kill you?"

"What for?" I said. "I was willing to get out of their lives. I still am. Why should they risk a murder rap just because they hated me?"

"Well. Hatred has been the motive for a lot of murders."

"Not with people like them," I said. "Not unless it would make them something. I'll tell you, Jeff. I don't see them risking a nickel to see the Holy Ghost do a skirt dance."

He grinned. Then, again becoming thoughtful, he raised another question.

"Why is your wife so opposed to divorce, d'you suppose? I know you'll give her money as long as you have it to give, but—"

"Money doesn't seem to have anything to do with it," I said. "She was that way right from the beginning, when I didn't have a cent and it didn't look like I ever would have. I just don't know." I shook my head. "There was a little physical attraction between us at one time, *very* little. But that didn't last, and we never had any other interests in common."

"Well," Claggett shrugged, "Bannerman was right about one thing. A woman doesn't have to give a reason for *not* wanting a divorce."

We talked about other matters for a few minutes, i.e., Mrs. Olmstead, my work for PXA, and the prospects for suing over the condemnation of my land. Then, he went back to Bannerman again, wondering why the latter had caved in so quickly when he, Claggett, had threatened to call the Underwriter's Bureau.

"Why didn't he try to bluff it out, Britt? Just tell me to go ahead and check? He had nothing to lose by it, and I might have backed down."

"I don't know," I said. "Is it important?"

"We-ell ... " He hesitated, frowning. "Yes, I think it might be. And I think it bears on the reason for your wife's not giving you a divorce. Don't ask me why. It's just a hunch. But ... "

His voice died away. I looked at his troubled face, and again I felt that icy tingling at my spine ... a warning of impending doom. And even as he was rising to leave, a pall seemed to descend on the decaying elegance of the ancient Rainstar mansion.

XXVIII

CLAGGETT DROVE OFF TOWARD TOWN TO GET SOME MONEY FOR MY FATHER-IN-LAW, Bannerman following him in his rattletrap old vehicle. Kay came back into the house.

While she prepared dinner for the two of us, I cleaned up the mess Luther Bannerman had left and carried the dishes out into the kitchen. She glanced at me as I took clean silver and plates from the cupboard; asked if I was still mad at her. I said I never had been—I'd simply tried to set her straight on where we stood. Moreover, I said, I was grateful to her for the several jolts she had given my father-in-law.

She said *that* had been a pleasure. "But if you're not mad, why do you look so funny, Britt? So kind of down in the mouth?"

"Maybe it's because of seeing him," I said. "He always did depress me. On the other hand . . . "

I left the sentence hanging, unable to explain why I felt as I did. The all-pervading gloom that had settled over me. Kay said she was sort of down in the dumps herself, for some reason.

"Maybe it's this darn old house," she said. "Just staying inside here day after day. The ceilings are so high that you can hardly see them. The staircase goes up and up and it's always dark and shadowy. You feel like you're climbing one of those mountains that are always covered with clouds. There are always a lot of funny noises, like someone was sneaking up behind you. And . . . "

I laughed, cutting her off. The house was home to me, and it had never struck me as being gloomy or depressing.

"We both need a good stiff drink," I said. "Hold the dinner a few minutes, and I'll do the honors."

I couldn't find any booze; Mrs. Olmstead apparently had finished it all off. But I dug up a bottle of pretty fair wine, and we had some before dinner and with it.

We ate and drank, and Kay asked how much Mrs. Olmstead had stolen from me. I said I would have to wait until tomorrow morning to find out.

"It really doesn't bother me a hell of a lot," I added. "If she hadn't gotten it my wife would have."

"Oh, yes. She tore up the checks you sent your wife, didn't she?"

"That's right," I said.

"Well, uh, look, Britt . . . " She paused delicately. "I've got some money saved. Quite a bit, actually. So if you'd like to—"

I said, "Thanks, I appreciate the offer. But I can get by all right."

"Well, uh, yes. I suppose. But"—another delicate pause. "How about your wife, Britt? How much do you think she'd want to give you a divorce?"

I told her to forget it. Connie had apparently made up her mind not to give me a divorce on any terms, and there was no use in discussing it.

"I don't know why. Perhaps she has a reason, and I'm too stupid to see it. But"—I laughed suddenly, then quickly apologized. "I'm sorry, Kay. I just thought of a story my great-grandfather used to tell me. Would you care to hear it?"

"I'd love to," she said, in a tone that gave the lie to her statement.

But I told it to her, anyway:

THERE WAS ONCE A HANDSOME YOUNG INDIAN CHIEF, WHO MARRIED A MAIDEN FROM A NEIGHBORING TRIBE.

SHE WAS NEITHER FAIR OF FIGURE OR FACE, AND HER DISPOSITION WAS TRULY UGLY. NEVER DID SHE HAVE A KIND WORD TO SAY TO HER HUSBAND. NEVER WAS HE ABLE TO DO ANYTHING THAT PLEASED HER. SHE WAS SIMPLY A HOMELY SHREW, THROUGH AND THROUGH. AND THE TRIBE'S OTHER SQUAWS AND BRAVES WONDERED WHY THEY REMAINED TOGETHER AS HUSBAND AND WIFE.

THE DAYS PASSED, AND THE MONTHS, AND THE YEARS.

FINALLY, WHEN THE CHIEF WAS A VERY OLD MAN, HE DIED.

HIS WIFE LAUGHED JOYOUSLY AT HIS FUNERAL, HAVING INHERITED HIS MANY PONIES AND BUFFALO HIDES, AND OTHER SUCH WEALTH. AND THIS, HIS WEALTH, WAS HER REASON, OF COURSE, FOR MARRYING HIM AND REMAINING WITH HIM FOR SO MANY YEARS.

Kay stared at me, frowning. I looked at her deadpan, and she shook her head bewilderedly.

"That's the end of the story? What's the point?"

"I just told you," I said. "She married him and stuck with him for his dough. Or the Indian equivalent thereof."

"But—but, darn it! Why did he marry her?"

"Because he was stupid," I said. "His whole tribe was stupid."

"*Wha-aat?*"

"Why, sure," I said. "A lot of Indians are stupid. That's why we wound up in the shape we're in today."

Kay jumped up and left the table.

XXIX

I WAS SORRY NOW THAT I HAD TOLD HER THE STORY, but it hadn't been a rib. My great-grandfather actually had told it to me, a bit of bitter fun-poking at Indians, their decline and fall. But there was wisdom in it for any race.

We all overlook the obvious.

Danger is so commonplace that we have become atrophied to it.

We wring the hand of Evil, and are shocked at the loss of fingers.

I left the dining room, pausing in the hallway to glance into the kitchen. Kay was aware of me, I am sure, but she did not look up. So I went on down the hall to the vast reception area, crossed its gleaming parquet expanse and started up the stairs.

I hadn't occurred to me before, but what Kay had said was true. The upward climb was seemingly interminable, and as shadowed as it was long. There were those strange sounds, also, like stealthy footsteps in pursuit. Sounds where there should have been none. And, due to a trick of acoustics, no sounds where sounds should have been.

I reached the landing, breathing hard, almost leaping up the last several steps. I whirled around, tensed, heart pounding. But there was no one behind me. Nothing but shadows. Cautiously, I looked down over the brief balustrade, which joined the top of the staircase to the wall of the landing.

The parquet floor below me was so distant that I would not have known that it was there had I not known that it was. So distant, and so cloaked in darkness. I backed away hastily, feeling more than a little dizzy.

I went on to my room, cursing my runaway imagination. Calling down curses upon Kay for her unwitting planting of fear in my mind. Cops should know better than that, I thought. It didn't bother cops to talk about darkness and shadows and funny noises, and people sneaking up behind other people. Cops were brave—which was not an adjective that could be applied to Britton Rainstar.

I was, at least figuratively, a very yellow red man.

I had a streak of snowy gray right down the middle of my raven locks. And I had a streak of another color right down the middle of my tawny back.

I got out of my clothes, and took a shower.

I put on pajamas and a robe and carpet slippers.

My pulse was acting up, and there was a kind of jumpiness to my toes.

They kept jerking and squirming of their own volition: my toes always do that when I am very nervous. I almost called out to Kay, when she came up the stairs. Because she was a nurse, wasn't she, and I certainly needed something to soothe my nerves.

But she was miffed at me, or she would have come to me without being summoned. And if I managed to un-miff her, I was sure, what I would get to soothe me was Kay herself. One of the best little soothers in the world, but one which I simply could not partake of.

I had screwed the lid on that jar, you should excuse the expression. She was forever forbidden fruit, even though I should become one, God forbid.

I tried to concentrate on non-scary things. To think of something nice. And the nicest thing I could think of was something I had just determined not to think of. And while I was doing my damnedest not to think of her, simultaneously doing my damnedest to think of something else, she came into my room.

Fully dressed, even to her blue cape. Carrying her small nurse's kit in one hand, her suitcase in the other.

"All right, Britt," she said. "I'm moving in here with you, or I'm moving out. *Leaving!* Right this minute."

"Oh, come off of it," I laughed. "You'd get a permanent black eye with the department. As big as your butt, baby! You'd never get a decent job anywhere."

"But you won't know about it, will you, Britt?" She gave me a spiteful grin. "After I leave, and you're all alone here in this big ol' house. ... "

She set her bags down, and did a pantomime of what would happen to me; clawing her hands and walking like a zombie. And it was ridiculous as hell, of course, but it was pretty darned scary, too.

" ... then the big Black Thing will come out of the darkness," she intoned, in ghostly tones, "and poor little Britt won't see it until it's too late. He'll hear it, but he'll think it's just one of those noises he's always hearing. So he won't look around, and—"

"Now, knock it off, dammit!" I said. "You stop that, right now!"

" ... and the big Black Thing will come closer and closer." (*She came closer and closer.*) "And closer and closer, and closer—*GOTCHA!*"

"Yeow!" I yelled, my hair standing on end. "Get away from me, you crazy broad!"

"Fraidy cat, fraidy cat!" she chanted. "B.R. has a yellow streak, running down his spine!"

I said I'd rather have a yellow streak running down it than pimples. She said angrily that she didn't have pimples running down hers. And I said she would have when my hex went to work.

"A pretty sight you'll be when you start blushing. Your back will look like peaches flambé in eruption. Ah, Kay, baby," I said, "enough of this clowning around. Just give me something to make me sleep, and then go back to your room and—"

"I *won't* go back to my room! But I'll give you a hypo if you really want it."

"If I want it?" I said. "What do you mean by that?"

"I mean, I won't be here. You'll be aww-ll all-alone, with the big Black Things. I thought you might be afraid to go to sleep aww-ll all-alone in this big ol' house, but—"

"All right," I said grimly. "We wound up our little affair, and it's going to stay wound up. You know it's best for both of us. Why, goddammit"— I waved my arms wildly. "What kind of a cop are you anyway? A cop is supposed to be something pretty special!"

She said she was something pretty special, wasn't she?—managing a demure blush. I said she could stay or get out, just as she damned pleased.

"It's strictly up to you, Miss Misbegotten! My car keys are there in the top dresser drawer!"

"Thank you but I'll walk, Mr. Mangy Mane. I'm a strong girl, and I'm not afraid of the dark."

She picked up her bags, and left.

I heard the prolonged creaking of the stairs as she descended them. A couple of moments later, I heard the loud slamming of the front door.

I settled back on the pillows, smugly grinning to myself. Dismissing the notion of going downstairs, and setting the bolts on the door. It would be a lot of bother for nothing. I would just have to go down and unbolt it, when Kay came back. As, of course, she would in a very few minutes. Probably she had never left the porch.

I closed my eyes, forcing myself to relax, ignoring the sibilant scratchings, the all-but-inaudible creakings and poppings, peculiar to very old houses.

I thought of the stupid Indian and his blindness to the obvious. I thought of Connie's senseless refusal to give me a divorce. I thought of Luther Bannerman, his quick admission that Connie had no insurance policy when he thought Claggett was going to check on it.

Why didn't Connie want a divorce? Why the fear of Claggett checking with the insurance company? What—

Oh, my God!

I sat up abruptly, slapping a hand to my forehead. Wondering how I could have missed something that an idiot child should have seen.

I was insured. That was what Claggett would have discovered. Bannerman had lied in saying that the insurance company had rejected me.

Why had he lied? Why else but to keep me from becoming wary, to allay any nasty suspicions I might entertain about his and Connie's plans for me.

Of course, the existence of the policy would have to be revealed in order to collect the death benefit. The double indemnity payoff of $200,000. But there was absolutely nothing to indicate that fraud and deception had been practiced to obtain the policy. Quite the contrary, in fact.

I myself had applied for it, and named Connie as my beneficiary. She had what is legally known as an insurable interest in me. And if I was the kind of guy—as I probably was—who might neglect or forget to keep up my premium payments, she had the right to make them for me. Moreover, she definitely was not obligated to make the fact known that I had the policy, an asset which could be cashed in or encumbered to her disadvantage.

If her marital status should change, if, for example, we should be divorced, I would have to certify to the change. And, inevitably, I would actually know what I had only been assumed to know—that I *was* insured. So there could be no divorce.

Connie and her father couldn't risk another automobile accident by way of killing me. Two such accidents might make my insurers suspicious. An accident of any kind there on their home grounds might arouse suspicion, and so I had been allowed to clear out.

I returned to my home. After a time, I began remitting sizable sums of money to Connie, and as long as I did I was left alone. They could wait. Time enough to kill me when the flow of money to Connie stopped.

Now, it had stopped. So now—

A blast of cold air swept over me. The front door had opened. I sat up abruptly, the short hairs on my neck rising. I waited and listened. Nerves tensing. Face contorted into a stiffening mask of fear.

And then I grinned and relaxed. Lay back down again.

It would be Kay, of course, I hadn't expected her to stay away this long. To say that I was damned glad she had returned was a gross understatement. But I must be very careful not to show it. Now, more than ever, Kay had to be kept at a distance.

After all, I had promised to marry her—when and if I was free. And Connie's attempt to murder me was a felony, uncontestable grounds for divorce.

Kay would undoubtedly hold me to my promise. Kay was a very stubborn and determined young woman. Once Kay got an idea in her head, she would not let go of it, even when it was in her own interests to do so. Maybe it was a characteristic of all blushing redheads. Maybe that was why they blushed.

At any rate, there must be no gladsome welcomes between us. Nothing that might develop into intimacy.

Perhaps I should pretend to be asleep, yes? But, yes. Definitely. It would show how little I was disturbed by her absence. It would throw figurative cold water on the hottest of hot-pantsed redheaded blushers.

I closed my eyes and composed myself . I folded my hands on my chest, began to breathe in even measured breaths. *This should convince her, I thought. Lo, the Poor Indian, at rest after the day's travail. Poor Lo, sleeping the sleep of the just.*

Kay finished her ascent of the stairs.

She came to the door of my room, and looked in at me.

I wondered how I looked. Whether my hair was combed properly, and whether any hair was sticking out of my nose. Nothing looks cruddier than protruding nose hairs. I didn't think I had any, but sometimes it shows when you are lying down when it would not show otherwise.

Kay crossed to my bed. Stood looking down at me. My nose twitched involuntarily.

She had apparently been running in her haste to get back to me. She had gotten herself all sweaty, anyway, and she stank like hell.

I am very sensitive about such things. I can endure the direst hardships; my Indian heritage I suppose. But I *can't* stand a stinky squaw.

I opened my eyes, and frowned up at her.

"Look, baby," I said. "I don't want to hurt your feelings, but—b-bbbbbbb-uht—"

It wasn't Kay.

It wasn't anyone I had ever seen before.

XXX

HE WAS A YOUNG MAN, younger than I was. I knew that without knowing exactly how I knew it. Perhaps it was due to cocksureness, the arrogance that emanated from him like the odor of sweat. He was also a pro—a professional killer.

No one but a pro could have had the incredible nervelessness and patience of this man. To loiter in a hospital lobby, say, until he could give me a murderous shove down its entrance steps. Or to wait in the fields adjacent to my house, until he could get me in the 'scope of his high-powered rifle. Or, missing me, to go on waiting until the house was unguarded and I was unprotected.

The pro knows that there is always a time to kill, if he will wait for it. He knows that when necessity demands disguise it must be quickly and easily used, and readily disposed of. And this man was wearing make-up.

It was a dry kind, a sort of chalk. It could be applied with a few practiced touches, removed with a brush of the sleeve. I could detect it because he had overused it, making his face a shocking mask of hideousness.

Cavernous eyes. A goblin's mouth. Repulsively exaggerated nostrils.

And why? Why the desire to scare me witless? Hatred? Why would he hate me?

There was a *click*. The gleam of a razor-sharp switchblade. He held it up for me to see—gingerly tested its murderous edge. Then looked at me grinning, relishing my stark terror.

Why? Who? Who could enjoy my torture, and why?

"Why, you son-of-a-bitch!" I exploded. "You're Manny's husband!" His eyes flickered acknowledgment, as I looked past him. "Get him, Manny! *Get him good, this time!*"

He turned his head. An impulse reaction.

The ruse bought me a split second. I vaulted over the end of the bed, and hurtled into the bathroom. Slammed and locked the door, just as he lunged against it.

A crack appeared in the inlaid panelling of the door. I called out to the guy shakily, foolishly. "I'm a historical monument, mister. This house is, I mean. You damage a historical monument, and—"

His shoulder hit the panel like a piledriver.

The crack became a split.

140

He swung viciously and his fist came through the wood. He fumbled blindly for the lock. I stooped, opened my mouth and chomped down on his fingers.

There was an anguished yell. He jerked his hand back so hard that I bumped my head against the door. I massaged it carefully, listening, straining my ears for some indication of what the bastard would try next.

I couldn't hear anything. Not a damned thing.

I contined to listen, and I still heard nothing.

Had he given up? No way! Not so soon. Not a professional killer with a personal interest in wasting me. Who hated me, was jealous of me, because of Manny.

"Look, you!" I called to him. "It's all over between Manny and me. I mean it!"

I paused, listening.

"You hear me out there? It's you and her from now on. She told me so herself. Maybe you think she's stalling by going to the hospital, but ... "

Maybe she was, too. Maybe her earlier hospitalization had also been a stall. Or maybe just the thought of being tied up with this guy again had driven her up the wall. Because he really had her on the spot, you know?

She had tried to kill him, had done such a job on him that she believed she *had* killed him. Thus, her long convalescence after his "death." Also, after his recent reappearance, he would have discovered her painful pestering of me in the course of casing her situation. So she was vulnerable to pressure—a girl who had not only tried to kill her husband, but who had also pulled some pretty raw stuff on her lover. And the fact that her husband, the guy who was pressuring her, was on pretty shaky grounds himself would not deter him for a moment.

For he was one of those bullish, dog-in-the-manger types. The kind who would pull the temple down on his head to get a fly on the ceiling. That was the way it was. Add up everything that had happened and that was the answer.

I called out to him again, making my voice stern. I said I would give him until I counted to ten, wondering what the hell I was talking about. *Until I counted to ten, then what?* But he didn't seem very bright, either, so I went right ahead.

"One-two-three-four—*Do you hear me? I'm counting!*—five-six-seven-eight—*All right! Don't say I didn't warn you!*—ni-un-ten!"

Silence.

Still silence.

Well, he could be gone, couldn't he? I'd chomped down on his fingers damned hard, and he could be seriously bitten. Maybe I'd even gotten an artery, and the bastard had beat it before he bled to death.

It just about had to be something like that. I would just about have to have heard him if he still remained there.

I unlocked the door. I hesitated, then suddenly flung it open. And—

I think he must have been standing against the far wall of the bedroom. Nursing his injured hand. Measuring the distance to the bathroom door, as he readied himself for the attack upon it.

Then, at last, hurtling himself forward. Head lowered, shoulders hunched, legs churning like pistons. Rapidly gaining momentum until he hit the door with the impact of a charging bull. Rather, he *didn't* hit the door, since the door was no longer there. I had flung it open. Instead, he rocketed through the opening and hit the wall on the opposite side. And he hit it so hard that several of its tiles were loosened.

There was an explosive *spllaat*! He bounced backward, and his head struck the floor with the sound of a bursting melon.

For a moment, I thought he must be dead. Then, a kind of twitching shudder ran through his body, and I knew he was only dead to the world. Very unconscious, but very much alive.

I got busy.

I yanked off my robe, and tied him up with its cord.

I grabbed up some towels, and tied him up with them.

I tied him up with the hose of the hot-water bottles.

I tied him up with the electric light cords from the reading lamps. And some pillow cases and bedsheets. And a large roll of adhesive bandage.

That was about all I could find to tie him up with, so I let it go at that. But I still wasn't sure that it was enough. With a guy like that, you could never be sure.

I backed out of the bathroom, keeping my eye on him. I backed across the bedroom, still watching him, and out into the hallway. And then I stopped stock-still, my breath sucking in with shock.

Connie stood flattened against the wall, immediately outside my door. And lurking in the shadows at the top of the stairs, was the hulking figure of my father-in-law, Luther Bannerman.

XXXI

I LOOKED FROM HIM TO HER, staring stupidly, momentarily paralyzed with shock. I thought, *"How . . . why . . . what . . . ?"* Immediately following it with the thought, *"How silly can you get?"*

She and Bannerman had journeyed from their homeplace together. Having a supposedly invalided daughter was a gimmick for chiseling money from me. So he had parked her before coming out to my house this afternoon, picking her up afterward. Since Kay wouldn't have volunteered any information, they assumed that she was no more than the nurse she appeared to be, one who went home at night. She had left. While they waited to make sure she would not return, they saw Manny's husband enter the house in a way that no legitimate guest would. So they followed him inside, and when he failed to do the job he had come to . . .

My confusion lasted only a moment. It could have taken no longer than that to sort things out, and put them in proper order. But Connie and Luther Bannerman were already edging toward me. Arms outspread to head off my escape.

I backed away. Back was the only way I could go.

"Get him, Papa!" Connie hissed. *"Now!"*

I saw a shadow upon the shadows—Bannerman poising to slug me. I threw up an arm, drew my own fist back.

"You hypocrite son-of-a-bitch! You come any closer, I'll—!"

Connie slugged me in the stomach. She stiff-armed me under the chin.

I staggered backwards, and fell over the rail of the balustrade.

I went over it and down, my vision moving in a dizzying arc from beamed ceiling to panelled walls to parquet floor. I did a swift back-and-forth re-view of the floor, and decided that I was in no hurry at all to get down to it.

I had never seen such a hard-looking floor.

I was only sixty-plus feet above it—*only!*—but it seemed like sixty miles.

I had hooked my feet through the balusters when I went over the rail.

Connie was alternately pounding on them and trying to pry them loose, meanwhile hollering to her father for help.

"Do something, darn it! Slug him!"

Bannerman moved down the stairs a step or two. He leaned over the rail, striking at me. I jabbed a finger in his eye.

143

He cursed, and let out a howl.

Connie cursed, howled for him to do something, goddammit!

"Never mind your damned eye! Hit him, can't you?"

"Don't you cuss me, daughter!" He leaned over the rail again. "It ain't nice to cuss your papa!"

Connie yelled, "Oh, shit!" exasperatedly, and gave my foot an agonizing blow.

Her father took another swing at me, and my head seemed to explode. I heard him shout with triumph, Connie's maliciously delighted laugh.

"That almost got him, Papa. Just a little bit more, now."

"Don't you worry, daughter. Just you leave him to Papa."

He aimed another blow at me. She hit my sore foot again.

And I kicked her, and I grabbed him.

He was off-balance, leaning far out over the rail. I grabbed him by the ears, simultaneously kicking at Connie.

He came over the rail with a terrified howl, clutching my wrists for dear life. My foot went between Connie's legs, and she was propelled upward as Bannerman's weight yanked me downward.

She shrieked, one terror-filled shriek after another. Shrieking, she flattened herself against my leg and hung onto it.

She shrieked and screamed, and then yelled and howled. And one jerked one way, and the other pulled the other way. And I thought, *My God, they're going to deafen me and pull me apart at the same time.*

They were really a couple of lousy would-be murderers. But they were amateurs, of course, and even a pro can goof up. As witness, Manny's husband.

I caught a glimpse of him as I was swung back and forth. Looking more like a mummy than a man, due to the variety and number of items with which I had bound him. He came hopping through my bedroom door, very dazed and wobbly-looking. He hopped out onto the landing, lost his balance and crashed heavily into the balustrade.

It creaked and scraped ominously. The distant floor of the reception hall seemed to jump up at me a few inches, and the terrified vocalizings of the Bannermans increased.

Somehow, the mummy got to his feet again, though why I don't know. I doubt that he knew what he was doing. He got to the head of the stairs, stood looking down them dazedly. He executed another little hop—and, of course, he fell. Went down the steps in a series of bouncing somersaults. Hitting the leg which Bannerman had just managed to hook over the rail.

The jolt almost knocked Bannerman loose from me. Naturally, I was yanked downward also, simultaneously exerting a tremendous yank upon the balustrade.

It was too much. Too damned much. It tore loose from its ancient moorings, and dropped downward. Connie skidded down my body head-first, unable to stop her plunge until she was extended almost the length of her body. Clutching her father's legs, as she clung to me by her heels.

She screamed and cursed him, hysterically. He cursed and kicked at her.

A strange calm had settled over me—the calm of the doomed. I was at once a part of things and yet outside them, and my overall view was objective.

I didn't know how the few screws and spikes which still attached the balustrade to the landing managed to stay in place. Why it didn't plunge downward, bearing us with it, into the reception hall. Moreover, I didn't seem to care. Rather, I cared *without* caring. What concerned me, in a vaguely humorous way, was the preposterous picture we must make. Connie, Bannerman and I balled together in a kind of crazy bomb, which was about to be dropped at any moment.

I waited for the weight to go off of me, the signal that we were making the final plunge. I waited, and I kept my eyes closed tight. Knowing that if I opened them, if I looked down at that floor so far below me, it would be about the last time I looked at anything.

There was so much racket from the Bannermans and the grating and screeching of the balustrade that I could hear nothing else. But suddenly the weight did go off of me in two gentle yanks. There was another wait then, and I expected to hit the floor at any moment. Then, I myself was yanked, and a couple of strong arms went around me. And I was hustled effortlessly upward.

I was set down on my feet. I received a gentle bearing-down shake, then a sharp slap. I opened my eyes. Found myself on the second-floor landing, with its ruined balustrade.

Connie and Bannerman were stretched out on the floor, face down, with their hands behind their heads. Manny's husband lay at the foot of the stairs in a heap.

Kay peered at me anxiously. "I'm terribly, terribly sorry, darling. Are you all right?"

"Fine," I said. Because I was alive, wasn't I, and being alive was fine, wasn't it?

To show my gratitude, I would gladly have gone down on my knees and kissed her can.

"I would have been back sooner, Britt, but a truck driver tried to pick me up. I think I broke his darned jaw."

"Fine," I said.

"Britt, honey . . . we don't have to say anything to Sergeant Claggett about my leaving you alone, do we? Let's not, okay?"

"Fine," I said.

"I'll think of a good story to cover. Just leave it to me."

"Fine," I said.

"You do love me, don't you, Britt? You don't think I'm awful?"

"Fine," I said.

And then I put my arms around her, and sank slowly down to my knees.

No, not to kiss her can, although I really wouldn't have minded.

It was just that I'd waited as long as I could—and I couldn't wait any longer—for something soft to faint on.

XXXII

KAY'S STORY WAS THAT SHE HAD GONE OUT OF THE HOUSE TO INVESTIGATE SOME SUSPICIOUS NOISES, and had found a guy apparently trying to break in. During her pursuit of him (he had got away) Manny's husband, and subsequently the Bannermans, had entered the house. But, fortunately, she was in time to overpower them and save me from death.

The story didn't go down very well with Jeff Claggett, but he couldn't call her a liar without calling me one, so he let it go. And Kay not only kept her job with the department, but she received a commendation and promotion. The increase in pay, she estimated, would pay for the all-white gown and accoutrements. Which, she advised me unblushingly, she intended to wear at our wedding.

To move on:

Connie and Luther Bannerman pleaded guilty to conspiracy to commit murder, and attempted murder. They received ten years on each count, said sentences to run consecutively.

Manny's husband remained mute, and was convicted of attempted murder. But other charges were dug up against him before he could begin serving the sentence—he was a very bad guy, seemingly. The last I heard, he had accumulated two life sentences, plus fifty years, and he was still standing mute. Apparently, he saw nothing to gain by talking.

Manny was taken from her hospital to the criminal ward of the county hospital. Pat Aloe could have got her out, I am sure, since the charge against her of harboring a criminal—failing to report her husband to the police—was a purely technical one. But Pat had grimly washed his hands of Manny. He wanted nothing more to do with her. He had no further need for her, for that matter, having begun the swift closing out of PXA's affairs.

Manny cooperated fully with the authorities, and their attitude toward her was generally sympathetic. She had attacked her husband without intent to kill him. His abuse had driven her temporarily insane, and when she recovered her senses, she was holding a steam pressing-iron in her hand and he was sprawled on the ground at her feet. The storm was gathering by now, and she was forced to flee back inside her resort cabin. When the police came in the morning to investigate the storm's havoc, she was near death with shock and she was never questioned about her husband's supposed death.

Actually, he wasn't even seriously hurt, but there was a dead man nearby—one of several who had died in the storm—who resembled him in size and coloring. Manny's husband made the features of the dead man unrecognizable with a few brutal blows, switched clothes with him and planted his identification on him.

He disappeared into the night then, and no one ever questioned the fact that he was dead. Possibly because so many people were glad to have him that way. Rumors had been circulating for some time that he had irritated people who were not of a mind to put up with it, and only his apparent death saved him from the actuality.

There followed an extended period of hiding out, of keeping out of the way of former associates. Finally, however, believing that feeling about him had cooled down, and having sized up Manny's situation, he had paid her a covert visit.

She was terrified. Anyone who knew him well would be. Also, she was vulnerable to his threats, thanks to the nominal attempt on his life and the malicious mischief she had made for me. She couldn't go to the police. She couldn't go to Pat, who was already furious with her. So she acceded to her husband's demands. She would go away with him, if he would leave me alone.

She collapsed after his visit, and was forced to go to the hospital. His reaction was to try to kill me. She hoped to buy him off, and he accepted the money she gave him. But, of course, he would not stay bought. Again, he gave her an ultimatum: She would go back to him, or I would go period. So she had agreed to go back to him, but the ugly prospect had brought on another nervous collapse with its resultant hospitalization.

Actually, he had no intention of leaving me alone, regardless of what she did. He was a handsome hood, and as vain and mean as he was handsome. And it was simply not tolerable to him to allow his wife's lover to live.

So he had tried to kill me for the third time. At the same time the Bannermans were attempting to kill me for the second time. And so much for them.

The charge against Manny was dismissed, with the urgent recommendation that she seek psychiatric help. She gladly promised to do so.

Mrs. Olmstead was caught up with in Las Vegas. She was drunk, thoroughly unremorseful and some twenty thousand dollars ahead of the game. She returned most of my money, I *think*. I'm not sure, since I don't know exactly how much she got away with. Anyway, I declined to prosecute, and she was still in Vegas the last I heard.

Still drunk, still unremorseful and still a big winner.

XXXIII

I WENT TO THE HOSPITAL A FEW DAYS AFTER THE BANNERMANS AND MANNY'S HUSBAND TRIED TO KILL ME. My house needed repairs to make it livable and it was kind of lonesome there by myself, so I went to the hospital. And I remained there while the courts dealt with my would-be killers, and certain other happy events came to pass.

The doctors hinted that I was malingering, and suggested that I do it elsewhere. Jeff Claggett gave me a stern scolding.

"You don't want to marry Nolton. You *shouldn't* marry her. Why not lay it on the line with her, instead of pulling the sick act?"

"Well ... I do like her, Jeff," I said. "And she saved my life, you know."

"Oh, hell! She was goofing off when she should have been on the job, and we both know it."

"Well ... But I promised to marry her. I didn't think I'd ever be free of Connie at the time, but—"

"That wasn't a promise, dammit! Anyway, you've got a right to change your mind. You shouldn't go ahead with something that's all wrong to keep a promise that should never have been made."

"I'm sure you're right," I said. "I'll have a talk with Kay as soon as I get some other things out of the way."

"What things?"

"Well ... "

"You've got a go-ahead on your erosion book, and a hefty advance from the publisher. You're getting a good settlement on your condemnation suit; my lawyer friend says it will be coming through any day now. So what the hell are you waiting for?"

"Nothing," I said firmly. "And I won't wait any longer."

"Good! You'll settle with Nolton right away, then?"

"You bet I will," I said. "Maybe not right away, but ... "

He cursed, and stamped out of the room.

The phone rang, and of course it was Kay.

"Just one question, Britt Rainstar," she said. "How much longer do you plan on staying in that hospital?"

"What's the difference?" I said. "My divorce hasn't come through yet."

"Hasn't it?" she said. "Hasn't it?"

"I, uh, well"—I laughed nervously. "I haven't received the papers yet, but I believe I did hear that, uh—my goodness, Kay," I said. "You surely don't think that I don't want to marry you."

"That's exactly what I think, Britt."

"Well, shame on you," I said. "The very idea!"

"Then, when are you leaving the hospital?"

"Very soon," I said. "Practically any day now."

She slammed up the phone.

I lay back on the pillows, and closed my eyes.

I was thoroughly ashamed of myself. My shame increased, as the days drifted by and I stayed on in the hospital. The naive, evasive-child manner I maintained was evidence of my general feeling of hopeless unworthiness. The I-ain't-nothin'-but-a-hound dawg routine set to different music.

Whatever I did, I was bound to make someone unhappy, and I have always shrunk from doing that. I am always terribly unhappy when I make others unhappy.

I wondered what in the name of God I could tell Manny. After all, I had told her that the only reason I didn't marry her was because I couldn't. I was married to Connie, and there was no way I could dissolve our marriage. Now, however, I was free of Connie, and Manny was free of her husband. So how could I possibly tell her that I was marrying Kay Nolton?

I was wrestling with the riddle the afternoon she came to see me, the first time I had seen her since that seemingly long-ago day when she had come to the house.

I stalled on giving her the news about Kay, staving it off by complimenting her on how nice she looked. She thanked me and said she certainly hoped she looked nice.

"You see, I'm getting married, Britt," she said. "I thought you should be the first to know."

I gulped and said, "Oh," thinking that took me off the hook all right—or sank it into me. "Well, I hope you'll be very happy, Manny."

"Thank you," she said. "I'm sure I will be."

"Is it, uh, anyone I know?"

"We-ell, no ..." She shook her head. "I don't believe you do. You're going to get acquainted with him, because I intend to see that you do. And I think you'll like him—the real *him*—a lot better than the man you think you know."

"Uh, what?" I frowned. "I don't understand."

"Well, you'd just better!" Her voice rose, broke into joyous laughter. "You'd better, you nutty, mixed-up mixedblood, or I'll take your pretty gray-streaked scalp!"

She came to me at a run, flung herself down on the bed with me. Naturally, the bed collapsed noisily.

We were picking ourselves up when the door slammed open, and a nurse came rushing in. She had red hair and beautiful long legs, and a scrubbed-clean look.

"Kay—" I stammered. "W-what are you doing here?"

She snapped that her name was Nolton, *Miss* Nolton, and she was there because she was a nurse, as I very well knew. "Now, what's going on here, miss?" she demanded, glaring at Manny. "Never mind! I want you out of here, right this minute! And for goodness sake—*for goodness sake*—do us all a favor and take him with you!"

"Oh, I intend to," Manny said sunnily. "I'm getting married, and he's the bridegroom."

"Well, I'm glad to hear it," Kay said. "I'm g-glad that s-some-one's willing to marry him. He said t-that—that I—"

She turned suddenly, and hurried out the door.

Manny came into my arms, and I did what you do when a very lovely girl comes into your arms. And then, over her shoulder, I saw the door ease open. And I saw that it was Kay who had opened it.

She stuck out her tongue at me.

She winked and grinned at me. And, then, just as she closed the door, she turned on a truly beautiful blush.

And when it comes time to close the door on someone or something I know of no nicer way to do it.

ROUGHNECK

I

I PULLED THE OLD FORD INTO THE CURB AND CUT OFF THE MOTOR. Badly overheated from its flattened crankshaft, it continued to run for a moment or two—pounding so hard from its exertions that the whole car shook. It was a sweltering August day in 1929. It had stopped on upper Grand Avenue in Oklahoma City. Wiping the sweat from my face, I stared glumly out the window.

Along this street I had hustled newspapers as a child, *The Oklahoman* in the morning and *The News* at night. Not far from here was the fine residence we had occupied when the Thompson family affairs took a sudden and fantastic turn for the better. And here, across the walk to the right, was the office building from which Pop had directed a multi-million dollar oil business ... So long ago, and yet it seemed like yesterday. Now Pop was in Texas and his money was there, too, sunk into one oil-less well after another. As for me—me and Mom and my kid sister, Freddie. ...

Freddie was a large girl, and she had always enjoyed an excellent appetite. She contended now, whimperingly, that Mom and I were deliberately trying to starve her to death. We had money, didn't we? We had *some* money, anyway. Well, why the heck didn't we eat, then? Just name her one good reason why we didn't eat!

"Shut up," said Mom. "Ask your big brother. He knows everything."

"Oh, for God's sake," I said.

"Well, I don't care," said Mom. "If you'd ever listen to anyone, you wouldn't get into such awful messes. We wouldn't be in this mess now. But, oh, no, not you. Now, I'm not going to say another word, Jimmie, but. ..."

Being very tired and worried, and no longer young, she said quite a bit more. It seemed I was stubborn, wilful, a consistent and deliberate flouter of convention. I seemed never to have used my very good mind for anything but involving myself in trouble.

I spent six years in high school, and I got out then only by falsifying the records. As a youth in my first long pants, I was an associate of chorus girls, grifters, gamblers and other ne'er-do-wells. By the time I was fifteen, I had been variously employed as a newspaper "man," a burlesque show hawker, a plumber's helper, a comedian in two-reel pictures and in a dozen-odd other occupations. With equal ease, I could quote the

155

Roman lyric poet, Catullus, or the odds against making four the hard way.

I was not yet sixteen when I became a night bellboy in a luxury hotel. (This through the intervention of a good natured thug and con man named Allie Ivers.) I earned big money there—and I acquired still more by gambling—and spent it all. At eighteen, I broke down with tuberculosis, acute alcoholism and complete nervous exhaustion.

I bummed through west and far west Texas for three years, slowly getting my health back in the high, dry climate. Then I returned to Fort Worth and went back to the hotel. A group of gangsters made me their distributor for bootleg whiskey. The dubious honor was thrust upon me, practically at gunpoint. I plotted to get even, simultaneously recouping my fortunes.

Starting off with a handle of a few cases a week, I gradually enlarged my order until, finally, the few had increased to twenty. In order to do this, I had to wholesale the stuff to other hotel employees at a very short profit and sometimes no profit at all. But that was all right. The total proceeds from the twenty cases were to be my profit. I intended to dump them for a minimum of three thousand dollars, and then skip town. My gangster associates could whistle for the dough I owed them.

Unfortunately, my cache of whiskey was discovered and confiscated by Federal prohibition agents. They took it all, but they only reported five cases. And this bit of official perfidy was an even harder blow than my financial loss. It prevented me from making a new start with the gangsters; it deprived me of any valid excuse for not paying their bill. I had the alternative of paying up or getting my head beaten off . . . or, of course, leaving town. So, with approximately a thirtieth of my anticipated three thousand—a little less than a hundred dollars—I loaded Mom and Freddie into the car and headed north.

Our destination was Nebraska, and we were not nearly so downhearted as we headed toward it as one might think. Mom's parents lived in a small Nebraska town, and she and Freddie would be welcome with them for a time. As soon as I could arrange it, they would join me in Lincoln where I hoped to enter the state university. I was sorely in need of some higher education, as an editor acquaintance had pointed out. He had also pointed out that I was much more apt to wind up dead, than as the writer I hoped to be, unless I abandoned the course I was following.

We chugged along quite cheerfully for a matter of five or ten miles. Then the car began to reveal its overall worthlessness. The motor steamed and smoked. It clattered, pounded and roared. I pulled off the road and lifted the hood. A brief examination uncovered the terrible truth.

The crankcase was filled with sawdust and tractor oil. It had been doctored thusly to conceal a flat crankshaft—the one incurable ailment of the Model-T Ford. No repair, as the term is usually used, would correct the difficulty for more than a few hours. We needed a new shaft, new bearings, new rods, and other internal accessories. Briefly—and it would have cost us little more—we needed a new motor.

It took us two days to get to Oklahoma City, a distance of two hundred and fifty miles. It also took almost seventy of our one hundred dollars. We had traveled no more than a fourth of the way to our destination, and more than two-thirds of our money was gone.

Here we sat, then, on that sweltering August afternoon in 1929—a tired, middle-aged woman, a tired, hungry young girl, and a tired, somewhat saturnine-looking young man. Here we sat, nominal beggars in a broken-down Ford, at the site of our one-time glory. I closed my eyes against the brilliant sunlight, and I could almost see Pop bustling out of this building—young, smartly dressed, hurrying toward his low-slung Apperson-Jack or the big Cole Aero-Eight. I could see us all riding home together, out to the big high-ceilinged house with its book-lined walls. I could see the friendly face of the cook as she dished up the dinner. I could taste—

I opened my eyes again. Mom gave me a frown.

"Now, that's a nice way to talk," she said. "That's nice language to use in front of your mother and sister."

"What did I say?" I said. "All I said was ship. I was thinking how cool it would be, you know, to be out on a ship and—"

"You did not!" said Freddie. "He did not say ship, Mama! He said s-h-i—"

"Well," I said hastily, opening the door of the car, "I guess I'd better be going. Wish me luck."

The man I went to see had come to Oklahoma from Germany in 1912. Due to some flaw in his immigration papers, he had been detained on Ellis Island for several months, and when World War I broke out he was taken into custody as an enemy alien. The case came to Pop's attention. Through his then powerful political connections, he got the man released and started on the way to becoming a citizen. Moreover, since the man seemed incapable of doing anything for himself, Pop set him up in business. He bought the guy three heavy-duty oil field trucks; he leased the trucks back from the man at a very fancy rental. He gave him a fat "bonus" of oil stock which climbed from its dollar-par to one hundred dollars a share. I don't know why Pop did such things, and I doubt that he knew. It was simply his way—until his money ran out.

Well, I went up to the guy's offices—they occupied a half floor in this building—and I was admitted to the inner sanctum the moment I sent in my name. With tears of pure joy in his eyes, he wrung my hand; and then, seemingly overcome with emotion, he gave me a bear hug. . . . Why hadn't we kept in touch with him all these years? What oil fields was Pop operating in now? Was he, perhaps, contemplating a return to Oklahoma? . . . He babbled on, firing questions about the family, telling me about his own. His wife and daughter were in Europe. His son had just returned to Harvard prep. They had a "nice little house"—the mansion of a former governor—out on Classen Boulevard, and he insisted that we come out and—

I finally managed to cut in on him, to make him listen. He heard me out, nodding sympathetically; and while I thought I detected a certain coolness in the atmosphere, I attributed it to my own hypersensitive feelings. He neither did nor said anything out of the way, and I incline to a defensive apprehensiveness when asking for favors.

Of course he would help me, he declared. It was no more than right. He was delighted to have seen me, even under these unhappy circumstances, and he wanted to see Mom and Freddie also. His car was about due to call for him, but there would still be time for a chat.

We rode downstairs together. He greeted Mom and Freddie as warmly as he had me. Then, his car pulled up at the side of ours, a chauffeur-driven, twelve-cylinder Packard, and regretfully he bade us goodbye.

He pressed a bill into my hand. He hopped into his limousine, and it glided away into the traffic. I looked down at the bill. Silently I handed it to Mom. She was still staring at it dazedly as I climbed in, and I winced at the stricken wonder in her eyes.

"It must have been a mistake," she said, slowly. "Don't you suppose it was a mistake, Jimmie?"

"With friends you're not careless," I said. "With people you care about, you make sure."

"Why don't we eat?" Freddie demanded. "That man gave you five dollars."

II

THERE WAS NO ONE ELSE WE COULD APPEAL TO. No one we could or would ask for help. My elderly grandparents could not be expected to provide traveling expenses. It would be burden enough on them to take care of Mom and Freddie for several months. Pop, who had remained in Texas, had no money. My married sister, Maxine, was on tour with a girl's orchestra and doing all right financially. But we had no idea of where she might be, or how we could get in touch with her.

I got the car's rods tightened at a cost of eight dollars. We pulled out of Oklahoma City, munching a dinner of day-old cinnamon rolls. There was nothing to do but go on. We couldn't stay there and we couldn't go back, so we went ahead.

The rods were working loose before we were well out of the city limits. By the time we reached Guthrie, a distance of about thirty miles, the car had reverted to its customary clattering, overheated crawl. Somehow we got through the town and chugged up a long grade on the other side. Just as we passed the crest, a car shot out of a side road and piled into us broadside.

It was a stripped-down Ford, loaded with road workers, and they were loaded with home brew. The vehicle skidded off of ours, piled into a telephone pole, and over-turned twice. They were all thrown clear and suffered only minor injuries, but their car was pretty well wrecked. We were unhurt, also, and except for a ripped-off fender and headlight and a blown-out tire, our car was undamaged.

They picked themselves up, and apologized handsomely. It was all their fault, they admitted, and they were more than anxious to make amends. Unfortunately, they had no insurance and no money, having exhausted their meager resources to buy beer, but if there was anything else they might do. . . .

I could only think of one thing. They gladly agreed to it. Hitching the two cars together, we coasted back down the hill and into a garage. There they left us, after further protestations of good will, and two mechanics took over. The crankshaft and its appurtenances were transferred from the wrecked car to mine. Also the battery, a headlight, a tire and certain other incidentals.

The job took all night, and until noon the next day. The bill came to forty-one dollars. I couldn't pay it, of course, as I proved by turning out my pockets to the manager. But I pointed out that there was more than enough salvagable material in the road workers' car to take care of the deficit. Rather grimly, he took what cash I had, filled our tank with gas and waved us on our way.

We parked by the roadside that night, eating a dinner and breakfast of purloined roasting ears. Shortly after we crossed the Kansas border the following day, we ran out of gas. I "borrowed" some from a passing motorist ("just enough to get to a filling station"). When that ran out, I hailed another car and received a similar "loan." Thus, we limped across Kansas—ten, twelve, fifteen miles at a time.

At a farm near Topeka, I got a half day's work laying drain pipe, and the proceeds took us almost to the Nebraska line. But here, it seemed, with several hundred miles still ahead of us, we could go no further. The car had to have lubrication, and an oil change. We were all exhausted and suffering from painful stomach troubles. We had been on the road for more than a week, with no real rest and almost nothing but raw or half-cooked vegetables. Some way or somehow, we simply had to get some money.

We had stopped in a small village, and Mom suggested that she might earn a dollar or two by doing some family's washing. But she obviously was not physically capable of performing any such chore even if, as was highly unlikely in a place like this, she had a chance to. And while I doubted that there was any work for me either I got out and looked around.

It took me about ten minutes to cover the place, to visit and be turned down by each of the business establishments. Turning onto a side street, I picked a cigarette butt from the gutter and lit up. There was a shade tree here between the walk and the street. I leaned against it, puffing hungrily, staring absently at the side of a feed store across the way. It was almost hidden by a gaily colored poster—an outsize twenty-four sheet—advertising some theatrical attraction in a nearby city. My eyes moved up from the trite legends of ONE NIGHT ONLY and STRAIGHT FROM BROADWAY to the line of smiling, evening-gowned girls.

I looked at the one on the end—up past the violin and into her face.

It was my sister, Maxine!

I let out a whoop of pure joy.

I sent a collect wire from the railroad station, and Maxine responded generously. Two days later, having left Mom and Freddie with my grandparents, I arrived in Lincoln.

I was practically broke again. I hoped to sell the car for enough to carry me until I could land a job. Meanwhile, since it was not yet quite daylight, I cleaned up in a restaurant men's room and ate a large and leisurely breakfast. An hour or so later, when I thought the auto sales lots might be open, I returned to my car.

A police tow truck was just hitching on to it. Overnight parking, it seemed, was a violation of the law in Lincoln, and no, no exceptions were made for newcomers. I could redeem the car by paying a fine, plus towing and storage charges.

I listened to this ultimatum, choked with a mixture of emotions, and then suddenly I sagged against a telephone pole and began to howl with laughter. The tow crew looked at me warily. They hopped into their truck and drove away, taking my car with them, and I sat down on my suitcase and laughed until my lungs ached.

That car—that damned lousy, heartbreaking, backbreaking Ford! And they thought I'd lay out dough to get it back! They thought *I* was crazy! They thought *I* was!

Any maybe I was. After ten days and a thousand miles in that car, it wouldn't have been surprising.

III

I WORKED THAT DAY AND THE NEXT TWO AS A SODA AND SANDWICH MAN. Relatively flush then, and well nourished with free meals, I quit the job and visited the university. I presented the letter of introduction from my editor friend in Texas. The recipient, a member of the administrative staff, was very cordial but was unable to offer me any assistance. He could not make me a loan himself. The university could not extend aid except to students with outstanding scholastic records. Perhaps if I appealed to another writer . . . some faculty member who was interested in writing . . .

At this time, the assistant chancellor of the university was Robert Platt Crawford, a big-name writer for *The Saturday Evening Post* and other large-circulation magazines. I knew him only by reputation and he, of course, did not know me at all. But I went to see him. I showed him some of my stories from regional periodicals, and requested a loan—one sufficient to pay a semester's tuition and buy textbooks, plus, if he had it to spare, a few dollars extra.

Dr. Crawford looked somewhat startled. After a moment of deep silence, he asked that I repeat my request. I did so. The good doctor looked relieved. The acoustics of his office were very poor, he murmured, and he had feared momentarily that a complete remodeling of it might be necessary. . . . Would I mind telling him a little about myself? Something about my background? Obviously, I had been out of high school for a number of years. Why was I starting college now and why had I chosen to come to this one?

I told him, rather brusquely at first, out of nervousness, and then, as he beamed and nodded at me, with increasing ease. I talked on and on, so interested and amiable did he seem, and so intertwined were the various events of my life. To describe my hasty exit from the hotel world, it was necessary to describe my entrance. And that led to an account of the burlesque houses and Allie Ivers, the whores' nemesis; and that, in turn, led back to other things. . . . Newspaper work, and my adventures as a dairyman, and the time I had almost cornered the French postcard market, and my abysmal failure to maintain the high standards of a millionaire's son. . . .

Dr. Crawford smiled. He chuckled. He leaned back in his chair and roared. Recovering himself, he declared that he had great faith in my talents as a writer, and that, moreover, I was obviously scholastic material

162

of the very highest type. He would consider it a privilege, he said, to finance me. And taking out his wallet, he proceeded to do so.

I took the money, gratefully but a little incredulously, for I had been afraid that in being completely frank with him I might have prejudiced my case. Now, having achieved the seemingly impossible, I realized that it could not have been achieved in any other way. The last man in the world to deceive is the man you hope to get money from. If he has it and you don't, the odds are that he is at least as shrewd as you and probably a hell of a lot shrewder.

Dr. Crawford refused my offer to give him a note for the money. "Now why would I want that?" he said; and thus another simple truth was pointed up to me . . . why *would* he want it? When a man's sole collateral is his word, why bother with his signature?

With my tuition taken care of, I applied at the newspapers for part-time work; I applied at the radio stations, the advertising agencies, the publicity firms—at every place which conceivably might be in need of literary talent. I was expensively dressed. The fast-money circles in which I had moved had compelled a fine head-to-foot wardrobe, and my attire represented an original investment of several hundred dollars. I suspect that many of the important executives who received me thought that I was either a majority stockholder in the company or wished to become one. Most of them were brusque and some were pointedly unpleasant when they discovered the true and humble purpose of my call. Just why did I think they would want to hire me? What did I have to offer, an ex-bellboy, ex-oil field worker, et cetera, with a few months' newspaper experience and a few unimportant manuscript sales? They could get better men than me for nothing. There were college graduates here in Lincoln—men with graduate degrees in journalism—who were glad to work without salary, solely for the practical experience it gave them.

I left some of these interviews cringing and more than a little shamed. Hell, I was actually sick, for my twenty-two-year-old hide had worn thin, instead of toughening, from the almost incessant onslaught of an outrageous fortune. I winced at each new blow to my pride, and the blows fell hard and fast.

Being very stubborn—and, no doubt, stupid—I persisted in my patently hopeless quest. And, finally, at the last place I expected to, I met with seeming success.

It was at a farm magazine. The two young editors looked me over fondly, ascertaining that I was entering the university, and, after a significant glance at one another, took me into firmly courteous custody . . . So I was from Texas, eh? (Here an awed look into the lining of my forty-dollar Borsalino.) And I wanted a job, eh? (A glance at label of imported tweed topcoat.) Well, they could understand that. It gave a man a certain

independence, helped his standing on the campus. Now, of course—
naturally—I had enrolled in the College of Agriculture?

"My God, no!" I said, and then, seeing the pained looks on their faces,
"Why would I want to do that? I'm in Fine Arts."

They shook their heads. I had made a terrible mistake, they said. No
one enrolled in Fine Arts, absolutely no one. The degree was worthless,
you know; one might as well have a diploma from a barber college. The
thing to do—and they would take immediate steps to arrange it—was to
switch to the College of Agriculture. I could take journalism there, also
as much English as I liked; and with a B.Sc.A., I would be fixed for life.
It was practically as good as an M.D.

Now, I was to become very cross with these young men in ensuing
months, but I will say—although I say it grudgingly—that I believe they
were sincere. A man with a Bachelor of Science degree in agriculture *can*
invariably get a job, and usually at a very handsome beginning salary. He
can and he should, for he's damned well earned it. To begin with, he
needs to have been raised on a farm and to have taken an active part in
Four-H work. He will also find it helpful if he attends a vocational high
school specializing in agriculture. Then he goes to an agricultural college—
Nebraska is one of the three or four best in the world—and he enrolls
for a heavy science curriculum, *plus*. He doesn't take just physics, which
is plenty tough in itself, but *agricultural* physics. Not just botany, but
agricultural botany. And so on down the line. Practically every subject is
a laboratory course. When he isn't peering through a microscope or
working a slide rule, he will probably be wielding a surgical knife—
dissecting the diseased and malodorous innards of some animal.

Well, I had less than no business in such a college; even less, say, than I
would have had in a theological seminary. So, of course, I enrolled in it.
Or, rather, the two editors enrolled me. And I suspect that they came to
regret it as much as I. They were also on the "rush" committee of an ag
college fraternity, and they regarded me as a highly solvent, and hence
desirable, prospect. They invited me to their "house" for dinner, and the
next thing I knew I was pledged and a student in the College of Agriculture.

Came the dawn—as they used to say in movies—and there were curses
and recriminations as bitter as they were mutual. I felt that I had been
swindled. They, my fraternity brothers, felt that they had been. And it
was too late to correct matters. We had to put up with one another, and
make the best of it.

They crammed me at every opportunity to get me through my courses
(a failing student could not belong to a fraternity). But naturally they
could get me no job. How could they, a guy as dumb, agriculturally, as I

was? It was up to me to find work for myself, and I couldn't be choosy about it. For the fraternity dues and assessments had added almost a third to my contemplated living costs.

Eventually, and largely among the faculty members, I made some wonderful friends at the Agricultural College of the University of Nebraska, and I actually learned quite a bit about agriculture. But my first few months there were the most miserable in my life. I detested everyone, or so I convinced myself. Everyone appeared to detest me. I lived in a turmoil of worry, disappointment, disgust and self-doubt. Meanwhile, I had taken the first job I could find—as night attendant in a funeral establishment.

IV

I WENT TO WORK AT SIX O'CLOCK AT NIGHT, and remained until seven in the morning. My pay was fifty dollars a month. My duties were mainly confined to answering the telephone, and to receiving the occasional callers who dropped by to look upon their late loved ones.

Since I was permitted to sleep at the place—thus saving the price of a room—and since there was plenty of time to study, the job was nominally a good one. But for me, ever squeamish and imaginative, it was a small-scale nightmare. I couldn't sleep in the eerie, softly-lit quiet. I couldn't concentrate on my books. My jittery nerves were always on the point of popping through my skin, and when Bill, the ambulance driver, would creep up behind me and address me in ghostly tones, I literally hit the ceiling.

A southerner and a college student like myself, Bill was the other night employee. He had practically as much time on his hands as I had, and when he wasn't pestering me he was usually down in the basement casket room. He said that I should join him down there—the coffins were beautifully padded and made excellent beds. And it was so peaceful, too, just like being in a nice quiet grave.

"You come along with me, Jim, boy," he would warmly insist. "You jus' let old Bill tuck you in. I got one all picked out for you—a big bronze job with a real heavy lid. I'm tellin' you, man! You get in that good old casket and I close down that good old lid, and you just naturally *got* to relax. . . . "

I was horrified, then puzzled by his antics. It just didn't seem reasonable that any man could be so perpetually merry in such depressing surroundings. The suspicion grew in my mind that there must be some attraction in the basement besides the caskets.

One night when Bill had laid hands upon me and was insisting that I climb into one of those "good ol' coffins," I grabbed him by the shoulders. Pulling him close to me, I ordered him to expel his breath. He did so, grinning guiltily.

"You sure won't tell no one, will you, Jim?" he pleaded. "The boss man'd just naturally pop his pumpkin if he found out about it."

"Lead the way," I said firmly. "We're wasting time."

He led the way, back into the deepest recesses of the basement. Reaching into a dust-covered pine casket, he withdrew two quarts of homemade beer. His landlady made it, he said, and he always arrived at work with a goodly supply.

We drank. He looked into my face expectantly.

"Not bad," I said. "Of course, it's pretty warm."

"Not bad, pretty warm!" Bill exclaimed. "Now, ain't that just like a Texas fella? Always belittlin' something!"

"Well, it *is* warm," I said. "Why don't you go over to the restaurant and get a bucket of ice? I'll pay for it."

"Huh-uh!" Bill rolled his head. "They'd wonder what it was all about, and the first thing we knew—wait a minute! I know what we can do, Jim boy!"

"Yeah?" I said.

"Why, sure. Now that we're both in on the deal, there ain't a thing in the world to stop us."

He explained. I choked and almost dropped my bottle.

"For God's sake," I said. "We can't do *that*! It's—well, it's just not right."

"You mean it ain't respectful? What about the Egyptians—I guess they didn't have plenty of respect for the dead, huh? What about the Chinese, all them fine ol' civilizations?"

"Well, sure," I said, "but that's different."

"Sure, it's different. The stuff they put around their dead folks was wasted. This ain't gonna be."

Bill went on to remark that I could drink my beer warm, if I liked, or I could do without entirely. Then, he gathered the remaining bottles from the casket, and trudged off up the stairs.

I followed him. He went into the cooling room, and pulled out one of the two long drawers that were set into the wall. Tenderly, he began tucking beer around the refrigerated body inside. He laughed scornfully as I snatched a bottle away from him.

"You just ain't makin' sense, Jim. Now, just looky here at this nice old fella. Am I botherin' him? Is it hurtin' him any? Why, I bet he likes it—looks like a fella that guzzled plenty himself."

I had to admit that the occupant of the drawer did look that way. His genially ruddy countenance spoke of many gay jousts with the so-called Demon Rum, and the bottles which nestled around him seemed anything but incongruous. There was a certain rightness about them. He looked much more natural in the close company of beer than he had without.

Still, I didn't like it, and I said so. Which, of course, was all I could do by way of protest. Certainly I couldn't report Bill to the management for what was no more than a breach of good taste.

The long night passed. The following night Bill came to work with a dozen quart bottles, giving four to me and placing the other eight in the cool custody of the "nice old fella." He had to go out around nine on an ambulance call. I was dozing comfortably in the chapel, with a half gallon of warm beer in me and another half at my side, when the night bell rang.

I shoved the bottles under my chair, and went to the door.

It was a party of three people, two middle-aged women and a man. They had just arrived from out-of-state, and must start back that very night. Cranky with weariness and sorely pressed for time, they demanded to be shown the remains of you-know-who.

I stammered inane excuses. I urged them to sit down for a few minutes. I was by myself at the moment, I stuttered, and it was against the rules to—to—

The door to the rear opened. Bill strolled in, a quart of beer tilted to his mouth. "How about a cold one, Jim boy?" he said. "Come on back an' see how nice this ol' fella is——"

He broke off, open-mouthed. He looked from the three people to me, and my contorted features told him the terrible truth. Very unwisely, although I could well understand the action, he turned and ran.

Grim and suspicious, our visitors followed him.

Now, seven quarts of beer can be very hard to handle, even if one is not frantic with alarm . . . as, of course, Bill was. They slid from his stricken fingers. They dropped out of his shirt front where he was futilely trying to stuff them. And save for one which burst on the floor, they all went back around the bosom of their recent host.

Our visitors discovered him thus. The ladies shrieked. The gentleman cursed and threatened to cane us. They stamped out then, to a telephone; some twenty minutes later the owner of the establishment arrived.

He fired Bill and me on the spot.

Somehow, while I do drink it, I have never cared much for beer since then.

V

MY NEXT JOB WAS IN A BAKERY. The hours were from six p.m. until midnight five days a week, plus all day Saturday and Sunday. The pay was twelve dollars a week. The work was hard and virtually incessant.

I was what is known as a "batch man," the employee who works in the storeroom and puts together the ingredients necessary for the various bakery products. The bakers and floor workers could rest between jobs, but there was no rest, no between, with mine. I had to "set up" for both the day and night crews. As fast as one batch was out of the way, the floor was crying for another. Bread dough, sweet dough, cake dough, pie dough, filling, topping, icing, frosting, eggwash, oil, and so on into infinity.

The work was not only backbreaking—try juggling hogsheads of lard and ninety-eight-pound sacks of flour and one hundred and eighty-pound sacks of salt, if you doubt my word—but it was also extremely exacting. There was almost no margin for error. A few ounces too much of this or that, and hundreds of dollars worth of dough would be ruined. It seemed to me that for work as difficult and demanding as this I should get more money.

I suggested as much to the manager of the place. He looked me up and down coldly. There was a depression coming on, he said, and he had a long waiting list of job applicants. So, if I was at all dissatisfied, if I felt that I wasn't making enough. . . .

I told him I was entirely satisfied: I loved the job and the pay was more than enough. I apologized humbly for bothering him.

Now eventually, and indirectly, the job paid me a great deal of money. It provided the source material for numerous trade-journal articles, and the background for my ninth novel, *Savage Night*. In all, I suppose, I cashed in at the rate of several hundred dollars for every week I spent at the bakery. But that was later—more than twenty years later in the instance of the novel—and it did me no good whatsoever at the time. With rent to pay and with all my other expenses, the twelve dollars I received for each seven-day period was ridiculously inadequate.

I considered dropping out of the fraternity. But that would be an involved and painfully embarrassing procedure, and besides, I simply couldn't do it. My "brothers" had their faults, as I was ever ready to point out, but poor scholarship was not among them. I had to have their

169

help scholastically. For the time being, at least, it was impossible to do without it. Moreover, I seriously doubted the wisdom of severing relations with a "house" which had many alumni on the faculty.

Meals were my biggest expense. The hard work gave me a terrific appetite, and it seemed that I could never get enough to eat. Nevertheless, since I could think of no place else to cut down, I cut down on meals. In fact, I practically eliminated them—stuffing myself instead with the various edibles in my stock room. I still get a little ill when I think of some of the messes I put together.

The basic item of my diet was bread—the "crippled" loaves damaged in the machinery. The garnish (or whatever you want to call it) might be raw frozen eggs and lard, mince meat and malt syrup, or some truly weird concoctions such as cooking oil, chopped chocolate, caraway seeds and raisins. I made myself sandwiches of these things, eating them on the job and sneaking them out when I left. And when my stomach revolted, as it frequently did, I bought it into subjection with stiff cocktails of lemon and vanilla extract.

I survived in this fashion for several months. Then, shortly after the college mid-term, when I had barely squeaked by the semester examinations, I was stricken with acute appendicitis.

I was rushed to a hospital. When I emerged from it, some six days later, I was appendix-less, penniless, jobless and considerably in debt. I felt pretty good about the situation. With things that bad, it seemed that they must take a turn for the better. And they did.

VI

U<small>P UNTIL THEN</small> I <small>HAD SCORNED ANYTHING LESS THAN A STEADY SALARIED</small> <small>JOB</small>. Now, since nothing of this kind was available to me, I began taking anything that was offered—a few hours work in one place, an hour or so in another. Some of these odd jobs cost me far more than I earned. As a cafeteria bus boy, for example, I spent sixty hours in paying for a huge tray of dishes which I had broken. Gradually, however, I eliminated such jobs from my agenda and substituted new ones, and finally—and after no great elapse of time—I had several which not only paid reasonably well but also were reasonably to my liking.

I read papers for the English department. I wrote campus news for the Lincoln *Journal*. I sold radios on commission. I worked as floorman in a dance hall. All irregularly, yes; seven or eight hours a week on each job. But my total pay aggregated more than I had been making at the bakery, and in my various bustlings about the city I ran across a salaried position. It was in a small department store, one of a midwestern chain of installment-sales houses. The hours were noon to six weekdays and all day Saturday. The pay was a magnificent eighteen dollars a week. I rearranged my classes to fit this schedule, and went to work.

Since I held on to my other jobs, there was little time for rest or relaxation in the months that followed. I seldom got to bed before midnight, and I had to be up at dawn to make my seven o'clock classes at the university. But I had never slept when I could find anything else to do (I still don't), and there were ample compensations for the unending round of work.

Mom and Freddie were able to join me. We took a large house, renting out part of the rooms to defray expenses. I studied harder and began to do better in my classes. It was easier to study, now that I was relatively free of financial worry, and with my education costing so much in money and effort I valued it more. I started writing again—free-lancing for myself. And I worked harder at that, too. As a result I sold a serial and several short stories to farm magazines, and placed two stories in the literary quarterly, *The Prairie Schooner*. Almost overnight, the outlook for the future turned from black to bright.

I worked at the store as a collection correspondent, and my immediate superior was the credit manager, a man named Durkin. We admired each other greatly. Barely literate himself, he thought I was a wonderful

171

writer. I thought he showed exceptional wisdom in holding this opinion. Our mutual admiration was to end disastrously, but not until many pleasant months had passed. During this time, about the only discord in the smooth harmony of my affairs was a re-encounter with Allie Ivers— the impish, larcenous, fantastic friend of my Texas nonage.

It happened one quiet summer evening when I was strolling home from work. A cab swept past me as I started across an intersection. It skidded around in a U-turn and headed back in my direction; it headed straight toward me, seemingly out of control, and as I leaped back to the side-walk, it climbed the curb and followed me. I was frightened out of my wits. Darting back into the street, I began to run for dear life, and I tripped and fell sprawling. The cab drew abreast, and Allie leaned out the window.

"How terrible," he said. "Such a fine young man to be lying in the gutter!"

Well, I had always liked Allie, and despite the weird doings which usually resulted from our association, I was glad to see him. So I cursed him out mildly and entered the cab, first making sure that he was carrying no concealed weapons or other items which might involve us with the police.

Allie pressed a pint of whiskey upon me. Uncorking another for himself, he drove off, bringing me up to date on his affairs. He had left Texas, he said, shortly after I had. The police had had nothing against him, actually, but they had intimated that all parties concerned would be happier if he traveled for a while. And Allie had thought it well to follow their suggestion. He had moved up through Oklahoma and the midwest, working "the twenties" and other small con rackets. Arriving here in Lincoln well-heeled and under no necessity to "work," he had taken this hack-driving job by way of divertissement. He intended leaving town in the morning. Meanwhile, tonight. . . .

He outlined his plans for the night's entertainment. I told him, firmly and profanely, he could count me out.

"What's the matter?" Allie coaxed. "All I want you to do is drive me and my lady friend around. What's wrong with that?"

"There's everything wrong with it!" I said. "For one thing I don't have a license to drive a hack."

"So what? I've got a dozen. The guy I bought them from gave me a quantity rate."

"Now I'm not going to argue with you, Allie," I said. "I'm tickled to death to see you, but I absolutely refuse——"

Allie wheedled. He reproached me sorrowfully. Was this his one-time protege—the youth he had rescued from the life of a burlesque house candy peddler? Was I so far gone in respectability that I could not do a small favor for an old friend?

"Just answer me one question," Allie demanded. "Are you going to drive this cab or are you going to be a horse's ass?"

We drove on, arguing and drinking. I began to waver. It had been almost a year since I had tasted real whiskey. For months I had been a model of hard-working respectability, and the existence was beginning to pall. College was over until the fall term. Why not, now that I had a little free time, make a break with tiresome routine?

"Well, all right," I said at last. "But no rough stuff, Allie. You've got to promise to keep it clean."

Allie removed the cap from his head and put it on mine. He promised, as I had asked.

"You'll have to promise, too," he said. "This is a very refined young lady we're picking up. I'm taking her to the country club dance."

"You're kidding," I laughed.

"You'll see," said Allie. "By the way, stop at this drug store, will you? I'm taking her a few cigars."

I pulled in at the curb. I turned and looked at him, startled. "Cigars! You're taking her some——"

"Havanas," murmured Allie. "Like I say, she's very refined."

He was in the drug store for some time, deliberately lingering, I suspect. When, finally, he emerged, I was finishing my first pint and much of my trepidation and curiosity about the expedition had vanished with it.

He directed me to a particularly execrable section of the city. I drew up at a house he pointed out—a tumble-down, unpainted shack—and Allie debarked again. He remained in the house for about five minutes. He came out with one of the fattest, ugliest women I have ever seen.

Her enormous legs were bare. Her hair frizzled out from her bloated head like the thongs of a mop. She was costumed in tennis shoes (with the toes cut out) and a filthy gray house dress.

Both she and Allie were smoking cigars.

He assisted her, waddling, across the yard. Helping her into the seat with a stream of courteous and honeyed patter, he climbed in at her side.

The door slammed. The rear curtains came down.

"James," said Allie. "Take us to the club."

"The club," I said suavely, and I put the cab into gear.

The place was several miles out in the country. By the time we arrived, there was a long line of cabs and cars waiting to debouch their passengers at the brilliantly lighted entrance. I fell in at the end of the line. As it moved up, I edged the cab forward with it. We got nearer and nearer the entrance, and from the back seat came sounds of high—very high—revelry.

I had a pretty good idea of what was under way back there, although I did not realize how far it had progressed. But being very merry by now, I saw no reason to admonish my passengers nor to remind them of their whereabouts. Allie had wanted to come to the club. All right, I had brought him and his lady friend here. The rest was up to them. As I saw it, the "lady" could look no worse than she originally had, whatever her present condition.

The cab crept forward, a car length at a time. Bathed in a boozy, rosy glow, I gazed out at the splendor immediately ahead . . . Men in tailcoats and tuxedos, women in evening gowns. They milled around beneath the gaily decorated canopy, roamed up and down the broad steps. Laughing, talking, calling hellos to each new arrival.

The last vehicle ahead of me drove away. I pulled up in its place. The doorman stepped forward smartly and flung open the rear door. There was a grunt, a gasp, a curse—and a thud.

And out into the entrance, the cynosure of a hundred horrified stares, tumbled Allie and his lady. Each puffing on a cigar. Both completely naked.

I took one startled glance at them. Then, sliding out of the door on the opposite side, I ran.

VII

THINGS WENT VERY WELL FOR ME UNTIL EARLY SPRING OF THE FOLLOWING YEAR. Then the manager of the store which employed me was fired, and everything began to go wrong. The former manager had been a quiet, gentlemanly sort, as kindly to everyone as his job would allow. The man who replaced him was a brassy loudmouth—one of the most deliberately offensive men I have ever known. I had barely got to my desk the day of his arrival when he called me on the carpet.

"Notice you're keeping a couple of women," he growled. "What I want to know is how you're doing it. How you buying stuff for whores on the dough you make?"

"Buying stuff for—for—?" I stared at him, open-mouthed. I didn't have the faintest idea what he was talking about.

"Maybe you've been knocking down a little, huh?" he went on. "Well, you'd better lay off. You want to buy stuff for whores, you have 'em co-sign the account with you. And no phoney names, see? None of this crap that it's for your mother and sister."

I understood him then, all right. But I could still only stand and stare, sick with a swiftly mounting fury. . . . Mom and Freddie. In one and the same breath he had accused me of fraud and referred to my mother and sister as whores.

I think I have never been closer to murdering anyone.

Apparently he saw how I felt.

"Well,"—he forced an uncomfortable laugh—"guess I kind of got my wires crossed, huh? No offense."

I didn't say anything; I couldn't. So, after a word or two more of grudging apology, he waved me out of his office.

My last class at the college let out at 11:50 in the morning, and I had to be at the store at noon. I had no lunch period, then, as the other employees had; and I usually grabbed a bite when I made our afternoon deposit at the bank. I was never more than a few minutes about it—just long enough to gulp down a sandwich and some coffee. Both Durkin and the former manager had consented to the arrangement.

The new manager, having given me a few days to cool off, called a halt to it.

Whether I ate or starved was strictly my own headache—see? I could drop my last morning class, or I could do without lunch; that was for me

175

to decide. All he knew was that I was not going to do any more "fugging around" on company time.

"Getting too goddamned much money, anyway," he grunted. "We could get a full-time employee for what we're paying you."

Well, I had to hold the job, at least until the end of the school term. So I restrained my temper—and went without lunch from then on—and I continued to swallow his insults and arrogance in the miserable days that followed. I had plenty of company in my misery. As boorishly rude as he was with me, he was often more so with the other employees. No one could do anything to suit him. He was always "taking over" on a sale or a credit interview, showing the "goddamned incompetents" (us) how it should be handled. And when the sale or the interview went sour, as it often did, he was furious ... Goddammit, couldn't we do anything right? How the hell could he do his job and ours, too?

The credit manager, Durkin, an executive in his own right, caught as much hell as the rest of us. But while he appeared a little hurt at times, he showed no resentment. As a new man, he said, the manager should be given every chance to make good. It was his job to give orders. It was ours to carry them out, insofar as we conscientiously could. That was the only way you could run a business.

"I'm sure he means well," Durkin would assure me earnestly. "After all, we're all here for the same purpose. We all have the store's best interests at heart."

I was sure the manager did not mean well, and that he had no one's interest at heart but his own. But I had learned the futility of arguing with Durkin. Not too intelligent outside of his work, he was utterly devoted to the store. And in his mind the absentee owners were minor gods. They *had* to know what they were doing, and since they had put the manager here, *he* had to, also. . . . That was that, as far as Durkin was concerned, and it continued to be that until early summer, a couple of weeks before the end of the school term. Then. . . .

By way of getting new customers into the store, the manager had written a sales letter. Durkin, who had been charged with having it mimeographed and mailed out, showed me a copy of it.

"You're a writer, Jim," he said. "You know all about these things. What do you think of it?"

I read it, shaking my head. It was filled with wornout catch phrases which were completely uninformative and brassily offensive. No one was going to believe that we were giving away merchandise. No one would believe that we were in business solely to "befriend the good people of Lincoln" and that we yearned only to be their pals and buddies.

"It's the worst kind of junk," I told Durkin. "If this doesn't put us out of business, nothing will."

"Oh?" Durkin frowned troubledly. "You really mean that, Jim? You're not just saying it because he wrote the letter?"

"It's the awfullest bunch of tripe I ever read in my life," I said, "and you can tell that stupid bastard I said so."

"Well," Durkin murmured, worriedly. "You certainly ought to know, Jim. You're an authority on writing. Maybe I'd better. . . . "

Turning away from my desk, he went into the manager's office. Almost verbatim he gave that gentleman my opinion of the letter. Then, as the manager gaped at him, apoplectic with fury, Durkin suggested that I be commissioned to write a "really good" letter.

Well, the manager finally found his voice, and all hell began to pop. He cursed Durkin out at the top of his lungs. Then he called me in and he cursed us both out together. He'd show us, by God. He'd teach us to make fun of our betters. He would have ten thousand of the letters printed up—ten thousand instead of the five thousand he had originally contemplated. And we—Durkin and I—would have the job of addressing, sealing and stamping them. We'd do it on our own time, with no assistance and no extra pay.

He dismissed us with another string of profanity. Putting through a rush order to the print shop, he got a delivery on the letters that very evening. And for the rest of the week, and part of the next, Durkin and I worked night and day. I was sore as a boil, naturally. Durkin, strangely enough, seemed completely at peace with himself. He remained stolidly polite to the manager. In fact, the more the latter gibed and nagged at him, the more polite he became.

It was the manager's idea to "sweep the town off its feet," to hit it such a blow that it would be "rocked to its heels." So the letters were allowed to accumulate instead of being sent out a thousand or so at a time. He kept close watch on our progress. Seeing that we were near the finish, he remained with us that last night, although he did not, of course, help us with the work. He looked on, grinning maliciously, as we packed the letters into boxes and loaded them into Durkin's car.

"I guess that'll teach you," he jeered when, at last, the job was finished. "Snap into it, now, and maybe you'll get that stuff mailed before midnight."

He drove away laughing. Durkin told me to go on home, that he would take the letters to the post office himself. I protested my willingness to help, and for the first time in our acquaintance he was curt with me. He didn't want my help, he said. He preferred taking care of the letters himself.

I went home. He got into his car and drove off. Late the following afternoon, I learned the reason for his unprecedented conduct.

I was working the cashier's window at the time. A quiet, nondescript little man came up to the wicket and asked to be taken to the manager. I suggested, according to store practice, that I might be able to help him.

"I'm not sure the manager is available at the moment, sir. If it's something about your account, some misunderstanding or——"

"Post office department," he said, displaying his credentials. "Are you in charge of the mail?"

"I handle some of it, yes," I said. "I'm not in charge, but——"

"I'm in charge." Durkin came up and stood beside me. "This young man has nothing to do with the mail."

"I see," the little man nodded. "Well, we received a call from the sanitation department a little while ago." He broke off cautiously. "I think I'd better see the manager."

"You can't. There's no need to see him," said Durkin.

The little man looked at him. Reaching through the window he tapped Durkin on the arm. "Mister," he said, and his voice cracked like a whip, "you get the manger for me and be damned quick about it!"

Durkin shook his head stubbornly. The manager, having heard himself referred to, came out of his office. Surlily, he inquired what the hell was up.

The inspector introduced himself. He explained. And what happened then is impossible to describe adequately. The manager gasped. He choked. His face purpled, puffing up like a balloon, and his eyes stood out from his head like doorknobs. He began to bellow, to scream.

Durkin was fired within the hour, as soon as approval could be obtained from the home office. I, a mere clerk, was discharged immediately—the suspected instigator of, if not an actual accessory to, the credit manager's crime.

"I'm certainly sorry, Jim," he apologized. "I tried to keep you out of it, you know. That's why I sent you on home instead of——"

"But why did you do it at all?" I said. "My God, Durk, you might have gone to the pen for a deal like that. We both might have, if the company wanted to get tough with us. Why the hell did you do it, anyway?"

"Why, Jim," he said, reasonably, "you know why I did it."

"Dammit, I don't know," I said.

"Sure, you do. You said the letters were junk; they'd hurt the store. So, naturally I . . . "

. . . so he had taken all ten thousand of them—all carefully addressed, sealed and stamped—and thrown them into the city dump!

VIII

WITH THE SCHOOL TERM FINISHED, I got a full-time job in another department store—a tumbledown old emporium on the outskirts of the business district which catered largely to the farm trade. It was a strange place, operated by a baffling network of absentee owners and concessionaires. Although an approximate fourscore people worked in it, the auditor and I, his assistant—and a few custodial employees—were the only employees of the store proper. The others were all in the pay of the various concession owners.

A man named Carl Frammich was the auditor. Our duty was to keep tabs on the concessions—the grocery and clothing departments, the cosmetics counter, the cream-buying station, the barber shop, the restaurant, and a dozen-odd other stores within our store. We collected their receipts, and supervised their help.

Complaint department? That was us. Credit and Collections? Us again. Personnel, Purchasing, Payroll? You guessed it. Everything that no one else did—and the clerks did nothing but sell—was handled by the auditor and his assistant. Frankly, I was soon overwhelmed by the job, and, for much of the time, didn't know what I was doing or why.

Carl Frammich. . . . Of all the weird, off-trail characters I have known, he was the weirdest, the most off-trail. Stacked up beside Carl, my old friend Allie Ivers was a dull-normal person. Carl looked like the devil—literally, not in the slang sense. He was Satan come to life, and he had the devil's own cynicism; and he could rarely say three words without two of them being blasphemies or obscenities. Yet his voice was angelic. It was the sweetly piping falsetto of a five-year-old. Musical and high-pitched, and with such pronounced lisp that it was often impossible to understand him.

"Tompn," he would say, "bwing at doddam fuddin cash ledger in here an ess oo an me twike a skewin balance on uh sonabitsin bastud." Or, "Tompn," he would say, "do down an tell at doddam assho in weddy-to-weah to top skewin up his salestickets or I'll tum down air an kick uh fuddin kwap outta im. . . . "

Despite my own errors in that direction, I have always said that no man can work while he is drunk. But I say this with one mental reservation—lisping, Satanic-looking Carl Frammich. Carl was dead drunk throughout the three months of our association. He came to work drunk, and he drank throughout the day. Straight alcohol when he could get it, anything from horse liniment to "female tonic" when the alcohol was unobtainable.

He would stagger up the stairs in the morning, bottles protuding from every pocket, and lurch wildly toward his desk. Sometimes he would make it on the first try, but more often than not he would wind up in a corner or sprawled on the floor. And once he almost went out the alley window. But whatever his difficulty before he gained his desk, he would never allow me to assist him.

"Need the fuddin etertise," he would explain solemnly. "Dot to teep in tundishun. Always watch oor doddam skewin helf Tompn an oo be awright."

Once seated, Carl seldom arose until the day was over . . . and the day we worked was never shorter than twelve hours. He didn't eat anything. He didn't go to the toilet. When he had to urinate, he simply scooted his chair around, hoisted himself up on the arms and let go out the alley window. Since the window opened on the store's parking lot, there were frequent and bitter complaints about this practice. Customers were constantly grumbling that Carl's urethral discharges had seriously damaged the paint on their cars, and one guy declared that several holes had been eaten in the hood of his vehicle. All these complainants got short shrift from Carl.

Could they prove that he was guilty? Did they have witnesses who would swear to the fact in court? No? "Well, skew oo, mithter!" And if they did have proof, they still received no satisfaction.

"Looky, mithter," he would explain. "Iss isn't any store—iss a doddam bookteepin tumpny. Oo uh hell oo donna sue, anyway? Oo dit anyfing out uh iss doddam outfit I'll split wif oo."

Except for me, to whom he was always kind, Carl had not a pleasant word for anyone. But he was at his most insulting when dealing with the home office or its representatives. "Now, ess dit one fing straight," he would say, addressing some traveling auditor or supervisor. "I'm wunnin iss doddam place, an I don't need any fuddin assho like oo to tell me how. I do as I doddam pwease, see? Oo don't like at oo can skwew orself an I'll quit."

The home office chose to like it. Very wisely. Carl worked for a pitifully low salary, and despite his drinking he was by far the best auditor in the chain. He could and did do the work of three men, and with an expertness, an unfailing accuracy, which surpassed genius.

Day after day, I saw him so drunk that his eyes were glazed and his head jerked and rolled on his neck in alcoholic spasms; I saw him weave in his chair, tilt perilously backward and forward and from side to side.

And with all that I never saw him hesitate in his work or make one single, solitary error! Sometimes I would have to put a pen in his hand, and place his other hand on the comptometer. But once that was done, he needed no further assistance. His left hand would flick over the keys of the machine, veritably playing a tune on it; his right hand would roam over the ledger, inscribing it with long columns of always accurate, excruciatingly neat figures. As often as I watched the miracle, I remained amazed by it.

"Nuffin to it, Tompn," Carl would lisp, grinning at me devilishly. "Jus a matter of teepin in tundishun. Jus dotta live wight, ats all."

This "teepin in tundishun" and "livin wight" was (or so Carl advised me) only part of his formula for doing highly complex work while stumbling-blind drunk. The truly important thing, he said, was to "fine 'em, fud 'em an fordet 'em," or, perhaps, to "skwew 'em all an the easy ones twice."

"Pith on 'em, Tompn," he declared a dozen times a day. "Hang it out uh window an skwew uh whole doddam world."

He was such a wonderfully good accountant and had followed the profession for so many years that, I suppose, he could have done his job in his sleep. He didn't need to think about it, in the ordinary sense of the word. Too drunk to see straight, or even to see at all, he was carried through one intricate task after another by his subconscious mind.

I wondered what he was doing in such a job as this one, why he drank as he did. Late one afternoon, some six weeks after the beginning of our association, I found out. I had been smiling about something, some joke one of the clerks had told me. Apparently I had been doing it for some time, and since our desks faced each other Carl got the notion that I was smiling at him.

"Sumpn funny, Tompn?" he demanded, his normally flushed face turning white. "Whynt oo laugh out loud? Did it out uh oore doddam skwewin system!"

"W-why, Carl," I stammered. "I was just——"

"Do ahead!" he lisped angrily. "Evey one else does, doddam wotten son-a-bitsin bastuhds! Tant do anywhere, tant say anything without some fuddin skwewball laughin his doddam head off. . . . Look like uh Devil, don't I? Look like uh Devil an talk like a skewin doddam baby! Tant dit a doddam decent job. Tant even thay hello to a doddam woman. . . . "

He raved on, cursing and spilling out obscenities, inviting me to "do ahead an have a dood laugh." Thus, at last, I saw why things were as they were with him—that his arrogance was only a cloak for a shamed and hypersensitive man. Fortunately, the right response came to me. I did not make the mistake of apologizing or sympathizing with him.

As soon as I could get a word in edgewise, I told him he was a damned fool. A man might look like the Devil and talk like a baby, but he did not need to *act* like either. "I'll tell you something," I said—and what I told him was quite true. "One of the best adjusted, happiest men I ever knew was a dwarf with club feet. He was one of the country's top corporation attorneys. He had a beautiful wife and four fine children. No one cared what he looked like. He was such a swell guy—and such a smart one— that no one noticed what he looked like. Oh, a few boobs might snicker at him, but what the hell did he care about them?"

Carl brushed at his eyes—in his self-pity and fury he had actually started to weep. He suggested that his case was different. "It wouldn be tho bad if I could juth thpeak plainly. Thath the worth——"

"It's always different," I said. "We've all got our own brand of trouble; I've had mine. If I'd acted like you do, I'd have died of tuberculosis or the d.t.s long ago."

"Yeth, but——"

"You're beating yourself over the head," I said. "You'd rather feel sorry for yourself than do something. If you're ashamed of the way you talk, why are you talking all the time? You never miss a chance that I can see. You're shooting off your mouth, getting into arguments, from the time you get here in the morning until you leave. You make a spectacle out of yourself with your drinking. If you don't want to be laughed at, why do you give people so many opportunities?"

I was pretty sore. My many failings do not include laughing at the infirmity of another, and the accusation that I had done so did not set well.

Carl heard me out, looking rather sheepish toward the last. Finally, he grinned and said, "Well, fud oo, Tompn. Fordet it, will oo?" and we both went back to work.

Well, it may have been wishful thinking, but it seemed to me that he did not get quite so drunk from then on. Also that he talked less to those outside the office, avoiding arguments where they could be avoided. Instead of mere working companions, we became quite good friends. Where before he had merely recited trite obscenities, he now conversed with me. . . . Did I really think he might be able to land a good job and not be laughed out of it? Did I really think that one such as he could lead a normal life, with all that the word implied? . . . I said of course he could— *if* he would stop thinking about himself and straighten up. For a man as brilliant and talented as he was, people would overlook any handicap.

"Oo weally mean at, don't oo, Tompn?"—studying me narrowly. "Oore not dus tiddin, are oo?"

"You know I do," I said. "You know what I say is true. If you go on like you've been doing, you've got no one to blame but yourself."

He thought about that, and a few days later it paid off.

It was now nearing the fall of 1930, and the economic depression was tightening over Nebraska. But the nation's political and business leaders still proclaimed it a temporary recession. It was merely a readjustment period, and prosperity was just around the corner, et cetera. To reachieve prosperity it was only necessary to "tighten our belts," "overcome sales resistance" and so on.

Well, the store tightened its belt—rather, by arranging salary cuts for the various concession employees, it tightened *their* belts. And by way of overcoming the aforesaid sales resistance it began a series of vigorous campaigns. The clerks were given sales quotas—to be met or else. They were organized into competing "armies," with the winner receiving a blue ribbon or a plaque or some such prize. One "bargain" sale followed another. Every week the home office shipped us a huge batch of advertising matter—flamboyant placards and pennants and counter cards. It was my job, one of my many jobs, to "decorate" the store with these.

In the midst of all this activity, Carl absented himself from work for two days on a plea of sickness. By the time he returned, I was virtually exhausted and he, incredibly, was *sober!*

He had brought two pint bottles with him—two bottles of good whiskey. He took a drink from one, passed it to me and waved me to a chair at his desk.

"Oo dotta help me dwink at, Tompn. We finis at, at's all eres donna be. I'm tuttin out uh doddam tuff."

"You've got another job," I guessed.

"Doddam wight," he said proudly. "Tart in nex Monday. Chief auditor for big gwocwey chain in Tansas Tity. An I dot oo a job ath my athithtant."

I congratulated him, and thanked him. I pointed out, however, that I would be returning to school the following week and could not take a job in another city.

"I'll just go on working here part-time," I explained. "It's a sweat shop and they don't pay peanuts, but——"

"Ats what ey tol you, huh?" Carl shook his head grimly. "Well, they tol me juth two dayth ago to fire you—inthithted on it. Thaid ey could dit a man full time for what eyd have to pay oo."

"But they promised!" I protested. "They said if I'd accept eighteen dollars a week and work real hard this summer they'd keep me on at the same money when school started."

"Oo dot it in writing?" Carl shook his head again. "Iss asho outfit! Work a manth ath off an en pith on him!"

He declared that he was not going to do another "dod dam lick of work" as long as he remained on the job and that I was not to do any

either. That was an order, he said—"pothitively not a doddam sonofabit-
sin bit of work." We would just sit around until the end of the week and
enjoy ourselves.

I didn't dispute the order. After a time, by way of conserving his
whiskey for him, I went out for a gallon of home brew. I returned to find
Carl examining the week's batch of advertising matter.

"Thith skwewin cwap," he said. "Let the bathturdth sthick it up ere
ath." Contemptuously, he started to toss a placard aside. Then, a truly
devilish grin spread over his face, and he picked it up again. "How about
it, Tompn? Long ath oore dittin uh date, oo dus ath thoon dit it tomorrow?"

"I suppose so," I said. "A couple of days won't make much difference."

"Thath uh way I feel. Tho we'll both leave tomorrow. But we'll div iss
doddam outfit thumpn to wemember uth by."

"Yeah?" I said. "I don't see——"

"How ith thingth in uh dwug department? Ey dot plenty of Totexth on
hand?"

"Totexth? Oh, Kotex," I said. "Why, yeah, I guess so. The inventory
shows around five hundred boxes. What——?"

"Wunnerful," said Carl. "Thwell! Loth of Totexth an iss fuddin meth
of thigns. Who could ath for anyfing more?"

That was the way, then, that it came about. Thus, the beginning of a
joke which was to throw our employers into embarrassed fury and to
keep the Lincoln area snickering for months to come.

As soon as the store closed for the day, Carl and I gathered up the
advertising matter and went downstairs. We requisitioned the drug departments's entire supply of sanitary napkins. With these, and our placards and pennants and counter cards, we proceeded to "decorate" the
store. It was after dawn before we finished. We unlocked the restaurant,
helped ourselves to breakfast, and retired to the office to await results.

We were hardly seated before the department heads began to arrive.
And as soon as they arrived and got one startled look at the store, they
came bounding up the stairs to confront Carl. . . . What the hell was the
idea, anyway? Was he trying to get the establishment laughed out of
business? The display would have to come down immediately.

Carl told them what they could do. If our decoration job was in any
way disturbed he would personally see to it that their concession was
yanked. "I'm uh doddam boss here," he pointed out. "Oo wun oor
skewin concession my way or oo don't wun it!"

One or two of the department heads accepted this dictum. The majority, however, headed for the nearest telephone and laid the matter before

their concession owners. The latter called our home office. The home office called us. It was what Carl had wanted.

He listened, grinning, to the outraged tirade which poured over the wire. Then, when there was a temporary pause for breath, he had his blasphemous and blood-curdling say. He was "fudding well twitting and Tompn was twitting." We had already paid ourselves to date, and now we were walking out. And since there would be no one around to carry out the management's orders, the decorations—or a large part of them— would stay right where they were. At least they would stay there until someone arrived from the home office.

"At'll teath oo to skwew people!" he yelled. "Doddam dirty pithanth! Do on an skweam oor fudding lungth out—ith muthik to my earth!"

He ended his remarks with a raucous raspberry—and if you have never heard a lisping raspberry, you have missed something. Then, he and I donned our hats, and left the office for the last time.

It was raining that day. As usual, when the weather made agricultural pursuits impractical, the farmers had come into town to shop. It was not yet ten in the morning, but already the store was filling up with customers—or, I should say, people. For few of them were buying any- ting. They stood around in little groups, the men haw-hawing and point- ing, the women giggling and blushing. Wherever they looked they saw the same thing, and each look brought a fresh outburst of amusement.

"Well, Tompn," said Carl happily. "Ith at sumpn or ith at sumpn?"

I said that it was, indeed, something. And it was.

Throughout every department, throughout the store, boxes of the things were arranged in neat pyramids and piles, each forming a pedestal for some bit of advertising matter—a pennant, placard, or counter card.

The pedestals were all of a kind, all made of boxes of sanitary napkins. The advertising matter all voiced the same slogan, the magic words-of- the-week intended to overpower sales resistance. That was all you saw, wherever you looked—stacks of s.n.'s, each crowned or draped with the same gaudily-lettered slogan:

HAPPY DAYS ARE HERE AGAIN

IX

My LITERAL-MINDED FRIEND DURKIN, the ex-credit manager, had an out-side sales and collection job with an installment store. On his recommendation, I got a job with the same firm. My hours were the same as they had been during our previous association, and permitted me to attend school in the morning. The pay was twenty dollars a week, plus car allowance, plus commission.

On the surface, it seemed to be a very fine job and the manager a very cordial fellow. Durkin, who was assigned to breaking me in on my duties, advised me not to be too optimistic.

"You wanted a job, Jim," he said, heading his car toward the shabbiest section of town, "so I helped you to get it. But I don't think you're going to like it. I don't, and I think I can take a lot of stuff that would throw you."

"I don't understand," I said. "Mr. Clark seemed to be——"

"Mr. Clark *is* a nice guy. As long as you produce. That's all he asks of you, to get the money, and he doesn't care how you do it. But, brother, you'd sure as hell better get it."

"Well," I shrugged, "that's our job. If a man doesn't do his job, he should catch hell."

"It's not quite that simple," said Durkin. "But you'll see what I mean."

We had crossed Salt Creek and entered a neighborhood of rutted dirt streets and unpainted shacks. Durkin stopped in front of one of them, took a collection card from the dashboard clip and got out. I followed him across the trash-strewn yard to the house.

Durkin knocked; he pounded; he stood back and kicked the door. There was no response. All was silent behind the drawn shades of the place.

"Well," I said uneasily, "it looks like there's no one home, Durk."

Durkin gave me a pitying look. Drawing back his fist, he jammed it through the screen and lifted the latch. Then, he turned the doorknob and walked in.

I tottered after him.

Seated at a table made of packing boxes was a burly unshaven man in undershirt and trousers. As we walked in, he set down his tin cup of coffee and directed a string of curses at Durkin.

186

"Ought to beat your goddamned head off," he swore. "Ought to call the cops on you. Breaking and entering—don't you know that's against the law?"

"Let's have the dough," said Durkin. "Come on, snap into it!"

"I ain't got any dough! I ain't been working."

"Come through," said Durkin. "You worked two days and a half last week."

"So I made a few bucks. I got to have something to eat on, don't I?"

"You don't do any eating on our money," said Durkin. "Let's have it."

The man ripped out another string of curses. Surlily, his eyes wavering away from Durkin's stern stare, he jerked a five-dollar bill from his pocket.

"All right. There's your goddamned dollar. Give me four bucks change."

Durkin put the five in his billfold, wrote out a receipt for it and tossed it on the table. "You were behind in your payments, Pete," he said evenly. "That brings you up to date."

The man's face purpled. Fists clubbed, he started toward Durkin, and, almost absently, Durkin turned to me.

"Jim, get that size forty-six coat out of the car—the sheeplined. I want Pete to try it on."

"But,"—I stared at him incredulously—"b-but he——"

"That's right. I brought it along especially for Pete. Winter's coming on, and he's going to need a good warm coat."

I got the coat out of the car, noting that it had cost six dollars wholesale according to the code number. Durkin slipped it on Pete, even as the big man glowered and grumbled threats.

"Fits you like a glove," he declared. "Isn't that a swell coat, Jim? Makes Pete look like a new man."

"Prob'ly fall apart in two weeks," muttered Pete. "What you want for the damned thing?"

"Oh, I'll make you a good price on that. Let you have it for twenty-five dollars."

"Twenty-five dollars!" Pete let out a howl. "Why you can get the same damned thing anywhere for eleven or twelve!"

"But you don't have eleven or twelve," Durkin pointed out, "and you can't get credit anywhere else. . . . Tell you what I'll do, seeing that you're an old customer. I'll make it twenty-two-fifty, and you can pay it out at four bits a week. Make your payments a dollar-fifty a week instead of the dollar you're paying now."

"Well . . . twenty dollars and two bits a week!"

"You're wasting my time," said Durkin, crisply. "Let's have the coat."

Pete hesitated. "Oh, hell," he said. "Okay. Twenty-two-fifty and four bits a week. What you got for me to sign?"

Having given me a demonstration of what the job was like, Durkin filled me in orally as we drove on to the next customer. The store was one of a nation-wide chain of eighty, all operating under the same unorthodox methods. They deliberately sold to poor credit risks—a market avoided by other stores. Thus, being without competition, they could operate from the most unpretentious side-street establishment and charge very high prices for inferior merchandise. Collection expenses were high, of course, but still low enough, percentage-wise to make the operation immensely profitable. And the losses on uncollectible accounts were not nearly so large as one might think. The chain was constantly on the lookout for good men—"aggressive, forceful men." Such men could earn very handsomely. There were minimum prices on all merchandise; anything a man could get above that price was split between him and the store. He also received a relatively high base salary, and a commission on collections.

"I run better than a hundred dollars a lot of weeks," Durkin said. "That's about three times what I'd get in this town on the average collection job."

"I'd say you earned it," I said. "Are all the customers like Pete?"

"Well, none of 'em are easy to get money out of, but some are worse than others. We've got a real tough baby coming up."

The "tough baby" lived in a place similar to Pete's, and like Pete, he did not appear to be at home. The front door was locked, also the back one. Durkin shaded his eyes with his hands and peered through several of the windows.

"Can't see him," he frowned, "but I know damned well he's here. I'm sure I saw him out on the steps when we rounded the corner. I wonder if . . . "

He broke off, staring speculatively at the back yard privy. With a significant wink at me, he headed for the edifice, pausing on the way to pick up two fist-sized brickbats.

He pounded on the door of the privy. He kicked it. He stood back and hurled the brickbats at it with all his might. There was a yell from the inside, a furious curse-filled sputtering. Durkin took a pair of pliers from his pocket and hefted them thoughtfully.

"Come on out, Johnnie," he called. "You'll have to do it sooner or later, so why not make it light on yourself?"

"To hell with you!" yelled the man within. "Try and make me come out, you goddamned thieving junk-peddler!"

"All right," said Durkin, reasonably, "don't come out, then. Just shove your money under the door."

Johnnie replied with an unprintable suggestion. He was not shoving any money under the door and he was not coming out; and that, by God, was that.

Durkin shrugged. He fitted the hasp over the staple in the door, and slid a handle of the pliers through it. Then, scooping up an armful of old papers from the yard, he walked around to the back of the privy.

Two planks had been removed from its base, apparently to provide ventilation. Durkin touched a match to the papers, and shoved them through the aperture.

Since they fell into the waste pit, there was no danger—or at least very little—of incinerating Johnnie. But the clouds of stinking smoke which welled up from the pit, soon had him on the point of strangulation. He yelled that he would murder Durkin—he would kill him if it was the last thing he ever did. The next moment he had ceased his threats and was beating wildly on the door, pleading hysterically for mercy.

"Three dollars, Johnnie," said Durkin. "Shove it through the crack and I'll let you go."

"Goddammit,"—*cough, cough*—"I can't. My wife's in the hospital. I've got to have——"

"Three dollars," said Durkin.

"But I—*all right!*"—a terrified scream. "There it is! Now for God's sake let me——"

Durkin took the three crumpled bills, slipped the pliers from the hasp and stepped back. Coughing and strangling, bent double, Johnnie staggered out into the yard.

He was no more than a boy, eighteen, perhaps nineteen years old. He was tall, six feet at least, yet he could not have weighed much more than a hundred pounds. His cheeks were colored with the rosy, telltale spots of tuberculosis. There was no fight left in him.

He stumbled and sat down in the weeds, coughing, staring at us.

"Starved," he said dully, as though he were talking to himself. "Just plain starved, that's all that was the matter with her. And it won't be no different when she gets out. Starvin', her and me together; freezin' when it's cold, scorchin' when it's hot, livin' like no one ever let a dog live. W-what—what's—"

He broke off, gripped in another paroxysm of coughing. He wheezed, spat and spoke again.

"What's a guy gonna do?" he said. "What's he gonna do when he does all he can and it ain't nowheres good enough? Huh? How about it?" He glared at us fiercely for a moment. Then, his eyes lowered and he addressed the question to the ground, to the soured, sun-baked earth. "What's a guy gonna do, anyway? What's a guy gonna do? What's a guy gonna ... "

Durkin gripped my arm suddenly, and steered me toward the car. "It's him or us," he said. "Them or us. What's a guy going to do?"

X

I HAD BEGINNER'S LUCK THAT FIRST WEEK. Perhaps I was assigned to some of the easier accounts, or perhaps my customers were feeling me out— taking my measure—before getting tough with me. At any rate, I did very well and without having to resort to the tactics which Durkin had used. The quaint notions grew in my mind that (1) I was the world's champion collector, and (2) that the store's clients were merely misguided and misunderstood. They didn't pay because they had not been made to see the importance of paying. Because they were approached with abuse, they responded with it.

Saturday night came, and Mr. Clark detained me after the other collectors had left for a few words of hearty praise. "I knew you'd be a top man," he declared. "You keep this up and you'll be making more dough than your college professors."

"Oh, well," I smirked, my head swelling three sizes, "I don't expect to make *that* much."

"You'll do fine. You've got the size—that's the important thing. Throw a good enough scare into these bastards to begin with and you can take it easy from then on."

"Well," I hesitated, uncomfortably. Somehow, the fact had evaded me that the store's four collectors and Clark as well were all very large men. "I don't think size has much to do with it, Mr. Clark. I mean——"

"Maybe not," he shrugged. "We always hire 'em big, but I suppose there are plenty of tough little guys. They wouldn't have the psychological advantage, of course, but——"

"I don't mean that," I said. And I went on to tell him what I did mean. That the customers should be treated with kindness—firmly but kindly. Treat them as oneself would like to be treated if in the same circumstances.

Clark stared at me blankly as I expounded my theory. Then, at last, his broad flat-nosed face puckered in a grin, and he guffawed. "By God!" He slapped his hand on the counter. "You really had me going there for a minute, Jim! . . . Treat 'em nice, huh? Be kind to 'em. I think I'll pull that one on the home office!"

"Well," I said, "I guess it does sound kind of funny, but——"

"What a sense of humor! What a kidder!" He burst into another round of guffaws. "Well, have a nice weekend and I'll see you Monday."

I spent the weekend working on the old car I had bought. Monday noon, still stubbornly convinced that I had solved the secret of successful collecting, I went back on the job. It was just about my last day on earth.

My first customer was an employee of a rendering plant, a place which, due to the hellish odor it exuded, was located in the outskirts of the city. Here the unfortunates of the area's animal population were brought— those that had died of old age or disease or accident. Here they were converted into hides and tallow, glue, bristles and bone.

I parked my car in the stinking, refuse-filled yard. Entering the building, I was almost knocked down by the stench and great clouds of blow flies swarmed over me. I gasped, and tried to brush them away. I went forward cautiously, brushing and gasping.

The lower floor of the building appeared to be one huge room, apparently the storage place, so far as any existed, for the animals that were brought in. From wall to wall, they littered the floor—cows, horses, sheep and swine; animals in various hideous states of mutilation and decomposition. All swarming and crawling with blow flies.

While I was peering around in the darkness, a man—some sort of foreman, I suppose—came in from the yard and inquired my business. I explained, tactfully, that I wished to see Mr. Brown on a business matter.

"Collector, huh?" he grunted. "How come you don't do your collectin' at his house?"

"I don't know," I said. "I'm a new man on the job. I imagine, though, that the store wasn't satisfied with the way he was paying so they instructed me to come here."

"Well," he grimaced, surlily, "I'll call him for you—this time."

Moving a few feet away from me, he cupped his hands and shouted up at the ceiling. He was preparing to shout a second time when a trapdoor opened high above him and a man looked down.

"Yes, sir? Was you callin' me?"

"You're damned right I'm calling you!" the foreman said, adding that the next time his work was interrupted by personal matters would be the last time. "I ain't going to have it, get me? You can't take care of your business without mixing it up with mine, you can get another job!"

He jerked his head at me curtly, and strode away. I moved over beneath the trapdoor.

The man above me was so besmeared and grimed from his work that I could see nothing of his features. But there was that in his attitude which spoke of murderous anger. I called up, apologetically, that I was sorry if I had caused trouble. "If you'll just drop your payment down to me. . . . "

"Tough guy aren't you?" The eyes in the smeared face gleamed broodingly. "Scare hell out of my wife, get her so upset she's half out of her mind. Then you come around here raising hell."

"You're mistaken," I said. "I've never talked to your wife or even seen her for—"

"The hell you ain't! She told me what you looked like. There wouldn't be two guys with that outfit as big as you are."

"But there——"

"You wait there," he said. "You wait right there, and I'll drop something down to you."

I waited. I stood looking upward until my neck began to ache, and then I looked down again. And that was when it happened.

I imagine he must have had someone help him, for the great bloated carcass—a dead hog—which shot down suddenly through the hole must have weighed all of four hundred pounds. It grazed my arm as it went past. Only the fact that I had turned slightly, to glance out the door, kept it from landing on me.

There was a tremendous thud, the sound of splitting hide and exploding flesh. I flung myself backward, instinctively, but not soon enough to avoid a sickening and smelly spattering. I looked down at myself, at the awful thing at my feet, and then I looked up at the trapdoor. Brown was there, peering downward casually.

"Little accident," he said. "Fella forgot that the door was open. Happens all the time around here."

I didn't wait. I was on my way out of the place as fast as my near-nerveless legs would carry me. My hands were trembling so badly that I could hardly get the car started.

I made myself fairly presentable again at a filling station washroom, but the damage to my morale was irreparable. I couldn't collect. I couldn't sell—which, ordinarily, was quite easy to do. I could not approach my customers with the "firm kindliness" which I had so grandiosely advocated (how could you be nice to people like that?). Neither could I get tough with them (tough with people who might kill you!). I didn't know what to do, what to say, how to act; and while I doggedly made every call assigned to me, I wound up the day without a single sale or one small collection.

I stalled at the store that evening until the other collectors had checked in and left. Then, with forced casualness, I sauntered up to the wicket and laid my collection cards in front of Clark. We were alone. Except in very large cities, the managers of the chain's stores were the sole inside employees.

He lighted a cigarette, spewed smoke from the corner of his mouth as he squinted down at the cards. His coat was open. For the first time I noticed the minute ornament that dangled from his watch chain—a tiny pair of golden gloves.

"Yeah, Jim," he said absently, having followed the direction of my eyes. "Yup, I was a pretty good man with the mitts. Might have made a champ heavy if I'd kept at it."

"I see," I said.

"Yeah, I might have and might not, but I figured I'd be better off in another line. Have the odds more on my side. You see, I look at it this way, Jim. It's hard to get anything and hold onto it, even if the other guys in your field are just *almost* as good as you are. You don't stand out, know what I mean? To really stand out you've got to move out of your own pasture—get into some line of work like, well, like this. Something where you don't have any competition; where you can slap hell out of any three guys you may come up against. Do you get my meaning, Jim?"

"I get it," I said.

"I don't see any sales slips here, Jim. . . . "

"No," I said. "I didn't sell anything."

"And there are no collections on these cards. . . . "

"I didn't collect anything."

He studied me, shook his head. "No, you wouldn't be that stupid. You wouldn't try to knock down the whole lot. Did you take the day off, Jim? No? You actually worked six hours without making any sales or any collections?"

"Yes," I nodded. "I know it sounds funny, but——"

"Funny? No, I wouldn't say it was. Come around the counter, Jim." He pointed. "Come right through that little gate there, and sit down in this chair." He pushed me into it. "And I'll sit down right in front of you." He did so. "Now, let's have the story."

He was sitting so close that his legs pressed against mine; he had also leaned forward, gripping the arms of my chair. Obviously, with our respective noses almost touching each other, the position was not one to put me at my ease. The explanation I stammered out sounded preposterously weak and foolish.

Nevertheless, and much to my surprise, Clark seemed to accept and understand it. "I've been afraid at times, too, Jim. There's been times when I've lost my nerve. I remember once in Chicago when I was working for a loan shark, a very tough outfit, incidentally. They sent me out to collect from a steelworker who owed us a hundred—half of it interest—and the guy went for me with a baseball bat. Damned near caved my skull in. Scared? Why, Jim, it took the guts right out of me. And then I sneaked back to the office, and I got them back. The boss gave me a break. He had a couple of boys take me down into the basement and *both* of them had baseball bats; and they didn't just threaten me with 'em, they used them. And pretty soon, Jim, I wasn't afraid of that other guy at all. I wasn't afraid to collect from him. All that

I was afraid of was what would happen if I didn't collect. . . . Now, to get down to your case, to get to the point, Jim—I'll lay you a little bet. I'll bet you'd like to go out to the rendering plant tomorrow and get the dough out of that jerk. I'll bet you'd a lot rather do that than come in here and tell me that you haven't done it, that you've pissed off a whole day. Am I right, Jim? Isn't that the way you feel about it?"

I would like to be able to say that I stood up at this point, told him to take his job and shove it, and walked out. But, inclined as I am to place myself in the most favorable light, I am incapable of such an outright lie. I had to work. I had grown up in a world, in jobs, where the roughest justice prevailed, where discipline was maintained, more often than not, with physical violence. And, now, in Clark, I recognized an all too familiar type. From such men, a nominal bluff is a warning. Their threats are promises.

"You weren't thinking of quitting, were you, Jim? I'd hate to see you do that. It costs money to break a man in, and I'm supposed to know how to pick 'em."

I shook my head. "No, I don't want to quit."

"That's on the level? You wouldn't just walk out of here tonight and not show up any more? If you have something of that kind in mind . . . "

"I don't."

"Good boy!" He grinned suddenly and took a playful poke at my chin. "You'll be all right now; you'll do fine from now on. You were just afraid—of the wrong things."

Well, to make an interminable story merely long, I did go out to the rendering plant the next day and I collected from the man who had tried to drop the hog on me. I cut my last class at school, and was thus able to arrive at the plant before noon. I was waiting at the door when Brown came outside to eat his lunch. Taken by surprise and being without the previous day's advantage, he paid up promptly. In fact, after one startled look at me, he was extending the money before I could ask for it.

Heartened by this success, I did fairly well that day. But the following day I went into another slump, and by Saturday I was selling and collecting next to nothing. Clark, whose manner had grown increasingly ominous as the week progressed, detained me that night for another "conference."

It began much the same way that the first one had. The stage setting was the same. Seating me in front of him, he pinned me to the chair with his knees and arms and thrust his face into mine. In a quiet, purring voice, he lectured me on the perils of misplaced fear. He was deadly serious. Now and then, he gripped my arm in emphasis and I almost yelled with the pain. And yet essentially, deep in that part of heart or mind which makes a man what he is, I remained unaffected. I was afraid of him, but the fear could not move me.

"Jim—" His voice snapped suddenly. "You think I'm kidding you? You think I'll let you get away with making a chump out of me? Boy, if you've got any ideas like that ... !"

"I haven't," I said. "I know how you feel. I wouldn't really blame you if you took a poke at me."

"It'll be more than a poke, Jim! By God, you're going to start hitting that ball Monday or——"

"I don't think I can," I said. "I'd like to—I need every cent I can get. But you'll be doing the smart thing to fire me."

"Huh-uh! I'm not firing you and you're not quitting."

I shrugged. He was calling the turns. He could keep me on the job— make it extremely unpleasant for me to leave—but he could not make me perform in it. If he thought that he could, I added (rather shakily) now was a good time to try.

"Yeah?" His jaw jutted out. "That's the way you want it, huh?"

"N-no. But—"

"Tell me, Jim ... " He paused and wet his lips. Then, he went on, his broad face puzzled, his tone almost wheedling. "You stacked up like my kind of guy. I figured you and me, we probably went to different schools together. So, well, what's the deal, boy? How come it rolls out like this?"

"I don't know," I said.

"You're sure you haven't let some of these deadbeats get you down? They haven't got the Indian sign on you so bad that——"

"It isn't them," I said. "It's me, something that sort of holds me back. I don't know quite how to explain it, but ... "

"Go on. Make a stab at it, Jim."

"I guess I'm not afraid of them enough," I said. "They may pull some stunt like that guy at the rendering plant did, but I know they're really no match for us. We've got everything on our side. The law, and a tough bunch of boys to ride them ragged. I can't fight people like that. I feel sorry for them."

"They don't feel that way about you, Jim. They hate your guts. You saw how that Brown character acted."

"I know," I said. "That's what started it. Seeing how they felt, and not being able to resent it. Feeling that I had it coming. If I'd been in Brown's place, if someone had charged me four prices for a bunch of junk and then shoved my wife around, I'd have probably done what he did."

"They don't have to buy the stuff, Jim. If they're stupid enough to do it——"

"They have to buy it or do without. No one else will sell to them."

"Yes, but ... " He paused. "Yeah, but, Jim ... " he said slowly, and paused again. "You see, Jim, it's—uh—uh—"

He stood up and paced around the office. Turning suddenly, he leveled a finger at me. "Now, here's the way it is, Jim. We're actually pretty damned nice to these people. We're just working to help 'em, but naturally—uh—help costs money, so we have to—uh—"

He broke off, scowling, fixing me with a glare that dared me to laugh. Then, following a long moment of silence, his face relaxed and he himself laughed. "All right," he said. "All right, Jim, we'll call it quits for to-night. But you're going to do it, get me? By God, you—you *got* to do it!"

Judson Clark—Jud Clark. Ex-college football star, ex-pug, ex-heavy in the loan shark racket: a literate thug, to state the case briefly. I worked with him for months—at least, I held my job with the store—and I came to like him very much. I liked him and pitied him.

I was, as he had indicated, "his kind of people." Our backgrounds roughly paralleled one another, and I should have responded to the demands of necessity and self-preservation. I should and I must—for in my failure he saw failure for himself. I represented something vital to him, a threat to the only way of life he could understand. His fear that the structure of that life might be crumbling was far greater than any fear he could inspire in me.

Our conferences became almost nightly affairs, by turns abusive and wheedling. He jeered me in front of the other collectors. He even called Mom one day to declare that I was letting him down sadly—he who had only my best interests at heart—that I was failing her and Freddie, that jobs were very, very hard to get and that it would be a shame if I was forced to drop out of school; and asking her to "lay the proposition" before me and to make me "see the light" and so on.

I told Mom that I wished to God he would fire me. The constant pressure was to do a job which I could not do, and yet being unable to quit, was becoming unbearable.

It goes without saying, of course, that I did not always check in at the store empty-handed. I usually had some small something to show for my day's efforts. Generally speaking, however, the nature of my successes was such as to leave Clark almost anything but reassured.

"I don't get it, by God!" he yelled one night. "This bastard—all the other boys gave up on him. Even I took a crack at him and I couldn't score. He's a mean, no-good son-of-a-bitch. He loaded up on that stuff without ever intending to give us a nickel, and he's got so damned many judgments against him it was a waste of time to sue. So I'm all set to charge him off, and then you get his card. And you, by God, you collect!"

"Yes," I said uneasily. "It looks like—uh—I did, all right."

"Well? If you can collect from guys like that, you can collect from anyone!"

I shook my head. We had had similar discussions before, and I had not been able to make him understand. I felt differently about this particular customer and the others like him. I could tackle them without any twinge of conscience.

He stood over my chair, scowling, and I thought that at last he would give way to his feelings by giving me a drubbing. Instead, he turned abruptly and marched over to the card files.

He began to thumb through them swiftly, occasionally jerking a card out and tossing it onto his desk. Then, when he had extracted about twenty of them, he gestured curtly to me.

"All right," he said, "there's your cards for tomorrow. And by God, Jim . . . Well, you know what I mean. You do it, get me? You do what you're supposed to do!"

I looked at the cards. I looked at him. "All right," I said. "I'll do what I'm supposed to . . . "

In the deepest black there is some white; and among our several thousand customers there were a few hundred whom any store would have been delighted to have on its books. If one of them fell behind in his payments, a polite note from Clark would usually elicit a prompt remittance. At the worst, a word or two from a collector would turn the trick. There was no, or practically no, collection expense in dealing with these customers. The store made recognition of the fact by selling them reasonably good merchandise and at reasonably fair prices, and in other ways— insofar as it was capable of that figurative act—leaned over backwards to retain their good will.

Collectors, naturally, love such clients . . . but they are not allowed to keep them. It is a collector's job to collect—not merely to accept payments. It is a manager's or credit manager's job to see that the collector devotes his expensive time to people who will not pay of their own free will. That is the rule. I, through Clark's fear-born stubbornness, became an exception to it.

To use the contemptuous installment house term, I was handed a "milk route." I worked it (you should excuse the expression) well into the following spring.

Occasionally, I would be called upon to take over some nominally uncollectable account—some deadbeat so completely lacking in scruples that I could feel free in abandoning my own—and then I would have to actually work. But most of the time I did nothing more arduous than write receipts and pocket payments.

So Clark had his way; he proved himself right and me wrong. But his triumph was even emptier than it appeared. For now, with one corner of his life's mudsill secured, the others began to waver and give way.

Clark had a saying, a ready retort for the collector who fell down on an account. "The guy's eating, isn't he?" he would say. "Well, if he's eating, he's got dough. He has to have, and by God you better get it!"

It was a pretty conclusive argument. Or, rather, it had been in the past. But in the end—as the end approached—the collectors had an answer for it. They came in at night, dogged and sullen and sometimes battered, men driven as far as they could be driven. And they faced Clark almost pleasurably, anxious to reply to his stock question, to deliver the retort beyond which there could be no other.

"Huh-uh. That's what I'm saying, Jud—they ain't eating. Ain't got a thing in the house but a pound or so of cornmeal."

"What the hell you trying to hand me?" Clark would say, his voice furiously desperate. "Goddammit, everybody's got to eat! You think I'm going to swallow any goddamned story like——"

"I'm telling you how it is, Jud,"—an indifferent shrug, perhaps a thinly disguised sneer—"Why don't you check on it yourself? Maybe you can get that cornmeal away from 'em."

Each week the inflow of cash dropped to a new low. Even some of the best accounts began to go sour. One of the collectors was laid off, then another; finally only Durkin and I remained. The home office issued instructions that no merchandise should be sold except for cash.

This last happening, Durkin told me, was the tipoff. It was all over now but the shouting. "The chain's getting ready to fold, Jim. It's finally sunk in on 'em that they can't beat this. They're just stalling for time, trying to grab off what they can without putting out anything more."

I was sure he was right, but Clark, when I asked him about it, furiously denied that the company was on the verge of bankruptcy.

He had grown quite thin in recent weeks. The flesh was drawn tight on his broad, strong face. He swayed a little as he addressed me, and his breath stank with the odor of rotgut whiskey.

"That goddamned Durkin," he jeered. "A goddamned rube! What the—*hic!*—what the hell does he know? Why, Jim, Jim, ol' pal—" He leaned forward, confidentially, dropping a hand on my shoulder to steady himself. "I've *seen* it, Jim. I know what I'm talking about. They got their own office building, hundreds, thousands of people workin' in it, an'—and they got their own factories and trucking lines an'—and warehouses that cover a city block. An' they got all these stores—stores in almost every state in the union, two'r three in some states. An'—*hup!*—they even control some banks, Jim. Just the same as own 'em. S-say our accounts are spread over a year's time, why they can take that paper to the banks an' get the cash on it. They got 'em by the balls, see? They crack the whip just like we do, an'—an' you know us, Jim. Long's the bastards've got a nickel to get, we—w-we—"

He swayed, staggered, and lurched back against his desk. He sat there, nodding owlishly into space, and mumbling and muttering to himself.

"G-got to be. S-saw it myself, didn't I? All the people'n the buildings'n the factories'n the b-banks'n the warehouses'n the ... the everything. Didn't let 'em jus' tell me. Saw it m'self. Know it's there—g-gotta be there. Somethin's there it's *there*. 'S'there an' thass all there is to it. Where—w-where the hell's it gonna be if it ain't there? What ... where'n hell is anything gonna be?"

Two weeks later the chain closed its doors.

XI

I SQUEEZED THROUGH THE SUMMER ON A VARIETY OF ODD JOBS, anything I could get that would bring in a few dollars. Early in the fall, the radio store for which I had been making an occasional sale came out with a line of low-priced table models—a decided novelty in those days—and I made money hand over fist. I was convinced that I had the depression licked. So much so that I not only reenrolled for the college fall term, but I also got married. My wife had a good job. Our understanding was that, if I should be caught in a pinch, she could give me enough financial help to get through college. Meanwhile, until I was solidly on my feet and a better arrangement could be worked out, she continued to live with her family and I with mine.

Alas, for the best laid plans of newly married couples. A horde of other salesmen jumped in on the radio bonanza. Within a few weeks, the depression-narrowed market was saturated and my earnings fell to nothing. I could find no other work. My wife's employers learned of her marriage (we had been keeping it secret), and having a no-married-women policy, they promptly fired her. Then, to further complicate the situation, she discovered she was pregnant.

Mom and Freddie went back to my grandparents' home. I withdrew from school, gave the remitted tuition fees to my wife and took to the road.

I think I must have hitchhiked the length and breadth of Nebraska ten times in looking for work. I found barely enough to buy myself an occasional meal; and finally I could no longer do that. It was late in November, in the city of Omaha, that I reached the end of my tether. I was light-headed from lack of food. Weeks of sleeping in fields and ditches had ruined my clothes. Cold water shaving and washing had left me smeared, scratched and sinister-looking.

Night came on. Snow began to fall. Shivering, I got up from my park bench and wobbled up the street. I came to an empty doorway and took refuge in it, huddling back against the rusted dusty screen. The building was on the edge of the business district—a poorly lit, semi-slum section. On the corner, a few feet away, was a bus stop. A bus drew up, and a middle-aged, well-dressed man got off.

He peered around in the darkness, frowning. Then with a muttered "Damn," he turned back to the curb. Apparently he had got off at the wrong stop and was now waiting for another bus. I stood staring at his pudgy, well-clothed figure. Never before had I had the nerve to bum anyone—to ask for money. I simply didn't know how to go about it. But I knew I'd better do it now unless I intended to freeze or starve. Perhaps, I thought, taking a preliminary gulp of my pride, it wouldn't be so bad. We were alone, he and I, and there would be no witnesses to my shame.

I stepped out of the doorway, and walked up behind him. I said—well, I don't know what I said. But I suspect that discomfort and nervousness made me rather gruff. He could hardly be blamed if he construed my appeal as a demand.

"Huh!" he grunted and looked startledly over his shoulder.

He gulped and faced straight ahead again. His hand went into his pocket and came out with two one-dollar bills and a quantity of change. He thrust it backwards at me. And without turning around, and before I could thank him, he started across the street at a run.

He dashed into a small cigar store, and I saw him speak excitedly to the proprietor. The latter snatched up a telephone, and . . . and the truth finally dawned on me.

The guy thought I had held him up. He was summoning the police.

I forgot all about being weak and giddy. For the next five minutes or so, I reclaimed the one athletic skill of my misspent youth—marathon running. When the cops arrived at the scene of the "holdup"—and they wasted no time about it—I was so far away that I could barely hear the frustrated whinings of their sirens.

A good meal and a visit to a barber college did wonders for me. But that night, in a fifty-cent hotel room, I decided to clear out of Nebraska. There was nothing here for me. Perhaps there was nothing elsewhere, either, but I *knew* there was nothing here.

The next morning I hitchhiked back to Lincoln and said good-bye to my wife. It was not a pleasant occasion, much less so than it would have been ordinarily, since her elderly parents felt—justifiably, no doubt, from their viewpoint—that I had treated their daughter badly.

Well, anyway. I walked down to the freight yards that night, and caught a train south. In the south, at least, a man could sleep out if he had to.

There were two empty boxcars on the train (empty of paying freight, that is), and they were already filled with travelers like myself. So, believing that it would offer me sufficient protection from the cold, I settled down behind a tractor that was loaded on a flat car.

I was wrong. As the train gathered speed, the sub-zero wind whipped and nipped at me from all directions. The snow piled on me and froze on me until I looked like something carved of stone.

I knew that there was a division stop a couple hours out of Lincoln, and

I decided to lay over there and thaw out. But apparently due to the cold and my weariness, I lost consciousness. When I came to it was daylight and I was still on the train, and so nearly frozen that I could barely move.

I rode on into Kansas City. There, with the assistance of two other bums, I managed to unload.

I stayed there for a week—I *laid* there, I should say—in the weeds of the hobo jungles, freezing and burning by turns, in the throes of pneumonia. Fortunately, I have a hereditarily tough constitution, and I was very lucky. I had fallen among old-time hoboes, men who had chosen the life of wandering workers, not the depression-born bums. We had been in many of the same places—the pipeline jobs, the "rag towns" of the south and west. I was one of them, a guy who could talk knowingly of Four-Trey Whitey and the Half-a-Half Pint Kid, who knew how to filter canned heat through a handkerchief and rubbing alcohol through dry bread, who knew all the verses to the *Gallows Song*. In a word, I was a brother in distress, and deserving of all the help they could give. And they gave it. I came out of my illness very weak, but, thanks largely to my hobo benefactors, I did come out of it.

The first day I was able to travel I tramped across the city and walked up into the freight yards on the other side. It was night when I got there, and a train was making up for the south. I walked up and down the cars, looking for an empty box. Finally, becoming very weary, I settled for a gondola.

It was loaded, although not quite full, with hardwood. I snuggled down at the end of the lumber. I was feeling quite pleased with my wisdom in boarding the train in its makeup stages. The other bums, who would hop it on the yard's outskirts, would not be able to choose their berth as I had.

The train humped and jerked and began to move smoothly. There were two short blasts from the locomotive, and its speed increased. Then, with one long wavering blast, we really began to roll. Nervously, I stood up and looked over the side of the gondola.

We were just coming out of the yards, and already our speed was a good forty miles an hour. Groups of men—bums—were standing back from the tracks, showing no interest whatsoever in the cars that whizzed past them. I looked up and down the freight as we shot past a lighted crossing and as far as I could see, every door was closed. I climbed up on the lumber and looked forward and backward.

No one up there. No one riding the tops. And no one, apparently, riding the boxes. Shivering, I heard another long wavering blast from the locomotive—unmistakably a highball—and I knew I'd made one hell of a mistake.

The gondola had fooled me; it had been my experience that open cars

were not included in manifest freights. Nonetheless, this was a manifest—
an express merchandise train—and tolerant as the railroads were in those
days, they tolerated no super-cargo on manifests. These trains carried
valuable freight. A man caught riding them was automatically presumed
to be a thief, and he was treated as such.

I stayed up on top of the lumber. After a time, I saw a light bob up at
the head of the long line of cars, and back at the end another light. They
came toward each other slowly, toward me; moving from side to side,
now and then sinking out of sight. Those would be trainmen, guards,
searching the freight from front to rear. How long would they be in
getting to me? And when they did get to me . . . ?

I watched their progress. Longingly I watched the lights of villages flash
past us in a blur of speed. The locomotive howled hauntingly, blasted the
night with its highball demand for right-of-way.

The speed-induced wind was near freezing, but I was dripping with
sweat. A little hysterically, I wondered what the hell I had better do. I
couldn't jump—not from a train traveling a mile or more a minute. Just
as certainly, I couldn't stay where I was. I was very apt to be shot. At
best, if the guards took a chance of my being unarmed, I would no doubt
be clubbed insensible.

From my extensive travels in the midwest, I knew we could not be very
far from Fort Scott, Kansas, a railroad division point. But just how far,
whether we would get there before the trainmen got to me, I didn't know.
Neither could I be certain that the train would stop at Fort Scott, or even
slow down sufficiently to let me hop off.

The trainmen came nearer, one from the front, one from the rear. At
last they were no more than three car lengths away. Leaning over the
edge of the gondola, I stared ahead into the night.

Lights. A lot of lights. It must be Fort Scott. And—and, yes, almost
imperceptibly, the train was slowing down. But it wasn't slowing down
enough; we weren't going to hit Scott soon enough. It was still several
minutes away, and the guards were now only seconds away from me.

They came over the last of the cars separating them from me. They saw
me and yelled. I yelled back, holding my arms over my head. But they
either did not see my gesture in the darkness, or, seeing it, still did not
care to take chances. I heard a shout of "*Get the bastard!*" and they came
forward at a lurching, menacing run. Each had a thick club thonged to his
wrist. Each was wearing a gun belt and gun.

They reached the end of their respective boxcars simultaneously, and
started down the ladders. They jumped down to the gondola and advanced on me, clubs upswung . . .

As a child, my maternal grandfather had used to tell me all sorts of wild stories, allegories thinly disguised as personal experiences. One of his favorites concerned a hunting dog, which, being attacked by a mountain lion, had climbed a tree and escaped. "But how could he?" I would protest. "Dogs can't climb trees." "All depends on the dog," Grandfather would retort. "This dog *had* to climb one." Now, at last, after the passing of decades, I saw what he meant.

We were just nearing the outskirts of Fort Scott. The train was still going at a terrifying clip, But I had to jump and a man does what he has to.

I swung over the side of the gondola. I looked over my shoulder— stared down into darkness. And, then, as the guards' lanterns flashed in my eyes and their clubs descended, I jumped. I swung myself outward and backwards and let go.

The tracks at this point were atop a high grade, and I seemed to fall for minutes before my feet touched the cinder-blanketed embankment. They barely touched, then bounced me into the air as though they were springs.

I turned a complete somersault, landed on my feet, and was again bounced into the air. I came down on my shoulders and went into a long skid. Skidding on my shoulders and back, I wound up at the foot of the embankment. There was a strange shrieking in my ears, an almost animal keening. A minute or two passed before I realized that I was listening to myself, screaming in an agony of shock and pain.

I laughed and sat up. I buried my face in my hands and rocked to and fro, laughing and sobbing, unable to believe that I was actually alive. After a time, I pulled myself together, climbed back up to the tracks, and limped into Fort Scott. There I was arrested for vagrancy, jailed for the night and floated out of town in the morning.

XII

I HAVE BEEN PRETTY CRITICAL AT TIMES OF MY NATIVE STATE, Oklahoma. For one thing, I believe it is and always has been the rottenest, politically, in the country. But on the whole I am fond of it and proud of it, and I am quickly annoyed with people who speak disparagingly of "Okies" and make uninformed remarks about the state's "backwardness." Where politics is concerned, Oklahoma may be, to use the Brookings Institution phrase, "the heart of Balkan America." But in many ways it is so far ahead of the majority of the commonwealths as to make comparison pitiful.

To cite a few statistics, it has more paved roads, more institutions of higher learning, and more playgrounds and parks per population than any state in the union. It has a really effective department of labor—not a mere letterhead conglomeration of spineless hacks. Its department of charities and corrections has long been held up as a model among penal and eleemosynary authorities. Unlike a certain state to the south, Oklahoma does not brag about its achievements—not nearly enough, anyway, in my opinion. Progressiveness, and the good life which is its objective, are considered a citizen's rightful due. Many of the state's wealthiest men came there broke and they have not lost touch with, nor sympathy for, those less fortunate than themselves.

I hopped off a freight in Oklahoma City late in a bitter November night, a half-starved and filthy bum. And almost immediately I was taken into custody by two patrol-car cops. Naturally, I thought it was a pinch, and their kindly words sarcasm. But such was not the way of Oklahoma City cops. They drove me to a city shelter where I was fed and able to clean up. Then, they turned me over to another pair who chauffeured me into the downtown district. These last two offered me a choice of "hotels" for the night—the city jail, a section of which was open to homeless men, or one of the several city courtrooms which were also left open at night for the benefit of such as I. Their advice was that, due to overcrowding at the jail, I sleep on one of the courtroom benches. I followed this suggestion, and got my first good night's sleep in weeks. I had no bedding, of course, but the benches were clean and the room well-heated. When morning came, and I again took to the street, I felt wonderfully refreshed and hopeful.

There were several soup kitchens about the city, such as the one I had been taken to the night before. But while I was a bum, and no better than any of the others, I winced at the thought of playing the "mission stiff"—of being drawn into the shabbiness and despair of men who had lost all initiative. I had had no choice last night. Now, being merely hungry instead of starving, I was determined to find some other way of procuring food, or to do without.

I wandered over into the south part of town, up and down Reno and Washington streets which were then a kind of poor man's paradise. There were signs offering new shoes for a dollar, complete men's outfits ("slightly used") for two-fifty, clean hotel rooms for five dollars a month. There were stores and markets pleading with customers to buy butter at ten cents a pound, choice porterhouse steak at twelve cents a pound and high grade coffee at three pounds for a quarter. Eggs were six cents a dozen, milk a nickel a quart, bread three loaves for five cents. As for the restaurants—clean, wholesome-smelling places with their menus posted in the windows—they were practically giving their wares away.

Three large hotcakes with sausage, butter and syrup and coffee—for *five cents!* Roast beef dinner with four vegetables and beverage, for fifteen cents. Ham or bacon and eggs with French fries, hot buttered biscuits, marmalade and coffee, for ten cents. A little mental calculation told me that a man could live handsomely in Oklahoma City for considerably less than a dollar a day. Unfortunately, I didn't have a dollar, nor even the one-hundredth part of one.

Mouth watering, I turned away from the menu I was studying, almost knocking down a brisk, bird-like little man who had taken up a position beside me.

"Jim Thompson's boy, ain't you? Sure you are, spittin' image of him." He bobbed his head, grinning at me happily. "What the hell you doin' in town? Your dad with you? Bet you don't remember me, do you?"

I was about to admit that I didn't know him, but he was rattling on, introducing himself before I had the chance. He was a one-time saloon owner from Anadarko, my birthplace, where Pop had been a United States marshal and later sheriff. Now, he and his wife were operating a rooming house here in Oklahoma City, and nothing would do but that I, the son of the "best damned friend" he'd ever had, should move into their establishment.

"I'd like to," I said. "I'm sure I'd be very comfortable, but I don't think I'll be staying in Oklahoma City."

"Why not?" he demanded promptly. "Best damned city in the best damned state in the union. What you going to find anywhere else that you won't find here?"

"Look," I said, "I can't rent a room anywhere. I'm broke, and I can't find a job and——"

"Hell," he snorted, "you think I thought you was dressed up for a masquerade party? Sure you're broke. Sure you ain't workin'. Who the hell is?"

I would feel perfectly at home at his place, he declared, for all of his other tenants were also broke. Now and then, they picked up an odd job and made a dollar or so, whereupon they paid him what they could. I could do the same and I must or he would feel highly insulted.

So I went home with him, and his wife fixed me a whopping breakfast. And all day long, he and she were running in and out of the room they had assigned me—the best in the house—doing their humble utmost to be friendly and helpful. They dug me up an old suit which, while ill-fitting and worn, was splendid compared with the one I was wearing. They even brought me an old but serviceable typewriter and a quantity of paper.

I have many sharp memories of that winter in Oklahoma City. Of writing two novels and selling neither. Of selling three hundred thousand words of trade-journal material and collecting on less than a tenth of it. Of distributing circulars at ten cents an hour, and digging sewer ditches at nothing per. Of being drawn into a wholesale swindle by Allie Ivers. And of a little streetwalker named Trixie.

The sewer job was sponsored by the state, as a so-called "relief" program. But as I saw it, the only relief it gave was to a handful of political fatcats, the project "supervisors," and to the real estate owners. The supervisors got fancy salaries for doing nothing. The real estate boys got valuable improvements on their property for next to nothing. We, the men who dug eleven-foot sewer ditches under hazardous, backbreaking conditions—well, I shall tell you what some of us got.

I was tipped off to the job by two former oil field workers, Jiggs and Shorty—of whom much more later—who were tenants at the place where I was living. Lacking carfare, we walked the eight miles back and forth to work. It was either raining or snowing throughout the time of our employment, and our clothes were never thoroughly thawed and dried out from one shift to the next. As for the project itself, I have never anywhere seen men treated with such cold-blooded shabbiness.

There were no men left on top of the ditch to keep the dug earth moved back. Thus, as the ditch deepened, it was virtually impossible to throw the dirt up and out as far as it had to be thrown. You would load your long-handled spoon (shovel), grip it by the very tip of the handle, and hurl the soggy earth upward with all your might. It would reach the crest of the ditch and balance there hazardously. Then, slowly but surely, it would topple and slide, and a fourth of it would fall back in your face. Worst of all, however, was the fact that the ditches were unshored. There was no bracing to keep them from caving in, and being deep in saturated earth they caved in constantly.

Those cave-ins were terrifying things. Just how terrifying you may understand if, like most people, you have a horror of being buried alive. There were two kinds of them, one a sudden bulging in of the sides which pinned you around the knees or the waist. In the other, the most frightening, the cave-in was from the top. The sky would suddenly disappear like a lamp blown out, and frenziedly you would hurl yourself forward, race madly away from the collapsing area. And a moment later, in the spot where you had been working, there was no longer a ditch. Only eleven feet of half-frozen mud.

I don't know why the job was managed as it was, for having to do much of the same work twice was certainly poor economy. I suppose the wretched state of affairs was due not so much to bad management as no management. Generally, the supervisors knew little or nothing about construction work and made only token appearances on the job. The supervising, such as it was, was done by relief-roll straw bosses, men too fearful for their own paychecks to point out planning errors or demand better conditions for the workmen.

When our two-week pay period ended—we were allowed to work only twelve days a month—Jiggs, Shorty and I tramped into town and presented our time numbers at the project offices. Our wage had been set at one dollar and a quarter for an eight-hour day, so each of us was entitled to fifteen dollars. But only Jiggs' check was for the full and correct amount. Shorty received five dollars and I drew a check for two-fifty.

We protested, of course, but the well-fed gentleman behind the wicket waved us away indifferently.

"Don't talk to me. All I do is hand out the checks. Go out and argue with your project timekeeper."

"That's swell," I said. "And how long am I going to have to wait for a check after I get it straightened out?"

"How do I know?" he shrugged. "I got nothing to do with it."

Shorty and I argued a while longer, but it was a waste of breath. Finally we gave up, and the following morning we went back out to the job. Our timekeeper wasn't there. Like us—although he was drawing a much better salary—he also was working only two weeks a month. I managed to get his home address, and Shorty and I went out to see him. A young man—and not a very bright one—he listened to us with an air of absent-minded virtue.

"You must be mistaken," he said absently. "Your checks had to be for the right amount."

"Look," I said, "maybe they had to be for the right amount, but they weren't. Are you sure you turned us in for the full twelve days?"

"I did if you worked."

"Well, don't you remember that we did work? Don't you know that we did?"

"Can't remember everyone," he said sullenly. "All I know is that if you worked, I marked you down."

Shorty, whose shoulders were almost as broad as he was tall, began to curse. He declared that he had ten dollars coming, and he intended to get it in cash or to collect it from someone's hide. Considerably alarmed, the timekeeper produced his records.

"There you are," he pointed out placatingly. "J. Thompson—fifteen dollars. And here, I got your friend down for the same amount."

I looked through the pages of names. As I had suspected, there were two other J. Thompsons, one with two days work to his credit and the other with six. Much the same situation existed in the case of Shorty, whose last name, like mine, was a common one. Obviously, due to the gross stupidity of the timekeeper, our earnings had gone to the wrong men.

What did he intend to do about it? Well, fellas, there was really nothing he could do. He suggested, however, that we might look up the men who had received our checks and demand an exchange.

"Fat chance," Shorty scoffed bitterly. "You think they'd hand 'em over, huh? How the hell we going to prove they even got 'em?"

"Well—uh—"

"Anyway," I said, "we've already cashed our checks. We've got no way of proving that we didn't get the full amount."

"Well, uh—" A fearful glance at Shorty—"I'm awful sorry, fellas, but ... "

Shorty stamped out, cursing, too murderously furious to trust himself in the young man's presence. We were rooked, he said, as we headed back to town. There was nothing we could do but take it and forget it and concentrate on finding a quick job to make up for our loss.

"I don't know," I said. "It probably won't do any good, but I think I'll go up to the state offices of the project and give them an argument."

"Power to you," he shrugged glumly. "Me, I know when I'm licked."

The project headquarters were in a major downtown office building. I spent the better part of the day there, shuttling from one hack to another, and of course I got no satisfaction at all. Late in the afternoon, I gave up and walked back to the elevators.

The door to one of the cars slid open. I was about to step into it when the operator barred my way. I had seen him and the other two operators staring at me while I was in the project offices. They had left their cars alternately and wandered down the corridor, glancing in at me through the open office doors. Now this man barred my way, a sly smile spreading under his deadpan expression.

"Can't carry you, chief," he said briskly. "Have to use the service elevator."

"What?" I said. "But I'm no delivery boy. I've got as much right to——"

"Sorry. Got my orders. Down the end of the hall and to your right. Man there will take you down."

It was an insult, a slur brought on, as I saw it, by my shabby appearance. In the south, a self-respecting person does not swallow such affronts. I tried to shove my way past him, and was firmly shoved back. Before I could force my way into the car, the door slammed in my face.

I punched the signal button. Another elevator came, and its operator treated me exactly as the first one had.

"Have to take the service elevator, fellow. Down to the end of the corridor and to your right."

"Now what the hell is this?" I said angrily. "Who the hell told you to do this? I'm here on legitimate business. If you think you can shove me around just because I'm not well-dressed——"

"Aahh, look fellow,"—he grinned at me pleadingly—"it's kind of a joke, see? An old friend of yours had us pull it on you. Me and the other boys are just doin' what we're told to."

"Joke?" I said. "An old friend of mine? But——"

"You'll see. And don't tell him I tipped you off, huh?"

The door closed. Bewildered, I went down the hall and pressed the bell for the service elevator. It arrived instantly, operated by a frail, blond, blue-eyed young man. The word STARTER was emblazoned across the jacket of his tuxedo-style uniform.

"What took you so long?" he said. "Been arguing with my hired hands?"

"I might have known it," I said. "Allie Ivers!"

XIII

ALLIE HAD CAUGHT A GLIMPSE OF ME WHEN I ENTERED THE BUILDING THAT FORENOON. Being his own boss, practically speaking, and with very little real work to do, he had chosen this elaborately backhanded way of renewing our acquaintance.

"And about time, too," he declared, as he headed the car upwards. "A smart guy like you hanging around relief job offices! I'm going to have to take you in hand!"

He stopped the elevator at roof level and motioned for me to follow him. I did so, and he unlocked the door of a penthouse with his pass key and waved me inside.

It was a very elaborate layout, a beautifully furnished combination apartment and office. Stepping over to the bar, Allie selected several bottles at random and mixed us two huge drinks. We clinked glasses and, rather cautiously, I sat down next to him on one of the leather-upholstered stools.

"Whose place is this, Allie?" I said. "And don't tell me it's yours!"

"Belongs to an oil man," he shrugged. "He's only here about a week out of the month. What are you so jumpy about, anyway? I've never got you into any trouble, have I?"

"Oh, no!" I said. "What about the time you hooked me into taking that cop's pants and the time you got me mixed up in the Capone gang, and the time—well, that last time in Lincoln when you had me drive the cab for you?"

Allie grinned and reached for the bottles. I asked him how he'd gotten away from the country club that night.

"Nothing to it," he said casually. "I gave the doorman my cigar to hold. Then, I helped the babe into the cab and drove off."

"Without any clothes on?"

"Well, it was a warm night. We dressed down the road a ways. . . . Speaking of clothes, incidentally, let's go back here."

We went into one of the outsize bedrooms, and Allie rolled back the closet doors. Inside were at least a dozen men's suits, three or four topcoats and racks of shoes and ties. Allie indicated that I was to help myself.

"They won't be a perfect fit, but it'll be good enough. And don't argue about it. You're just going to borrow them for the night."

212

"But why? I can't——"

"How would you like to edit a magazine? Be the publicity man for a big fraternal order?"

"Well, fine, but——"

"Then do what I tell you, and I'll order up dinner for us."

I could get no further information out of him at the moment, so with considerable hesitation I exchanged my clothes for some of the splendid garb in the closet. Except for the shoes, which were a trifle large, everything fitted me perfectly. By the time I had finished dressing, the waiter arrived with our dinner—two outsize porterhouse steaks with all the accessories for a modest banquet. Allie signed the check (using the tenant's name, of course) and wrote in a five dollar tip for the waiter.

"The guy never checks his bills," he explained as we sat down to the meal: "I throw parties up here all the time."

He went on to explain at some length and somewhat apologetically that he had not, appearances to the contrary, sunk to doing an honest day's work for an honest day's pay. With the elevator boys and charwomen acting as his agents, he was working several small but profitable rackets in the building—selling chances on punchboards, peddling raffle tickets and so on, collecting a cut from the office to office peddlers. Also, needless to say—although he said it—he was stealing.

"Nothing very big, you understand. A few bucks worth of stamps in one place and a few typewriter ribbons in another and a box or so of stationery in another. I got a guy that takes the stuff for a short profit."

I shook my head. "Allie, what makes you go on like this? Why don't you do something with your life? You're smart. You've got a nice personality and you make a good appearance. If you'd act sensible, stop making like a cheap crook——"

He was grinning at me thinly, looking me up and down. "Yeah, Jimmie? What would it get me? Rides on freight trains? Ten-cent meals and a job digging ditches? Rags for clothes and a weedpatch for a bed?"

"Well, all right," I said, stubbornly. "Maybe I'm not doing so good right now, but I'll pull out of it. I——"

"Right you are," Allie nodded. "You're on your way to pulling out of it right now. After tonight you'll be sitting pretty."

"How? Just what am I supposed to do, anyway?"

"You know all about publicity, don't you? How to put out a small magazine?"

"Well, I don't know *all* about it, but——"

"You know enough. Just let these guys that I introduce you to know that you know. I'll do the rest."

Again, I could get no more information from him. He did insist—he swore to it—that he would involve me in no trouble, and I had to be satisfied with that.

We finished eating. Urging me to help myself to the liquor, he went down to the locker room and changed clothes. He returned with a briefcase which he filled with bottles from the bar.

By this time, naturally, I had had more than a little to drink and the qualms which I usually felt in Allie's presence were fairly well desensitized. As I have indicated, I was very fond of him. In his own peculiar way, he had always tried to be kind to me; and now, I hoped, in my hour of need, he might pull a plump rabbit from the fiscal hat.

I accompanied him downstairs, and we taxied to an address on upper Broadway. We debarked there, and I followed him upstairs to the second-floor lodge rooms. The men he introduced me to, as I saw them, were semi-prosperous, lower middle class citizens—master barbers, delicatessen owners, head bookkeepers and the like. Genial men, wise enough in their own way, but not too well-informed when they strayed outside of it. Allie seemed very popular with them. With him vouching for me as "the well-known author and editor," I was looked upon with almost embarrassing awe.

After a score or so of introductions, Allie ushered me into a kind of board room and seated me at the head of the long table therein. Then, having distributed the bottles around at strategic points, he advised me that everything was going nicely and departed for the outer rooms.

Some thirty minutes elapsed before the door reopened and Allie ushered in a group of the brothers. They ranged themselves around the table, and the bottles began moving from hand to hand. As the room filled with tobacco smoke and the gentlemen with high-grade bourbon, Allie got down to the business of the evening.

For some months past, he pointed out, the lodge had considered the establishment of a small magazine or newspaper—something which every self-respecting fraternal order had and which this one certainly must have if the brothers were to go on holding their heads high. The delay in inaugurating such a periodical had reached the point of becoming a lodge disgrace; there was no longer any excuse for it. Here before them sat one of the country's most renowned publicists and editors. Purely out of friendship and the desire to help along a good cause, he (*me, that is*) had consented to get the publication started without fee ... except, of course, his personal expenses. All that was required now, was that the good brothers present, these more substantial members who comprised the backbone of the lodge, should underwrite the proposition and——

One of the brothers cleared his throat. Just how much was this—uh—this thing going to cost?

"Three thousand dollars," said Allie. And then, as his eyes swept the table, weighing the brothers, seeing a troubled expression spread from one face to another—"That's Mr. Thompson's offhand estimate, I should say. What about it, Jim? Could we put out something a little smaller for about—uh"—another lightning-sharp glance at the brothers—"about two thousand?"

I nodded, looking, I suspect, not a little troubled myself, for I had given him no offhand estimates nor any other kind. Before I could do more than nod, Allie was proceeding:

"Call it two thousand. That'll be one hundred and fifty each for you gentlemen, or a total of eighteen hundred, and I'll throw in the remaining two hundred. Until the loan is repaid, we'll hold a lien on all advertising and subscription fees—that's Mr. Thompson's suggestion—and each of us will receive a lifetime subscription free of charge. In other words, we'll have the honor of funding the publication and be liberally repaid for——"

"Allie," I said, rising to my feet. "You can't—I can't—"

"Of course," said Allie smoothly, "I'd forgotten you had another appointment. You run right along now, and I'll see you later."

"But——"

"You don't have to apologize. We all understand," said Allie. "Go right ahead, and I'll get on with the meeting."

He got on with it, drawing the attention of the brothers away from me to him. After a moment of standing there awkwardly, with the group but not of it, I left. It was all I could do, as I saw it. There would be later opportunities to block Allie's swindle, and I would crack down on him then.

Waiting at the foot of the stairs outside, I wondered what his next step would be, how he intended to extract eighteen hundred dollars from a group such as this. Certainly they wouldn't have so much cash on them tonight. Neither, with their slender resources, would they hand over their checks for one hundred and fifty each. They were doing very well for the times, yes, but they were still very small fish in the puddle. To men like these, the loss of one hundred and fifty dollars would be a severe financial blow.

I was still wondering how Allie intended to swing it when he came hustling down the stairs. He was obviously expecting an assault of reproaches and questions, so, just to confound him, I said nothing at all. We returned to the penthouse in an almost dead silence, and silently I went into the bedroom and redressed in my own clothes. Allie looked at me quizzically as I returned to the living room.

"Well, we pulled it off, Jim."

"We did?" I said.

"Sit down and have a drink and I'll tell you about it."

I hesitated but I sat down and accepted a drink. Allie told me about it. The lodge brothers would draw personal notes in our favor, co-signed by one another. Since they were all good credit risks there would be not the slightest trouble in discounting the notes for cash. All he and I had to do was accompany the various lodge members to the bank and collect the money.

"We can wind it all up in a day or two, and then——"

"And then we skip town?"

"I'm telling you," said Allie. "These little job printing shops are all screaming for work. We go to one of 'em and sign him up to put us out a little throwaway for a year—a few dozen copies each month of the cheapest thing he can put together. He does everything, see, even collects news from the lodge. We give him maybe three hundred bucks, and he bills us for a thousand. The rest of the eighteen hundred is your expenses."

I sat staring at him. Allie's pleased grin slowly changed to an uncomfortable frown.

"Well, what's the matter with it? Just show me where there's room for a rumble."

"There isn't any," I said. "It's airtight. Your friends at the lodge may squawk, but there's nothing they can do."

"Friends, hell! They're chumps. I've been trying to figure out a way of taking 'em ever since I joined the outfit. . . . We're the only friends in this deal, just you and me. I've known you half your lifetime and I've always liked you, and——"

"And I've always liked you," I said. "You were always on the make, but you did it in such a way that it seemed more humorous than criminal. When you took anyone it was usually a sharpie or at least someone who could afford to be taken. . . . Guys like these tonight, poor trusting bastards with some little job or business—you wouldn't have touched them in the old days, Allie. I can't really believe that you'd do it now."

I set my glass down and stood up. Scowling, he stepped in front of me.

"You're not going to play, Jim? You come in here today flat on your ass and I practically hand you a grand—hell, I'll make it a grand; you can have a thousand for your end and I'll——"

"I'm not going to play," I said.

"This isn't the old days, Jim. We can't call our shots any more. Why, Christ, I'm really doing this for your sake, anyway. You can't back out on me, leave me to try to explain to those birds, after all the trouble I——"

"I'm not backing out," I said. "I was never in. I warned you in the beginning that I wouldn't go for any swindle."

"What the hell are you going to do, then? Dig ditches or sponge off your friends? I've got a pretty sweet setup here, but if you think I'm going to—to—"

I gave him a level look. He turned his head, scowling but shamefaced. "Aahh, hell, Jim, you know I didn't mean that. It's just that I'm pretty damned disappointed. You know how you'd feel if a guy you'd always kind of, well . . . ?"

"I know exactly what you mean," I said. "Now, do I walk downstairs or do you take me on the elevator?"

We rode down on the elevator. Diffidently, each of us hurt by the other, we parted at the entrance. We had several casual encounters in Oklahoma City after that, but the diffidence, the stiffness, remained. Allie was ashamed of himself. He was angry with me for making him ashamed.

Years passed before we met again in another city, and Allie, still sore and shamed, yet wanting to crack the ice between us, found a way of reestablishing our friendship. The medium he chose virtually frightened me witless—more so, I should say, than I ordinarily am. But though it almost turned my hair gray, I think it was worth it.

I'll tell you about it at the proper time.

XIV

SHORTY AND JIGGS KNEW THE LOCATION OF A POT OF GOLD, figuratively but none the less golden: an abandoned oil well with a mile of high-grade pipe in it. The well was deep in the heart of eastern Texas on part of a one-time plantation. For years past the worn-out soil of the area had gone unfarmed, and was now a jungle of weeds, bush and second-growth timber. Its present owner would gladly permit the removal of the pipe for a fraction of its resale value.

As Shorty told the story, the plantation owner had been so embittered at the drilling contractor's failure to strike oil that he had chased him and his employees from the property at gunpoint. The contractor had sued for recovery of his machinery and equipment. The plantation owner had filed counter suit. Having more money than the contractor, he won after years of litigation. But his victory was an empty one. News of the gentleman's bad temper and stubbornness had spread among the oil field fraternity, and no one would touch the job on a share-salvage basis. It was cash-on-the-line or no deal. So, with the land owner now nearly bankrupt and still as stubborn as ever, it was no deal.

When he died, his heirs split and sold off the property as small farms. As the land went bad, the farms moved from one owner to another. One of them was no longer sufficient to support a family. It took several, and the original forty-acre plots were consolidated and reconsolidated. And even then large areas were so depleted as to be not worth tilling. Thus, the case with the land on which "our" well stood.

"I don't know, Shorty," I said, when he first told me the story. "It sounds like another oil field fairy tale, just too damned good to be true. You actually saw it yourself?"

"Damned right I did. I didn't believe the story myself when I first heard it, so not having nothing else to do, I looked the place up. I talked to the guy that owns the land, and then I waded on out through the jungle and looked at the well. It's there, by God. More than five thousand feet of highgrade casing. And it's free—I mean, it ain't frozen in the hole. I rocked it and I know."

"But it might be cemented part way down. If it was cemented, say at a thousand feet, you could still get some sway."

"Why the hell would it be cemented? They didn't strike oil."

"Well," I shrugged, "I don't know. Maybe that plantation owner did it.

218

He might have been afraid that someone would steal the pipe, so——"

"But he couldn't have got it out himself if he did that! Ain't that right? . . . I know how you feel, Jim. It sounds so bee-yoo-tiful you figure there's just got to be something wrong, but there ain't a danged thing."

"The derrick and the rig and the tools are still there? They're still in good shape?"

"Good enough to do the job. Naturally, they ain't first-class after all these years."

"Why couldn't we just truck the above-ground stuff off and sell it?"

"Aah——" Shorty gave me a disgusted look. "An oil field hand like you asking a question like that? It ain't oil country down there. What'd you have left by the time you hauled twenty tons of machinery out of the backwoods and shipped it a thousand miles? Pipe—casing—is different. There's a dozen pipe yards within a hundred miles. We get it trucked to the railroad on credit and sell our bill of lading."

Shorty was a driller and Jiggs a tool dresser—a full cable-rig crew. They needed a third man—I was their candidate—to help with the rigging up, and serve as boilerman and roustabout when the job proper began. They also needed about three hundred dollars for supplies, repairs and fuel oil for the boiler.

Three hundred dollars. That was all that stood between us and the three-way split of a small fortune!

We talked about it endlessly. It got so that we could talk about nothing else. We would sit around our freezing rooms at night, dining off of stale bread and tea, squeezing the last crumbs from a nickel sack of tobacco and passing the butt from hand to hand: three half-starved ragamuffins talking and dreaming of riches. We got out pencil and paper, and we argued and we haggled and we figured and we *figured*. And that awesome, that terrible and frustrating three hundred dollars began to shrink. . . . Food? Well, we would get that farmer to help us out for an increased share in the profits. Travel and other expenses? Well, we would travel by foot and freight, and nuts to the other expenses. New parts for the machinery? Well, Shorty and Jiggs both had hand tools and our time was worth nothing. We would simply rebuild the old parts.

We cut the three hundred down to one hundred, but there we seemed to be stuck. For we would need at least a hundred for fuel oil, and that was something we could neither beg, borrow nor invent.

Since we didn't stand a chance of raising a hundred, I gave up at this point. But my mechanically inclined friends were not so easily defeated. After conferring together several days, and making liberal use of paper and pencil, they came to me with a solution to the problem.

There were acres of brush and timber around the well. We would simply convert the oil/gas feed boiler to a wood burner, rigging a blower to obtain the necessary high degree of heat. . . . So that was taken care of, but still I hung back. I had several promising manuscripts in the mail (manuscripts which *I* felt were promising) and I was about to complete a novel. Too, and this I suppose was my main reason for delaying, I was reluctant to exchange my present situation, poor as it was, for weeks and perhaps months of certain and undiluted hardship.

I begged for time, and grudgingly Jiggs and Shorty gave it to me. It was the aforementioned Trixie who sped me, or caused me to be sped, upon my way. And when I say sped I mean exactly that.

Trixie had come to my door in the guise of a necktie peddler, a waif with a heart-shaped face, indiscernible breasts and a pair of the largest feet I have ever seen. Naturally, I was not buying any neckties, nor was I interested in the commodity which she was actually selling. But I invited her in anyway for a cup of the tea I had just fixed, and she remained to chat and rest her outsize feet.

The poor girl was undoubtedly a moron; I have seen very few prostitutes who were not. But as she began dropping in on me daily and we got to know each other better, I acquired a high regard for her intelligence in at least one respect. Moron or no, Trixie was a damned good literary critic.

She would lie on my bed, her toes hanging over the footrail like bananas, while I read to her from my latest efforts. And always her response was the one I had hoped to achieve. She laughed in all the right places, she wept in all the right places. By turns, as I turned the pages, she was pensive, gay, frowningly thoughtful. And when I got a rejection, ah, then indeed was she a tonic beyond price for my withering ego.

I have heard some pretty good cussing in my time, but never anything like the epithets which Trixie applied to the editors in faraway New York—those malicious imbeciles who turned down my manuscripts. The obscenities which spewed effortlessly from her rosebud lips were occasionally such as to make me blush, and I would suggest that she was allowing partisanship to carry her away. But Trixie, deferential as she usually was, would have none of this milksop attitude.

Trixie and I became very fond of each other. But she was depressed and disturbed by my insistence on a purely platonic friendship. I had been "awful nice" to her. Now why wouldn't I let her be nice to me, return favor for favor, in the only way that she could?

I tried to persuade her that her company and conversation were more than ample recompense for any small kindnesses I had extended, but this she was unwilling to believe . . . Was there something—uh—wrong with me, perhaps? Didn't I like "it"? Did I think she wasn't clean? Well, then?

Not only did my continence trouble Trixie, it was also, she advised me, seriously upsetting her "boyfriend, Al" ("Owl," she pronounced it). Al, it seemed, had a great deal of pride. He liked to keep things even-Steven, and he didn't take nothing off of no one. Unless I allowed her to do the "right thing," he was going to call a halt to her visits.

Well, I had some ideas about the pride of a man like Al—if a pimp can be called a man—and I passed them along to her. And that, of course, was a serious mistake. Trixie's face turned white, then red, then white again. She cursed me, she raked, she wept. . . . Al was "wunnerful," she scream-sobbed. He was the finest, kindest, nicest man in the world and no one had better say he wasn't because she'd kill 'em if they did!

Finally, she stamped out, tearfully vowing that I was nine kinds of a bastard and that she would never speak to me again as long as she lived. Two days later, around noon, she returned.

Her little head was high in the air. In place of the customary plough shoes, her gondola feet were squeezed into runover satin slippers, and she was otherwise decked out in rummage-sale finery. There had been a big change in her life's station, she haughtily informed me. She was now a "hostess" in a combination whore house-blind pig, a position which the all-wise and kindly Al had obtained for her. And if I didn't think I was too goddamned good, she and he hereby invited me to attend the grand opening.

I murmured congratulations, squeezing out a compliment to be conveyed to Al. Immediately, Trixie's haughtiness vanished, and weeping, she flung her arms around me. . . . Honest, she'd been just sick about the way she'd acted, calling me all those dirty names. But she simply hadn't been able to help it. Anything that hurt Al, it hurt her a thousand times worse. It just drove her out of her mind, and—and, well, would I please come? Al would be there, and I could see how wunnerful he was. By accepting their hospitality for the evening, I would free them of their onerous feeling of obligation toward me.

"But—" I hesitated, uncomfortably. "But what about your boss, Trixie? The guy that owns the place?"

"It's all fixed, Tommy. You an' Al are gonna get all you want to drink all evening long, and it won't cost you a penny!"

"But I can't let you pay for——"

"I already *did* pay for it. You know." She blushed prettily. "I spent all last night paying for it. Me an' the boss—well, he took it out in trade and I'm taking it out in trade, and if you don't come . . . "

She looked up at me anxiously.

I told her I would come, and she squealed with delight. "An' you be sure and drink plenty, too," she said, as she gave me the address of the establishment, "because plenty's what I paid for."

The place was a barn-like old building, a former residence on upper Washington Street. The thug who looked me over and admitted me waved me toward the living room area which was now equipped with tables, chairs and a homemade bar. A sign behind the latter fixture announced that choc beer was fifteen cents, whiskey two shots for a quarter. Beneath this announcement was the large lettered word C-A-S-H and the legend, In God We Trust And You Ain't God.

Although it was still early in the evening, the room was already crowded with guests—largely of the type one would shun from meeting in a dark alley. Trixie spotted me in the doorway, greeted me with a hug and led me back to a rear table. At it was seated a burly, slack-jawed giant, none other than the wunnerful "Owl."

Trixie introduced us and scurried away for refreshments. He looked me over and I looked him over, and it was one of those things . . . hate at first sight. Probably I would have detested him just as much if I had not known what he was.

We were still giving each other the cold-eye when Trixie returned, but she was too happy at having brought us, her dearest ones, together to notice the congealing atmosphere. Advising us to holler when we ran dry, she gave us each a bright smile and returned to her party.

The whiskey was white corn and was served in heavy glass jelly jars of about three and a half ounces capacity. Owl took his down at a swallow, and without any change in expression, and chased it with an infinitesimal sip from the choc pitcher. He set his glass down with a look that dared me to repeat the performance. I did so and somehow, miraculously, managed not to strangle or cough. Then, by way of pointing up my feelings about him, I poured my chaser into the glass instead of drinking from the pitcher.

A brief flash of his eyes told me that the insult had scored, but ostensibly he took no notice. Turning suddenly genial, he obtained another round of drinks from a passing hostess, and called for bottoms up again. We downed them. A third round arrived. We downed that, too.

He weaved slightly in his chair, then leaned forward bracing his elbows on the table.

"T-Tommy—" he coughed, "Tommy, you're a nice guy an' it's a real pleasure to meet you."

"Swell," I said, flatly.

"Y-you like me, too, Tommy?"

"How," I said, "could I help it?"

"But you don't like Trixie, do you? Think you're too good to take favors off'n me an' Trixie?"

"Now, look," I said, "let's get this straight, once and for all. Trixie doesn't owe me anything, and even if she did I wouldn't——"

"S'all right, Tommy. No need to apologize. If you think you're too goddamned good to lay my girl—*hic!*—it's perfeckly all—*hic!*"

He weaved again, and his meaty right hand came out. Obviously, or so I thought, he intended to give me a friendly pat on the shoulder, and for Trixie's sake I decided to endure it.

"—s'all right. Unnerstand perfeckly. Think you're too damned good for Trixie, why—*hic!*" The hand wobbled, suddenly, and swung sideways. It landed on my ear with an agonizing *cr-aack*!

The blow almost knocked me from my chair. Righting myself, I started to make a grab for him, but he was beaming at me waterily, too drunk—apparently—to realize what he had done. Moreover, Trixie had suddenly returned to our table, frowning at me, smiling tenderly at him.

"Tommy hurt you, Owl? Did he? What'd you say to him, Tommy?"

"Naah." He waved her away grinning. "Tommy an' me are buddies, ain't we, Tommy? Just havin' a friendly little conversation. Bring us some more whiz an' leave us alone."

"That's right, Trixie," I said. "Bring us some drinks and leave us alone. Owl and I are getting along fine."

Trixie gave me a doubtful look, something between an apologetic smile and a frown. But she brought more of the white lightning and choc, and left us alone again. As usual, we downed the drinks at a gulp.

It was simply too much too fast, particularly in view of the fact that I had eaten almost nothing all day. A thunderbolt seemed to race up my spine and explode in my skull, and for a split second I lost consciousness. When I came to, Owl had returned to his grievance.

So I thought I was too good for him and Trixie? Thought they were some kind of white trash, maybe? Well, that was all right. If that's the way I wanted to feel, why——

His heavy hand wobbled and swung again. Again it cracked painfully against my ear.

Trixie started for us at once, of course. But I smiled at Owl amiably and he grinned at me woozily, still the innocent unaware, so Trixie went back to her own table.

Someone brought us more whiskey. Rather slowly now, studying each other covertly, Owl and I took it down. I wasn't quite sure yet about his condition and intentions. I was reasonably confident that he knew what he was doing, that he was doing it deliberately and with malice afore-thought. Believing that I would do anything to keep the peace for Trixie's sake, he intended to sit here and gradually slap me silly.

That was his scheme, I thought. But I was not absolutely positive of it, and I had to be positive before starting a riot in a place like this. Also, I needed just a little more to drink to put me in the proper fettle.

The jelly glasses were refilled. Emptied. Surreptitiously, I lowered mine below the table edge and thence into my pocket. Owl licked his lips cautiously and picked up his favorite conversation piece. His hand began its preliminary wobbling.

It darted, swung and landed. Smack on my ear for the third time.

By now we had become the cynosure of all eyes, to coin a phrase, one pair of which belonged to the proprietor. So while Trixie, confident that all was well between us, stayed where she was, we received a visit from the bouncer.

"What the hell's going on here?" he demanded. "You guys want to fight, get the hell out in the alley."

"Fight?" I grinned bewilderedly. "Alley? Do you want to go out in the alley, Owl?"

"Not me," said Owl firmly, and in extremely clear accents. Then, remembering his pose: "We're ol' buddies, mister. Whash all this stuff 'bout fightin'?"

The bouncer scowled, shrugged and walked away. I pushed back my chair.

"'Scuse me a minute, ol' buddy," I said. "Got to go to the john."

"S-sure." He bobbed his head drunkenly. "I'll jusht—hey, where's your glass?"

"The girl must have taken it away," I said. "You order up another while I'm gone."

I walked back to the men's room. Stepping up on the filthy sink, I pushed up the narrow window to the alley and unlatched the screen. I stepped back down again, removed one of my socks and slid the jelly glass inside. I knotted the open end, dropped it into my pocket and returned to the table.

Apparently Owl had got the notion that I had not intended to return, and now seeing me meekly before him again—a sitting duck as he saw it—he could scarcely conceal his malicious pleasure. It was a situation made to order for pimps, being able to beat hell out of someone who could not strike back. Tossing his drink down, he started working up to the fourth blow almost before I had finished mine.

I slipped the sock out of my pocket and waited.

His hand waggled and found its target. I swung the sock.

He saw it coming and tried to fling himself sideways. It caught him on the side of his head, and the blow combined with his lurch sent him sprawling and stumbling across the room.

He landed on top of a table occupied by four oil field workers and their ladies. But this was not, I am happy to say, the end of his travels. Showered with whiskey, beer and splintered glass, the outraged group laid hands on him, men and women together. They hoisted him up and hurled him, even as children might hurl a doll. And Owl went sailing through the air, screaming and kicking, scattering people and furniture and glassware until he crashed against the far wall.

It was a wonderful brawl, with Owl the center of attraction, but I got to see very little of it. The bouncer and the proprietor were heading toward me. So was Trixie, a beer pitcher swinging in each hand as she ploughed through the growing riot and wreckage. I fled into the toilet, and out the window.

I trotted down the alley, wondering if it might not be an excellent idea to leave town for a while. By the time I reached my rooming house, I had come to a decision.

I talked with Jiggs and Shorty, and we all conferred with our landlord. He generously allowed us to make up blanket rolls from our bedding, and also lent us five dollars. Early the next morning we caught a freight south.

XV

JIGGS HUGGED THE TOP JOINT OF CASING AND BRACED HIS FEET AGAINST THE DERRICK FLOOR. He rocked his body to and fro, then stepped back frowning.

"Well?" said Shorty nervously. "What's the matter? It's just like I told you, ain't it?"

Jiggs shook his head ambiguously. "You try it, Jim. See what you think."

I hugged the pipe—it was twenty-four inches in diameter here at the well's top—and tried to rock it. I stepped back, avoiding my friends' eyes.

"Well, how about it?" Shorty blurted out. "Goddammit, what's wrong with you guys? You—you ain't going to tell me that pipe's cemented!"

"Well," Jiggs shrugged, "maybe it ain't *cement*, but——"

"'Course it ain't! What sense'd there be putting cement in a duster?"

"——but it'll sure as hell do until cement comes along. I don't think— I'm afraid we ain't ever gonna ..." He broke off, and there was a heavy silence for a moment. "Oh, Christ," he said at last "What the hell, anyway?"

Shorty looked at us, and we both looked away. He said, almost pleadingly, "Now, look, you guys. It's just mudded up—silted down. What d'you expect after all these years?"

"Sure," Jiggs sighed. "Bound to be something like that. Be damned funny if it did rock free."

"Ain't that the way you feel, Jim?" Shorty looked eagerly at me. "Don't you figure it's just silt or mud?"

"Sure," I said. "We hook the bull wheel into it, and it'll pull slick as snake oil."

"Sure," Jiggs repeated. "Sure it will."

I was practically certain that it wouldn't, and so was he. And so, for that matter, was Shorty. Perhaps he had been able to get some motion from the pipe on his original visit to the well, but he must have known that something had been gripping it solidly and not too many hundreds of feet below ground. He had deceived himself nourishing an almost baseless hope until it had become belief. And now here we all were, and there was nothing to do but go ahead.

Silently, we cleaned out the tool house and spread out our blanket rolls. We built a fire, and set a lard-can "kettle" on to boil. The farmer who owned the land had given us a grubstake—blackeyed peas (fifty pounds), cornmeal (fifty pounds), coffee, salt pork and other staples. We would eat, at least, as long as we worked on the project.

We had been on the road three days, walking the last thirty-five miles. But worn out as we were, we tossed sleeplessly for most of the night. We were all too worried to sleep, too disappointed. At the first crack of daybreak, we were up drinking coffee, and by dawn we were at work.

There was a great deal to be done. Basically, the rig and tools were in good shape, but that long-ago contractor had left things in a mess and the vandal, Time, had made mess into chaos. Thousand-pound timbers had sagged and slipped. Collapsed spools of cable were spewed every which way, mingled and intermingled in Gordian tangles. A twenty-foot stem— tons of solid steel—was jammed back into the calf wheels. The walking beam had toppled down into the belt house. The—but let it go. You would have to know your drilling rigs and terminology to appreciate the damage.

Our first task was not with the rig proper but on the pump to the adjacent water well. For while we could carry water for ourselves from the farmer's house, it would take thousands of gallons a day to keep the boiler going. We stripped the engine down, sandpapered its twin pistons and relined the bearings with our single precious bar of babbitt. We filled the tank from the farmer's precious supply of gasoline. And after a mere seven or eight hours of cranking, the damned thing ran.

We all felt better after that. There is something about having water, when you have been without, that does things for a person's spirits. We all took a bath, and flushed out the tank and boiler lines. Using the farmer's tools, we all fell to chopping wood which we stacked in cords before the boiler's feed box. In all, we were about three weeks securing our water and fuel supply. With that taken care of, we were ready to start on the rig.

Now, there are no light objects around drilling machinery. The stuff all weighs into the hundreds and thousands of pounds. It is meant to be moved with winches and cranes—with machine power. And we had a great deal of clearing away to be done before we dared cut steam into the rig. Everything had to done by hand, ours alone, ostensibly, and since ours were simply not adequate. . . . Well, I can't explain it, how we got the necessary help. All I can do is tell you about it.

We would be struggling futilely with some immovable object, when suddenly, from north and south and east and west, men would come plodding through the tangles of underbrush and blackjack. Negro and white, share-croppers and tenant farmers. Poor ragged devils, even poorer than ourselves if that were possible, bonily emaciated with the ravages of hookworm and malaria. Exactly the right number came to get the job done—no more, no less. They expected no pay and they seemed surprised and embarrassed by our thanks. As soon as the task at hand was completed, they departed again.

It was an eerie phenomenon, one that I have observed nowhere else but in the "lost country" of the Deep South. There were no telephones in the area, and many of our helpers came from miles away. Incredible as it seemed, we were forced to accept the fact that these men could anticipate our need hours before it arose. They knew what we were going to do before we did! We would start to work in the morning, faced with so many tasks that we didn't know which to tackle first. Or, perhaps, we would start on one job, then shift to another. In any case, when the time came that we needed help, it was there and in the right amount.

Unlike Shorty and Jiggs, I could not shrug off this weird state of affairs as "just one of them things." There is a peculiar twist of my mind which impels me to fly into every puzzle as though dear life depended on it. So I pestered our farmer friend about it whenever he put in his appearance. And while I never got a straight explanation of the riddle, I did achieve some understanding of it.

The "how" I never learned. But the "why-for," to use the dialect of the section, became clear.

The occasion was one morning some five weeks after our arrival. We were practically through with the rigging up, and the farmer had been standing around watching us. With an almost abrupt adieu, he stepped down off the derrick floor and started for the backbrush. I asked him where he was going.

"Over to Lije Williams'—" He paused uncomfortably. "Figger I'd he'p him clean out his cellar. Got a plumb big beam to tote back in place after the cave-in."

I asked him when the cave-in had taken place. He mumbled evasively, somehow abashed by the question.

"It hasn't happened yet, has it?" I said.

"Didn't say that," he mumbled. "Just said I was goin' to he'p him."

"How do you people know things like that?" I asked. And he shook his head awkwardly: he didn't know; he couldn't say; he didn't like to talk about it.

"If you knew this cave-in was coming, why didn't you warn Lije? Maybe he could have stopped it."

"Caint," he said simply, his face clearing a little. "Couldn't hardly do that. Suthin's what's goin' to be, it is."

"So you do know," I said, "you just admitted it. How?"

He was growing increasingly uncomfortable at the quizzing, and my friends were nudging me to get on with the work. But I kept after him, and his inherent politeness restrained him from telling me what he should have: viz, to mind my own business and let him mind his.

"Looky, friend," he blurted out at last. "I caint—I don't rightly know how to—to—"

"Make a stab at it," I encouraged him. "Put it in your own words. How do you folks know when somebody needs help?"

He frowned troubledly, scuffing his overrun shoes in the rocky and ruined soil. He looked around at the desolate wasteland. And then his eyes lifted to the bleak, unpromising sky, searching perhaps for a Deity whose head seemed forever turned.

"Got to," he said, bluntly.

That was the end of his explanation.

It was enough.

With the wreckage cleared out of the machinery, we were able to complete the rest of the cleanup with power, and we got it done in a matter of hours. We used the remainder of the day to rig our casing cable and blocks; then, early the next morning, we fired up for the big event.

Since the well had been a deep one, the steam lines were outsize, extra-heavy duty. Similarly, the boiler was something to warm the cockles of an oilman's heart. It had a capacity of one hundred and twenty-five pounds pressure (the safety valve was set to pop off at that point) which is enough power to move a mile-long freight train. It was certainly enough to move a mile of pipe, we felt . . . if the pipe was movable.

I started off with the water glass (gauge) at the third-full mark, gradually opening the injector valve. The first fifteen or twenty pounds of pressure were hard to get, but after that, with the steam-driven blower cut in, the pressure rose swiftly. Shorty and Jiggs retired to the derrick floor, and readied themselves. At seventy-five pounds, I shouted a high sign.

Shorty manipulated the gear lever. Jiggs kept an anxious eye on the cables and blocks. The derrick creaked as the line tightened. The guy wires began to hum. Then a sound like a monstrous groan rent the air, and there was a high-pitched, ear shattering whining—and the bull wheel spun uselessly in its belt.

We took the belt off, tightened it with a splice and put it back in place. It spun almost as badly as ever. No power was being transmitted to the machinery.

We took it off again and resurfaced the wheel with bits of old belting. This time it held; there was not the slightest skidding or slipping. But when Shorty "hit it" with ninety pounds pressure, the seven-eighths inch casing cable snapped like a thread.

We re-rigged with two lines instead of one. With the boiler pop-off valve shrieking, with a full one hundred and twenty-five pounds pressure, Shorty began to "run" at the pipe—to let the lines go slack and then hit it with everything he had.

That went on for two days, at the end of which we had to knock off to chop wood. The pipe hadn't budged. Jiggs said it wasn't going to.

"I ain't sore, understand," he told Shorty. "You musta known that pipe wouldn't pull, and you oughta have your butt kicked for draggin' me and Jim down here. But——"

"It'll pull." Shorty's face flushed. "We're gonna re-rig with four lines."

"What good'll that do? The two we got can take anything we can put on 'em."

"You'll see," said Shorty sullenly. "You guys don't want to help, you don't have to. I'll do it myself."

Well, we weren't going to let him do that, naturally. So we finished the wood-cutting, and strung an additional two lines through the blocks and down to the stubborn pipe. Shorty then ordered a double-guying of the derrick—two guy wires for each of those we now had.

We asked the reason for them. He was sullenly uncommunicative. The rig was going to be double-guyed, and to hell with us if we didn't want to help.

Curiously, Jiggs and I did our share of the job.

"Now," said Shorty, when finally everything was as he wanted it, "you think that derrick'll hold? You figure there's anything we can put on it, it won't stand up to?"

There was only one answer to the question; the rig, of course, was bound to hold up. It was inconceivable that it shouldn't.

"And them four casing lines? You figure they'll hold—three and a half inches of solid steel line?"

Yes, we nodded, the lines also would hold. They could no more give way than the rig could. *But——*

"What the hell you drivin' at, anyway?" Jiggs demanded angrily. "The derrick an' them lines could stand up against three boilers like the one we got. They could take four hundred pounds of steam an' never feel it. But we only got *one* boiler and we only got a hundred and twenty-five pounds, so——"

Shorty walked off, leaving Jiggs talking. We followed him out to the boiler. He stepped up on the firebox door, and braced his body against the barrel. Taking a piece of wire from his pocket, he firmly wired shut the safety valve.

By no means a professional oil filed worker, I did not immediately grasp the significance of this action. But Jiggs' face turned slightly green beneath the tan.

"Are you crazy?" he snapped, as Shorty leaped back down to the ground. "Why you think that's set to pop at one-twenty-five? Because it'll blow up if it don't!"

"No, it won't," said Shorty grimly. "They test these things high. If it's set for one-twenty-five, it ought to take a hundred and seventy-five or two hundred. For a while, anyways."

"Yeah, but for how long a while? And how you going to know if it ain't built up to two-fifty or three hundred? The gauge only reads to a hundred and twenty-five."

"It won't raise more than two hundred. It just ain't got the fire and water capacity."

"Well," Jiggs said, "I wouldn't want to be around it if it was carrying a hundred and fifty pounds pressure, but ... "

He turned and looked at me. So did Shorty. The decision was mine, their attitudes said. They worked up on the derrick floor, more than seventy-five yards away from the boiler. If it blew up, I would be the one to be blasted into the next county.

I hardly knew what to say. We had put in almost two months here, and it was agonizing to think of going back to Oklahoma City empty-handed. But I naturally preferred returning empty-handed to not going back at all.

"I don't like to ask you, Jim—" Shorty broke the silence. "But I honest-to-God think it'll be safe enough. You don't need to hang around the old pot ... very much. Just crowd that pressure needle around until she hits zero again; then you can load the firebox with all it'll hold and head for the bushes."

"Yeah. But suppose it blows while I'm doing all that?"

"All right," he said dejectedly. "I'm not asking you to."

"Anyway, the steam won't hold. You start hitting it in the rig and——"

"It'll hold long enough, Jim! A half hour or so. That's all I need to get the pipe started."

"And you think it will start?"

"By God, it's *got* to!" he declared. "With all that power on it, it can't help but come, even if it's cemented. The rig and the lines won't give, so the pipe has to!"

Jiggs scratched his head, remarked that for at least once in his life Shorty seemed to be making sense. I wasn't so sure, but as they waited, silently, looking at me, I felt compelled to go along with the stunt.

"All right," I said. "I think I'm making a hell of a mistake but—all right."

We drew the fire from the boiler, swabbed the flues and cleaned the firebox of its last speck of ashes. The next morning, while Jiggs and Shorty made a final check of the rigging, I refired.

The pressure needle moved steadily toward the pop-off point. It swung past it with a sinister lurch, and on around to the zero pin. I wanted to run at this point; never in my life have I wanted to do anything so badly. But the box had to be well-stoked first and the ash was banking up so high that there was little room for the necessary wood.

I flung open the door to the grates and began raking at them furiously. I slammed it shut again, and snatched frantically at the wood pile. I hurled in wood by the armloads—jammed it in until it was hanging out of the firebox. I turned the blower on full blast, opened the water-injector valve to its widest. And ran.

I reached the safety of the bushes, and dropped down breathless on the ground.

Shorty hit the steam.

He jolted the pipe a few times, slackening then suddenly tautening the lines. Then he braced his feet against a post, pulled the long lever out as far as it would go, and held it there.

The guy wires hummed. They began to howl with the strain. There was a vast creaking of timber, and the gears shrieked and groaned and screamed. Louder and louder grew the tumult; and then gradually it dimmed. We had lost our head of steam.

And the pipe had not moved an inch.

I fired up three times that day, lingering a little longer each time before running. It was no good. Maybe, by all the laws of physics, the pipe *should* move, but apparently it was not law-abiding pipe.

I told Shorty that we were throwing good time after bad. He implied, rather sourly, that I was at fault.

"I just ain't gettin' the steam, Jim. You give me *enough* steam and that pipe'll pull all right."

"What the hell do you call enough?" I sputtered. "How can I give you any more?"

"Well, I got a little idee about that. I'll think it over tonight—kind of work it out in my head—and we'll give it a try in the morning."

He arose ahead of Jiggs and me in the morning, and when we yawned out into the chilly dawn his invention was ready. It was a stoker, rigged from odds and ends of pipe and a length of sheet iron. Amidst an uncomfortable silence, he demonstrated its operation. He looked at me, and abruptly let go the contraption.

"All right, Jim, forget it. We'll just pack up an' get, and to hell with the damned pipe."

"No, we'll try it," I said. "If we don't get that casing, it won't be my fault."

"You're sure you want to? You know what you'll have to do?"

"I'm dying to do it," I said, not too pleasantly. "And that's probably exactly what I will do."

We had breakfast. Shorty and Jiggs retired to the derrick, and I fired up again.

The steam rose. I cut in the blower, and began to fire more rapidly. The pressure gauge rose to a hundred and twenty-five pounds; the needle swung around to the zero pin. I flung open the grate doors, began to rake ashes with one hand and feed the firebox with the other.

At last the ashes were all removed, while, at the same time, wood bulged from the firebox. I swung the stoker up to the door, and loaded it out to the end.

It was a cold day—bitter with that gnawing, seeping-in cold peculiar to the southern low country. Yet despite this, and the fact that I was stripped to the waist, I was sopping with sweat. It ran down over my body in rivers, and my feet seemed to float in my shoes . . . out of fear, partly, I suppose. But equally, at least, because of the heat. If I had not been sweating so much, I think I should have literally caught fire.

The boiler plates began to glow with an ugly, warning pink. The pink became a dull cherry-red, and then, slowly, a bright scarlet. Threads of steam curled up ominously from the rivets.

God only knows how much pressure was straining beneath those plates. But the steam had to hold, and already the stoker was practically empty. The intense blaze was gulping down wood as though it were so much paper.

I fed and raked ashes, blind with exhaustion and sweat, numb with fear. The boiler began to quiver and shimmy, but I kept on. And at last I had what Shorty wanted. The grates were clean, the firebox full, the stoker loaded. All at the same time. There was as much steam as could be got, and the steam would hold.

I stumbled back from the glowing, shaking monster. I tottered up the hill and fell down among the bushes, fighting to get my breath.

Down in the derrick, Shorty grasped the long lever to the casing reels. It was hot—even *that* was hot. He yelled and did a little dance of pain. Then, he grabbed hold again with a piece of sacking, and pulled it all the way out. And Jiggs jammed it there with a crowbar. They stood back, then, Jiggs looking up into the tower—alert for any breakage—Shorty with his eyes on the pipe.

The by-now familiar and threatening clamor began, but a dozen times louder than it had been on any of our previous attempts. The guys sang; there was an insane howling of tortured wood and metal. It grew to an unbearable pitch, until it seemed to pierce down through your flesh and bones and into your very vitals. And, then, suddenly, it was almost quiet.

Every tiny cell and molecule of the equipment had been stretched and squeezed to its limits. There was no longer any give in them, no room for friction nor clashing, and hence it was silent. The only noise was the hissing of steam.

Around me the earth began to tremble, the bushes to weave and sway. Fascinated, I waited and watched. I had heard about this all my life and now I was seeing it; the legendary meeting of the irresistible force and the immovable object.

A shout from Shorty snapped me out of my reverie. I got up and trotted down the hill.

"It's coming, Jim! The pipe's moving! You gotta give me some more steam!"

"You're crazy!" I stammered. "I wouldn't go near that boiler now for all the——"

"Get movin'! Just a little bit more, Jim, an'—*oof!*"

Jiggs had dived into him like a football tackle, knocking him off of the derrick floor. He had come off of it at a run, and now still running he propelled us ahead of him.

"Run, damn you, run! The pipe—it's—"

"Damn you, Jiggs!" Shorty tried to jerk away from him. "That pipe's just startin' to move an' if Jim would——"

"Sure, it's moving! It's stretching!"

"Stretch? Why, goddammit, it couldn't—*Yeeow!*" yelled Shorty. And he led the race for the bushes. For, fantastic as it seemed, the pipe *was* stretching.

And suddenly it snapped.

It soared up out of the hole, some forty feet of "indestructible" twenty-four inch casing. Like a giant lance, it rose up through the tower of the derrick, smashing through the crown block, batting the heavy gear and pulleys high into the air. And then, snared by the attached lines, it whipped sideways and plunged earthward again.

It came down on the rig, splintering braces and cross-braces, leaving the derrick a wobbling ruin. It landed thunderously amidst the machinery . . . and, for all practical purposes, that machinery ceased to be. Steam spouted from the maze of broken lines—rose mercifully over the ruin. When it cleared away, we trudged back down the hill.

There was nothing to salvage. The rig was utterly and completely beyond repair. At any rate, we were ready to admit that the pipe could not be pulled.

We could not trust ourselves to speak. Case-hardened wretches that we were, we were that near to weeping. Our farmer friend took the disappointment much more philosophically.

"Didn't lose nothin'," he pointed out, as he fed us a farewell banquet of jackrabbit stew. "Didn't have nothin' to begin with."

XVI

I RECEIVED SEVERAL SMALL MANUSCRIPT CHECKS IN A ROW THAT SUMMER, and Mom fell heir to a modest sum. She and Freddie came down to Oklahoma City, bringing my wife and baby with them, and we continued on together to Fort Worth, Texas. Pop had got a job of sorts there. I got one, shortly after my arrival, as a hotel doorman. It was easily the lousiest job I have ever had.

I worked a seven-day, eighty-four-hour week. My salary was fourteen dollars per, less certain arbitrary deductions by my employer which usually totaled two or more dollars. Even with the low prices prevailing in those days, it was a starvation wage for a man with a wife and child.

I was not allowed to sit down during the shift, nor did I have any relief period. I *could* go to eat or to the toilet if I chose to. But if a motoring guest checked out during my absence, his garage charges were on me. After paying one gentleman's nine-dollar bill out of my twelve-dollar wage, I chose to stick to my post.

The omission of a lunch period didn't bother me; I couldn't afford to eat anyway. But the interminable and unrelieved standing on a hard sidewalk, and the compulsion to ignore the demands of nature, were something very nearly like torture. Let it go at that. This is one period of my life I don't like to talk about.

A few pennies at a time, I saved enough money to rent a typewriter and buy some fancy letterheads. I circulated the quality business magazines, and got a number of assignments. Mom and Freddie did the necessary interviewing for me. I wrote their findings up in my "spare time." From business writing, I gradually moved into the relatively high-paying field of fact-detective stories. And after more than a year, I was able to quit the doorman job. I still have numerous mementoes of it, swollen joints and weakened kidneys being the least unpleasant of the lot.

I had for a long time inclined to a youthful bemusement with the *genus Texan*, and as a result I failed to achieve the high Texas standards of character and intelligence. Now, years later, as I moved about the state in search of detective stories, there seemed to be signs that I had improved, or that the professional Texan had. I got along very well with the type, and they were at least tolerant of me. I was beginning to have high hopes of a solid and permanent rapprochement when, one day in Dallas, the futility of such fond imaginings was ignominiously borne home to me.

Fact-detective stories cannot be sold without pictures, and I had found it convenient to become acquainted with many newspaper photographers. They were invariably first-class workmen. They could get stuff from their morgues that was ordinarily unobtainable, and they didn't charge me anything. We were always ol' friends—ol' Texas friends—after a few drinks, and were thus above paying each other for favors. The loans to them and the liquor that went into them got to be a rather frightening item of expense. But in view of my ol' friends' magnanimity, I shut my eyes to it.

Well, after an afternoon's "shooting" expedition with one of these ol' friends, during which we had imbibed a quart of whiskey and started on a second, he suggested a call upon some practitioners of the oldest profession. I demurred. He asked for a loan.

"Jus' lend me a couple dollahs, Jim, ol' boy. That's all it takes. You can come up an' wait in the hall, and have some nice drinks for yourself."

"But I haven't got two dollars—dollahs—Hank, ol' boy," I said. "I spent—I done went an' spent all the money I had on that last jug of whiskey."

"You ain't got no money, *a*-tall?"

"Well, I got this—this here—four-bit piece," I said.

"Well, gimme it, then. I'll match this gal, double or nothin'. I feel pretty lucky."

"But what if you lose?"

"Why, I'll just do without. Naturally."

I murmured that this hardly seemed ethical. "Do you really think you ought to, Hank? I mean, if you lose you'll have to back out. You'll be cheating her."

"Faugh! Fie!" he said, disgusted at this insult. "I'll be teachin' her a very valuable lesson. No tellin' how much it'll be worth to her in future years!"

I went along with him, and he matched the girl and won.

She was a large, bloated woman, somewhat past the first flush of youth. I would hesitate to say exactly how much somewhat. But I think it safe to state that however old the oldest profession is, she must have been a charter member.

Cursing her luck, she led my friend into a room and slammed the door. I sat down on a bench, took a big drink and began fooling with the camera. I lit a cigarette and had another drink. I took a couple more. I examined the camera again.

What seemed like a very brilliant idea popped into my mind.

Creeping across the hall, I turned the doorknob silently and eased the door open an inch or two.

Slowly, I raised and poised the camera.

I don't know whether the "girl" was merely unconventional, or whether she was trying to acquire a suntan. Or whether, perhaps, having worn out her original equipment, she was now employing ersatz. It was impossible to tell whether her pose was a whim or dictated by necessity. At any rate, she was kneeling crosswise on the bed, her stern to my ol' friend, and gazing languidly downward into a crockery chamber pot.

It occurred to me that I would need a flash bulb, and I turned to go back to the bench.

Of course, I bumped and rattled the door.

The woman turned, startled. She stared at me stupidly for a moment. Then, choking with anger, she opened her mouth and let out a bellow of rage. The bellow ended in a sibilant splash as her teeth fell out and dropped into the pot.

Crawling from the bed and holding her hand over her mouth so that we might not see her indecently exposed, she made motions for my colleague to get his clothes on and get to hell out. I beat him down the stairs by a few paces.

"Jim," he said stonily as he buttoned his shirt, panting, "Jim—me an' you, we ain't friends no more."

"Aw," I said, "don't take it that way, Hank. Come back to my hotel with me and I'll get another five for you. You can go to a good place."

"Naw, sir," he declined firmly. "I wouldn't borry another nickel from you, Jim, if you was the last man alive. I thought you was a friend of mine . . ."

"Well, I am."

"From Texas."

"Well, I've lived here for a long time," I said.

"But you ain't a *Texas* man." He shook his head in gloomy triumph. "You couldn't give a Texas man enough liquor to make him look in on a fella while he was with a gal. Why, Jim, you ain't—you're im—im—" He faltered, then came out with the hideous epithet.

Of all my critics, he is the only one ever to call me *immortal!*

XVII

In the spring of 1936, I heard of a chief of police who was making a big name for himself in a small Oklahoma city. I queried a magazine about him, and was given the go-sign. I paid him a visit. He seemed to be everything that rumor said, and then some. In fact, his exploits were so many and so well handled as to comprise the stuff for a long serial. I wrote the magazine to that effect, and again I got a go-ahead.

They did not give me a flat promise to buy, of course. Irrevocable commitments are almost unheard of in the publishing world. But they did think it would make a swell serial, and they were anxious to see it. And that was good enough for me.

I moved my family to Oklahoma City (there would be much research to do in the capital's appeals' court files). I did my writing there, traveling back and forth to the police chief's town for the numerous interviews we had to hold. It was a long, drawn-out job. What with my traveling and research, I was almost three months getting it done and my slender financial resources were exhausted. I was anything but worried, however. I had forty thousand words of the best damned detective story I had ever written. Counting payment for the pictures, I would receive around two thousand dollars for it, and two thousand in those days was equal to six or eight thousand now.

I was very happy as I caught the bus for the police chief's city. I knew that there would be no difficulty in getting his approval of the story, and once that formality was taken care of, my work was finished. It would take a couple weeks to get my check, but that was all right. I could hock my typewriter for enough to ride a couple weeks.

I arrived at my destination. Grinning dreamily, I mounted the steps to the police station. Two thousand dollars—*wow!* And it couldn't come at a better time. My wife and I could have a real home for the second baby we were expecting.

Well, I went into the police station, grinning like a fool. I came out staggering, so sick and faint that I almost fell down the steps. My story was worthless. No magazine in the world would have it as a gift. For throughout its forty thousand words, it held the chief as a model of public officialdom—a man unflinchingly honest, unswerving in his devotion to duty. And those things were exactly what he was not. He had lived a lie for years, and the lie had at last caught up with him.

I came to a trash receptacle, tossed the thick, carefully prepared manuscript inside. I boarded a bus for Oklahoma City.

A police chief—and he had been head of an interstate auto theft ring! A police chief—and now he was locked up in his own jail! It was a ludicrously comic situation, but somehow I couldn't laugh a bit.

Back in Oklahoma City, I broke the bad news to my wife. The next morning, after pawning my typewriter, I started looking for a job. I had to have one, at least temporarily. Free-lance writing, like any other business, requires capital.

I was briskly turned down at the first newspaper I applied to, the city's leading daily. I went on to another one, and the city editor, while pretty crotchety and curt, invited me to sit down.

"Might have something opening up on rewrite," he said. "Nothing certain about it, but . . . how long you lived here?"

"About ten years," I said, omitting to mention that those years were mainly during my childhood. "I know the city well."

"Wouldn't be much good to us if you didn't," he grunted. "Don't want any floaters, anyway. This is a home-town paper for home-town people."

I told him that I was his man, a bona fida home-town boy. "I was away at college for a couple of years, but . . ."

"All right. Give me your telephone number, and I'll call you in a day or two."

He picked up a pencil. He waited, looking at me impatiently. Helplessly, I looked back at him.

I had no telephone of my own, and I couldn't remember my landlady's number as many times as I had called it. In most respects, I have a pretty good memory but telephone numbers have always eluded me.

"I—I guess I'll have to look it up," I said. "I just moved recently, and——"

"Give me your old number, then. The operator will make the switch."

"Well, I——" I cursed myself. I should have told him that I didn't have a phone, but I hadn't been able to think that fast.

"Hmmm." He stared into my reddening face. "This place you're living now, that address. Right down on the edge of the business district, isn't it? What is it, a rooming house?"

"Y-yes, sir. But——"

"You've got a wife and baby—you're a permanent resident—and you're staying in a rooming house? Where'd you live before that?"

It was useless to lie to him. Now that his suspicions were aroused, he would run a check on me in the file of city directories which every newspaper maintains, and a lie would be promptly detected.

"All right," I said. "I'll be frank with you, sir. I——"

"Thought so," he grunted, bending back over his desk. "Sorry, nothing for you. Nope, nope, that's all. Don't have a thing."

I started for the door, very dejected as you may guess.

An elderly copy-desk man followed me out into the hall.

"Too bad, son," he said. "If you're not too particular about money, I may be able to put you next to another job."

I said that I would be grateful for anything at all, for the time being. He told me where the prospective job was, and my face fell again.

"Writers' project? But that's relief work, isn't it? I'm not a relief client."

"They have a few non-relief people—men who really know writing and editing. Sort of supervisors, you know, for the non-professionals. One of the fellows who got laid off here is over there now."

"Well," I said dubiously, "I suppose it won't hurt to look into it."

"Sure it won't." He gave me an encouraging slap on the back. "They've got a big set-up over there, a hundred and twenty-five people, I understand. Maybe you can get to be boss of the whole shebang!"

I grinned weakly at the jest, and thanked him for his kindness. Reluctantly, and without any real hope of landing a job, I applied at the writers' project office.

I was hired immediately.

Eighteen months later I was appointed director—"boss of the shebang."

That was how it happened, how the whole course of my life was changed: because I couldn't remember my telephone number . . .

Except for a very small executive staff, which I did not become a member of for almost a year, project employees worked only two weeks a month. The wage wasn't enough for me to live on, with my increased responsibilities, and I originally intended to quit as soon as I sold a story or two. But my work was appreciated—something which means a great deal to a writer. And having some kind of steady income, however small, meant a great deal to my wife. She had become justifiably bearish on the business of free-lance writing after the police chief fiasco. If a story like that could blow up, she pointed out, then there was none we could be sure of, and with two children we had to be reasonably sure of something. I thoroughly agreed with her.

I stayed on the job, writing detective stories in my off-weeks. Little by little, we acquired a degree of solvency. She and the kids returned to Nebraska the following spring for a visit. I went down to Fort Worth to cover a story. My folks were living in rather cramped quarters, so I stayed at the house of my married sister, Maxine.

I was back in the bedroom one afternoon, putting the finishing touches to the story, when Maxine announced that I had a caller.

"An awfully nice young man," she said innocently. "A Mr. Allison Ivers. He's driving a brand new convertible, and——"

"—and it's probably hot," I cut in grimly. "That guy will snitch your silverware and throw it away. Just for the hell of it!"

Allie had showed up in Fort Worth during my tour of duty as a doorman, and I knew that he was now managing a wildcat taxi and rental car service. In view of the constraint that existed between us, I was surprised that he had traced me here to my sister's house. I was also far from pleased by the visit.

I still liked him and was anxious to patch up our misunderstanding. But this, I felt, his coming here to a stranger's house, was damned presumptuous. He was taking advantage of me, as I saw it, putting me in a position where I would be compelled to be polite whether I chose to or not.

I shook hands with him coldly. He took a tall paper sack from his coat pocket and politely pressed it upon Maxine.

"A cold bottle of prepared cocktails," he explained. "Perhaps if father doesn't mind, we might all have a drink."

"My father?" Maxine looked blank, then tittered delightedly. "Did you hear that, Jimmie? He thinks you're my father!"

"He doesn't think anything of the kind," I said. "He's the biggest goddamned liar in the country, and he's got a hell of a lot of guts coming out——"

"Dearie me!" Allie rolled his eyes. "Such language to use in front of a young girl."

He and Maxine stared at me reprovingly. She brought glasses from the sideboard, and I glumly accepted a drink. Allie made primly polite conversation with Maxine.

"It's such a beautiful day," he said in his piping choirboy voice. "On a day like this, I love to be out in the country with the birds and the flowers."

He sighed and fluttered his eyelids. Maxine gave him a fond look. "You hear that, Jimmie? Why can't you ever be interested in nature and—uh—nice things like Mr. Ivers?"

"Mr. Ivers," I said, "is just about three sheets in the wind."

"Why, he is not! I guess I could tell if a person was drunk."

"You couldn't tell with Allie," I said, "not unless you knew him as well as I do. Now, if he'll just tell me why he came out here——"

"Why—" Allie seemed honestly hurt. "I just thought we might take a little ride, Jim. Thought we might be able to iron out a few things. I know you've come up a long way in the world, and I'm still in the same old rut. But——"

"Now, wait a minute," I said uncomfortably. "You know I wouldn't high-nose you, Allie. It's just that——"

"Then how about that ride? It's a company car. You can see the commercial license plates from here."

I looked out through the screen door. "All right," I said, not too graciously. "Let's get going."

We pulled away from the house and headed out West Seventh Street. Allie drove superbly—a reassuring but by no means surprising fact. Drink had never seemed to do the things to him that it does to most people. Its sole effect on Allie was to excite his fantastic sense of humor.

We reached the outer limits of the city and sped down the highway. Allie began to talk quietly. He said I had become stiff-necked, a stuffed shirt, too uncompromising in my dealings with onetime associates. The publishing swindle in Oklahoma City was a case in point. It had been an error on his part, and he would have been quick to admit it—if I had possessed the live-and-let-live attitude which I had once had. But I had lost my tolerance. Instead of kidding with him I had humbled him, made him feel cheap and of no account. And I had persisted in my high and mighty air in our subsequent meetings.

"What about you?" I said. "You got pretty rough yourself that night in Oklahoma City."

"That's different, and you know it. I can rough talk you and it doesn't mean anything. Who in the hell am I, anyway? But when you start pouring it on me, like you did there at your sister's house——"

"Aaah," I scoffed, "I was just kidding, Allie. You know that. Anyway, you started it yourself."

"I told you," said Allie, "that was different. A man with a club foot, you don't kid him because he limps."

I could see his point vaguely, but I didn't know quite what to do about it. I said so.

"You could laugh occasionally for one thing. You could crawl out of that shell you're in, and start acting like a human being."

"I laugh when there's anything to laugh about," I said, "and quite a few people think I act like a human being."

"Well, I don't," said Allie. "I—hey! Look at that!"

I turned and looked out over the prairie in the direction he had pointed. "Look at what? I don't see——"

"That airplane—over there in that patch of clouds! A guy just fell out of it!"

I cupped my hands over my eyes, stared intently at the clouds. I could see nothing resembling an airplane nor a falling body.

"What the hell are you trying to—to—" I turned back around in the seat. "Allie!" I yelled. "*Allie!*"

The blood drained from my face. I almost dropped dead from sheer fright. For the car had suddenly gathered speed, and Allie was no longer at the wheel.

He was slumped in the back seat, a lap robe thrown over his knees, his head lolling foolishly.

The car swerved suddenly and shot toward the ditch. Righting itself at the last instant, it sped toward the opposite ditch. I yelled and flung myself on the steering wheel. It wouldn't turn. It was jammed.

This last circumstance should have been the tipoff for me, but I was not thinking clearly. As the car shot down the road, swinging crazily from side to side, I could only think of one thing: the booze had at last caught up with Allie, and this hideous predicament was the result.

We were traveling far too fast for me to jump. My terrified shouts and screams elicited nothing from Allie but foolish, slit-eyed grins. I tried to apply the brakes. There was no response. I turned the ignition switch—and the car kept right on going. Faster and faster.

I don't know what other motorists must have thought as we roared in and out of the traffic: probably, I suppose, that their eyes were playing tricks on them. I was yelling at the top of my lungs, fighting frantically with the useless wheel. Allie remained slumped in the back seat, apparently unconscious that anything at all was amiss.

It seemed like hours but it was all over in a few minutes. When I could no longer muster a yell, when my terror had exhausted itself and I was resignedly awaiting my seemingly inevitable demise—then the insane ride ended. The car turned smoothly into a side road and came to a gentle stop.

I rubbed my eyes, incredulous. Every nerve standing on end, I turned around in the seat.

Allie was not, of course, drunk. He grinned at me, the lap robe kicked aside, and pointed down at his feet. I looked. I began to curse him.

"Dual controls! Allie, I'll murder you for this if it's the last damned thing——"

I stuttered and choked up with fury. Then, suddenly, reaction set in, and I began to howl with laughter. I laughed until I was breathless and my face streamed with tears.

"Allie," I gasped at last, "what did those controls cost you?"

"Oh," he shrugged, "around sixty dollars. Of course, it'll cost something more to get them taken out."

"And you did that just for this—just to break the ice between us? It was worth that much to you?"

"Well . . . "

"Why don't we go out on the town tonight?" I said. "Have a real beer bust, like we used to in the old days, and make a tour of the burly houses, and——"

"About your question—" Allie climbed back behind the wheel, beaming—"It was worth it."

XVIII

I HAD LESS THAN NO PULL IN OKLAHOMA POLITICAL CIRCLES, and as chief editor of the state writers' project I did not endear myself at Washington headquarters. I went out of my way to be unaccommodating to politically "right people." I would not accept a foolish directive simply because it came from Washington. I got my directorship by hard work—and because (or so a Washington official informally informed me) it would have shrieked of misfeasance to appoint another.

I soon began to wish that someone else had got the appointment.

To begin with, I did not, for a long time, draw a director's salary. The former incumbent had accumulated months of annual leave, and he continued to draw his pay throughout those months. Since the budget allowed for only one director, I was stuck with my relatively meager editor's salary. It was an irksome and embarrassing situation.

It was bad enough to be doing an executive's work at a subordinate's pay. But the struggle to meet my increased expenses, the newly imposed obligations to entertain, became downright maddening. I had practically given up free-lance writing to devote myself to the project. Our third child had just been born, and we were head over heels in debt. Several times, in order to finance an unavoidable dinner party, my wife and I pawned everything but the clothes we were wearing.

I got back into free-lance writing fast, and finally worked my way out of the financial mess. But the holding of two full-time jobs, which was what it amounted to, was beginning to tell on me. And finances were only part of my troubles.

My predecessor had been left relatively free of political interference, and so had I for the first few months. There were hints—some pretty strong ones—that it might be well to favor this person or that group, but there was never an outright demand followed up by retaliation if one refused. The national administration felt itself too strongly entrenched. It saw little need anywhere to curry political favor, and it saw none at all in the "Solid South." Now, however, the situation changed.

A national election was not far off. There were signs that the administration might have trouble achieving a third term. So it began making up to the local boys, giving in to their hitherto evaded demands. In effect the actual control of the various projects passed from Washington to the states.

Well, I was and am a long way from puritanism, but I could not stomach the squandering of relief moneys for political purposes. Also, I could not (and cannot) be shoved very far along a course which I believe to be wrong. So I resisted the pressure, and was promptly punished.

Travel orders and expense accounts were held up. Requisitions for supplies were delayed interminably. My worker quota and the quota of available workers shifted swiftly from month to month. I couldn't get the people I needed, or I was in danger of employing workers without authorization, having to pay their wages out of my own pocket.

Interested as I was in the job, it seemed foolish and futile to stick with it. I sent in my resignation to Washington.

Washington refused to accept the resignation. It was pointed out to me—with considerable truth—that I held the threads of the various project endeavors and that they would become hopelessly snarled if I should let go. Much time and work would be lost if a new man had to take over. As for my complaints, well, I was doubtless "looking on the dark side" and had unwittingly "exaggerated the situation" but perhaps something could be done about it.

Apparently, Washington did protest to the state officials, and the latter thought it wise to ease up a little. Then gradually they reapplied the pressure, and I fired in another resignation.

This one was also refused with much the same sort of letter as the first. Again the pressure went off and on, and again I resigned.

In all, I sent in four resignations before I finally got an acceptance, but it is not yet time to relate the tragi-comic circumstances surrounding that event. Moreover, in rushing ahead, I am giving the impression that the job was an unrelieved headache. It was not at all.

The phrase "big happy family" has become so abused as to be ridiculous. But, in the main, it accurately describes my project. My people knew that I was fighting to protect their jobs. They knew that they could advance themselves with good work—and in no other way—and the knowledge gave them a dignity and pride that was far from common among relief-roll workers. Many were poorly educated, while others had had no previous work experience. I set up after-hours classes in a number of such subjects as spelling, typing, shorthand and business etiquette. And, as a result, any number of hitherto "unemployables" found jobs in private industry.

This was no more than I should have done, of course, and I don't mean to hold myself up as a model of virtue. It is only that, in relating so much that is ribald and unflattering about myself, I feel compelled to show something of my better, or at least more socially acceptable, side.

And, now, having done this. . . .

One Saturday, I and one of my editors—I'll call him Tom—drove down to a town in southwestern Oklahoma. An Indian celebration was being held there which we intended to cover. Our travel authorization being held up as usual, we went on our own time and at our own expense.

We took in the afternoon events of the "celebration," and they proved to be pretty poor stuff. As long as we were there, however, we decided to stay through the next day. So we checked in at a hotel, had dinner and started to drive around the town.

It was much more colorful than the ceremonies had been. Reservation Indians were everywhere. Many of them appeared to have been drinking, and were having a hell of a time for themselves. But no one interfered. The Federal law, ordinarily unbending in the matter of whiskey and Indians, seemed to have been temporarily—if unofficially—suspended.

Tom and I were stopped at a street light, when two slangy female voices hailed us:

"Hey, you writer fellows—where you going?" and "How about giving us a ride?"

Startled, we looked toward the curb.

Two reservation squaws stood there, grinning at us. Blankets were draped around their beaded dresses; their hair hung in long black braids. They were about fifty years of age, I imagine. One was some six feet tall and extremely thin. Her companion was around five feet, and must have weighed a full three hundred pounds.

I pulled in at the curb. They peered through the car window, and I got a whiff of very good bourbon.

"How about that ride?" the thin one asked. "You guys got nothing else to do."

"I'm afraid we do have," I said. "We're here to write up your celebration, and——"

"Nuts!" Fatty scoffed. "We saw you out there this afternoon—just wastin' your time. That's missionary stuff. We don't do any real dancing for those yokels. You want to see the genuine article, we'll show you where to go."

Tom murmured that it might be a good idea; it was probably the only way we could see any truly authentic dances.

I hesitated, glancing at the large, suspiciously bulging handbag which each of the squaws was carrying.

"What about the whiskey? You're not supposed to have it, are you?"

"What do you care?" said Skinny on a note of belligerence. "I figure we're old enough to drink if we want to."

"Well, of course you are but——"

"So what's the argument?" said Fatty comfortably. "You didn't sell it to us or give it to us, so there's no need to worry. Just open the door and let's get going."

The car springs groaned as she climbed into the back seat. Skinny joined her and, rather uneasily, I drove on.

We were quite a while in reaching our destination, an isolated section of the river bottoms. The ladies liked their drinks mixed—their bags contained several bottles of pop—and it was necessary to stop for the mixing. Naturally, we took a drink out of courtesy. Naturally—after that first one—we took a great many more. When we finally rolled up at the dance site, we were all four the warmest of friends and in a state of high hilarity.

About twenty-five or thirty Indians, male and female, were gathered there. The women were dressed as our friends were; the men wore breechclouts and paint. Tom and I waited in the car while our erstwhile companions conferred with their tribesmen. They beckoned to us after a moment; we had passed muster. We got out, shook hands all around and were presented with tin cups of a potent beverage which one of the squaws dipped from a large iron pot.

I can't recall the name of the stuff now. But it was made, I learned later, from a base of corn and saliva. The squaws chewed corn to a pulp and spit it into the pot. When they had a sufficient quantity of this mash, they filled the pot with water, added sugar and allowed it to ferment. That was all there was to it, except for an occasional skimming. In a few weeks the stuff had a kick like an army mule.

Things began to get a little fuzzy after our first few drinks. But somehow or another we were divested of our clothes and equipped with breechclouts, and someone—or several someones—decorated us from head to foot with bright clay paint. Tom and I preened and strutted. The braves shouted their approval. Then the fire was built up and the squaws formed in two opposite lines, creating an aisle to the flames. The men arranged themselves single-file at the head of this lane. Tom and I fell in at the end of the line.

There was a wild warwhoop; the squaws began a rhythmic stamping and clapping and the dance was on.

Whooping, weaving and bobbing, the Indian at the head of our line danced down the aisle and made a whirling leap over the flames. He started back around to the end of the line, and the next man did his dance and leap. Then, the next, and the next, until everyone had performed but Tom and me. We decided to do a duet.

I wish someone could have gotten a picture of us, for it must have been one of the prize comedy bits of all time. Every time we revolved in the dance one of us socked or kicked the other, and when the crucial moment of our leap arrived we were off-balance and groggy. We leaped, anyway, whirling and whooping.

Tom's flailing feet booted me in the back. I clutched at them instinctively. Thus entangled we soared up and above the fire. We hung poised over it for a moment; then, our forward momentum lost, we dropped smack down into the middle of the flames.

Our friends had been prepared, I suspect, for some such fiasco; otherwise, there would have been a couple of barbecued writers. As it was, however, we were snatched out and rolled in the dust before we could even be singed. And we suffered nothing more than a slight and temporary tingling in our painted hides.

An intermission was declared for refreshments and to allow us to recover. The dance resumed then, and Tom and I resumed our places in the line. But you may be sure that we did no more double acts.

A sudden downpour of rain put an end to the festivities. I had gotten a little too close to the fire on some of my leaps, with a consequent mild toasting of my feet. But the furious exercise had been an antidote for the drink, and except for my smarting soles I was about as near normal as I ever am. Still, Tom insisted that I was in no condition to drive. He would take over, he said, with Skinny to give him directions. The fat squaw and I should sit in the back.

I let him have his way. We started off. In the blinding rain, Skinny became confused; and an hour later we were still wandering around the narrow trails of the back country.

The better to see, Tom rolled down the window and leaned out. He yelled and swung the wheel. He was too late. In the instant that his eyes were off the road, the car had slid onto the rain-caved shoulder.

It lurched, wobbled, and toppled. Then it was lying on its top in the bottom of the ditch, and three hundred pounds of squaw were lying on top of me.

Neither of us was injured, but she had passed out from the booze and all her avoirdupois was so much dead weight. I couldn't move. I could hardly breathe. Tom and Skinny climbed out and tried to pull her off of me, but they could get no leverage, due to the position of the car, and with that much to heft they needed a chain hoist. They tickled her feet, pinched her—did everything they could to revive her. She remained inert, snoring peacefully, and I remained pinned down.

I told them for God's sake to get into town; doubtless they could find their way on foot. "Send out a tow car! And *hurry!* I can't take much of this!"

They set off for town. The hours passed and they didn't come back, and there was no sign of a wrecking car. I squirmed and struggled to free myself. All it got me was exhaustion. Finally, breathless and numb and worn out, I gave up the futile struggle.

It was around dawn when I heard the creak of harness and wagon wheels. I shouted and there was an answering hail. The sounds quickened and came nearer. They ceased, and a grizzled face appeared at the car window.

It was a farmer, on his way to town with a wagonload of corn. He stared in at me and the squaw, eyes widening incredulously. Then, guffawing and slapping his knees, helpless with merriment, he collapsed against the embankment.

I could see nothing at all funny about the situation. But my profane remarks to that effect seemed only to make him laugh the harder. Finally, upon my angry statement that he was laughing at a dying man, he got himself under a modicum of control.

He unhitched his mules and hitched them onto my car. It came easily upright, and back onto the road.

The farmer refused payment for his help. Gasping, tears of amusement streaming down his face, he claimed that he was actually in my debt.

"Ain't—*haw, haw, haw!*—ain't laughed like that since I don't know when. How in the heck did you get in such a dagnabbed fix?"

"Never mind," I said grimly. "Just never mind."

I drove off. The last I saw him he was hugging the neck of one of the mules—haw-hawing hilariously while the animal hee-hawed.

A few hundred yards down the road I encountered the tow truck, Tom and Skinny riding with the driver. They had been confused about the location of my car and had toured the countryside all night attempting to find it.

We got Fatty revived. The driver agreed to take her and the other squaw to wherever they wanted to go. He also made us a present of a gallon can of gasoline, which, he mysteriously insisted, we were "cert'n'y gonna need."

He was right. Tom and I sneaked in the side door of the hotel, and reached our room unobserved. And we remained there, with the shades drawn, for the next twelve hours. We had to. It took us that long to remove the warpaint, and we didn't quite get it all off then. There were certain areas of our anatomy which were just too tender for the brush and gasoline treatment.

Fortunately, their location was such as to make public exposure unnecessary.

XIX

In the fall of 1938, I received a visit from two old-timers in the Oklahoma labor movement. They were pioneers in the state, and men of some substance. They bore warm letters of introduction from several members of the Oklahoma congressional delegation. They wanted the writers' project to do a history of labor in the state.

Well, I liked these gentlemen very much, and I was personally sympathetic to their plan. But it was inadvisable on a great many counts. I explained this to my callers and they left—quite friendly, but intimating that the matter would be carried over my head. I immediately sent a long letter to Washington.

I wrote that we would undoubtedly be politically pressured to do the book, but that we should and must withstand it. Labor was sensitive about its mistakes. It would consider unfriendly a book that was merely accurate and complete. Then, there were the various inter-union quarrels— long-standing jurisdictional disputes, for example. We could hardly ignore them in the proposed history, but the skimpiest mention was certain to offend some organization. Before the book was finished, we would have pleased no one and angered everyone.

I did not believe (I wrote) that labor was yet sure enough of itself to accept an honest, factual history. And even if this were not the case, there was an excellent reason for steering clear of the job. Federal expenditures were intended to benefit all the public. The one contemplated would not. If we did a history of labor we would lay ourselves open to demands from other segments of the population. We could be asked for a history of the state chamber of commerce, or some other such group, and we would have no legitimate grounds for refusing.

I got no reply to my letter; no acknowledgment of it. Washington simply wrote me, a couple of weeks later, to proceed with the labor history.

I did so.

All the problems that I had foreseen, and then some, arose. I could never get the different labor leaders together without the danger of a knock-down, drag-out brawl. Any unfavorable mention of a union was invariably "a goddamned lie" and "that guy sittin' over there" (the leader of an opposition union) should be compelled to admit it. As for me, I was charged with everything from stupidity to personal prejudice to taking pay from the National Association of Manufacturers.

I was fortunate in having the confidence of Pat Murphy and Jim Hughes, respectively the state commissioner and assistant-commissioner of labor. Their help in oiling the troubled waters was invaluable. Oddly enough, however, I received the most assistance from a man who had profanely declined to appear at publication committee meetings and who had threatened to kick me out of his office if I ever walked into it.

I called on him. He didn't give me the promised booting, but I did get an ear-blistering cursing out. He had "heard all about" the way his union had been slandered; an acquaintance of his on the committee had tipped him off. Well, if I let one word of it get into print, all hell was going to pop in Congress. And if I thought he couldn't make it pop, I was a bigger damned fool than I looked.

I asked him why he thought I would want to injure his union. He grumbled that he didn't know, but he knew damned well that I had. Laying the manuscript before him, I asked him to look at a portion dealing with another union.

The section was not flattering to the organization involved, and as he read he began to nod approvingly. I had those bastards dead to rights, he said. Someone had at last told the truth about them, and about time, too. I pointed out some other sections to him—likewise unflattering and dealing with other unions. He read through them beaming.

"Could have made it a little stronger, though," he said. "I could tell you things about those sons-of-bitches that would make your hair curl."

"I imagine we'll have to tone it down a lot," I said. "They've been kicking about it."

"Naturally, they're kickin'," he declared. "The truth always hurts."

He nodded to me, piously. Then, after a moment, a slow flush spread over his face, and he cleared his throat uncomfortably.

"Of course," he said, "we shouldn't be too hard on people. Now, I got just about the biggest union in the state, and there's bound to've been a few times when—we—uh—got out of line a little, but——"

I looked at him, torn between the desire to laugh and blow my top. Suddenly, I stood up and reached for the manuscript.

"Let's have it," I said. "I thought I could talk sense to a man as big as you are, but you're even worse than the others."

"Now, wait a minute. All I said was——"

"At least they don't insist on a brag-book. That's what you want. You're good at dishing it out, and when it comes to taking a little you start crying. Everyone's picking on you and you're going to raise hell in Congress, and——"

"Sit down," he said firmly. "Maybe I had you all wrong and maybe you've got me a little wrong. Let's start all over again."

I sat down, and we went through the manuscript together. He was by no means pleased with some of the references to his union, but he felt impelled to prove his fairness—to show me and the other labor organizations how a *big* man operated. And with his example to point to, I was able to swing the others into line.

I don't mean to say that we, the writers' project, got everything into the manuscript that should have been in it. But this was as much due to the lack of publishing funds as it was to the attitude of the unionists. We published as comprehensive a book as we could for the money we had.

I should mention here that the government furnished no funds for publishing, *per se;* only for the actual preparation of the manuscript. So, at the beginning, I had set up an apparatus among the unions for soliciting and handling money. It did not function; there were too many conflicts among its members. Too much distrust. In the end, or rather, long before the end, I became the treasurer-solicitor.

By later summer of 1939, we had the funds to publish a modest volume and the manuscript was finished. Washington approved it. I sent it to the printer. A few days later, with the type already set, I was called into state headquarters of the various work projects. They flatly ordered me to kill the book.

Flabbergasted, I wanted to know why. If there was any part of the book which they had a justifiable objection to I would gladly cut it out. So much had been cut already that a little more wouldn't be missed. I was told that they "had not had time" to read the manuscript (they had had a copy for days), and the matter was not pertinent. The book simply should not be published *period*.

I said it would be published *period*.

I returned to my office . . . and found a long-distance call from Washington awaiting me. They had just talked with the state officials.They agreed with the latter that the book should be killed.

I was so furious that I could hardly talk. "You shoved this thing down my throat," I said. "I didn't want to touch it and I told you why—and you ordered me to go ahead anyway. Well, now we've spent a fortune in government funds on research and writing. Now we've collected publishing funds from the unions and contracted with a printer and got the book set in type. And now, without any explanation, you tell me to forget the whole thing. I'm not going to do it. I couldn't do it if I wanted to, and I don't want to."

I slammed up the phone. Calling my secretary, I wrote my fourth and very final resignation.

I knew what lay behind the ultimatum handed me—a very shabby kind of politics. A national election was impending. The administration had decided to take a sharp turn to the right, to do nothing that might even remotely offend the conservatives. It was not necessary to do anything for labor or to show any particular regard for it. Labor could be kicked in the teeth, and it would still tag along with the administration. It had no place else to go. The conservatives, on the other hand, must be appeased. No chances could be taken with their vote.

Washington responded to my "insubordination" by sending an official out to see me. We met at his hotel room. A rather prim, old-maidish guy, he was much more conciliatory than I had expected. Washington did not want me to resign, he said. They were sure, and so was he, that some kind of compromise could be worked out to the satisfaction of all parties.

I said that nothing would make me happier, and that, meanwhile, I would delay my resignation.

To abridge events considerably, we got quite companionable as the afternoon waned. He brought out a bottle, and with the first few drinks his prim manner disappeared. I was a swell guy, he declared—a pleasant relief from the stuffed shirts who usually surrounded him. We had been talking business for hours, so now how about a little fun? What could we do tonight by way of relaxation?

Well, in a city without night clubs or a legitimate theater, there was not a very wide choice of entertainments. Anyway, he was not interested in more of "the same old things." We kicked the subject around, continuing to drink, and finally we went out to an amusement park.

We went on a number of the rides, he getting gayer and gayer. We arrived eventually at the penny arcade, and here the bag-punching device caught his eye.

"Challenge you," he said. "Go ahead and hit it, and then I will. Bet I can sock it harder than you can."

I dropped a coin in the slot, pulled the bag down on its chain and hit it. He glanced at the dial which registered the impact, and waved me to stand aside.

He wound up, more in the manner of a ballplayer than a boxer. Grunting for me to "just watch this one," he swung. The bag crashed against the dial. It came hurtling back. And since he had not removed himself from its path, it smashed squarely into his face.

That ended the evening's entertainment. In an icy, accusing silence, I drove him back to his hotel. He was going to have a couple of very unlovely black eyes. I, who had seen him at a gross disadvantage, was to receive a figurative shiner. At least, I had a strong hunch that he would slam me as soon as he got back to Washington.

All my life, it seemed, things had been turning out this way. I would work myself into exhaustion, maintain the most correct of attitudes. Then, flukish Fate would take a hand and something preposterous and wholly unrelated would edge into the picture. And all my work and rightness would be as naught.

My hunch was correct.

The gentleman returned to Washington.

Washiongton "regretfully" decided to accept my resignation.

I refused to quit. My project funds were cut off. I remained at work unpaid, as did my executive staff, until the labor history was through the printers.

With a little string pulling, my staffers were relocated in other jobs. I then did some very earnest pulling on my own behalf.

A few weeks later, through the instrumentality of the University of North Carolina Press, I received a year's research grant-in-aid from the Rockefeller Foundation.

XX

A FEW NIGHTS AGO, during one of the rare periods of quiet around our domicile, my wife and I fell to reminiscing about the "good old days" when we and our children were young.

"I don't know how we stood it," said Alberta, with a mixture of fondness and horror. "Of all the nutty, headstrong kids anyone ever had! I guess they must have got it from you, Jimmie."

"Oh, undoubtedly," I said. "It's unthinkable that *you* might——"

"Well, naturally," Alberta shrugged. "Naturally, no woman in her right mind would have married you in the first place. Or if she did, she'd soon go crazy. And speaking of marriage, Mr. Thompson . . . "

"Yes?"

"You still owe me the twenty you borrowed for us to get married on."

"To get back to the subject," I said, "those children were really a handful, weren't they? Of course, they still go their own merry way, but compared to how they used to be—when Patricia was about six and Sharon three and Mike two . . . "

. . . those kids—our kids—Pat, Mike and Sharon. They took one long look at us as they entered the world, decided that we were no more than well-meaning imbeciles, and thenceforth paid us no heed whatsoever. As far as authority was concerned, one would have thought that they were the adults and we the children. They would have nothing to do with high chairs, sleeping cribs, toidy pots or the other impedimenta of infancy.

Each insisted on his own double bed. Each insisted on using the regular toilet, nor were they at all chagrined when, as frequently happened, they fell into it. High-chairs, milk, baby food—such was not for them. Before they could walk, they were sitting at the table; they demanded to so sit, backing up the demand with hunger strikes. Elevated by stacks of books, they wielded their long razor-sharp carving knives—each had his own pet blade. And while Alberta and I looked on in helpless horror, a whole ham or a nine-pound roast would disappear as though by magic.

They smoked my cigarettes. They appropriated my beer. They took full charge of our household, three firmly autonomous powers, and everything there in or around that household.

Pat, our eldest, and seemingly the least loony of the lot, gave us relatively little trouble. *Relatively*, mind you. Pat seemed to have been

257

born with a college professor's vocabulary, also a penchant for dramatics, and she used the first attribute to satisfy the second. Left alone with a telephone for five minutes, Pat became "Mrs. Thompson" or "Mrs. Thompson's social secretary." She would call store after store, ordering stuff that she wanted as theatrical props. And she was so damnably glib about it that she frequently obtained credit where Alberta and I ourselves had been turned down flat.

Mike, our youngest, was what I have always regarded as the most horrid of humans, the direct bane of humanity—a practical joker. Visitors to our house invariably found diapers stuffed into their hats, purses and the like. Diapers which looked much more unwholesome than they actually were. Like Pat, Mike had an artistic bent. Mixing dinner leftovers with mustard and mayonnaise, he achieved messes so hideously realistic as to deceive even his mother and me.

Sharon, our middle child, the second oldest . . . Sharon. I could write a book about her—a dozen books. But being limited spacewise, perhaps I had better concentrate on her principal and most troublesome peculiarity.

Sharon collected, and ran a school for, wild animals.

Pushing a perambulator which we had bought during Patricia's infancy, and which she and our other kids had flatly declined to ride in, Sharon patrolled the alleys and byways, taking into custody the biggest, the ugliest cats and mongrels she could find. She loaded them into the buggy, dogs and cats together. And there was such a peculiar charm about her, such a fey-ish quality, that they never fought nor protested.

"You be dood," she would say, hoisting a bulldog in one arm and a tomcat in the other. "Be fwiends." Then, into the buggy they would go, and while they did not become friends, their behavior was impeccable.

When she had a full cargo, she wheeled them home and into the bathroom. She washed them there, bandaging any wounds they might have, then escorted them into the kitchen. Stuffed with several dollars worth of groceries, they were next taken into the living room—her "school." And here, having seated them in a row, Sharon lectured them on personal hygiene, the importance of being "fwiends" and similar assorted subjects.

I don't know what the qualifications were for "graduation," but some classes met them very quickly, were dismissed within an hour or so, while others were held far into the night. In any event, no post-graduate work was required; and each day's student body was composed of a new group of animals.

Well, to get on with my story: with three kids like ours, a home of our own began to seem imperative. So, a few months before I left the writers' project, we moved into one. I didn't buy it outright, of course. As with the furniture—eight rooms of brand-new stuff—I made a substantial down payment and mortgaged my earnings into eternity for the balance.

But with all my dread of debt, I felt that the move had been a wise one.

The house was a rambling, roomy tapestry-brick cottage, with an enormous back yard, a garage and sevants' quarters. The price was incredibly cheap. It was so low, in fact, that I had been a little alarmed, feeling that there must be something seriously amiss. But I knew quite a bit about building, and even a very superficial investigation of the premises told me that this was first-rate construction. So, as I say, we bought it and moved in.

It was a happy time, that first afternoon in our own home. The kids were pleased with it, impressed with the new furniture. Pat promised to lay off the charge accounts. Mike agreed to forego the diaper-and-mustard trick. Sharon . . .

"That child," Alberta sighed wearily. "One minute you see her, and the next one she's gone."

"Well," I said, "at least we know where she's gone. She took the perambulator with her."

"Well, go out and find her, for goodness sake! We've got a nice place now, and I want to keep it that way. Tell her—ask her—please not to. . . . Now what are you grinning about, Mike?"

Mike's grin widened. "Sha'n," he said. "Sha'n unner house."

"*What?*"

"Uh-huh. Unner house wif tats an' dogs."

It was true, we discovered by stamping on the floor. We went out into the yard, and Sharon presently emerged through the foundation air-vent, covered with cobwebs and dirt and followed by her coterie of animals.

"Buds unner house," she explained placidly. "Otsa bad buds. Twied to dit wid of 'em."

Alberta said that of course there were bugs under the house: there were bugs under any house. "What I want you to get rid of," she said, "is those animals. And for heaven's sake get yourself cleaned up."

Sharon dismissed her class without protest; apparently their practical experience in "bud hunting" had earned them a diploma. We were about to reenter the house when Pat yiped suddenly, slapped a four-inch centipede from her neck, and took a hearty swing at Mike.

"Doggone little brat! I'll teach you to put spiders on me!"

"Did not." Mike kicked her on the shin, his face puckered indignantly. "Don't wike buds."

"Tol' you," said Sharon. "Buds unner house. Inna house. All over everywhere."

"Well, they probably are now," said Alberta grimly. "You dragged them all out with you. Now, get cleaned up and stay out of trouble for a few minutes!"

We dragged Mike and Pat into the house and locked them in separate rooms. With Sharon occupied in the bathroom, Alberta and I began preparing dinner.

All was peace for a time, while Alberta pounded the steak and I peeled potatoes. Then, abruptly, she too let out a yipe, and dropped the frying pan she was holding to the floor.

"Jimmie! L-look at that!"

I looked. And my skin crawled. For a small army of centipedes was oozing up from the stove, dropping down from its sides and slithering over the floor.

I got rid of them, stomped on every one in sight. But Alberta remained shuddery and nervous. Probably, she admitted, a thing like this was to be expected in a house long unoccupied; but couldn't we have a cold dinner tonight?

I said we could, naturally, and drove to a nearby delicatessen. When I returned some thirty minutes later, she and the kids were all out in the front yard. And all were squirming and scratching uneasily.

"Jimmie," said Alberta desperately, "we just can't stay in there! The place is literally crawling. The beds and the chairs and the tables and— and they're even in the refrigerator! The more we move around the worse they seem to get."

"Oh, now," I said, "they surely can't be that bad. We'll all get busy killing them, and——"

"Well, they *are* that bad, and the centipedes are only part of it. That house is just absolutely alove with bedbugs, millions of 'em! You can't even sit down in a chair without getting all bitten up."

Well, I investigated personally, and found that she had not exaggerated the situation. Every stick of our brand-new furniture was infested. Just looking at it closely, at the swarms of ugly brown bugs, made me itch from scalp to toes. I could think of only one explanation, that they must have been in the furnishings when we bought them.

Since it was not yet six o'clock, I called the manager of the furniture store and told him what had happened. Or, I should say, what I believed had happened. He sputtered indignantly.

Vermin in the great B——furniture store? Incredible! Outrageous! "I think it much more likely, Mr. Thompson, that——"

"You made the delivery from your warehouse," I said. "Probably they were in there. Some of the second-hand furniture you handle was infested, and they got from it onto mine."

"B-but—" he hesitated uncertainly, "but all our second-hand items are thoroughly fumigated before storing! It's one of our strictest rules. I'm sure that none of our workmen would ever be so remiss as to——"

"Let's face it," I said. "I've had this furniture barely three hours, and it's damned near jumping with bugs. It couldn't have got that way out here, so they must have been in it all along. It's the only plausible explanation."

"Well—" he coughed uncomfortably—"if we are at fault, and it seems we must be. . . . "

"Get the stuff out of here," I said. "Get it out tonight, and replace it with new. And for God's sake look it over good before you deliver it."

"Yes, yes," he said hastily. "But—uh—tonight, Mr. Thompson. I'm not sure that we can——"

"You'd better," I told him. "You won't get another penny out of me unless you do, and I'll sue you besides."

He surrendered, mumbling apologetically. Within less than two hours, the buggy furniture had been removed and replacements installed. The family and I examined them carefully. Satisfied that they were bug-less, we ate our long-delayed dinner and retired.

I can't say which of us hollered first, who was the first to leap scratching and clawing from his bed. The insect attack seemed to have been launched on all of us simultaneously, and we reacted en masse.

Cautiously, our hides smarting with welts, we reexamined the furniture. Only Sharon seemed unsurprised at the result.

"Tol' you," she said placidly. "Buds unner house, inna house. Wiv wight inna bwicks an' wood."

Alberta and I looked at her, looked worriedly at each other. "Jimmie, do you suppose—I mean, could it be that way?"

"I don't know," I said, "but I'll sure as hell find out."

I called the real estate dealer who had sold me the place. He was completely blunt and unapologetic.

"I sold you that house as is, Thompson, remember? If you don't remember, you'll find the fact stated clearly in your sales agreement."

"Then you knew it was like this?" I said. "You deliberately and knowingly——"

"As is, Thompson. There were no guarantees. It's your house . . . as long as you make your payments. The bugs are your problem, not mine."

He slammed up the telephone. I tried to call him back and got no answer. Cursing, I called an insect exterminator who advertised night service.

It would cost several hundred dollars, I supposed, to get a house this size renovated. But if I didn't spend it—and, offhand, I didn't know where in the hell I could get it—I would lose everything I had invested.

The owner of the exterminating company answered my call. He promised to send some men out right away, and then he broke off abruptly and asked me to repeat the address.

I repeated it.

"Oh, oh," he said, softly. "Mister, you are stuck."

"How do you mean?" I said. "How do you know when you haven't even——"

"I've been out there. Been there twice in the last year, and the job looked worse the second time than it did the first. For one thing, that house is built right on top of a centipede city—a big colony—and God only knows how far and how deep it extends. And them bedbugs, now; when they get dug in like they are, you've practically got to take a place apart to get 'em.... I'm not saying that the job can't be done, understand. It could be, but——"

"Yes?"

"It would cost you more than the place is worth."

I hung up.

Pretty drearily, we shook out our blankets and bedded down in the backyard.

For a week after that, until I could scrape up the money for an apartment, we camped out there, cooking over an open fire and sleeping on the ground.

With so much space available, Sharon enlarged her animal classes and Pat staged theatrical spectacles and Mike's practical joking expanded to ultra-hideous proportions. In a word, the kids loved every minute of it, and we were only able to get them to move with threats of flagellation and promises of expensive treats.

As for Alberta and me, with a small fortune in savings and borrowings gone down the drain, the less said about our feelings the better.

XXI

Pop, Mom and Freddie settled in Oklahoma City about a year after my return. Freddie got a cashier's job and Mom found part-time work as a saleswoman. Pop also got a job, but he held it briefly. It was menial and monotonous. He could not, willing as he was, give it the necessary attention. He became increasingly absent-minded, retreating into the memories of better days, and his employers fired him.

Poor as the job had been, its loss was a severe blow to Pop's morale. He felt useless and cast aside, and his distress saddened and worried me as nothing else could. As boy and youth, it had been impressed upon me that I fell far short of Pop's standards. He was always kindly, but I was obviously not the son he had hoped for. Well, that was past, and I could do nothing about it. But I felt now that I had to do something to lift him out of his despondency. Help given now, when no one else could give it, would do much to offset my failings of the past.

Pop had always been a rabid and knowledgeable baseball fan. And, at this time, baseball betting books ran wide open in Oklahoma City. The gambling was unorganized—the syndicate boys who tried to move in got the fast heave-ho. But a "local" who wanted to set up a small book was unmolested, nor was he required to pay off to the authorities.

I asked Pop if he would be interested in such an enterprise. He was not only interested but enthusiastic. I talked the proposition over with an acquaintance of mine, a man who ran a pool hall−beer parlor, and found him glad to oblige. He wouldn't take any cut from the book, he said. He had plenty of space for the setting up of a blackboard and Western Union ticker, and the betting would bring him trade.

So the installations were made, and, with a hundred dollars in cash, Pop began business. Like all books around the town, he took the long end of the bets: six to five, say, regardless of the team bet on. And the wagers were limited to a five-dollar top. Operating in this way, he was certain to win—he could not possibly make any serious inroads into his hundred. It was more as a formality than because I had to leave town for a week, that I asked the proprietor of the establishment to take care of him if he needed anything.

The week passed. Pop called on me my first morning back in the office. The betting had gone fine, he said absently. He had managed the bets as he should and had wound up each day a modestly comfortable winner. . . .

But he was broke.

"But you couldn't be!" I said. "Even if you'd lost every day you couldn't be. Did you"—I looked at him sharply—"did you give it away? Have some of your old friends been around to see you?"

Pop immediately took umbrage at my tone. Certainly he'd given nothing away, he said; his friends were not beggars. Perhaps he had seen fit to extend a few "small loans," but——

I was pretty bitter about it. Pop's generosity with his "friends" was largely responsible for reducing him from millionaire to pauper, and for years during my childhood it had forced us—his family—to make our home with relatives.

"All right," I said at last. "It took every penny I had to set you up, but I'll refinance my car and bankroll you again. But this time, Pop ... "

"I know," he said, a little testily. "You don't need to say anything more on the subject."

"I'm going to make sure of it," I said. "If any of those bums come around you again, there's going to be trouble."

I arranged for the loan by telephone. Then, leaving Pop stiff-necked and hurt, I went to see my beer parlor friend.

I was pretty sure of the identity of the men who had "borrowed" from Pop. Relatively young and able-bodied, they simply sponged because they preferred not to work; they were the kind who would beg with a bankroll in their pockets. I described the pair and the proprietor of the place nodded grimly.

"They've been around, all right. Showed up the first day your dad operated, and they've been here every day since. Two of the worst chiselers I ever seen. Why, I'd never seen the characters before, but they even tried to put the bite on me!"

"I'll tell you what," I said. "I'm going to sit in your back room for a while this afternoon. If they show up today, they'll get worked over with a pool cue."

"Well, now—" He scratched his head uneasily. "Don't think I could let you do that, Jim. Run a nice clean store here, never no trouble or anything, and I want to keep it that way. Anyhow——"

"All right. I'll catch 'em outside, then."

"—anyhow," he continued, "it wouldn't do much good. I dropped some pretty strong hints to your dad, and it didn't stop him. Just got huffy with me. I reckon he's been a pretty big man at one time, huh? Well, he can't get over the idea that he ain't one now—and maybe it's just as well that he can't. Prob'ly couldn't live with himself any other way."

"But look," I said, "I can't let him——"

"Better forget about this book or anything else where he's got to handle money. Know it cost you a nice little wad for that ticker and everything, but—oh, yeah, speaking of money ... "

He punched the keys of his cash register, took several small slips of paper from the drawer. They were I.O.U.'s—Pop's. The total just about equaled the pending loan on my car.

"Didn't think I ought to do it, Jim," he said apologetically, "but you said to take care of him, y'know, an' I done it."

I paid him, of course. And subsequently, unable to meet the loan, I lost my car. Needless to say, Pop's book did not reopen.

There was nothing much wrong with Pop physically, according to the doctors. But no man who feels useless and can see nothing to look forward to can long remain in good health. Pop's condition worsened rapidly. He came to require a great deal of looking after. When I, with my grant-in-aid about to expire, decided to go to California, he was in no condition to make the long trip.

This posed quite a problem, for Freddie's job was about to play out and she and Mom also wanted to make the move to California. Finally, since no other solution offered, Pop entered a small sanitarium.

We hoped that he would be able to come out on his own in a month or so. If that proved impossible, we meant to have him brought out with a nurse in attendance, just as quickly as we could get the necessary money.

For the time being, we had no such sum and no way of getting it. The car I drove was borrowed from a friend; he himself had borrowed it from his brother while on a visit to California. As payment for its use on the trip, I was to return it to that brother, a San Francisco car dealer.

Well, we arrived in San Diego where I intended to headquarter. After getting the folks settled there, I headed on toward San Francisco. It was only about five hundred miles distant—an easy day's drive, I supposed. But to one unfamiliar with the fantastic California traffic, five hundred miles can be a very long way. It was noon before I reached Los Angeles. Hours later, not long before sunset, I was just edging out of the city.

Being very short on money and still shorter on time, I had picked up a snack to take with me at a highway-side delicatessen. It consisted of cheese, crackers, a dill pickle and a bottle of port wine. I opened these purchases, now that I was through the city traffic, and ate and drank as I drove.

Not since I was a child at my grandfather's house had I drunk any wine. And this, by comparison, seemed wonderfully mellow and mild. I gulped it down, feeling the tenseness flow out of me as it flowed into me. I came to another wayside store and purchased another bottle. It sold for twenty-five cents a quart, cheaper than almost any drink but water. Since it was drawn from a keg into an unlabeled bottle (you can't buy it that way any more), I could only judge its potency by taste. And my taste said it was innocuous.

The error had almost fatal consequences.

Without realizing it, I drifted into a rosy haze. I came out of it just in time to keep from going off the highway. I stopped the car immediately, and rubbed my eyes. They didn't want to focus, it seemed, while my head showed a stubborn tendency to nod. I drove on slowly, intending to fill up on black coffee at the first lunch stand I came to.

Mile after mile passed. No lunch stand appeared. Night came on and it was all I could do to keep my eyes open, then suddenly, a few hundred yards ahead of me, the headlights picked out the figure of a man.

He was signaling for a ride. Possibly, I thought, he was the answer to my predicament. I slowed the car to a crawl, looking him over.

Young—seventeen or eighteen, perhaps. Pretty hard-bitten and rugged looking . . . but what of it? I had looked a hell of a lot worse many times.

I came even with him and stopped. "How far you going?" I called blearily.

"San Francisco." He hesitated with his hand on the door. "I mean, almost to San Francisco. A little place this side of——"

"Can you drive? Well, pile in, then," I said; and he piled in.

He was a fast driver but a good one. After watching him a few minutes, I uncorked the wine and leaned back.

"Sure glad you stopped for me, mister," he said. "It was beginning to look like I was going to have to stand there all night."

"Glad to have you along," I told him. "But how come you're out on the highway this late?"

"CCC camp." His face tightened with bitterness. "You know, relief work. Thirty bucks a month to your family, and they treat you like you were a convict. They kicked me out tonight."

"That's too bad. How did it happen?"

"Well, I had this knife, see, and this other kid claimed it was his. And me and him got to fighting, so they kicked *me* out."

I murmured sympathetically. He went on talking.

He didn't know what his folks were going to think of him. Probably that he was just no good, and probably they would be right. He'd quit high school to work two years ago and since then he'd had three jobs— not counting the CCC—and they'd all blown up on him. The guy he was working for would go out of business or he'd get jumped about something he hadn't done, or—well, something would happen. It looked like there just wasn't any use in a fellow trying to do the right thing. The harder he tried the harder he got it in the neck.

"You've just hit a run of hard luck," I said. "Just stay in there pitching, and you'll come out of it."

"Yeah," he muttered. "It's pretty easy for you to talk. A swell car an'——" He caught himself. "Sorry, mister. Feeling pretty sorry for myself, I guess."

He lapsed into silence for a time. I grinned, boozily, in the darkness.

Easy for me to talk. Me with "my" swell car and my one good suit of clothes and little more than enough money for a wildcat bus ticket back to San Diego! My plight was many times worse than this youngster's. I had driven myself too hard, too long; I had become soul-sick with the drivel— the unadorned commercial writing—which I had poured into the popular magazines. And now I could do no more, even if my life depended on it.

Yet if I did not do that . . . ?

It was quite a question. What does a man of thirty-five do who has lost his one negotiable talent? What does he do, this man, with his history of alcoholism, nervous exhaustion, tuberculosis and almost uninterrupted frustration? What about his wife and three children? What about his father, whom he has promised to——

Abruptly, I cut off this chain of thought. Pop had cried when we left him.

But—I took a long drink of the wine—this was certainly a good joke on my hitchhiker. I should be envying him, instead of the other way around.

" . . . kind of work you do, mister?"

"What?" I said. "Oh, I'm a writer."

"Must be pretty good money in that."

"Well, I've made quite a bit," I said.

"How do you—uh—how do you do it, anyway? Just drive around the country looking at things until you get an idea, and——"

I laughed, choking on the drink I was taking. He gave me a sour look.

"I don't get it, by gosh," he said. "Me, I don't drink or smoke or, well, anything like that. Never even could afford to take a girl to a show. And all these other people, they go zipping around in big cars havin' a heck of a time for themselves an'—. It just ain't right, mister. You know it ain't!"

"Things will get better for you," I said. "They can get just so bad and then they have to get better."

"Yeah? What if they don't?"

"Then you'll probably be dead anyway, and it won't matter."

I was drowsy, more than a little weary of the conversation. Unconsciously, and quite unfairly—for no two people are alike—I was comparing his situation with the one I had been in at his age. And I felt that he was rather too ready to despair.

He was silent for fifteen or twenty miles. Finally, he said, hesitating:

"You—uh—you like to take a shortcut, mister? Up through the mountains?"

"Suits me," I shrugged.

Silence again. Then: "I r-reckon you're pretty tired, ain't you, mister? You want to go to sleep, I'll wake you up when we get there."

"Well, thanks," I said. "I think I'll do that."

I took the last drink in the bottle, and tossed it out the window. I leaned back and was instantly asleep.

At what seemed to be only a moment later, but which was actually several hours, I suddenly woke up.

The car was stopped, motor off, lights extinguished. I rubbed my eyes, tried to penetrate the darkness.

"What the hell?" I grunted. "Why are you stopped here?"

His head was slightly turned away from me; one hand was in his pocket. "I—I t-tell you, mister," he stammered tensely. "G-gonna tell you somethin'. I—— I——"

"Well, go ahead, dammit," I said, my head still fuzzy with the wine. "Spit it out!"

"I g-gotta——" His voice broke in a sigh. "I g-got to go to the toilet."

I laughed, not very pleasantly. "That's an idea but let's not make a production out of it. Come on! What's the matter with you, anyway?"

He levered the catch on the door.

I climbed out the door on my side.

And fortunately I held onto it. For at my second step my foot came down into empty space.

I gasped, and flung myself backward. Too frightened to speak or cry out, I peered around me in the pale, near-lightless light of the quarter moon.

We were in the mountains—high among them. And I was standing on the brink of a precipice, on a triangular strip of road bounded on one side by the cliff and on the other by the car.

It was a bad spot to get in: there was no getting past those cut-in front wheels.

It was a very bad spot: there was no getting out the other way, at the base of the triangle.

For the kid was standing there, silently, one arm shakily outthrust, and the dim moonlight sparkled wickedly on the long blade of his knife.

He took a nervous step toward me, knife circling in his hand. I squeezed backward an inch or two.

Then, I could retreat no further, nor could he advance further without actually attacking. So we stood there poised, staring at one another. Breathing heavily. Waiting.

I was terrified, sick and paralyzed with terror. I thought, *Well, you asked for it. You've been asking for it all your life and you finally got it.* I thought: *What a hell of a way to die; tossed down a mountainside with your throat cut.*

Then . . .

Well, it was a strange thing, but suddenly all my horror and sickness were for this boy. I could think only of the monstrous joke of which he was about to be victim.

A few dollars, an inexpensive wristwatch, a car that would get him pinched before he had it a day. That was what he was going to get— nothing. Nothing but the gas chamber or a life sentence in prison. And in a way it was all my fault.

I could have set him right about my financial situation. I could have shown some real interest in him, made an effort to give him some constructive advice. Instead I had chosen to spout platitudes, to egg him on with seeming callousness. To drink and sleep.

Now it was too late to tell him the truth; he would never believe me. It was too late to plead. He had begun the preliminaries of a holdup murder. Much as he might want to—and I was sure he did want to—he would be afraid to back out now.

If only there was some way of letting him know, of making him think that . . .

I swayed unconsciously. The action seemed to tap something in my mind, to set in motion the horror-frozen cells. And I swayed again, exaggeratedly, and spoke:

"Thass the knife you were tellin' me about? Le's see the damn thing."

I put out my hand, slowly. I held it there, the tips of my fingers almost touching the tip of the blade.

"Well, come on," I said. "You wanted to show it to me, didn't you? Can't see it with you hangin' onto it."

"M-mister, I——" His hand jerked convulsively, and the blade described an arc. Then, still holding the haft, he let it come down in my palm.

"Nice knife," I said. "But y'know somethin'? Some people see you carryin' that an' they might think you were goin' to hold 'em up."

I gave a gentle tug on the blade. I said, "Le's throw it away, huh?"

He let go.

I threw it away, flipped it over the precipice.

. . . We reached his hometown around midnight, and his folks, simple, good-hearted people, insisted that I stay over until morning. They were delighted, incidentally, that he had been dismissed from the camp. His father had landed a job that very day and there was one waiting for him, the boy, at the same place.

The kid and I slept in the same big old-fashioned bed that night. And, yes, I slept soundly. Why not? He was no criminal. Opportunity and necessity had conspired to make him one, but it was doubtful that he would ever again be gripped in such a sinister conjunction. Or, if he was, he had this recent experience to remember and to strengthen him.

The next morning I drove the car into San Francisco and turned it over to the dealer-owner. My arrival interrupted a telephone call he was making.

"Wired me you were coming in yesterday," he explained. "Figured you might have been hijacked, so I was putting out an alarm with the highway patrol."

"I'm glad you didn't have to," I said.

XXII

THE WAR BOOM, or, rather, the boom incident to the impending war, was just getting under way in San Diego. There was still a great deal of unemployment. Prices, following the oldest of economic laws, were racing far ahead of wages.

The seven of us—Mom, Freddie and my family—had to squeeze into a three-and-a-half room apartment. Freddie's job, as a switchboard operator, just about paid the rent on it. I was faced, then, with meeting our other living expenses, and I responded to the emergency quite ignobly.

I had been proud of my research grant, one of the two awarded yearly in the United States. It was an unusual honor for a man without a college degree, and the field I had been assigned—the building trades—was an important one. The immediate financial return was not large, but that did not matter. A book was to be published from my findings; there would be substantial royalties. Not only that, but it was entirely possible that I might receive academic recognition—an honorary degree. Maybe even a doctorate. I, Jim Thompson, the stupidest guy in high school, the college misfit and bumbler—that Jim Thompson would no longer be, nor his painful memories and gnawing, growing self-doubts. And into his place would step a redoubtable *Doctor* Thompson.

Having always detested affectation, I would never have used the title. But I needed it for what it represented—to disprove the almost unbearable implications of a long list of failures. If, I told myself, I could just this once achieve a real distinction—an honor unmarred by fluke or my own shortcomings—if I could just this once do a job that allowed me to keep my pride, meanwhile rewarding me handsomely. . . .

Well, I got the bad news a few days after we settled in San Diego. The war boom, with its immense leavening of the nation's economy, had made or would make my material obsolescent. The six room, five thousand-dollar house permanently vanished. So also did the dollar-an-hour building craftsman. It was "extremely regrettable" and I was not to consider it a reflection on my research or writing . . . but the book could not be published.

I started looking for a job.

I could find nothing—no position that paid even reasonably well or that carried any semblance of responsibility. I felt dispirited, licked, and I looked it. Appetiteless and unable to sleep, I had begun to drink great quantities of cheap wine. The stuff told on my appearance. It also, so thoroughly had I become impregnated, smelled.

I began applying for menial jobs (*"Just anything at all, mister."*). I found one just in time to keep us from starving.

One of the San Diego aircraft factories had begun an extensive expansion program. The building was being carried on simultaneously with the making of planes; and they needed a man to go around on his hands and knees, chipping up the spatterings of plaster and paint.

I leaped at this "opportunity," to use the personnel manager's term. If I made good (his phrasing again) I would be promoted to a full-fledged janitor. For the present, I would draw twenty-five dollars a week.

Well, poke fun at it though I do, the job was good for me. It kept me from drinking for at least eight hours a day. Through it, my interest in life was rearoused.

Roaming the plant from one end to the other, I got a broad and original conception of the workings of a great factory. The snatches of conversation I overheard, the things I saw, began to intrigue me. I tried to resist, but the constant challenge to the imagination was too strong to be ignored. I had to—as we used to say down south—"get in the big middle" of things.

One day I got up from the floor, wiped my hands against my pants and accosted the general manager. "I understand you're having a lot of trouble with your parts records," I said. "I'd like to have the job of straightening them out."

He gave me a quick glance. Grinning out of the corner of his mouth, he started to turn away.

"Give me a chance," I pleaded. "I've held some pretty important jobs in my time. What——"

"Have, huh?" He gave me another look. "You wouldn't be an expert accountant would you? Or a CPA?"

"Well, no, but——"

"You're an engineer, then."

"No, I'm——"

"But, of course, you read blueprints?"

"Well . . . "

"Better get back to your work," he said.

As soon as dinner was over that night, I hastened down to the public library. I drew out every book I could find on accounting and blueprint reading and took them home. I was still reading the next morning when my wife set toast and coffee before me.

Red eyed, and with a top-heavy feeling in my head, I accosted the general manager again.

"I can do any accounting job you've got around here now," I said. "And I can sight-read blueprints. I sat up all night studying."

Before he could turn away or order me back to my work, I reeled off the titles of the books I'd read. Some of them apparently struck a familiar chord, for he gave me an appraising look.

"All right. What do you think our trouble is?"

"Everything," I said. "Whoever installed your records system didn't know what they were doing."

"That's pretty hard to believe. It was installed by a very good firm of industrial engineers."

"Well, however good they were," I said, "they didn't know much about people. The system's good enough in theory, but it doesn't work out in practice. It overlooks the human element; it would take a corps of high-paid experts to keep it going. Now what you need is something simple, foolproof, and I can ... "

While he fidgeted, wavering between interest and irritation, I went on talking. In the end, doubtless as the only way he saw of shutting me up, he gave me my chance. I was put in the parts-control department for a week at my regular salary. During that week, I was to study the system and recommend changes which I felt would rectify the trouble.

I did better than that. In less than a week, I invented and installed a new system. And I gave such a convincing demonstration of its advantages that the former involved and expensive system was permanently discarded.

In the seven-odd months I remained at the factory, I was steadily promoted to better jobs and I received five pay increases. I quit at the end of that time.

I had progressed to a point where I was in competition with the professionals of aircraft building, men who had made and were making it their life's work. I couldn't hope to compete with them; I had no strong desire to. After all, I had my own profession, and I had spent almost twenty years in it. I would have to capitalize on that experience, and quickly, or remain the rest of my life in a modestly padded rut.

I had managed to labor out two short detective stories. With the slender proceeds from these, my wife and children returned to Nebraska for a visit and I caught a bus for New York. I was confident that I could turn up some kind of writing or publishing job there. Also, by being able to talk directly with editors and publishers, I would improve my chances for doing some really worthwhile free-lancing.

I took a bargain-rate bus, and the fare included meals. You can probably guess what those meals were like. I became violently ill after the first one, nauseated and racked with dysentery. And if there is any worse complaint to have on a cross-country bus—with, of course, no toilet and infrequent rest stops—I cannot think what it is. I began buying my meals but the poison was already in me, and it continued to manifest itself, painfully and embarrassingly.

The bus driver became annoyed, then infuriated. Due to my getting off "at every damned bush and signboard," he was hours behind in his schedule. The next time I made him stop, he declared, he would go off and leave me and I could by God walk to New York.

"But I can't help it," I said. "I'm sick."

"Well, get yourself some medicine, then! Get a jug of whiskey an' sip on it—that oughta help. Do *somethin'*, for God's sake!"

I bought a bottle of anti-colic compound. Its only effect was to put me to sleep . . . with almost disastrous results. So I tried sipping on whiskey, and that did help. The griping stopped and stayed stopped—as long as I drank.

We arrived in Oklahoma City the third day out, and I laid over there a day to see Pop. He could not believe it was I when I first walked in on him. The seven long, lonely months must have seemed like years to him, and I think he had begun to feel that we had abandoned him.

I made him understand the truth: that his remaining here was due to circumstances beyond our control. He began to brighten up.

"Well, it's all over now," he said. "You just help me get my things together, and I'll clear out of here right now."

"Pop," I said. "I—"

"Well?" He looked at me. "You're going to take me away, aren't you? T-that's why you've come back?"

I hesitated. Then, I said, yes, that was why. "But I can't go with you, Pop. I'm on my way to New York."

"Oh?" He frowned troubledly. "Well, I guess I could travel by myself if——"

"I've got a swell job there," I lied. "Give me a—well, just give me a month and I can send you to California by stateroom. Get you a nurse if you need one. But the best I can do now is a bus ticket."

"I don't know," he said dubiously. "I'm afraid the doctor . . . I'm afraid I couldn't . . ." He sat back down on the bed. "You're sure, Jimmie? If I wait another month, you'll——?"

"That's a promise. And I never break a promise."

"No," he nodded, and his face cleared, "you never do. . . . That'll be fine, then. I won't mind so much now that I know I'm really leaving."

He was very weak, but organically, considering his age, his condition was at least fair. As to the acute mental depression he had sunk into, the doctor felt that this would be greatly relieved once he was back with his family.

I stayed over in Oklahoma City that night. The next morning, leaving Pop happily laying his plans for his trip, I caught another bargain-rate bus for New York.

I had not counted on having to buy my meals on the trip, nor, of course, the purchase of some twenty dollars worth of whiskey. And I arrived in the big town with one lone quarter in my pocket. It was November of 1941, a cold, bitter night. I was still violently ill, and the cold seemed to congeal my California-thinned blood.

I stood on a street corner for a time, shivering, frightened by the crowds, wondering what to do. It was like a bad dream, like one of those nightmares where one is plunged into a strange world—where running is both imperative and impossible. I had to have rest. I had to have some whiskey. I had to, in a month's time—in less than a month, now ... My family had not been in Nebraska for several years, and they wanted to make a long visit. So there was no big hurry where they were concerned. But Pop—there could be no delay there. I could not fail him.

Meanwhile, first things first.

My baggage, a briefcase and Gladstone, was worn but substantial looking. I had no trouble in checking in at a first-class hotel and charging a quart of whiskey to my room. I gave my quarter to the bellboy. Slugging down a few drinks, I tried to map out a plan of action.

It would be impossible to hold a job until this bowel ailment was cleared up. At any rate, a job would not get me the money I had to have as quickly as I had to have it. I thought and thought, turning a thousand wild schemes over in my mind. And the one I finally settled on was probably the wildest of them all.

I would write and sell a novel.

This solution to my dilemma seemed even more preposterous the next morning. But I gave myself a pep talk—and several stiff drinks—and sallied forth into the city. After all, I was a writer, wasn't I? And publishers needed books, didn't they? And it was no crime to be broke, was it? So what was the difference if the proposition I had to make was just a trifle unusual?

It made quite a bit of difference, it seemed. I never got past the receptionists at the first few publishers I called on. At the fifth—or maybe it was the sixth—an editor heard me out sympathetically, and suggested that I wire whatever friends or relatives I had for a ticket back to California. He lent me two dollars for this purpose. I spent it for breakfast, cigarettes and a few more drinks. Then, I tackled another publisher.

This was a small but reputable firm which had published many first novels. I was promptly admitted to an editor's office. He listened to me incredulously, burst into laughter and took me in to see the publisher. That gentleman also listened, a frown of wonder creasing his forehead.

"Let's see," he said at last. "You want us to bail you out of your hotel, then——"

"It's just a small bill."

"Then you want us to lend you a typewriter and stake you while you're writing a novel, a book which you yourself don't have very clearly in mind."

I said I had it clear enough. "I talk a very bad story. And you only need to stake me for two weeks. When I turn in the novel, you can deduct anything you've given me from your usual advance."

"*When* you turn it in, and *if* it's publishable."

"You'll have it," I said, "within two weeks. And it will be publishable."

He hesitated, moved against his better judgment. "I'm sure your intentions are good, but I don't think you will. I don't see how you can. But perhaps . . . "

I walked out of that office with a battered typewriter in one hand and a check in the other. I checked out of my hotel, rented a three-dollar-a-week room on Seventh Avenue and started to work. Working an average of twenty hours a day, I finished the book in ten days.

It got a mixed reception at the publishing company. Some of the editors were very enthusiastic about it; others were just as unenthusiastic. So, as is often done, the manuscript was farmed out to another writer for reading and opinion.

This young man was the scion of a wealthy Hollywood family, and the author of one novel. He reported that I showed promise "for a beginning writer" but that I obviously did not know enough about life to attempt a novel. I needed to "meet the stark realities of existence at first hand"— not merely to read about them in books, as (he added) I patently had.

Sick and nearly hysterical with worry as I was, I burst into laughter when I read that report. The publisher gave me a friendly wink. He was no more impressed with the young man's opinion than I was. He would, he said, pass the manuscript on to a couple of other writers.

"Louis Bromfield and Richard Wright. I'm sure they'll like it. And now, as long as we're holding you up on the thing . . . "

He advanced me another twenty-five dollars. Since I had been practically living on whiskey, and whiskey was very cheap in those days, I still had part of the original advance left. If I had to, I could live two weeks with no additional money.

"Do you think—" I hesitated as I shook hands with the publisher. "Do you think you'll have your reports in within the next two weeks?"

"Well, we'll certainly try to. If we can't, and you should need a few more dollars, we can——"

"It isn't that," I said. "It's something that would be pretty hard to explain, and I won't try to. I've burdened you enough with my personal problems. But——"

"Sure." He clapped me on the back. "I'll let you know just as soon as I can."

XXIII

THE CALENDAR BLURRED AND SWAYED IN FRONT OF MY EYES. I braced my hands against the dresser, leaned forward squinting.

"Let's see," I mumbled aloud. "T-two days from Oklahoma, plus ten days, plus four f'r that Hollywood bastard, plus—plus— What the hell day is it?"

I couldn't figure it out. My eyes wouldn't focus. My mind was satiated with worry over the inevitable.

It was probably as well that I didn't know the truth, or, knowing, did not accept it. Sodden drunk for days, I was near enough dead already.

"G-got to eat," I thought, again mumbling the thought aloud. "Got to . . ."

I stumbled around the room, looking for my clothes. I discovered that I was dressed, and laughing crazily I flopped back down on the bed.

There was a knock on the door. I shrugged, and dug a bottle out from under the pillow. . . . Lot of knocking lately. Lot of funny-looking things. Take a drink, and they went away.

The door opened and two men came in. My landlady stood behind them, wringing her hands.

"I just didn't know what to do, gentlemen. I tried to call a doctor, but——"

"Sure. The doctors don't like to fool with us drunks. . . . What do you say, Bill? You thinking the same thing I am?"

"I'm afraid so. And I think we'd better get him there fast."

They took me by the arms, hoisted me to my feet. Suddenly panicked, I tried to jerk away.

They held onto me firmly.

"It's all right, fellow. We're from Alcoholics Anonymous. We're going to take care of you."

"H-how? Where you takin' me?"

"Don't you worry at all. We're on your side. Been through this thing ourselves."

We went down to the street and got into a car. Then on to Bellevue Hospital where I was committed.

Many scare stories have been circulated about Bellevue Alcoholic Ward. Perhaps I am not the most competent critic, but I saw nothing to justify them. The food was good, the beds comfortable and immaculate.

Surrounded by some pretty trying customers, the attendants remained accommodating, the doctors and nurses courteous and capable.

In a word, I was very well treated. So much so that by the afternoon of the fifth day I was able to be discharged.

I started across town toward my rooming house, worrying again—continuing to worry. It was a day short of five weeks, since I had left Oklahoma. Not much over a month, to be sure, but to an old man, a lonely old man who secretly feared that he might be forsaken . . .

I reached Fifth Avenue. Instead of crossing it, I suddenly turned and headed uptown. Surely the publisher would be able to make his decision by this time. By God, he simply *had* to.

Well, he had.

He walked me into his office, his arm around my shoulders. "Got some good reports from Louis and Dick. They're going to fix us up with blurbs to put on the cover. . . . Now, I do feel that quite a few revisions are necessary. There are a couple of chapters I'd like to see excised, and new ones substituted. But——"

"Oh," I said, pretty drearily. "Then it'll still be quite a while before——"

"What? Oh, no, we'll pay you for it right now. We're definitely accepting it. Incidentally, when you get this one out of the way, we'll be glad to—Yes?"

The receptionist was standing in the doorway. She murmured an apology, held out a yellow Western Union envelope. "This came in yesterday, Mr. Thompson. I tried to reach you by phone, but——"

"It must be from my mother," I said. "I wasn't sure how long I'd be at that rooming house, so I told her to—to—"

I ripped the envelope open.

I stared down at the message.

Blindly. Stricken motionless.

"Bad news?" The publisher's hushed voice.

"My father," I said. "He died two days ago."

THE GOLDEN GIZMO

I

IT WAS ALMOST QUITTING TIME WHEN TODDY MET THE MAN WITH NO CHIN AND THE TALKING DOG. Almost three in the afternoon.

House to house gold-buyers cannot work much later than three nor much before nine-thirty in the morning. The old trinkets and jewelry they buy are usually stored away. Few housewives will interrupt their after-breakfast or pre-dinner chores to look them up.

Toddy stopped at the end of the block and gave the house before him a swiftly thorough appraisal. It was the last house in this neighborhood. It stood almost fifty yards back from the street, a shingle and stucco bunga-low virtually hidden behind an untended foreground of sedge and cedar trees. Crouched at the end of the weed-impaled driveway was a garage, or, rather, Toddy guessed, one end of a three-car garage. An expensive late-model car was in view, and a highly developed sixth sense told Toddy that the other stalls were similarly occupied.

Hesitating, wanting to quit work for the day, Toddy flipped open the lid of the small wooden box he carried and looked inside.

In the concealed bottom of the box were the indispensables of the gold-buying trade: a set of jeweler's scales and weights, a jeweler's loupe—magnifying eyepiece—a small triangular-faced file and a tiny bottle of one hundred per cent pure nitric acid. In the tray on top was a considerable quantity of gold-filled and plated slum, mingled with the day's purchases of actual gold. The latter included almost an ounce of high-karat dental gold—bridges, crowns and fillings—plus an approximate two ounces of jewelry, most of it also of above-average quality.

A man who buys three ounces of gold a day is making very good money . . . if he buys at the "right" prices. And Toddy had bought right. For an investment of twenty-two dollars, he had acquired roughly eighty dollars' worth of gold.

It had been a good day, as good as the average, at least. He was under no financial pressure to work longer. If he knocked off now, just a little early, he could miss that clamoring and hopeless chaos which is Los Angeles during rush hours. He could be back in town inside an hour or less.

Elaine always slept late—of necessity. If he got back to the hotel early enough, he might be there before she started stirring around. Before she had a chance to raise any of that peculiarly hideous hell of which only she was capable.

Toddy lighted a cigarette fretfully, all but decided to begin the long trudge back to the bus stop. Still, if he quit early today, he would do it again. It might become a habit with him, complemented by the equally dangerous habit of starting to work late. Eventually, he would be working no more than an hour a day. And then the day would come when he would not work at all. That would be the end, brother. The end for him and a much quicker and more unpleasant end for Elaine. For regardless of her vain and frequent boasting, no one else but he would put up with her indefinitely.

With a shrug, he ground out the cigarette beneath his heel and took a decisive step up the walk. Swearing silently, he stopped again. Dammit, it was *almost* three—only ten minutes of. And it was such a hell of a gloomy day. Smog had settled over the city like a sponge. Gray, dank, sun-obscuring smog. Even if Elaine was all right when she awakened, the smog would start her off. She'd be depressed and blue, and if he wasn't there . . .

Not only that, but he would be wasting his time at this particular house. Obviously, wealthy people lived here, despite the air of desolation. And wealthy people, even when they were inclined to dispose of their old gold, usually knew its value too well to make the transaction profitable.

"Sharp" gold-buyers have no contact with the law . . . willingly. The law, as they well know, takes a very dim view of their activities. Their licenses may be in order; they may have done nothing provably illegal. Still, a steady stream of complaints flows in their wake, and the police become irritated. The police reason that a man who persuades a house-wife to sell him a hundred-dollar watch for five possesses no very high moral tone. He need get out of line very little, rub them the wrong way in the slightest, to be jailed for investigation and eventually "floated" out of town.

Toddy had stayed clear of the police so far, and he intended to keep right on doing so. There'd be no floater for him if he was ever picked up. Once they fingerprinted him, they'd be passing him from city to city until he got train sick. He couldn't remember all the places where he was wanted, but he knew there were a great many.

But—and he hated to admit it, in this instance—he was in little danger from the police unless he deliberately and flagrantly annoyed them. If he had run out of cards, the situation would have been different. But he had not run out; he was always careful to keep supplied. His reluctant fingers found one now, drew it from the breast pocket of his smart tweed coat.

> Mr. Toddmore Kent
> *Special Representative*
> Los Angeles Jewel & Watch Co.

Brokers In
Gold Silver Platinum

The Los Angeles Jewel & Watch Co. was a side-street watch-repair shop. Its owner was a beer-loving, bighearted little Dutchman named Milt Vonderheim.

Most wholesale buyers of precious metals give their door-to-door men the same kind of skinning that the latter deal out to their clients. They downgrade your ten-karat gold to eight; they weigh coin and sterling silver together; they "steal" your platinum at a price merely twice as high as that of twenty-four-karat gold. But tubby little Milt, with his beer breath and perpetual smile, was the golden exception to the base rule of other buyers. . . . So a man needed his money every night—was that a reason to rob him blind? So he had no regular residence in the city and was at the mercy of one who did—should you charge him a profit for not speaking to the police?

Milt didn't think so. Milt's prices were only a few cents lower than those of the U.S. Mint to whom he sold the stuff which Toddy and a number of other young men sold to him. Milt paid five dollars a penny-weight—one twentieth of a troy ounce—for platinum. If you'd had a lean day, he was very apt to upgrade your stuff; pay you fourteen-karat prices, say, for ten.

Nor was that all Milt did: fat, shabby little Milt, edging deeper and deeper into poverty. Milt supplied these cards which were literally worth their weight in gold if a cop stopped you. A cop wouldn't bother you when you showed that card, unless he had to. A transient gold-buyer was one thing. A special representative of a long-established local firm, no matter how small, was something else.

Milt had started Toddy out as a gold-buyer a year ago. He had trained him, stood by him through the perils that beset the trade. He had trained other men, too, Toddy knew, most of those who now sold to him, and he stood by them also. But he did not treat them quite the same as he did Toddy. He was always inviting Toddy back into his shop apartment for a beer or a chat. He was always bragging of him.

"That Toddy," he would boast to the other buyers, "from him you could well take a lesson. Regularity, steadiness, that iss the lesson vot Toddy should give you. While you boys are putting on your pants or drinking coffee, Toddy has already made fife dollars."

Toddy's lean face flushed a little as he remembered those boasts. Resolutely, he brushed a bit of cigarette ash from his whipcord trousers, made a slight adjustment on the collar of his tan sports shirt, and turned his pebbled-leather brogans up the walk to the house.

It was even farther away than it had appeared from the street, and he had an uneasy feeling of being watched from the dark interior behind the rusted screen door. But, hell, what was there to be nervy about? He wasn't giving the police any trouble and they weren't giving him any. And what else was there besides a slammed door or a dog? If he was starting to let things like that bother him, he might as well do a high brody right now. He and Elaine together.

He stepped lightly across the porch, splattered with green segments from the cedars, and raised his hand to knock. He jerked it back, startled.

"Yes?" said a man's sharp-soft voice. "What is it? You are selling something, please?"

The man must have been standing right in the door, hidden by the rusted screen and the shadowed room inside. Toddy blinked his eyes, trying to get the daylight out of them, but he still couldn't see the guy. All he knew about him was his voice—a Spanish-sounding voice.

"Not at all, sir," said Toddy, with energetic joviality. "I'm not selling a thing. A friend of yours suggested that I call on you. If I can give you my card . . ."

The screen opened and a bony, hair-tufted hand emerged. Deftly, it plucked the card from his fingers and disappeared. Toddy shifted uncomfortably.

This was all wrong, he knew. The spiel was off-key here, the gimmick was out of place. He had learned to use the card as a door-opener—to get 'em curious. To force them outside, or to get him in. He had learned to mention a neighbor, or, better still, a "friend." If they fell for it—and why shouldn't some neighbor or friend have suggested a call?—it was all to the good. If they got funny or sharp, he could have the "wrong house," lie out of it some way.

You had to do those things.

Toddy wished that he hadn't done them here.

He looked behind him, down the long inviting walk. He gave a slight hitch to his trousers and snuggled the box firmly under his arm. He'd give some excuse and beat it out of here. Or just beat it without saying anything. After all, he—he—

The screen door swung open, wide.

Through it, with stately but threatening grace, stalked the biggest dog Toddy had ever seen. He did not realize just how big it was until a moment later.

He knew very little about dogs, but he recognized this one as a Doberman. Slowly, it lowered its great pear-shaped head to his feet and examined each in turn. With awful deliberation, the animal sniffed each leg. It looked up at him thoughtfully, appraising him.

Silently, it reared up on its hind legs.

The front paws came down on Toddy's shoulders. The black muzzle almost rested against his nose.

Toddy stared into the beast's eyes. He stared unwinkingly, afraid to move or speak. He stopped breathing and was too fear-stricken to know it.

The screen door closed, slammed at last by its aged spring. As from a great distance, Toddy heard the man's amused chuckle, a seemingly unending chuckle; then, a sharp "Perrito!"—Spanish for "little dog."

The dog's ears pricked to attention. "Ssor-ree," the dog said courteously. "Ssss ssor-ree."

"D-don't m-mention it," Toddy stammered. "A mistake. I m-mean—"

The dog dropped back down to the porch and took up a position behind him. The screen door opened again.

"Please to come in," said the man.

"I don't—that d-dog," said Toddy. *Dammit, was he dreaming this?* "Won't he ... will he hurt anyone?"

"On the contrary," the man said. And, helplessly, Toddy stepped inside. "He kills quite painlessly."

II

Todd Kent (the *more* was phony) had been born with a gizmo. That—the GI term for the unidentifiable—was the way he had come to think of something that changed in value from day to day, that was too whimsical in its influence to be bracketed as a gift, talent, aptitude or trait.

For most of the thirty years of his life, the gizmo had pushed him into the smelly caverns where the easy money lay. All his life—and always without warning—it had hustled him out through soul-skinning, nerve-searing exits.

A runaway from a broken home, Todd had first hit the big dough when he was sixteen. He had landed as a bellboy in a big hotel. From that he advanced to bell captain, and he was in; the gizmo went to work. Before it was all over the job of bellboy in that hotel was priced at one thousand dollars—a sum which the purchasers grimly went about recovering (along with considerably more!) in various shady ways. Before it was all over—when the beefs flowed over Toddy's young head and those of the minor executives he had fixed—many of the bellboys were in jail and the hotel had a thoroughly bad name.

Toddy was too young to prosecute on a job-selling rap. But there was such a thing as a juvenile authority which could take charge of him until he was twenty-one. Not at all pleased with this prospect, he had a confidential talk with the hotel's lawyers. The result was that he left town . . . but without his spanking new Cadillac, his diamond rings and the contents of his safety deposit box.

In a trackside jungle, he watched an ancient and browbeaten bum toss dice from a rusted can. The bum put the dice in the can, shook them vigorously and threw a point. Then he reshook them, rolled them again, and there was his point. Not immediately—it usually took several throws—and not always. But almost always. Often enough.

Toddy's gizmo swung into action.

Yeah, the flattered bum agreed, it was quite a trick. Any hustler could throw hot dice from his hand, but who'd ever seen it done from a cup? Many big gambling houses insisted on cup shots, particularly where there was heavy money down. They were supposed to be hustler-proof.

No, he'd never got a chance to put the shot to work; stumbled onto it too late for that. But if a guy had the front, the dough, this was how it was done . . .

You held one die on your point. You didn't put it inside the cup. You palmed it and held it outside, pressed against the cup in your shooting hand. Say you were shooting for Phoebe, little five. You held onto three of it, then you rolled, letting the held die spin down at the exact moment the other shot came from the cup. Yeah, sure; maybe fever didn't make. Maybe the free die came out on four and you'd crapped. But you'd lowered the odds against yourself, see, kid? You'd knocked hell out of 'em. And how you could murder them big joints on come and field bets!

Months later . . . but this episode shall be cut short. Months later, in the secluded parlor of a Reno gambling house, a lean taffy-haired young man sat watching a slow-motion picture of himself. The picture had been shot, apparently, from a concealed camera above the crap table, and it showed little but the movements of his hands. But that was enough. That was more than enough. Before the film was half-unwound, Toddy was drawing out his wallet, his bank passbook, and—oh, yes—the keys to a spanking new Cadillac.

He moved into the con games as naturally as a blonde moving into a mink coat. He rode them through Dallas, Houston, Oklahoma City, St. Louis, Omaha, Cleveland. New Orleans, Memphis. . . . He rode them and was ridden, to use a police term. The gizmo was fickle, and he was ridden, rousted and floated.

Since he shunned working with others, he was confined to playing the "small con"—the hype and the smack and the tat. Those, however, with the new twists he added to them, were more than sufficient to provide him with a number of pleasant possessions, not the least of which was a substantial equity in another Cad.

Then, the gizmo becoming frivolous again, it removed these belongings and added his biography (handsomely illustrated) to a volume compiled by the Better Business Bureau. It also left him wanted on seven raps in Chicago, his then base of operations.

That was the gizmo for you. Pushing you into clover one day, booting you into a weedpatch the next.

The gizmo pushed him into the Berlin black market and sixty-three grand in cash. But, naturally, it didn't let him out of the Army with it. What it let him out of the Army with was a six-months' brig tan and a dishonorable discharge.

He wandered out to Los Angeles, hating the gizmo, determined to be rid of it. But the gizmo was stubborn. Wash dishes, drive a cab, peddle brushes?—don't be foolish, Todd*more*. Use your head. You can always see a turn if you look for it. . . . What about all these winos and bums? The town's full of 'em, and they'd sell you their right legs for a buck. They'd sell you their—*blood!* The big labs pay twenty-five a pint for blood. If you did the fronting, sold for fifteen and bought for five . . .

Toddy was in and out of the blood business fast. He stayed only long enough to get a roll. The scheme was entirely legal. For the first time in his life he was playing something strictly legit . . . and he couldn't take it. If it was legal to nourish the desire to drink with a man's own blood, then he'd go back to his own side of the fence.

He was resting on his roll, deliberating over his next move, when the gizmo shoved Elaine at him. He hadn't had a real roll or even time to take a deep breath since then. He couldn't make enough, no matter what he made, to do the thing that Milt, the gizmo having introduced them, persuaded him he should do. There was good money, legit money, in buying from dentists and other commercial users of gold.

Toddy couldn't have the dough and Elaine, too. Somehow, though he knew Milt was right in so advising him, he couldn't bring himself to boot her out on her tail.

. . . So, now, now the gizmo had led him into this house, into the money *or*. And he had a sneaking hunch that this was going to be something fantastic, even for the gizmo, in the way of *ors*.

III

For the size of the house, the affluence which it outwardly bespoke, it—this living room, at least—was badly, even poorly, furnished. The few chairs, the undersize divan, the table, all were of maple, the cheapest thing on the market. Except for a throw rug or two, the floor was bare.

Toddy looked at the table where, as a matter of habit, he had placed his open box. He saw now that there was another box on it, a kind of oblong wooden tray. A set of tong-type calipers partly shielded the contents; but despite this and the deep gloom of the room, Toddy could see the outline of a heavy gold watch.

He had taken this in at a glance, his gaze barely wavering from the man. The guy was something to look at. He was the kind of guy you'd automatically keep your eyes on when he was around.

He had no chin. It was as though nose and eyes and a wide thin mouth had been carved out of his neck. Either a thick black wig or a moplike bowl of natural hair topped the neck.

He stared from Toddy to the card, then back again. He waited, a faint look of puzzlement on his white chinless face. He smiled, suddenly, and held the card out to Toddy.

"I can read nothing without my glasses," he smiled, "and, as usual, I seem to have misplaced them. You will explain your business please?"

Toddy retrieved the bit of pasteboard with a twinge of relief. There was something screwy here. It was just as well not to leave his or Milt's name behind him.

"Of course, sir," he said. "I—that dog of yours took my breath away for a moment. I didn't mean to just stand here, taking up your time."

"I am sure of it," the man nodded suavely. "I am certain that you do not mean to do it now. Perhaps, now that you have recovered your breath, Mr.—?"

"—Clinton," Toddy lied. "I'm with the California Precious Metals Company. You've probably seen our ads in the papers—world's largest buyers of scrap gold?"

"No. I have seen no such ads."

"That's entirely understandable," Toddy said. "We've discontinued them lately—well, it must have been more than a year ago—in favor of the personal contact method. We—we—"

He stopped talking. He'd seen plenty of pretty girls in his time, many of them in a state which left nothing of their attributes to the imagination. But this . . . this was something else again . . . this girl who had come through the doorway to what was apparently the kitchen. She wore blue levis and a worn khaki shirt, and a scuffed pair of sandals encased her feet; and if she had on any make-up Toddy couldn't spot it. And, yet, despite those things, she was out of this world. She was *mmmm-hmmmm* and *wow* and *man-oh-man!*

Toddy stared at her. Eyes narrowing, the man spoke over his shoulder. "Dolores," he said. And as she came forward, he caught her by the bodice and pivoted her in front of Toddy.

"Very nice, eh?" His eyes pointed to her buttocks. "A little full, perhaps, like the breasts, but should one quarrel with bounty? Is not the total effect pleasing? Could one accept less after the warm promise of the mouth, the generous eyes, the sable hair with—"

"Scum," said the girl in almost unaccented English. "Filth," she added tonelessly. "Carrion. Obscenity."

"*Vaya!*" The man took a step toward her. "*Hija de perro!* I shall teach you manners." He turned back on Toddy, breathing heavily, eyes glinting. "Now, Mr. . . . Mr. Clinton, is it? I have allowed you to study my ward to the fullest. Perhaps you will confine your attention to me for a moment. You said you were sent to me by a friend?"

"Well, I'm not sure she was a friend exactly, but—"

"She?"

"A neighbor of yours. Right down the street here. I—"

"I know none of my neighbors nor are they acquainted with me."

"I—well, it's this way," said Toddy, and his gaze moved nervously from the man to the dog. The big black animal had been lying down. Now he had risen to stand protectively in front of the man, and there was a look about him which Toddy did not like at all.

"I buy gold," said Toddy, flipping open the lid of his box. "I—I—"

"Yes? And just what led you to believe I had any gold to sell?"

"Well, uh, nothing. I mean, a great many people do have and I just assumed that, uh, you might."

The man stared at him unwinkingly, the dog and the man. The silence in the room became unbearable.

"L-look," Toddy stammered. "What's wrong, anyway? Like I say, I'm buying gold—" He picked up the watch on the table. "Old, out-of-date stuff like this—"

That was all he had a chance to say. He was too startled by what followed to realize, or remember, that the watch was ten times heavier than it should have been.

Cursing, the man lurched forward and aimed a kick at Toddy.

Then the dog called Toddy an unpleasant name, the same name the man had called him.

"*Cabrone!*" it snapped. *Bastard!*

And then the dog howled insanely and leaped—at the man. For he had received the kick intended for Toddy and in a decidedly tender place.

The watch slid from Toddy's nerveless fingers. He slammed the lid of his box and dashed for the door.

In his last fleeting glimpse of the scene, the dog was stalking the man and the man was kicking and shouting at him. And in the doorway to the kitchen, the girl clutched herself and rocked with hysterical, uncontrollable laughter.

"I," said Toddy, grimly, as he raced toward the Wilshire line bus, "am going to call it a day."

The box seemed unusually heavy, but he thought nothing of it. Late in the day, like this, it had the habit of seeming heavy.

IV

LIKE MOST PEOPLE WITH A TENDENCY TO ATTRACT TROUBLE, Toddy Kent had a magnificent ability to shake it off. Hot water, figuratively speaking, affected him little more than the literal kind. He forgot it as soon as the moment of burning was past.

This afternoon, then, he was not only troubled and worried but troubled and worried at being so. Sure, he'd had a bad scare, but that had been more than an hour ago. An hour in which he'd ridden into town and had three stiff drinks. Why keep kicking the thing around? What was there to feel blue about? It was even kind of funny when you looked at it the right way.

Irritated and baffled by himself, Toddy turned in at the twelve-foot front of the Los Angeles Jewel & Watch Co.

Most of the shop was in darkness, but the door was unlocked and a light burned at the rear. Milt was reading off a buyer, one of the new ones. And his brogue was as broad as the young man's face was red.

"So! Yet more of it!" Milt slapped aside his brilliant swivel lamp and jerked the jeweler's loupe from his eye. "Did you look at dis, my brilliant young friend? Did you feel of it, heft it—dis bee-yootiful chunk of eighteen-karat *brass?*"

"Why—why, sure I did, Milt! I—"

"You did not!" the little wholesaler proclaimed with mock sternness. "I refuse to let you so malign yourself! Better I have taught you. Better you would have known. I vill tell you what you felt, my friend, vot you looked at! It was dis bee-yootiful young housewife, was it not? Dot vas where you were feeling and looking!"

A chuckle arose from the other buyers. The young man's voice rose above it.

"But it's stamped, Milt! It's got an eighteen-karat stamp right on it!"

Milt threw up his hands wildly. "Vot have I told you of such? On modern stuff, yess. The karat stamp is good. It means what it says. But the old pieces? Bah! Nodding it means because dere vas no law to make it. It means only dot you must have good eyes. It means only dot you have a file in your box and a vial of acid, and better you should use dem!"

The young man nodded, downcast, and started to move away. Milt beckoned, spoke to him in a harsh stage whisper.

"Tell no vun, but dis time I make it up myself. Next time"—his voice

294

rose to a roar—"FEEL DER GOLD AND NOT DER LADY!"

Everyone laughed, Milt the loudest of all. Then he saw Toddy and hailed him.

"Ah, now here ve have a *real* gold-buyer! What has my Toddy boy brought, heh? Good it will be! Always a good day it is for hot Toddy!"

His voice was a little too hearty, and he stood up as he spoke and jerked his head toward the curtained doorway to his apartment.

"If these gentlemen will excuse us for a moment, I would have a word with you in private."

"Sure," said Toddy. "Sorry to hold you up, boys."

He followed Milt back through the drapes, and the little jeweler whispered to him for a moment. Elaine. Again. He cursed softly and raised his shoulders in a resigned shrug.

"Okay, Milt. I'll come back later and check in."

"You understand, Toddy? There was not much I could do. I could not get away at this hour, for one thing, and the money—I was afraid I would not have so much as was required."

"Forget it," said Toddy. "You've done enough for me without having to take care of her."

Jaw set, he shouldered his way through the drapes again and strode out of the shop. Milt watched him through the door, then sank heavily down into his worn swivel chair. He took a long swig from an opened quart of beer and wiped his mouth distastefully. He looked up into the shrewd-solemn circle of his buyers' faces.

"There," he said, sadly, his dialect forgotten, "is one of the best boys I know. Brains he has, and looks, and deep down inside where it counts, *goodness!* And wasted, all of it is. Thrown away on a—on—"

They nodded. They all knew about Elaine. Toddy didn't talk, of course, except to Milt. And Milt wasn't a gossip either. But they all knew. Elaine got around. Elaine was hot water, circulating under its own power.

"Why don't he dump her, Milt?" It was a buyer named Red. "You can't do anything with a dame like that."

"I have asked myself that," said Milt, absently. "Yes, I have even asked him. And the answer . . . he does not know. Perhaps there is none. The answer is in her, something that cannot be put into words. She is vicious, selfish, totally irresponsible, physically unattractive. And yet there is something . . ."

He spread his hands helplessly.

One by one, the buyers drifted out, but Milt remained at his bench. He was musing, lost in thought. As if it were yesterday he remembered that day a year ago, the first time he had seen Elaine and Toddy Kent.

... It had been raining, and Toddy's bare head was wet. He had left Elaine up at the front of the shop and come striding back to the cage by himself.

"I have a watch here," he said, "that belonged to my grandfather. I don't suppose it's worth much intrinsically, but it's very valuable to me as a keepsake. Give it a good going-over, and don't spare any expense. I'll pick it up in a couple of days."

Milt said he would. He would be glad to. He was considerably awed by the young man's manner.

"Oh, yes," said Toddy, and he slapped his pockets. "Just put an extra five dollars on the bill, will you? Or, no, you'd better make it ten. I lost my wallet a little while ago. Think it must have been out in Beverly Hills when I was leaving my bank."

He did it so smoothly that Milt's hand moved automatically toward the cash drawer. Then it stopped, and he looked at the watch and at Toddy, and down the aisle at Elaine.

"It is a disagreeable day," he said. "You and the lady—your wife?— are both wet. If you will step back here, have her step back, I have a small electric heater ... "

"Some other time," Toddy said, imperiously pleasant. "Just make it ten and—and—"

"Yes," nodded Milt. "My suggestion is good. It is very, very good. Come back, sir, you and your wife."

So they had come back, warily. And Toddy had accepted a brandy in silence. And while he was sipping it, Elaine drank three.

She saw Milt watching her, amazed, and she grinned at him impudently. He looked hastily away.

"Where," he said, "did you lose your wallet?"

"At our hotel." Toddy laughed shortly. "We lost our baggage there, too. And our clothes. Not to mention ... not to mention anything."

"Ten dollars would do you no good."

"It would get us dinner and breakfast," Toddy shrugged. "It'd get us into some fleabag for the night. Tomorrow, I'll probably run into something."

"Not tomorrow. You have already run into it. Now."

"Yeah?"

"Yes," nodded Milt. "So I will give you ten dollars and you will visit me tomorrow morning. By tomorrow night, you will have the ten back and twenty, twenty-five, maybe fifty dollars besides."

"Oh, sure," said Toddy. "Sure, I will."

"Surely, you will," said Milt, gravely. "And even if you are not sure, you will be here in the morning. You will be here *because* you are not sure. Is it not so?"

Toddy had looked blank for a moment. Then his eyes narrowed and he grinned. "You've got my number, mister," he said. "I'll be here. And if there's fifty dollars to be made I'll make it."

They had gone out, then, taking Milt's ten dollars with them; and when Milt looked around for the brandy bottle, he found it gone, too.

V

AIREDALE AAHRENS HAD ONCE BROKEN A MAN'S JAW FOR ASKING WHY HE'D BEEN GIVEN THE HANDLE. It was like asking a one-armed man why he is called Wingie. Airedale had a long thick neck on a short stocky body. His hair was a crisp brownish-yellow, and his eyes were large and liquid and brown.

He didn't speak when Toddy entered the bail bond office. He simply picked up a pencil and the telephone and dialed the police station. After a moment he grunted, "Airedale. What's the score on Mrs. Elaine Kent?"

Toddy drew a chair up to the bondsman's desk and sat down. Elbows on his knees, he studied the familiar abbreviations which Airedale scrawled on a scratchpad:

"DD."

"*Drunk and disorderly.*"

"Assoff."

"*Assaulting an officer.*"

"Rear."

"*Resisting arrest.*"

It was quite a list, even for Elaine. She had obviously been in unusually good form today.

Airedale stopped writing for a moment. Then he wrote "four-bits" and cocked an eye at Toddy. Toddy sighed, made a loop with his thumb and forefinger. Airedale said, "Oke," and slammed up the receiver.

Toddy counted fifty dollars onto the desk, and the bondsman recounted them with thick stubby fingers. He made a balling movement with his hand and the money vanished. He discovered it tucked beneath Toddy's chin, shook his head with enigmatic disapproval, and dropped the bills into a drawer.

Toddy grinned tiredly. He didn't ask why the bond was not put up. He knew it was up. Airedale was in the real estate business. He sold lots. He bought them, too—cheap ones that were plenty adequate for dumps. He'd hold on to them until he needed them, and in the meantime a few hundred bucks slipped to his cousin in the city hall would miraculously produce an official assessment of the land at several times the purchase price—and the value.

Every once in a while somebody would wonder what had happened to all the forfeited bail. Where was the cash? What did the city have to show for it? The cash was in Airedale's pocket, but he'd give the city something to show for it, all right. He was no crook. He'd let the city have a nice thousand-dollar lot for ten or twelve grand in forfeited bail.

Airedale said, "How come they're going after Elaine? They trying to roust you, kid?"

Toddy shrugged. "You know how Elaine is."

"I do," Airedale nodded. "I thought maybe you didn't. You workin' full time as her chump, or can I rent you out? Let me be your agent, kid. They's millions in it."

Toddy chuckled wryly. *Characters,* he thought. *Ten thousand characters and no people.* "Maybe we'd better talk about something else," he suggested.

"Maybe we had," Airedale agreed promptly. "What do you hear from Shake's boys these days? Still trying to chisel in on you?"

"Still trying," Toddy said.

"You don't think they mean business, huh?"

"Probably," Toddy shrugged. "Where they slip up is in not thinking that *we* mean business, too; guys like me. Anyone tough enough to make it in the gold-buying game is plenty tough enough to hold onto what he makes. I'm not going to let a bunch of punks like Shake's tap me for protection. If I scared that easy, I wouldn't be in the racket."

"So? How come Shake's so stupid?"

"He had a little luck. He tapped a few Sunday buyers—old-age pensioners, kids, college boys, people like that."

Airedale nodded appreciatively. He looked toward the door. "Here she comes," he said. "God's little gift to Los Angeles—or why people move to Frisco."

Elaine didn't look bad, for Elaine. She always looked mussed and sloppy and she looked no more than that now. Though she was grinning, a delightful, elfin, heart-warming grin, it was immediately apparent that she had heard Airedale's remark. She made an obscene gesture with her forefinger.

"You can kiss my ass, you fat-mouthed, nosey son-of-a-bitch!"

"You mean that one under your nose? Not me, honey. I'm strictly an under-the-skirts guy—the clean stuff, y'know."

"Why, you dirty bas—"

"Knock it off." Toddy grabbed her by the elbow and dragged her toward the door. "That wasn't very funny, Airedale."

"So who's joking?" said Airedale. He broke into a roar of laughter as they went out, the legs of his chair banging against the floor with the rocking of his body. He stopped at last: wiped his eyes on the sleeve of his checkered shirt. He looked thoughtfully into his cash drawer, then firmly pushed it shut.

Meanwhile, riding toward the hotel in a taxi, Toddy was barely aware of the profane and obscene words which streamed softly, steadily from Elaine's mouth. It wasn't that he was used to such talk; somehow he had never got used to it. In the always-new fascination of watching her face, he simply lost track of what she was saying.

She had perfect control of her expressions. In the space of seconds she could register sorrow, elation, bewilderment, terror, surprise—one after the other. And unless you knew her, and sometimes even when you did, you could not doubt that the pantomimed emotions were anything but genuine.

Her expression now was one of angelic resignation, gentle entreaty. And her words were, "How about it, you stingy bastard? I want a bottle and, by God, I'm gonna get one!"

Toddy shook his head absently, not really hearing her. Her leg slid under his, and the heel of her tiny pump swung back against his crotch. He swore and jerked away. Involuntarily, he swung out and the back of his hand struck her in the face.

It wasn't a hard blow, but it was a noisy one. The cab stopped with a jerk. The driver pushed his hard face over the glass partition.

"What you tryin' to pull there, Mac?"

"She—" Toddy repressed a groan—"Mind your own business!"

"Like that, huh?" The driver reached for the door. "Maybe I'll make this my business."

"Wait," said Elaine. "Wait, please! It's this way, driver. My husband just got out of jail and his nerves are all on edge—" She let her hands flutter descriptively. "He wanted something to drink, and I didn't want him to have anything. But I guess . . . well, maybe he *does* need it."

"Dammit," snapped Toddy. "I don't want any—"

"Now you know you do, honey." Elaine laid a sympathetic hand on his arm. "He really must, driver. He hardly ever strikes me unless h-he's like this."

The cabbie grunted. "Okay, Mac. You got your own way."

"Give him some money, sweetheart," said Elaine. "You go right ahead and have your whiskey and I won't say a word!"

"I tell you, I'm not—Oh, hell!" said Toddy.

They had stopped in front of a liquor store, of course. Elaine had timed this little frammis right to a *t*. Toddy literally threw a five-dollar bill at the driver. And when the latter returned with a pint of whiskey, he literally threw it and the change at Toddy.

Elaine beamed at both of them. Then she took the bottle with a prettily prim movement and placed it in her outsize purse.

The hotel where Toddy and Elaine lived was a two-hundred-room fleabag a little to the north of Los Angeles' north-south dividing line. Coincidences excepted, its only resemblance to a first-class hotel was its rates.

It was the kind of a place where the house dick worked on a commission, and room clerks jumped the counter on tough guys. During the war it had paid for itself several times over by renting rooms to couples who "just wanted to clean up a little." People lived there because they liked such places or because they would not be accepted in better ones.

Toddy's insistence on a second-floor room had immediately identified him to the clerk as a hustler. All the hot guys liked it low down. Down low you could sometimes smell a beef before it hit you. You could sometimes get out ahead of it.

So Toddy had paid an inflated rate to begin with, and, three days later, when his primary reason for wanting a room near street level became apparent, the rent was boosted another ten a week. The clerk was sympathetic about it, insomuch as he was capable of sympathy. He even declared that Elaine was a mighty sweet little lady. But the rent went up, just the same.

He just had to do it, get me, Kent? The joint's liable, know what I mean? Now, naturally, the best little lady in the world is gonna cut it rough now and then, but people ain't got no sense of humor no more. Toss a jug on 'em from the second floor, an' honest to Christ you'd think they was killed!

Toddy had paid the extra ten without protest, and in return strong iron-wire screens went over the windows. And a hell of a lot of good they did! And empty bottle couldn't be hurled through them, but heavier objects could be—and were. So Toddy rented a room on the alley, the single window of which was protected pretty adequately by the fire escape. Of course, you could get stuff past the fire escape if you tried hard enough.

From the standpoint of comfort, it was by far the worst room Toddy and Elaine had lived in. It was badly ventilated and poorly lit. Even in the coldest days of winter (Oh, yes, it does get cold in California!) it was almost unbearably warm. The virtually uninsulated stack of the hotel's incinerator passed through one corner of the room, and the heat from it was like an oven's. Once, on one of her rampages, Elaine had loosened the clamp which held the square metal column to the wall. And before Toddy could get it back into place, re-join the loosened joints, his face was scarlet from its blast.

He had complained about the thing to the management, not asking its removal, of course, which was impossible, but requesting that its dangerously loose condition be corrected. The management had advised him that if the stack was loose, so was his baggage. There were no nails

holding it to the floor, and if he disliked his environment he could move
the hell out. The management was getting a bellyful of Toddy and Elaine
Kent.

On this particular evening, Toddy followed Elaine down the long
frayed red carpet of the hall, past the smells of gin and incense, the
sounds of sickness, sex and low revelry. He unlocked the door of their
room and stood aside for her to precede him. He closed it, set his gold-
buyer's box upon the writing table, and sank into a chair.

Elaine sat half-on half-off the bed, her back to its head. She loosened
the foil on the bottle with her teeth, tossed the cap away, and took a long
gurgling drink.

"How do you like them apples, prince?" She crinkled her eyes at him.
"Prince—spelled with a *k*. What do you say we have another one?"

She had another one and again lowered the bottle. "Well, let's have
the sermon, prince. If you don't get started we'll be late for prayer
meeting."

"Kid, I—I—" Toddy broke off and rubbed his eyes. "Where do you
get the dough to do these things, Elaine? Who gives it to you?"

"Try and find out. Everyone's not as chinchy as you are."

"I'm not stingy. You know that. I'd do anything in the world to help
you—really help you."

"Who the hell wants your help?"

"Wherever you get the money, whoever gives it to you, they're not
your friends. They're the worst enemies you could have. Can't you see
that, kid? Can't you see that some day you're going to get into something
that you can't get out of—that neither I nor anyone else can get you out
of? You've got intelligence. You—"

He broke off, scowling; for a moment he wanted nothing but to get his
hands on her, to—to . . . And then his scowl faded, and the near-murder-
ous impulse passed; and despite himself he chuckled.

Elaine had drawn her face down into a ridiculous mask of solemnity. It
was impossible not to laugh at her.

"Okay. So it's no use." He sighed and lighted a cigarette. "Go on and
get yourself cleaned up. I'll check in with Milt, and we'll have dinner
when I get back."

"Who the hell's dirty? Who wants dinner?"

"You are," said Toddy, rising. "You do. Now, get in that bathroom
and get busy!"

Elaine scrambled off the bed and ran to the bathroom door. She
paused before it, clutching the knob in one hand, the bottle in the other.
Eyes twinkling venomously, she screamed.

The blood-chilling, spine-tingling shrieks piled one upon the other—

rose to a crescendo of terror and pain. Then they ended abruptly as she slammed and locked the door.

Above the noise of the shower, he heard her spitefully amused laughter. Trembling a little, he crossed to the phone and waited. It began to ring. He lifted it and spoke dully into the transmitter.

"All right . . . we'll stop. Yeah, yeah. I know. Okay, you don't hear anything now, do you? Well, all right!"

He slammed up the receiver, hesitated glowering. He lighted another cigarette, took a deep consoling puff, and flipped open the lid of his box. He blinked.

What the hell? he thought. *How the hell? Let's see . . . I'd just picked the thing up, and, yeah, the lid of the box was open. And then Chinless tried to kick me, and the dog cut loose, and . . .*

Very slowly his hand dipped down and lifted out the watch . . . the watch from the house of the talking dog.

VI

HE NOTICED ITS WEIGHT THIS TIME; it sagged in the hand that held it. If he had any ability at all to estimate weights—and he had a great deal—this thing weighed a full pound. Of course, most of that weight would be in the works he knew. Even on the thick old-fashioned jobs like this, the maximum weights on cases seldom ran over thirty penny-weight, one and a half ounces. The case on a modern watch, with its thin movement, would weigh little more than half that much.

He took the loupe from his box and carried the watch over to the dresser. Snapping on a lamp, he made a small scratch in the case with his nail. Loupe in eye, he studied the now-magnified indentation. He whistled softly.

Twenty-four karat. *Twenty-four karat!* The stuff was practically never used in jewelry; never except, perhaps, in insignia and tiny plated areas. It was too soft, not to mention its cost. So . . . ?

Toddy lowered the watch and stood striking it absently against the palm of his hand. There was a tiny *plipping* sound, and the movement, face and crystal flew off. Flew off in one piece. Toddy stared at them, at it—looked from it to the case. He took it in one hand and *it* in the other, and balanced them.

The movement was little larger than a dime. With the things it was affixed to, the crystal and face, it weighted a "weak" five pennyweight. The case, then—the case weighed almost a full pound. There shouldn't be much more than a pound of pure gold in all of Los Angeles County—outside of government vaults, of course. And yet here was a pound of the stuff in his hand.

He snapped the two sections of the watch back together, a tremor of excitement in his fingers, a slow grin lining his tanned jaw. In a quiet recess of his mind, the gizmo was awakening. It was kicking back the covers and reaching under the bed for its bulging kit of angles.

So he'd picked up the watch by accident. So it didn't belong to him. So what? Maybe the chinless guy would like to claim title to it. Maybe he'd like to explain what he was doing with—well, call it by its right name—a pound of twenty-four-karat, .999 fine bullion.

Of course, Chinless didn't look like a guy who'd make many explanations. He didn't look like a nice guy at all to tangle with. Still, he wouldn't be stupid enough to raise a stink over this. Or would he? Toddy

304

wasn't sure—but then he'd never been a sure-thing player. This was worth gambling on; he was sure of that.

The movement was worthless as a timekeeper. It wouldn't run more than a few hours before it gave up the ghost. It served only to disguise the true nature of the watch. And no one would take such pains, go to such expense, with only one watch. There would be others—yes, and other items besides watches. Articles that weighed many times the amount their appearance indicated. If a man could move in on a setup like that—

Toddy paused in his scheming, listening to the chatter of the bathroom shower. The light of excitement dulled in his fine gray eyes. What was the use? What good would it do? No matter what he made it would all go the same way. Down the bottomless rat-holes which Elaine burrowed endlessly.

... Box under his arm, he closed the door of the room and walked down the long hall to the stairs. He went out through the side entrance of the lobby, reconnoitered its smog-bound environs with a glance as deceptively casual as it was automatic. He strolled up to the corner and stood leaning against a lamppost.

Ostensibly, he was waiting for the traffic signal to change. Actually, he was waiting for the man who had been lurking in the shadows of the entrance, a small man with a sunken chest and a snap-brimmed gray hat that was almost as wide as his shoulders. One of Shake's boys—a shiv artist named Donald.

The man approached. He sidled up to the opposite side of the post and spoke from the corner of his mouth.

"Let's have it, Kent. Shake ain't waitin' no longer."

"Cow's ass?" said Toddy, with the inflection of "How's that?"

"I'm not tellin' you again. The next time I see you, you'll have your balls in that box instead of gold."

"Why, Donald!" said Toddy. "How would I close the lid?"

Donald didn't answer him. Donald couldn't. Toddy's arm had curled around the post, around his head, and his nose was flat and getting flatter against the rusty iron. He mumbled "*Awwf-guho,*" and managed to free the thin steel knife from its hip sheath. Toddy's arm tightened, and he dropped the knife into the gutter.

"Now," said Toddy, "get this clear, once and for all. I'm not paying any protection—not one goddam penny. Don't try for it again. If you do . . . well, just don't."

He released the little shiv artist with a contemptuous twirl. He crossed the street and vanished into the darkness without looking back.

Milt's shop was dark, of course, but the door was unlocked. For a man in the gold racket, Milt's faith in human nature was astonishing.

Toddy made his way down the dark aisle with practiced ease, pushed through the wicket which adjoined the jeweler's cage, and shoved aside the drapes. Milt wasn't in the living room, but an excited clamor from the kitchen told Toddy where he was. Toddy set his box upon the old-fashioned library table, and went on back to the rear room.

As usual, the swarthy and sullen Italian who delivered Milt's beer was late, and, as usual, Milt was reading him off. He followed the man to the back door, gesticulating, complaining with humorous querulousness.

"Have you no sense of the importance of things? Is there no way I can appeal to you? Suppose I had run out! What then, loafer? That means nothing to you, eh, that I should be left here without so much as a swallow—"

The roar of the delivery truck shut off his protest. Muttering, face pink with outrage, he faced Toddy.

"I ask you, my friend, what should I do with such a dummox? What would you do in my case?"

"Just what you do," Toddy chuckled. "You wouldn't know what to do if you didn't have that guy to fight with every night. Anyway, I'll bet you've got your refrigerator full of beer."

"But the principle involved! The fact that I exercise a certain foresight does not affect the principle."

"Okay," said Toddy. "I think I'll drink a bottle of this warm, if you don't mind. On a night like this, I—"

"*Stop!*"

"Huh!" Toddy jerked his hand away from the beer case.

"Never!" said Milt with mock severity. "Never in my house will such a sacrilege be permitted. Warm beer? Ugh! Aside from the shock to the senses, there is no telling what the physical results might be."

"But I like—"

"I will do nothing to nourish such an unnatural appetite. Come! I will get us some that is only mildly cold."

Milt took two bottles from the bottom of the overflowing refrigerator and carried them into the living room. They took chairs on opposite sides of the table, toasted each other silently, and then went to work at grading and weighing the gold.

This, checking-in time, was virtually the only time of day when the scales were in use. Simply by hefting it, any good gold-buyer can tell what an article weighs within a margin of a few grains. His clients can't, of course. They have only the vaguest idea as to the weight of the things they sell. They live in a world of ounces and pounds ... and they remain there, if the buyer has his way. He won't use his scales unless he has to.

In dealing with Milt, a wholesale buyer, the scales were, naturally, necessary. Estimated weights, correct within a few grains, were not good enough. A grain is only one-four-hundred-and-eighth of a troy ounce, but multiplied by several dozen purchases it might cost the wholesaler his week's profit. As for the grading, that went swiftly. The quality of gold is determined by its brightness, and it was seldom that either Milt or Toddy lingered over an article.

Toddy took the bills which Milt gave him, and stuffed them into his wallet. A good day, yes, but if he could turn that watch, that pound of twenty-four-karat bullion now hidden in the back of his dresser drawer . . . If there was some way of tapping the source of that watch—

"There is," said Milt, "something troubling you, my friend?"

"Oh no." Toddy shook his head. "Just daydreaming. Tell me something, will you, Milt?"

"If I can, yes."

"Where would—how much scrap gold like this would it take to make a pound of twenty-four karat?"

"Well," Milt hesitated. "Your question is a little vague. Scrap of what quality—ten, fourteen, eighteen karat? Say it was all fourteen, well, that is easily estimated. Fourteen karat is sixty per cent pure. Roughly, it would take not quite two pounds of fourteen to refine into one pound of twenty-four."

Toddy whistled. "Where would you get that much gold, Milt?"

"I would not. So much gold, why it is more than two or three of my boys would take in in a week. And if I did buy it, I would not refine it into twenty-four? Why should I? It would gain me nothing. The mint would pay me no more for a pound of twenty-four karat than it would for two pounds, or whatever the exact figure is, of fourteen."

"Suppose you didn't sell it to the mint?"

"But where else would I . . . Ohh," said Milt.

"Now, wait a minute—" Toddy held up a hand, grinning. "Don't leap all over me yet. I'm just thinking out loud."

"Such thoughts I do not like."

"But, look, Milt . . . why couldn't a guy do this? Pure gold is staked at thirty-five dollars an ounce in this country. Abroad, it's selling for anywhere from seventy-five to a hundred and fifty—depending on how shaky a nation's currency is. So why couldn't you refine scrap into twenty-four, have it made up into jewelry, trick stuff, you know . . . "

"Yes," said Milt. "I see exactly what you are driving at. The jewelry could be worn into Mexico—for a few dollars; for a task so safe, wearers could be readily secured. And from Mexico, there would be little difficulty in getting the gold abroad. Yes, I know. I see."

"Well?"

"It is not well and you know it. There are severe penalties for removing gold from this country. Even to be in possession of bullion is a federal offense."

"But the profit, Milt! My God, think—"

"Yes," said Milt sternly. "The profit. My God. My God, is right. How many such profitable enterprises have you undertaken in the past? What was your profit from them? Heh? Shall I refresh your memory, my oh-so-foolish Toddy?"

"Oh, now," said Toddy, coloring a little. "There's no need to bring those things up. Anyway, this is an entirely different deal."

"Now you have your feelings hurt," Milt nodded. "You have given me your confidence and now I remind you of things you would rather forget. Good. I shall continue to hurt your feelings. I shall continue to remind you of the unpleasant conclusions of your past escapades. Better to do that than see you repeat your errors."

"But—" Toddy caught himself. "Oh, well," he said, "what are we arguing about? I told you I was just thinking out loud."

"And I told you it was not good to entertain such thoughts. Why should you dwell on them? At not too great a risk, you are making very good money. You are not known to the police here. Without some deliberate bit of foolishness, you are assured of an excellent income and, more important, your freedom. If, on the other hand, you—"

"I know," said Toddy, a trifle impatiently.

"You do not know. You place too great a store by the fact that you have not been fingerprinted by the police of this, the City of Angels. You are forgetting the brief but telling physical description of you which is on file at the license bureau. You are forgetting the bureau's reason for having such data—the fact that gold-buyers are always suspect, that it may be necessary to lay hands on them at a moment's notice. You see? You are safe only as long as you commit no overt act. Once you do, the fingerprinting and the discovery of your record will follow as a matter of course."

Toddy took a long slow drink of his beer. "Yeah," he said slowly. "I know ... But tell me one thing, Milt, just to satisfy my curiosity. Then I'll shut up."

"If I must."

"Say that you did—I know you don't—say that you did want to buy enough scrap of all kinds every week to refine into six or eight pounds of twenty-four karat. Enough to take care of the kind of overhead you'd be bound to have and still make enough of a killing to pay you for the risk. How would you go about it?"

"For me, it would be impossible, as I told you. Some of the larger refineries might buy that much gold."

"But they're checked, aren't they? If their shipments to the mint started falling off—"

"They are checked, yes. There is a check even on such relatively unimportant wholesale buyers as I."

"Huh," Toddy frowned. "How about this, then? Why couldn't you spread your buying through a group of wholesalers—take a pound or less of scrap from each one?"

"Because you could not pay them enough for the risk they were taking. And the secret of your enterprise would be dangerously spread with your buying. . . . So, there is my answer, Toddy. It is an impossibility. It cannot be done."

"But it—I mean—"

"Yes?" said Milt.

"Nothing. Okay, I'm convinced," Toddy grinned. "How about another beer?"

Uncomfortably conscious of Milt's curious and troubled gaze, Toddy left shortly after he had finished the beer. But he was by no means free of the tantalizing reflections which the watch had inspired. They expanded and multiplied in his mind as he strode back through the hazy streets.

Dammit, that gold *was* being bought, regardless of what Milt said. And this *was* entirely different from anything he had ever touched. He'd have to be careful, certainly. He'd have to do some tall scheming. But just because he'd had a few bad breaks in the past, there wasn't any reason to—

Toddy was almost running when he reached the hotel. He ignored the elevator and raced up the steps. He went swiftly down the hall. He shouldn't have left Elaine alone. He shouldn't have left the watch in the room.

His hand trembled on the doornob. He turned it and went in. The room was dark. He found the light switch and turned it on.

She lay sprawled backwards on the bed. Naked. Sheets tumbled with her strugglings, damp from her bath. Eyes glazed and bloodshot; pushing whitely, enormously from the contorted face. Veins empurpled and distended.

One of the stockings was tied around her throat, knotted and re-knotted there, and her stiffening fingers still clawed at it. The other stocking had been stuffed into her mouth; the toe of it, chewed, wet from gagging, edged out through the open froth-covered oval of her lips.

Toddy swayed. *How could I know . . . something I read . . . she was always asking for trouble . . .* He closed his eyes and opened them again. He put a hand out toward her—toward that hideously soggy fragment of stocking. Hastily he jerked the hand back.

The room had been ransacked, of course. Every drawer in the dresser had been jerked out and dumped upon the floor. Toddy's eyes moved from the disarray to the window. He went to it and flung up the shade.

There was a man down there near the foot of the fire escape. He was a small man with a hat almost as wide as his shoulders. One of his feet had slipped through the steps, and he was struggling frantically to free it.

VII

TODDY HAD BEEN SITTING ON HIS ROLL WHEN HE MET ELAINE IVES. He'd built up his wardrobe, had several grand in his kick, and was driving a Cadillac—rented, alas—while he tried to hit upon a line.

Toddy like nice things. He liked to live in good places. He found that it paid off. In the swank apartment hotel where he resided, he was believed to be the scion of a Texas oil millionaire. No one would have thought of associating the tanned, exquisitely tailored young man with anything off-color.

He was sitting in the bar of his hotel the day he met Elaine. Apparently she had followed him in from the street, although he had not seen her. The first he saw of her was when she slid onto the stool next to his and looked up at him with that funny, open-toothed smile.

"Order yet, darling?" she said. "I believe I'll have a double rye, water on the side."

He looked at the bartender who was giving Elaine a doubtful but chilly eye. "That sounds good enough for me," he said. "Two double ryes, water on the side."

In the few seemingly casual glances he gave her, while she drank that drink and three others, he checked off her points and added them up to zero. She was scrawny. Her clothes, except for her hat—she was always careful with her hats—looked like they had been thrown on her. The wide-spaced teeth gave her mouth an almost ugly look. When she crinkled her face as she did incessantly, talking, laughing, smiling, she looked astonishingly like a monkey.

Yet, dammit, *and yet* there was something about her that got him. Something warm and golden that reached out and enveloped him, and drew him closer and closer, yet never close enough. Something that even infected the bartender, making him solicitous with napkins and ice and matches held for cigarettes—that held him there wanting to do things that were paid for by the doing.

Toddy glanced at his watch and slid off the stool. "Getting late," he remarked. "Think we'd better be getting on to dinner, don't you?"

"No," said Elaine promptly, crinkling her face at him. "Not hungry. Gonna stay right here. Jus' me an' you an' nice bartender."

The bartender beamed foolishly and frowned at Toddy. Toddy gave him an appraising stare.

311

"I think," he said, "the nice bartender is in danger of losing his nice license. Which is worth a nice twenty-five thousand for a nice place like this. It isn't considered nice, it seems, to provide liquor to obviously intoxicated people."

"Not 'tox-toxshi-conshtipated! Ver' reg'lar—"

But now the bartender had become even more urgent than Toddy. And Elaine was holding herself in a little; she wasn't ready to open all the stops. Toddy got her out of there and into the Cadillac, and she passed out immediately.

He opened her purse, looking for something that would give him her address. Its sole contents, aside from compact and lipstick, was a wadded-up letter. He read it with a growing feeling of gladness.

Of course, he'd been sure from the beginning that she wasn't peddling, another b-girl, but he was glad to see the letter nonetheless. Any girl might blow her top if something like this happened to her—having a studio contract canceled before she ever started to work. Hell, he might have gone out hitting up strangers himself. Now, with the letter in his hand, he saw why he had felt that he had known her.

He had seen her several years before in a picture. It had been a lousy picture, but one player—a harried, scatter-witted clerk in a dime store— had almost saved it. She had only to fan the straggling hair from her eyes or hitch the skirt about her scrawny hips to set the audience to howling. They roared with laughter—laughter that was with her, not at her. Laughter with tears in it.

Toddy drove her around until she awakened, and then he drove to a drive-in and fed her tomato soup and coffee. She took these attentions matter-of-factly, trustingly, either not wanting to ask questions or not needing to. He took her to her home, a court apartment in North Hollywood.

He went in with her, steered her through the disarray of dropped clothes and empty bottles and overturned ashtrays to a daybed. She collapsed on it, and was instantly asleep again.

Toddy stared at her, perplexed, wondering what to do, feeling a strange obligation to take care of her. The court door opened unceremoniously and a woman stepped in.

She had a bust on her like a cemetery angel and her face looked just about as stony. But even she looked at Elaine and spoke with a note of regret.

So this was Mr. Ives—the brother Elaine had insisted would arrive. And just when she was beginning to believe there wasn't any brother! Well. She knew how perturbed he must be, she was fond of Elaine herself, and—and such a great talent, Mr. Ives! But it just couldn't go on any longer. She simply could not put up with it. So if Mr. Ives would find her another place immediately, absolutely no later than tomorrow—And since he'd want to get started early, the back rent—six weeks, it was . . .

Toddy paid it. He stayed the night there, sprawled out on two chairs. In the morning, he helped Elaine pack. Or, rather, he packed, stopping frequently to hold her over the toilet while she retched, and washing her face afterward.

He found and paid for another apartment. He put her to bed. Not until then, when she was looking up at him from the pillows—a bottle of whiskey on the reading stand, just as "medicine"—did she seem to take any note of what he had done.

"Sit down here," she said, patting the bed. And he sat down. "And maybe you'd better hold my hand," she said. And he held it. "Now," she said, her face crinkling into a frown, "what am I going to do about you?"

"Do?" Toddy grinned.

"Now, you know what I mean," she said severely. "I'm broke. I'm not working and I don't know when I will be. I guess I should ask you to sleep with me, but I've never done anything like that, and anyway it probably wouldn't be much fun for you, would it? I mean I'm so skinny I'd probably stick you with a bone."

"Y-yes," nodded Toddy. He had the goddamnedest feeling that he was going to bawl!

"Maybe I could wash some clothes for you," said Elaine. "That's an awfully pretty suit you have on. I could wash it real nice for you and hang it out the window, and it . . . would that be worth fifty cents?"

Toddy shook his head. He couldn't speak.

"Well"—her voice was humble—"a quarter, then?"

"D-don't," said Toddy. "Oh, for Christ's sake . . . "

Toddy hadn't cried since the night he ran away from home. He'd half-killed his stepfather with a two-by-four, bashed him over the head as he came into the barn. He'd tried to make it look like an accident, like one of the rafters had broken. But he was shaking with fear, with that and the bitter coldness of the night. He'd huddled down in a corner of the boxcar, and sometime during the night a tramp had crawled into the car also. Observing the proprieties of the road, the tramp had gone into a corner, that corner, to relieve himself. And Toddy had been soaked, along with his thin parcel of sandwiches. The stuff had frozen on him. He'd cried then, for the last time.

Up to now.

He was down on his knees at the side of the bed, and her arms clutched him in an awkward, foolishly sweet embrace, and she was talking to him like a child, as one child to another, and there had never been another moment like this in the history of man and woman. They cried together, two lost children who found comfort and warmth in each other. And then they started to laugh. For somehow in the extravagant and puppyish outpouring of her caresses, she had hooked the armhole of her nightgown around his neck.

While she shrilled gleefully that he was tickling her, and while her small breast pounded his face with merriment, he lifted and stood her on the bed. Then, since there was no other way, he slid off the other shoulder strap and drew the gown off her body, lowering his head with it.

He shucked out of it and turned around. She was still standing upright, examining herself in the wall mirror.

She twisted her neck and gazed at her childish buttocks. She faced the mirror and bowed her back and legs. She raised one leg in the air and looked.

She turned around, frowning, and nodded to him. "Feel . . . no, here, honey. That's where you do it, isn't it?"

Toddy felt.

"Not bad," he said gravely. "Not bad at all."

"Not too skinny?"

"By no means."

Elaine beamed and put her legs back together. Pivoting, arms stiff at her sides, she did a pratfall on the bed. When she stopped bouncing, she lay back and looked at him.

"Well," she said, puzzledly. "I mean, after all . . . Hadn't we better get started?"

Thus, the story of the meeting of Toddy and Elaine. Funny-sad, bittersweet. It put a lump in your throat; at least, in put one in the throat of Toddy, who lived it. Then, they flew to Yuma that night and were married. And the lump moved up from his throat to his head.

Literally.

They were in their hotel room, and Elaine was teasing for just one "lul old bottle, just a lul one, honey." All her charm was turned on. She pantomimed her tremendous thirst, staggered about the room hand shielding her eyes, a desert wanderer in search of an oasis. Then, she broke into an insanely funny dance of joy as the oasis was discovered— right there on the dresser in the form of his wallet.

Laughing tenderly, Toddy moved in front of her. "Huh-uh, baby. No more tonight."

Elaine picked up the empty bottle and hit him over the head with it. "You stupid son-of-a-bitch," she said, "how long you think I can keep up this clowning?"

VIII

SHAKE'S HEADQUARTERS WERE IN A WALK-UP DUMP ON SOUTH MAIN, a buggy, tottering firetrap tenanted by diseases-of-men doctors, a massage parlor ("cheerful lady attendants") and companies with uniformly small offices and big names. The sign on his smudged windows read, "Easiest Loans in Town." It was true in the same sense, say, that death solves all problems is true.

Without co-signers, collateral or even a job, in the usual meaning of the word, you could borrow from one to a maximum of ten dollars from Shake; and you could—and usually did—take the rest of your lifetime to pay it back. Shake liked to get along with people; he liked to live and let live. He said so himself.

If you objected to these lenient arrangements, things were still made easy for you; there was a swift and simple alternative. Shake's *pachucos*, his young Mexican toughs, would pay you a visit. They would drop around to your one-chair barber shop or your shoeshine stand or the corner where you hustled papers and kick the holy hell out of you. They'd lay you so flat you could crawl under doors. Shake pointed to the expense of these kickings as justification for his whimsical methods of compounding interest.

When Toddy pushed Donald into the office ahead of him, Shake and two of the *pachucos* were in the back room. They'd been splitting a half-gallon of four-bit wine while they stamped phony serial numbers into an equally phony batch of Irish sweepstakes tickets. Their minds were a little muggy and they were jammed around a littered table. Before they could snap together, Toddy had dutch-walked Donald inside and kicked the door shut.

They got to their feet then; they advanced a step in a three-cornered half-circle. But Toddy jerked his head toward the windows and the movement stopped abruptly.

"Come on," he invited grimly. "I won't do a damn thing but toss this bastard out on his skull."

"N-now, T-Toddy . . . " Nervous phlegm burbled in Shake's throat. "Now, Toddy," he whined, "is this a way to act? Bustin' into a office after business hours?"

He was a swollen dropsical giant with an ague, probably syphilis-inspired, which kept his puffed flesh in faint, almost constant oscillation.

"I've got something to say," said Toddy. "If you don't want those punks to hear it, you'd better send 'em out."

"Well, now—" Shake made a flabbily deprecating motion. "I don't know about that. We're settin' here having a nice little party, Ramon an' Juan an' me. Just settin' here minding our own business, and then you come along an'—"

"All right," said Toddy "I gave you a chance. I went up to my room tonight and—"

"*Wait!* Send 'em out, Shake!"

"Oh?" Shake looked doubtfully at the little shiv artist. "You been up to somethin' bad, Donald?"

"Send 'em out!" Donald gasped, teetering painfully in Toddy's grip. "Do like he says, Shake!"

"Well . . . How far you want 'em to go, Toddy?"

"How good can they hear?"

Shake hesitated, then waved his hand. "All the way down, boys. Clear down in front."

The *pachucos* left, duck-tail haircuts gleaming, heel-plates clicking on the ancient marble. When Toddy heard the outer door close, he released Donald with a shove.

"All right, strip."

"Goddammit, I done tole you I—"

"Take 'em off, Donald." Shake's pig eyes gleamed with interest as he sank into a chair.

Sullenly, Donald shed his clothes until he stood naked before them.

"You're awful dirty, Donald." Shake clucked his tongue reproachfully. "He have a chance to ditch it anywheres, Toddy? Could he of tossed it away?"

"No," Toddy admitted, "he couldn't."

"How big was it? . . . Donald, maybe you better bend over an'—"

Toddy chuckled unwillingly and Donald spewed out outraged obscenities.

"All right, then!" Shake said. "You just get them clothes back on before you catch cold. And, Toddy, maybe you better . . . "

Toddy nodded slowly. "Here it is," he began. "Donald hit me up for protection again tonight, and I gave him a brushoff. One that he'd remember. Then—"

"But that was just business, Toddy! Just because a man's ambitious and wants to expand, it don't prove—"

"It proves you're stupid enough to try anything. Jesus—" Toddy shook his head in wondering disgust. "Trying to shake down a gold-buyer! A bunch of cheap hoods like you. Why the hell don't you work out on Mickey Cohen?"

Shake looked embarrassed. "Well, now," he mumbled. "Maybe it wasn't real smart, but—"

"Smart!" snarled Donald. "You see what the son-of-a-bitch done to my nose?"

"I met Donald on the way to Milt's shop. I went on down to the shop and checked in, then I went back to my room. I couldn't have been gone more than thirty or thirty-five minutes at the outside. When I went in I found the room turned upside down, I found Donald heading down the fire escape, and I found my wife on the bed . . . strangled with her own stockings."

"Sss-strangled? . . . Y-you mean h-he . . . ?"

"I didn't!" Donald snapped, fearfully. "Dammit, Shake, why for would I do a thing like that?"

"W-why for was you in Toddy's room?"

"I—well, I—"

"Spill it!"

Donald edged toward the corner of the room, keeping a cautious eye on Toddy. "I j-just went up there to wait for him. Kind of surprise him, you know."

"Yeah?"

"I was—I was just goin' to cut him up a little when he came back."

Shake sighed with relief. "You see, Toddy? Donald wouldn't of killed her. Donald ain't that kind of boy. He was just goin' to cut you up a little."

"Uh-huh. And Elaine jumps him, so he gives her the business."

"You're a goddam liar!"

"Now you know better than that, Toddy," said Shake. "You been around too long to think a thing like that. In the first place, he ain't a killer. In the second place, he's a shiv man. Why for would he screw around with stockings when he had a shiv? It ain't his—his—"

—modus operandi, Toddy supplied silently. It was true; the operation method of a criminal almost never changes. The police would have a hell of a time if it did. Still, Donald had had the opportunity. He'd been caught at the scene of the murder.

"You think I'm—I'm immortal or somethin'?" Donald demanded with genuine indignation. "You think I'm a pervert? You think I killed the Black Dahlia?"

"I think you're a very sweet little boy," said Toddy. "The whole trouble is, people just don't understand you. Like me, for example. How'd you know it was safe to go into my room? How'd you know my wife wasn't in there . . . alive?"

"I could look under the door an' see it was dark. I knocked an' didn't get no answer, so I went in."

"The door was unlocked?"

"I'm tellin' ya."

"How long was this after you left me?"

"Well . . . fifteen-twenty minutes maybe."

"Just long enough to work your nerve up, huh? How long had you been there when I came in? It couldn't have been much more than ten minutes."

"It wasn't." Donald scowled peevishly. "Look. Why don't you cut out the third degree an' let me tell you."

"Okay. Keep it straight."

"I knocked on the door," said Donald. "I knocked an' waited a minute. I thought I heard someone movin' around—kind of a rustlin' sound—and I almost took a powder. But I didn't hear it no more, then, after the first time, so I figured it must be the window shade flappin' or something like that. I opened the door just a crack an' slid in . . . "

"Go on."

"I"—Donald wiped sweat from his face—"I stood there by the door, hugging the wall and waiting . . . an' . . . an' I don't know. I begin to get kind of a funny feeling, like someone was staring at the back of my neck. Well, you know how it is in that room, You can't really see into it up there by the door. You can't see the bed or nothing hardly until you get past the bathroom. Not with the lights off, anyways . . . "

"I know that," said Toddy impatiently.

"Well, I got this feeling so . . . so I slide down along the wall until I'm out of that little areaway. I came even with the bed and my eyes are gettin' kind of used to the dark an' I can see. A little. I can see they's someone on the bed. I—I—Jesus! I can't even think what I'm doin'! All I can think of is lightin' a cigarette—I mean, I don't really think of it. I do it without thinkin'. And then the match flares up an' I see everything, I see what's happened. An' then I hear you at the door, an' I try to beat it down the fire escape an'—"

Toddy nodded absently. Donald was in the clear. He'd been pretty sure right from the beginning. But under the circumstances, there'd been nothing to do but grab him.

Donald stepped to the table, poured out a water glass of sherry, and killed it at a gulp. Shake stroked his chins and stared interestedly at Toddy.

"If you was so sure Donald killed your wife," he said, "why didn't you just call the cops? That's what cops is for, to arrest criminals."

"So that's it," said Toddy. "I often wondered."

"You know what I think?"

"Yes."

"I think you killed her yourself. You either bumped her off before you left the room or—"

"—Or I went up the fire escape and did it, then beat it down and came up the front way." Toddy's tone was light, satirical, but there was a heavy feeling around his heart. Something seemed to struggle there, to fight up toward the hidden recesses of his mind. "Sure. That's what the cops will think. That's what *I'll* say after they work me over a few days."

Shake shook his head with a complete lack of sympathy. "They sure swing a mean hose in this town. You wouldn't believe what it does to a man's kidneys. I had a *pachuco* workin' for me; you remember him, Donald—Pedro? You remember how he went around after the cops had him? All bent together like a horseshoe. Had to take off his collar to pee."

"Think of that," said Toddy.

"Me an' Donald has got a duty to do, Toddy. The only thing is, how long should we take to do it? Now if we was real busy—say, we had some money to count—"

"Huh-uh."

"Huh-uh?"

"In spades."

"Too bad." Shake stared at the telephone. "That certainly is too bad, ain't it, Donald?"

"Oh, it's not too bad yet," said Toddy. "Let's see, now. It would take your *pachucos* a couple of minutes to get up here. That's not much, but I don't think you and Donald can take much. I really don't think you can, Shake. Of course, if you'd like to find out . . . "

He spread his hands, beaming at them mirthlessly. Shake drew the back of his hands across his mouth.

"So you'll sit here the rest of your life?" he burbled.

"All right," said Toddy. "Say that I walk out of here and you use the phone. I know every big-time con man in the country, and con men stick together. I'd make bond eventually. I'd be around to see you. You wouldn't enjoy that, Shake. I tell you from the bottom of my heart you wouldn't."

He stared at them a moment longer, white teeth bared, eyes gray and cold. Then he broke the tension with an easy, good-natured laugh.

"Now why don't we stop the clowning?" he said. "You boys know I'm all right. I know you're all right. We're all a little upset, but we're all big men. We can forgive and forget . . . and do business together."

Donald's narrow shoulders straightened unconsciously. Shake emitted a ponderous wheeze. "Now that's good sense," he declared. "Mighty good. Uh—what kind of business did you have in mind, Toddy?"

"Elaine was murdered for a watch. There was just one guy who knew I had it, the man that killed her. He's got rid of the watch by now. He'll also have an airtight alibi. So I'm stuck. All I can do is skip town ... "

"This watch ... Did it belong to this guy in the first place?"

"No," Toddy lied. "It belonged to an old lady. I fast-talked her out of it. ... God, Shake, I wish you and Donald could have seen the pile of stuff that woman had. Brooches, rings, necklaces. A good fourteen-fifteen grand worth or I don't know lead from platinum!"

"An' you just clipped her for the watch?"

"A *two-thousand dollar* watch. I couldn't bite her any harder without raising a chatter. And, of course, I didn't dare go back for another try."

"Sure, uh-huh." Shake bobbed his jowls understandingly. "How come you hadn't turned the watch, Toddy?"

"Too hot. Milt wouldn't have touched it. I'd just about decided to take the stones out and cut it up for scrap, but I hadn't got around to it yet. I'd only had it three days."

"Mmm," said Shake. "Uh-hah!" he said briskly. "All right, Toddy, it's a deal. You just give us this old lady's address an' we'll see that you get your cut."

Toddy smiled at him.

"Now what's wrong with that?" Shake demanded. "We'll cut him in for a full half, won't we, Donald?"

"Well, it's been nice," said Toddy, rising. "I'll drop you a card from Mexico City."

"Now, wait a minute ... !"

"I'll wait five minutes," said Toddy. "If I don't have two hundred bucks by that time, I'm on my way."

"Two *hundred!*"

"Two hundred—for almost a hundred times two hundred." Toddy's eyes flickered. "I won't say it'll be a cinch. She's about the crankiest, orneriest old bitch I ever tangled with. She lives all alone, see; doesn't have anyone she can pop off to. And she's got this game leg. I guess that makes her crankier than she would be ordinarily."

Shake licked his lips. "Game leg? An' she lives all alone?"

"Well," Toddy said conscientiously, "she *does* have three or four big Persian cats. I don't know whether they'd give you any trouble or not."

"I could handle 'em," said Donald grimly. "I could handle the dame. I ain't seen no dame or cats yet that I'm afraid of."

Toddy gave him an admiring look. Shake still hesitated.

"How do I know you ain't lying to us?"

"Because you've got *brains*," said Toddy. "Elaine was murdered. Murders aren't done for peanuts. It all adds up. Donald sees it. You're as smart as Donald, aren't you?"

"Yeah, but—but—" The words Shake searched for would not come to him. "But two hundred!"

"Two hundred as of the present moment," said Toddy, glancing at his watch. "I just thought of another party I can go to who'll give me—"

"Two hundred!" Shake scrambled hastily from his chair. "It's a deal for two hundred!"

. . . Toddy sat in a quiet booth in the bar, sipping a Scotch and soda while he studied the classified ads in the evening paper. He was not content with what he had done. No revenge could be adequate for the brutal and hideous death Elaine had suffered. He had, however, done all he could. For the time being, at least, it would have to do.

He had felt for a long time that Shake and Donald needed a lesson. Their threats tonight had done nothing to ameliorate that impression. Now they would get that lesson, one they might not live to profit by, and Elaine's murderer, the chinless man—the "old lady" they expected to rob—would get one. There'd be enough ruckus raised, perhaps, to bring in the cops. It was too bad that Chinless wouldn't know he'd been paid off, that Toddy had got back at him. But nothing was ever perfect. He'd settled two urgent accounts. He'd got a nice piece of scat money. He'd done all that he could, and no man can do more.

He took out his billfold and, under cover of the newspaper, inventoried its contents. Three—three hundred and twenty-seven dollars all together. Not very good. Not when you had to buy some kind of car out of it; and he would have to buy one. He had no way of knowing when Elaine's body would be discovered. He did know that the bus, plane and railway terminals would be watched as soon as it was. They might be looking for him already. He couldn't take any chances.

He slid out of the booth, sauntered past the bar stools and out to the walk.

It was quite dark now, and the dark and the smog condensed the glare of neon signs to a blinding intensity. Still he saw. He had to see and he did, although nothing in his manner indicated the fact.

He strolled straight to the curb, his attention seemingly fixed on the large wire trash basket which stood there. He dropped the newspaper into it and stared absently at the large black convertible. It was no more than ten feet away, parked in the street with the motor idling. The back seat was empty. The girl was at the wheel. The talking dog sat hunkered at her side, his front paws on the door.

With an effort Toddy suppressed a shudder.

He saw now that he hadn't really taken a good look at the dog that afternoon. The damned thing wasn't as big as he'd thought. It was bigger. And his imagination hadn't been playing tricks on him; it *did* talk.

The girl beckoned to Toddy. "Come," she called softly. The dog's jaws waggled. They yawned open. "C'm," he said. "C'm, c'm, c'm . . ."

Toddy looked over them and through them. He turned casually and stood staring into the bar. No way out there. The place had a kitchen, a busy one, and the rear exit lay beyond it. Up the street? Down? Pawnshops. A dime store. A butcher shop. All closed now.

He heard the softly spoken command in Spanish. He heard the scratch of the dog's claws as it leaped.

IX

In one swift motion Toddy stooped, grabbed the base of the basket, and lofted it behind him. Either his luck or his aim was good. There was a surprised yelp, the rattling scrape of wire. But Toddy heard it from a distance. He rounded the corner and raced down the gloomy side street.

It was not good, this way, but no way was good. He was entering a semi-slum section, the area of flyblown beaneries, boarded-up buildings, flophouses and wine bars which lies adjacent to the Union Station. No cab would stop for him here.

So now he ran. Now for the first time he knew the real terror of running—to run without a goal, to be hunted by the upper world and his own; to run hopelessly, endlessly, because there was nothing to do but run.

Sweat was pouring from him by the time he reached the end of the street. And just as he reached its end he saw a huge black form, a shadow, whip around its head. . . . The dog on his trail, behind him; the girl circling the block to head him off. That was the way it would be. He'd have to get in someplace fast. In and out. Throw them off. Keep running.

The dusty windows of a deserted pool hall stared back at him blankly. Next, a barber shop, also dark. Next, a burlesque house.

Across the grimy front, cardboard cutouts of bosomy women. Purple-eyed, pink-haired women in flesh tights and sagging net brassieres. Sprawled beneath them and gazing lewdly upward, the cutout of a man— puttynosed, baggy-trousered, derby-hatted. Names in red and white paint, Bingo Brannigan, Chiffon LaFleur, Fanchon Rose, Colette Casitas. And everywhere on streamers and one-sheets and cardboard easels, the legend: "Big Girl Show—DON'T DO IT SOME MORE."

"Yessir, the beeg show is just starting!" A cane rattled and drummed against the display. "Yessir," intoned the slope-chested skeleton in the linen jacket. "Step right in, sir."

He coughed as he took Toddy's ten-spot, but there was no surprise in it. He had always coughed; he could not be surprised. "Yessir"—he was repeating the instructions before Toddy had finished them—"Split with the cashier. Haven't seen you. Close the door."

"Exit?"

"Tough." The skeleton coughed. "Over the stage."

Toddy went in, anyway. It was too late to turn back. He moved past the half-curtains of the foyer and stood staring down the long steep aisle.

Not that he wanted one, but there didn't seem to be an empty seat in the joint. It was packed. Twin swaths of heads, terrazos of grays and blacks and bald-pinks stretched from the rear of the house to the orchestra pit. In the pit there was only a piano player, banging out his own version of the "Sugar Roll Blues." It must have been his own; no one else would have had it.

Toddy's nose crinkled at the stench, a compound of the aromas of puke, sweat, urine and a patented "perfume disinfectant." All the burly houses used that same disinfectant. It was the product of a "company" which, by an odd coincidence, also manufactured stink bombs. It was the only thing that would cover up the odor of a stink bomb.

He went slowly down the aisle, ears strained for sounds of the danger behind him, eyes fixed on the stage. Three chorus "girls" were on it—the show's entire line, apparently. They were stooped over, buttocks to the audience, wiggling and jerking in dreary rhythm to the jangling chords of the piano.

As Toddy advanced, the women straightened and moved off the stage, each giving her rear a final twitch as she disappeared into the wings. A man in baggy pants and a red undershirt came out. In his exaggerated anxiety to peer after the girls, he stumbled—he appeared to stumble. His derby flipped off, turned once in the air, then dropped neatly over his long putty nose.

Laughter swelled from the audience and there was a burst of hand clapping. The comic removed the derby and spat into it. He pulled the baggy pants away from his stomach and went through the motion of emptying the hat into them.

"Keep our city clean," he explained.

More laughter, clapping, stamping feet.

"Mi, mi, mi," chortled the comic, tapping his chest and coughing. "With your kind indulgence, I shall now sing that touching old love song, a heart-rending melody entitled (pause) 'If a Hen Lays a Cracked Egg Will the Chicken Be Nutty?'"

Laughter. A chord from the piano.

Toddy swung a foot to the pit rail and stepped across to the stage. The comic stared. He grasped Toddy's hand and wrung it warmly.

"Don't tell me, sir! Don't tell me. Mr. Addison Simms of Seattle, isn't it?"

No laughter. It was over their heads. Beneath the grease paint, the painted grin, the comic scowled. (*"What you pullin', you bastard?"*) "Why, Mr. Simms," he said aloud—simpering, twisting. "We can't do *that!* Not with all these people watching."

Howling laughter; this was right up the audience's alley. The scowl disappeared. The comedian released Toddy's hand and flung both arms around him. Head cuddled against Toddy's chest, he called coyly to the audience:

"Isn't he dar-ling?"

("How do I get out of here?")

"Don't you just lah-ve big men?"

("Dammit, let go!")

"You won't hurt me, will you, Mr. Simms?"

Above the whistling roar of the crowd, Toddy heard another sound. In the back of the house a brief flash of light marked the opening of the door. . . . A shouted, distant curse; the stifled scream of a woman. Toddy tried to jerk free and was held more tightly than ever.

"Kee-iss me, you brute! Take me in yo-ah ahms and—*oof!*"

Toddy gave him another one in the guts for luck, then a stiff-arm in the face. The comedian stumbled backwards. Stumbling, waving his arms, he skidded across the top of the piano and fell into the audience.

Over his shoulder, Toddy got a glimpse of people rising in their seats, milling into the aisle. He did not wait to see more. He darted into the wings, ducked a kick from a brawny man in an undershirt, and gave a blinding back-handed slap in return. A chorus girl tried to conk him with a wine bottle. He caught her upraised arm and whirled her around. He sent her sprawling into another girl—a big blonde with a pair of scissors. The third girl whizzed a jar of grease paint at him, then fled screaming onto the stage.

The exit was locked. He had to give it two spine-rattling kicks before the latch snapped. He stumbled out into the night, wedged a loaded trash barrel against the door—*that wouldn't hold long*—and ran on again.

He came out of the alley onto another side street. And this was more hopeless than the first one. No lights shone. Several of the buildings were in the process of being razed. The others were boarded up.

He started down it at a trot, panting, nervous sweat pouring into his eyes. He ran wearily, and then his head turned in an unbelieving stare and he staggered into a doorway. There was a double swinging door with small glass ports on either side. Through the ports drifted a dim, almost indiscernible glow. He went in.

He was looking up a long dimly lit stairway, a very long stairway. What had once been the second floor was now boarded off. Except for the former second-floor landing, the stairs rose straight to the third floor.

Gratefully, he saw that the swinging doors were bracketed for a bar; not only that, but the bar was there, a stout piece of two-by-four, leaning against the wall. He picked it up and slid it into the brackets. He put a foot on the steps. The boards gave slightly under his tread, and somewhere in the dimness above him a bell tinkled.

He hesitated, then went on. A man was standing at the head of the

stairs. He had a crew haircut and a mouthful of gum and a pair of pants
that rose to his armpits. He also had a sawed-off baseball bat. He
twiddled it at his side as he stared at Toddy with incurious eyes.

"Yeah, Mac?"

"Uh—I want to see Mable," said Toddy.

"Mable, huh? Sure, she's here. Agnes and Becky, too." The man
chuckled. He waited, then jerked his head impatiently. "You can't jump
'em on the stairs, Mac. That's the only way they won't do it, but they
won't do it that way."

Toddy ascended to the landing. He reached for his wallet, and the man
moved his hand in a negative gesture. "Just pay the gal, Mac . . . Now,
le's see . . ."

Doors, perhaps a dozen of them, extended the length of the hallway.
Doorways with half-doors—summer doors—attached to the outer casing.
The man nodded, pointed to a patch of light.

"Ruthie's free. Go right on down, Mac."

He gave Toddy's elbow a cordial push; then his arm tightened on it in a
viselike grip. "What the hell's that racket?"

"Racket?" said Toddy.

"You heard me. You bar that door down there?"

"Why the hell would I do that? . . . Wait a minute!" said Toddy. "I had
to boot a wino out of the doorway to get in. He must have come back
again."

The man cursed. "Them winos! And the goddam cops won't do a
thing about them!" He headed down the stairs scowling, twirling the
sawed-off bat. Toddy moved away from the stairwell.

There was no window at either end of the hall. There was nothing to
indicate which of the rooms opened on the fire escape. There'd be one,
surely, even in a whorehouse. But he'd have to hunt for it.

Come on, gizmo, he thought. *Be good to me.*

He rapped once, then entered the room the man had indicated. He
hooked the summer door behind him. He grinned pleasantly as he closed
and locked the other door.

"Hi, Ruthie," he said. "How've you been?"

"How you, honey?" She made a pretense of recognizing him. "Ain't
seen you in a long time."

She might have been twenty-five or ten years older, depending on how
long she'd been at it. Red-haired. Piled together pretty good. She wore
sheer silk stockings, high-heeled black pumps and a black nylon brassière.
That was all she wore.

She was sitting on the edge of the bed, shaving her calves.

"You mind waitin' a second, honey? I kinda hate to stop an' start all over again."

"Let me help you," said Toddy promptly.

He took the razor from her hand and pushed her gently back on the bed. He said, "Sorry, kid," and snapped his free fist against the point of her chin.

Her eyes closed and her arms went limp. Her feet slipped from the mattress, and he caught and lowered them to the floor.

Stepping to the window, he ducked under the shade and looked out. Wrong room. The fire escape opened on the next one. He might—but, no, it was too far. He could barely see the damned thing. Trying to jump that far in the dark would be suicide.

Ducking back into the room, he stepped to the tall Japanese screen and moved it aside. There was a low door behind it, a door blocked by a small bureau. Toddy almost laughed aloud at the sight of it. A bureau joint, for God's sake! He'd thought that gimmick had gone out with "Dardanella." Probably it had, too. This one probably wasn't used any more . . . but it might still be working.

In this little frammis, one of the oldest, you were persuaded to leave your clothes on the bureau . . . You see, honey? No one can touch 'em. The door swings in this way, and the bureau's in front of it. You can see for yourself, honey . . .

Toddy pulled out the top drawer and laid it on the bed. Reaching into the opening, he found the doorknob. Would the dodge work from this side, that was the question. If it didn't—

The knob turned slowly. There was a quiet *click*. Then, a little above the level of the bureau, the mortised panels of the door parted and the upper half swung toward him.

The head of a brass bedstead blocked the doorway on the other side. The man in it stared stupidly through the rails at Toddy. He was a young man, but he had a thick platinum blond beard. Or so it seemed. Then, he raised his head, bewilderedly, and Toddy saw that the hair spread out on the pillow beneath him was a woman's.

"F-for gosh sake!" the man gasped indignantly. "What kind of a whorehouse is—"

Toddy's hand shot out. He caught the guy by the back of the head and jerked it between the bedrails.

The man grunted. The platinum hair stirred frantically on the pillow to an accompaniment of smothered groans. Toddy gave the bed a push. It slid forward a few inches, and he entered the room.

He stepped out the window, and started down the fire escape. He took two steps, a third. The fourth was into space. Except for his grip on the handrail, he would have plunged into the alley.

He drew himself back, stood hugging the metal breathlessly. . . . Should have expected this, he thought. Building's probably been condemned for years. Now . . . He looked upward. No telling what was up there, but it was the only way to go.

All hell was breaking loose as he started up again. Doors were slamming, women screaming, men cursing. There was the thunder of overturning furniture—of heavy objects swung wickedly. And with it all, of course, the fearsome threatening snarl of the talking dog.

Suddenly, arms shot out of the window and clutched at Toddy's feet. He kicked blindly and heard a yell of pain. He raced up the remaining steps to the roof.

Stepping over the parapet, his hand dislodged a brick, and he flung it downward, heard it shatter on the steel landing. He pushed mightily with his foot, and a whole section of the wall went tumbling down. That, he thought, would give them something to think about.

Slowly, picking his way in the darkness, he started across the roof. There was no way out on either of the side streets he had been on. That meant he'd have to try for something on the parallel thoroughfare—up at this end, naturally, as far as he could get from the burly house.

He bumped painfully into a chimney, stumbled over an abandoned tar pot. He paused to flex his agonized toes and shake the sweat from his eyes. Unknotting his tie, he stuffed it into the pocket of his coat and swung the coat over his arm.

He was almost to the street now, and the majority of the buildings should be occupied. At any moment, he should be coming to a roof-trap or a skylight where—*Ooof!*

Glass shattered under his feet; there was a flash of light. He tried to throw himself backward and knew sickeningly that it was too late. He shot downward.

With a groaning wirish *whree* something caught his body in a sagging embrace. It hugged, then shoved him away. Upward. He landed on his side, unhurt but badly shaken. He opened his eyes cautiously.

He was lying on the floor beside a metal cot—a cot which, obviously, would never be slept in again. Down this side of the room and along the other were rows of other cots. At one end of the room, easily identifiable despite the half-partitions around them, were shower stalls and a line of toilets.

A flophouse, Toddy thought. Then he noticed the multitudinous chromos on the walls—GOD IS LOVE . . . JESUS SAVES . . . THE LORD IS MY SHEPHERD . . . and he amended the opinion. A mission flophouse. Heb. 13:8.

He got up and brushed the glass from his clothes. Picking up his coat, he crossed to the other side of the room and looked out a window. The stale air and the almost complete absence of light told him what he could not see. An air shaft. He'd have to go out through that door at the end of the room, and, if he knew his missions, there'd be plenty of people to pass.

Pondering drearily, desperately, a hope born of utter hopelessness entered and teased at his mind. Maybe Chinless *hadn't* got to Elaine. Maybe he didn't want to get Toddy. He might not have missed the watch. He might—uh—just want to talk to him.

Oh, hell. Why kid himself? Still, the idea wasn't completely crazy, was it? Elaine's murder had taken careful timing, a complete disregard for danger on the part of the murderer. Anyone as ruthless and resourceful as that would not waste time with dogs. Not if they wanted to bump you.

Chinless must have missed the watch. He'd missed it and he was holding off on killing him, Toddy, until he got it back. He—but wait a minute! If Chinless had got to Elaine, he already had the watch! Why else would he have killed—

"Is this right, brother?" said a severe voice. "Is this how we live in God's way?"

The man wore that look of puffed elation which seems to be the trademark of do-gooders, an expression born of a conscious constipation of goodness: of great deeds and wondrous wisdom held painfully in check; a resigned look, a martyred look, a determinedly sad look—a perpetual bitterness at the world's unawareness of their worth, at the fact that men born of clay take no joy in excrement, regardless of its purveyor. The man had a thick, sturdy body, a bull neck, and a size six and five eighths head.

He gripped Toddy's arm and marched him swiftly toward the door. "Don't do this again, brother," he warned. "The physical man must be provided for, yes. We recognize the fact. But before that comes our duty to God."

Toddy made sounds of acquiescence. This guy obviously wasn't used to having his authority questioned.

They went down a short flight of stairs which opened abruptly into a small sweat-and-urine scented auditorium. Tight rows of wooden camp chairs were packed with the usual crowd of mission stiffs—birds who were too low, lazy or incapacitated to get their grub and flop by other means.

The man shoved Toddy into a chair in the front row, gave him a menacing glare, and stepped to the rostrum.

"I apologize for this slight delay, brethren," he said, with no trace of apology. "For your sakes, I hope there will be no more. You are not entitled to the comfortable beds and nourishing food which you find here.

They are gifts—something given you out of God's mercy and goodness. Remember that and conduct yourselves accordingly. . . . We will rise now and Praise Him from Whom All Blessings Flow."

He nodded to the woman on the platform, and her hands struck the keys of the upright piano. Everyone rose and began to sing.

There was a comedian immediately behind Toddy. He liked the melody to the hymn, apparently, but not the lyrics; and he improvised his own. Instead of "Praise Him from Whom All Blessings Flow," he sang something about raisin skins and holy Joe.

The next song was "Onward, Christian Soldiers," which the comedian turned into a panegyric on rocks and boulders, the padding, in his opinion, of mission mattresses.

Toward the end of the hymn, the preacher cocked his head to one side and sharply extended his hand. The pianist stopped playing; the bums lapsed into silence.

"Someone here—"he said, staring hard at Toddy, "someone thinks he is pretty funny. If he persists, if he commits any further disturbance, I am going to take stern measures with him. Let him be warned!"

Toddy stared intently at the song book. There was a heavy silence, and then another song was struck up—"Nearer My God to Thee."

The comedian behaved himself this time, but some guy in the back of the house was sure giving out with the corn. He was gargling the words; he seemed to be trying to sing and swallow hot mush at the same time.

The preacher looked at Toddy. He stood on tiptoe and stared out over the congregation. They went on singing fearfully, afraid to stop, and the corny guy seemed to edge closer.

Toddy stole a glance up from his book. The preacher's mouth had dropped open. He was no longer singing, but his hand continued to move through the air, unconsciously waving time to the hymn.

Then, at last, the owner of the preposterous voice came into Toddy's view. He sat down at his side, on the floor, and laid his great pear-shaped head against Toddy's hip. Having thus established proprietorship, he faced the rostrum, opened his great jaws to their widest, and "sang":

"Nrrrahhhh me-odd t'eeeee . . . "

He was best on the high notes, and he knew it. He held them far beyond their nominal worth, disregarding the faltering guidance of the piano and the bums' fear-inspired determination to forge ahead with the song.

"Nrrrahhh t'eee," he howled. "Neee-rroww t'EEEE . . . "

There was a crash as the preacher hurled his hymnal to the floor. Purple with rage, he pointed a quivering finger at Toddy.

"Get that animal out of here! Get him out instantly!"

"He's not mine," said Toddy.

"Don't lie to me! You sneaked him in here tonight! That's why you were skulking upstairs! Of course he's yours! Anyone can see he's yours. Now get him OUT!"

Toddy gave up. He had to. The guy would be blowing the whistle on him in a minute.

He turned and started for the door. The dog hesitated, obviously torn between desire and training. Then, with a surly I-never-have-any-fun look, he followed.

Toddy paused on the sidewalk and put on his coat. The dog nudged him brusquely in the buttocks. He walked toward the curb, and the front door of the convertible swung open.

Toddy climbed in, heard the dog thump into the back seat, and leaned back wearily.

"What the hell's it all about?" he demanded. "What do you want with me?"

"You will know very soon," the girl said, and she would say no more than that.

X

Up until he met and married Elaine Ives, Toddy's world, despite its superficially complex appearance, was remarkably uncomplicated. Sound and practical motives guided every action; whims, if you were unfortunate to have them, were kept to yourself. Given a certain situation, you could safely depend upon certain actions and reactions. You might get killed for the change in your pocket. You would never get hurt, however, simply because someone felt like dishing it out.

Thus, on his wedding night, as he pushed himself up from the floor and slowly massaged his aching head, he couldn't accept the thing that had been done to him. He couldn't see it for what it was.

She'd been playing, putting on a show for him. Obviously, she'd just carried the act a little too far. She couldn't have meant what she'd said, what she'd done. She just couldn't have!

"Gosh, honey," he said, with a rueful smile. "Let's not play so rough, huh? Now what kind of whiskey would you like?"

"I'm sorry, T-Toddy. I—" She choked and tears filled her eyes.

"Forget it," he said. "You've just had a little more excitement than you can take. I should have seen it. I shouldn't have made you beg for a drink after all you've been through."

That was the way the incident ended. It was the way a dozen similar ones ended during the next few months. He gave in, and with each giving in her charm became thinner, the pretense of affection a leaner shadow. Why bother with charm, with pretending something she was incapable of feeling? It was easier and more to her taste simply to raise hell.

Still, Toddy couldn't understand; he refused to understand. She'd married him. Why had she done that unless she loved him? He wouldn't accept the contemptuous explanation she gave—that marriage, even to a chump like him, was better than working. She couldn't mean that. How could she when he'd done nothing to hurt her and was willing to do anything he could to help her? The fact that she'd make such a statement was proof that she was seriously ill. And so Toddy took her to a couple of psychiatrists.

The first had offices in his own building on Wilshire Boulevard, and he charged fifty dollars for a thirty-minute consultation. He allowed Toddy to spend one hundred and fifty with him before curtly advising him to spend no more.

"Your wife is not an alcoholic, Mr. Kent," he said. "In alcoholic circles

332

she is what is known as, to speak plainly, a gutter drunk. A degenerate. She could stop drinking any time she chose to. She does not choose to. She is too selfish. In a way, you are fortunate; she might have had a penchant for murder. If she had, she would probably pursue it as relentlessly as this will to drink."

The opinion of the second psychiatrist coincided pretty largely with that of the first, but he was longer in arriving at it. He spent much more time talking to Toddy than to Elaine, usually detaining him for an hour or so after each consultation. Toddy didn't mind. The guy was obviously a square shooter and interesting to talk to.

"Toddy," he said quietly one afternoon, the last afternoon they talked together, "why do you stick with her, anyway? I've told you she's no good. I'm sure you must know it's the truth. Why continue a relationship that can only end in one way?"

"I don't know that she's no good," said Toddy. "I know that she needs help, that I'm the only person—"

"She doesn't need help. She's been helped too much. She got along most of her life without you, and she can get along very well without you for the rest of it. The Elaines of this world have a peculiar talent for survival."

"Put it this way, then," said Toddy. "I married her for better or for worse. I'm not going to pull out—and, no, I'm not going to let her—just because things don't break quite the way I think they should."

The psychiatrist nodded seriously. "Now we're getting somewhere," he said. "We're approaching your real reason, at last. Let's examine it and see how it stands up. Your parents were divorced and your mother remarried. From then on, until you ran away, you lived in hell. The experience gave you an undying hatred of divorce. You made up your mind that you'd never do what your parents had done. All right. I can understand that attitude. But,"—he pointed with his pipestem—"it's ridiculous to maintain it in this present case. You're married to a virtual maniac. You haven't any children. Now stop living with the past, and use that intelligence I know you have."

"I—" Toddy shook his head. "What did you mean, Doc, when you said the marriage, Elaine's and mine, could only end in one way?"

"I don't think I'll tell you. I think it would make a greater impression if you told yourself."

"How do I go about doing that?"

"Well, let's start back with the time you ran away from home. Your reason for leaving, as I remember, was that one of the barn rafters had broken and struck your stepfather. You were afraid you might be held responsible for the accident, so you ran away."

"Well?" said Toddy.

"It was an accident," said the psychiatrist, "and yet you had a package of sandwiches, a lunch, all prepared. You were able to get away just in time to catch the evening freight out of town. . . . That, Toddy, is just about the most opportune accident I ever heard of."

Toddy looked blank for a moment; then he grinned.

"And so on down the line," the psychiatrist sighed. "You're easy to get along with; you'll suffer a great deal before you act. If you'd been treated fairly by your stepfather or the county attorney or that gambling house proprietor in Reno or the detective in Fort Worth or . . . But that isn't important. It's not what I'm talking about."

"What are you talking about?"

"You must know, Toddy: the fact that you can't admit the things you've done, even to yourself. At heart you're what you'd call a Square John. You're peaceful. You don't ask much but to be left alone and leave others alone. That's your basic pattern—and life hasn't let you follow that pattern. You've been forced into one situation after another where your strong sense of justice has impelled you to acts which were hateful to you . . .

"Get away from Elaine, Toddy. Get away and stay away. Before you kill her."

XI

THE CHINLESS MAN CHUCKLED SOFTLY AND MASSAGED HIS HANDS. "I present my proposition a little too fast, eh? It was not what you expected. I must apologize, incidentally, for the manner in which you were induced to return here. It seemed necessary. It was important that I talk to you, and I felt you might not respond to a simple request to call ... "

He waited, beaming, apparently for Toddy to make some polite disclaimer. Toddy didn't. For the moment, at least, he was incapable of saying or doing anything.

"As you can see," Chinless continued, "I mean you no harm. Quite the contrary, in fact. Despite the perhaps regrettable preliminaries of our meeting, I mean to benefit you—and, of course, to benefit myself. I would like to have you believe that, Mr. Kent; that I hold nothing but the friendliest feelings toward you."

He paused again, his beady black eyes fixed on Toddy's.

"Well ... " said Toddy; and his head moved in a vague half-nod.

"Good!" said the man promptly. "Now we will go into the matter in detail, take up details in their proper order. First of all, my name is Alvarado; I am known by that name. You, of course, are Todd or Toddy Kent ... also known as T. Jameson Kent, Toddmore Kent, Kent Todd and various other aliases. As you can see, I took the liberty of looking into your record after your visit here this afternoon. It interested me very much. It is largely why I have prevailed upon you to make this second visit."

"I—" Toddy swallowed. "I see."

"As you have probably observed," Alvarado went on, leaning forward earnestly, "extra-legal careers seldom attract the type of men which their successful pursuit demands. A willingness to flout often-foolish laws, yes—that characteristic is so common as to be unnoteworthy. But much more than that is required. Such men as yourself are indeed rare. I do not flatter you, Mr Kent, when I say that some episodes in your past reflect positive genius."

Toddy nodded again, his tense nerves relaxing a little.

"You find the dog disturbing, Mr. Kent? You need not. He is a working dog—quite harmless, actually, unless ordered to be otherwise."

"I was just wondering," said Toddy, "how you found out so much about me so fast."

335

"Nothing could have been simpler. A description of you, and a generous retainer, naturally, to one of the better private detectives. A brief check at the city license bureau. Then, a few cautious long-distance calls here and there . . . By the way, Mr. Kent"—Alvarado chuckled—"I should not show myself around Chicago, if I were you."

"I don't intend to," said Toddy. "Now, about this proposition of yours— you'd better not tell me about it. I don't think I can take it."

"But . . . I do not understand."

"The police are looking for me. Or they will be before long. My wife was murdered tonight—strangled in our room at the hotel."

"Murdered?" Alvarado frowned. "Strangled in your hotel room? What time was this, Mr. Kent?"

"Early this evening. Between six-thirty and seven, approximately." Toddy forced a smile. "To tell the truth, I thought you did it."

"I? Why did you think that?"

"Whoever killed her took the watch. Since it was your watch and you were the only one who knew I had it, I naturally thought you'd done it."

Alvarado stared at him in dead silence, the frown on his fish-pale face deepening. Then, unaccountably, the beady eyes twinkled and he laughed with genuine amusement.

"The watch was taken, eh? That is very funny. Ha, ha. You are very amusing, Mr. Kent. Like me you have a sense of humor. I am glad to know it!"

"But—now, wait a minute!" Toddy protested. "I—"

"I understand. Ha, ha. I understand very well. Perhaps for the moment, however, we had better continue with our business."

"But you—"

"As I was about to explain," Alvarado said firmly, "my original motive in having you investigated was precautionary. I wished to discover whether you were of the type to take the watch—with all it would reveal to the knowing—to the police. Happily, I found you were not. You have every reason to avoid contact with the police. That is right, is it not?"

"Yes, but—" Toddy gave up. He couldn't see why Alvarado thought the murder so funny. But since he did, that was that. For the moment, he wasn't in a position to question the chinless man. Right now, he was on the receiving end of the questions.

"Yes," he said, "that's right. I can't go to the police."

"As I so ascertained,"Alvarado nodded. "And having done so, I invited you here. For some time, Mr. Kent, a change in the personnel of this organization—of one of the personnel—has been strongly indicated. In fact, I have recommended such a change. But since no substitute for the incumbent was available, the recommendation did not carry much weight. In you, I think, I have found that long-needed replacement."

"You say you recommended the change?" Toddy asked.

"Yes. My superiors are not in this country, and it is necessary to consult them on such matters. Within reasonable bounds, however, they will act on my recommendations."

"I don't know," said Toddy, casually. "I can't see any big money in running gold across the border. Not for the individual runner."

"That was not what I had in mind."

"Well. You know I'm not a goldsmith."

"I know."

"I see," said Toddy. "Who's your present supplier?"

"Really, Mr. Kent." Alvarado laughed. "But I do not condemn your curiosity. It would be a splendid thing to know, would it not?"

"That's the spot you're planning for me?"

Alvarado shrugged. "For large rewards, Mr. Kent, one must expect to take certain chances. Your history indicates a willingness to do so."

"Up to a point," Toddy qualified. "There's one thing I don't understand. How can you get enough scrap gold to keep this racket running?"

"Another secret. You will understand when it is necessary for you to."

"I—" Toddy spread his hands helplessly. "I just don't see much point in discussing it, Mr. Alvarado. It sounds like a good proposition—one I'd jump at, ordinarily—but I can't take it now."

"No?"

"No! My wife was murdered tonight. I'm the logical suspect. I can't show myself anywhere. If I could, I'd be hunting down the murderer."

Alvarado started to smile again. "Ah, yes. Your wife . . . the watch. Perhaps you had better give me the watch now, Mr. Kent."

"Dammit!" Toddy snapped. "I just got through telling you that—"

"You want to keep it, of course," Alvarado nodded, understandingly. "You would be unintelligent if you did not try to. I do not blame you in the least, but it is impossible."

"But I haven't—"

"It is a sort of pattern, a template, you see. Without it, our work here would be seriously delayed. So,"—Alvarado's eyes glinted fire—"the watch, Mr. Kent."

Toddy got to his feet, carefully holding his arms out from his sides. The dog rose also, turning an inquiring eye toward the chinless man.

"Go ahead and search me," said Toddy hoarsely. "I can't give you something I haven't got."

"Since you are willing to be searched, you obviously do not have it with you. You will please tell me immediately where it is."

"I told you! I don't know—it was stolen!" He moved back a step as Alvarado rose. "Good-God, do you think I'd make up a yarn like that? I thought you'd killed her. That's why I tried to get away from the girl. I—"

"What you thought, Mr. Kent, was that I was a fool. I am afraid you still think so. . . . Did you dispose of it to that loan shark you visited—that petty racketeer? Or to that watch shop where you sell your gold? Carefully, now! I can discover the truth of your answer quickly enough."

"I've told you the truth," said Toddy simply. "I can't tell you anything more."

Alvarado's hand dipped into the inside pocket of his coat and emerged with a snub-nosed automatic. He held it pointing squarely at Toddy's stomach.

"This is embarrassing," he sighed, "as well as vastly annoying. Before telling me that your wife had been murdered, you should have made sure that I could not prove the contrary."

"Prove?"

"Now you will accompany me to the hotel and extricate the watch from wherever you have hidden it."

"The hell I will!" Toddy shook his head.

"Really, Mr. Kent," Alvarado grimaced. "You must know you are being preposterous."

"I know I'm not going to walk into a roomful of cops," snapped Toddy. "Not if I had a dozen popguns like that pointing at me."

The talking dog whined softly and looked up at them, then padded away unnoticed in the tension of the moment. Ever so little, the chinless man's eyes wavered. He moved back a step or two until he was no longer standing on the rug. He stamped his foot on the floor.

A door opened and clicked shut. There was a gasp and then the girl swept into the room.

"Alvarado! You promised me that—"

"Silence!" The word cracked like a whip. "I have not broken that promise yet. I would much prefer not to. Tell me . . . Where did you pick up Mr. Kent's trail tonight?"

"Why, I—I—" The girl looked at Toddy. "Didn't he tell you?"

"Answer me! Quickly, truthfully, and in complete detail!"

"I picked him up—him and the other man I told you of—about three blocks from the hotel. They were going south on Spring Street. As I told you, I had to circle a number of blocks, driving up and down before—"

Alvarado's hand jerked sidewise. The gun barrel whipped across the girl's breasts and back again.

"You were listening at the door, eh? You would remove Mr. Kent from the difficult position in which his stupidity has placed him? I will give you one more chance. Why was it, when you were given Mr. Kent's address, you were forced to pick him up several blocks away?"

"Because . . . he got away from me."

"Yes?"

"I . . . it was as I told you. He was leaving the hotel when I first saw him; that was at about six o'clock. I followed him from there to the watch shop, then back again. In my haste to park, I passed through a red light. A police officer saw me. He insisted on giving me a lecture, then on trying to arrange a later meeting . . . "

A rosy flush spread under the cream-colored skin, and her eyes lowered for a moment. "I do not know exactly how long it was before I got away. Perhaps twenty minutes. Perhaps a total time of thirty minutes elapsed before I parked the car and got up to Mr. Kent's room . . . "

"Go on. You knocked on the door. You tried it and found it unlocked. See? I save you the repetition of tiresome details."

"I went in. Mr. Kent was not there . . . "

"But the room was in great disarray, eh? You were shocked by its condition."

The girl shook her head.

"No," she said dully. "There was no disarray. The room was in quite good order."

"Now wait a minute!" Toddy exclaimed. "I left that room just—"

"Quiet, Mr. Kent. You will have ample opportunity to talk in a moment. I shall even assist you." Alvarado grinned at him fiercely, then nodded to the girl. "You say the room was in reasonably good order, Dolores? Surely, you are overlooking one very important item. Only a few minutes before—or so he tells me—the body of Mr. Kent's wife was in that room. Brutally murdered. Strangled with her own stockings. Killed and robbed of the watch which Mr. Kent had hidden in a dresser drawer . . . You recollect it now, eh? You remember this shocking sight now that I have refreshed your memory? The body of Mr. Kent's wife was in the room, yes? Answer me!"

Poised at the front door, the Doberman turned his great head and stared at them thoughtfully. Then he bellied down at the threshold, moved his muzzle back and forth across the lintel. A quiet, whining purr ebbed up from deep in his throat.

"Well? We are waiting, Dolores."

The girl hesitated a moment longer, her lip caught between her small white teeth.

Then she looked up. She spoke staring straight into Toddy's eyes.

"No," she said. "There was no body."

XII

AIREDALE AAHRENS (Need Bail?—Call Airedale) let the telephone jangle for a full minute while he lay cursing bitterly. Then he kicked back the bedcovers, snapped on the reading lamp, and literally hurled himself across the room.

"George!" he howled into the wall telephone. "How many times do I gotta tell you I . . . Oh," he said, after a minute. "Well, okay, George. Send him up."

Unlatching the door, he slid his feet into house slippers and shuffled out to the kitchenette. He poured himself a glass of milk from the refrigerator and carried it back into the other room.

The door opened, and City Councilman Julius Klobb came in.

"Look," he said. "This Elaine Ives—Kent. You've got to have her in court in the morning."

"I do, huh?" Airedale took a sip of milk. "Who says so?"

"Yes—you—do! And I say so. And you know why I say it."

"She'll have to do her time?"

"Naturally. Part of it, anyway; until the heat goes off."

"Heat," said Airedale, sourly. "Nine grand he takes off of me last year and still we got heat. Maybe I ought to fix through a beat cop. Or one of them guys that cleans out the washroom. Maybe they could earn their money."

Councilman Klobb spread his hands. "That's not being reasonable, Airedale," he said reproachfully. "The lid's been off now for well over eighteen months. Almost two years now without the slightest kind of rumble. I can't help it if we have an opposition party and they squeeze out from under once in a while. Frankly, I wouldn't have it any other way and I know you wouldn't. It's what makes America great—competition— unceasing struggle—"

Airedale groaned. "Unceasing horseshit. Put it away, will you? Save it for the Fourth of July."

"You'll have her there?"

"If it has to be her. We couldn't throw 'em another chump?"

"Of course not. Twenty-three arrests in a year and she's never laid out a day. She's the one they'll tie into. You know what'll happen when they do. Good God, man, do I have to draw you a picture?"

He didn't have to, of course. Airedale had known what to expect from the moment Elaine's name had been mentioned.

340

In many cities, bail is set to approximate the fine for a misdemeanor, and its forfeiture automatically closes the case. Usually, however, often in those places where the practice is most thoroughly entrenched, there are periods when it becomes inoperative. Bail then gives the lawbreaker his freedom only until court is held. And if he fails to appear he is considered a fugitive.

This, as Airedale well knew, must not be allowed to happen in Elaine's case. Obviously, the political opposition intended to use her as a broom in a thoroughly unpleasant house-cleaning. This woman, they'd say— they'd shout—has forfeited almost two thousand dollars in bonds. Where is that money? What is there to show for it? What besides a parcel of land which has already been obligated for twenty times its appraised value?

Airedale shook his head ruefully. To stave off an investigation, Elaine would have to face court on charges which, under adverse circumstances, could total up to months in jail and/or several thousand dollars in fines. She'd be sore as hell—which didn't trouble Airedale in the least. Toddy would be sore—and that did trouble him. Toddy had laid his money on the line. Now he wouldn't get anything for it. Airedale would return the dough he had paid, of course, but that wouldn't help much. Once a rap was squared, it was supposed to stay squared.

"How about this?" he said. "Can't we get our paper back and put up the cash in its place?"

"Would I be here if we could?" Klobb demanded. "Can't you see they planned this so we wouldn't have time to squeeze out?"

Airedale nodded. For Elaine to face court was bad, but the alternative was indescribably worse: to face it himself.

"Okay. I don't like it, but okay. She'll be there."

"Good." Councilman Klobb stood up. "Better get her on the phone right now, hadn't you?"

"Get her on the phone." mocked Airedale. "Yessir, that's all I need to do; just tell her to go down and turn herself in."

"But ... " Klobb frowned. "Oh, I see."

"Do you see that door?" said Airedale.

Klobb saw it. Rather hastily, he put it to use. Airedale began to dress.

Some fifteen minutes later he stepped out of a cab at Toddy's hotel and went inside. He was acquainted with the room clerk. He was acquainted with practically everyone in a certain stratum of the city's society. The clerk winked amiably, and extended a hand across the counter.

"How's it goin', boy? Who you looking for?"

"Might be you, you pretty thing," said Airedale. "But I'll settle for Toddy Kent."

"Kent? I'm not sure that he's regis—Oh," said the clerk, glancing at the bill in his hand. "Yeah, we got him. Want me to give him a buzz?"

"Not now, Is his key in his box?"

"That don't mean nothing. People here carry their keys mostly. He should be in, though, him and the missus both. I ain't seen 'em go out."

Airedale deliberated. He had a deputy sheriff's commission but he was reluctant to use it. It was always much better, particularly when you were dealing with a friend, to have someone else do the strong-arm work.

"Where's old lardass, the demon house dick?"

"Up with some broad, probably. No, there he is,"—the clerk pointed— "in stuffing his gut."

Airedale glanced toward the coffee shop. "Okay, I'll drag him out. About three minutes after you see us catch the elevator, you ring hell out of Kent's phone."

Airedale got hold of Kennedy, the house detective, and together they went upstairs. They stopped at Toddy's door. Almost immediately the phone began to ring. It rang steadily for what must have been a full two minutes. There was no other sound, either then or after it had stopped.

Airedale raised his fist and pounded. He stood aside, and nodded to Kennedy. The house dick gripped the doorknob with one hand, with the other he poised a peculiarly notched key before the keyhole. He slowly turned the knob and pushed gently. He dropped the key back into his pocket, drew out a shot-weighted blackjack, and abruptly flung the door open.

"Okay," he growled, "come out of it!" Then, after a moment's wait, he went in and Airedale followed him.

They looked in the bathroom, the closet and under the bed. Panting from the unaccustomed activity and his recent meal, Kennedy dropped into a chair and fanned his face with his hat.

"Well," he said, "they ain't here."

"No kidding," said Airedale.

Airedale went to the window and looked out. He looked down at the once-white enameled sill—at the streaked out-line of a heelprint.

Kennedy said, "She gave ol' Toddy a little more than he would take tonight. Boy, you could hear her yelling a block away!"

"Yeah?"

"I'm tellin' you, Airedale. It sounded like he was killin' her. If I'd had my way he'd of gone ahead and done it."

"So what did you do?"

"Gave him a ring. She'd already shut up by then, though, and there wasn't another peep after that."

Airedale stared in unwinking silence, and the house detective shifted uncomfortably. "Guess they must of gone out," he remarked, averting his eyes from the bondsman's liquid brown gaze. "Must of."

Absently scratching his nose, Airedale started for the window again, and his protruding elbow struck against the stack of the incinerator. He leaped back with a profane yell. Kennedy roared and pounded his knee.

"Oh, J-Jesus," he laughed. "You should of seen yourself, Airedale!"

"What the hell is this?" Airedale demanded. "A hotel or a crematory? What you got a goddam furnace goin' for in weather like this?"

Panting, shaking with laughter, the house detective explained the nature of the stack. Airedale made a closer examination of it. He kicked it. He removed a wisp of hair from the clamp. He measured the stack with his eye, and knew unwillingly that it was quite large enough . . . to hold a woman's body.

. . . Strolling back toward his hotel, he considered the smog through doggish eyes, reflecting, unsentimentally, that Elaine was doubtless part of it by now. That would be like her, to remain a nuisance even in death. Certainly it had been like her to get herself killed at such a completely inopportune time. When she failed to show in the morning, the cops would come after her. They'd do a little investigating, a little talking here and there, and the dragnet would go out for Toddy.

There was an all-night drugstore on the next corner. Airedale went in, entered a telephone booth and closed the door firmly behind him. He consulted a small black notebook and creased a number therein with his thumbnail. Fumbling for a coin, he checked over the contemplated project for possible pitfalls.

Fingerprints? No, they'd gotten her prints on her first arrest, and they hadn't bothered with them since. Pictures? No, they already had her mug, too, the newspapers and the police. And as long as she showed up in court—a woman of about the same age and size and coloring—Yeah, it could be done all right. Hundreds of women were in the Los Angeles courts every week. Elaine would draw the interest of papers and police only if she *didn't* show up.

Airedale dropped a slug into the coin box and dialed a number:

"Billie?"—he stared out through the door glass—"Airedale. How's it goin'? . . . Yeah? Well, it's slow all over, they tell me. . . . How'd you like a cinch for a while? . . . Oh, a buck—no, I'll make it a buck and a half. . . . Sure, don't you understand English? A hundred and a half a week. . . . Well, I'll have to talk it over with you personally. I don't like to kick it around on the phone . . . *Ex*penses? Sure, you get 'em, Billie girl. Board and room . . . absolutely free."

XIII

Toddy stared at the girl stonily. That reluctance of hers, the way she'd seemingly made Alvarado drag the story out of her, had been very well done. He'd almost believed for a moment that she was on his side. And now she'd lied. It *had* to be a lie. Either that or it was about time to wake up. It was time to give himself a pinch, put on his clothes, and go out for coffee.

With the body there in the room, the murder made sense. It put a frame on him like a Mack truck. Without the body, it was just plain damned screwy. It was nuts with a plus sign.

"Well, Mr. Kent?" Alvarado grinned satirically.

Toddy shook his head. "I've said all I've got to say."

"I see. Dolores, you will remain here. You, Mr. Kent, in front of me and through that door. I think you will be interested to see our basement."

"Wait!" The girl's voice was a sharp whisper. "Perrito, Alvarado! The dog!"

Alvarado looked. His gaze moved sufficiently from Toddy to take in the front door. He asked a soft question in Spanish.

"Hombres, Perrito? Si, hombres?"

Eyes shining with excitement, the dog took a few prancing steps toward him. His jaws waggled with the effort to articulate.

"Bueno, perro!" said Alvarado. "Stand!"

The dog became a statue—a waist-high ebony menace pointed motionlessly toward the door. "The lights, Dolores . . . "

Alvarado moved behind Toddy, jabbed and held the gun against his back. The lights went off. Dead silence settled over the room.

It was like that for minutes. Absolute silence except for the restrained whisper of their breathing. Then, distantly, from outside and overhead, came a soft *ping*. That, the cutting of the telephone wire, ended the silence. Having removed their sole danger, or so they thought, the prowlers were actually noisy.

There was a scraping of feet against wood, a noisy thud. Footsteps clattered across the porch. A whining, scratching sound marked the slashing of the screen.

The door shivered. The knob turned, and out of the darkness came a profane expression of pleased surprise. Feet scuffled. The door clicked shut again.

The lights went on.

Shake and Donald stood side by side on the threshold. Their eyes blinked against the light. Then they ceased to blink, grew wider and wider in their greenish-white faces.

"J-j-j-jjjjj . . . " said Donald.

Shake's pudding head wobbled helplessly. Oscillating, he sagged back against the door.

Alvarado's icy voice snapped him ludicrously erect.

"Take three steps forward! Now lock your arms behind you! Dolores—" He jerked his head.

The girl went in back of the two men. She searched them with contemptuous efficiency. Donald, of course, was equipped with his long thin-handled knife. From Shake's hip pocket she withdrew a man's sock, weighted and knotted together at the top. She was about to toss it to the floor when Alvarado held out his hand.

"If you please . . . " He hefted the sock, grinning at the two thugs as he moved slightly away from Toddy. "The chicken claws, eh—the sock loaded with broken glass. To what do I owe this honor, gentlemen?"

"It—that don't really hurt, mister," Shake blurted foolishly. "W-we wouldn't—"

"I am familiar with its possibilities. I wonder if you would still maintain it doesn't hurt if I should swing it vigorously against your crotch?"

Shake turned a shade greener.

Donald pointed an angrily indignant finger at Toddy. "He's the guy you ought to do it to, mister! He got us to come here!"

"Did he, indeed?"

"Just ast him if he didn't! Told us they was an old lady livin' here all by herself—an old crippled dame with a pile of jewelry!"

"That's just what he done, sir," Shake chorused righteously. "Got us to give him two hundred dollars for tippin' us off."

Alvarado glanced quizzically at Toddy. Toddy shrugged.

"I see. You,"—nodding at Donald—"is that what you were discussing with him earlier this evening?"

"It ain't *all* we was discussing." Donald eyed Toddy venomously. "What we was really discussing was murder. We—that's how we happened to make the deal with him. He killed his wife and he needed the money to blow town on."

"Oh, now," Alvarado laughed. "Murder his wife? I find that hard to believe. Doubtless he only told you that as a means of obtaining your money."

"I tell ya, he killed her! Anyways," Donald qualified reluctantly, "she got killed. She was layin' on the bed—right there in his hotel room!"

Alvarado made a sound of disbelief. "He invited you up to pay your respects, I suppose? At what time was this?"

"Right around six-thirty. An', no, he didn't invite me up there! I sneaked up while he was out, see? I was gonna cut him up when he came back."

He babbled on eagerly, anxious to make the evidence against Toddy as damning as possible. Shake tried to interrupt him once; he seemed to sense that there was much more here than met the eye. A cold word from Alvarado, however, and Shake was reduced to flabby quaking silence.

Donald concluded the recital with a vicious leer at Toddy.

Slowly, the chinless man turned to the girl. "Well?"

"I told you what I saw. There is nothing more I can say."

"So," sighed Alvarado, "we are confronted with two contradictory truths. Apparently contradictory, I should say. I wonder . . . But we must not bother these gentlemen with our petty problems. They are obviously men of large affairs. We must speed them on their way—with, of course, some small memento of their visit."

He moved, smiling, toward the two. "You would like to leave it that way, gentlemen? After all, breaking and entering is a very serious crime."

They nodded vigorously.

Alvarado's smile vanished. "I will do you a favor. Turn around!"

"B-but—"

"I withdraw the favor!" He swung the sock—once, twice. He dropped it and grabbed the dog by the collar. "The blood scent arouses him, gentlemen. I advise you to run very fast."

They stared at him stupidly; dazed, not grasping his meaning. The blows had reddened their faces. There was no other sign of their impact.

Then it came, the blood. It spurted out from ten thousand pinpoint fountains, formed into hideous red-threaded masks. The dog snarled and lunged.

"Quickly!" snapped Alvarado, and there was no doubting the urgency of his voice.

Shake and Donald came alive simultaneously. They hurled themselves at the door and wedged there. Clawing and cursing hysterically, they broke free. They stumbled and fell down the steps. The sound of their frantically pounding footsteps receded and vanished into the night.

Alvarado closed the door and stood with his back to it. He smiled at Toddy as he delivered a firmly admonitory kick in the dog's ribs.

"I seem to owe you an apology, Mr. Kent. I wonder if you will be generous enough to forgive and forget—if, in short, you are still of a mind to accept the offer I made you earlier."

Toddy's brow wrinkled. "Maybe. But what about my wife? Regardless of what's happened to the body, my wife's absence is going to be noticed. It's just a matter of time until the police will be looking for me. I can't show myself. I don't see how you can afford to be tied up with me."

"I am planning, Mr. Kent, to absolve you of the murder. Naturally, you would be of no use to me otherwise."

"You're *planning?*" Toddy said. "But how—why?"

"How I cannot yet tell you. As to the why, I have a double reason. Not only do I wish to have you associated with me, but I think it highly possible that the murderer may be my enemy as well as yours." Alvarado held up his hand. "Please! For the present, there is little more that I can tell you. And you have not accepted my offer . . . or have you?"

"All right." Toddy made up his mind. "It's my only chance. You've got yourself a boy."

"Good. Now, who knew that you had the watch?"

"You did."

"Of course. And Dolores. But who else? You told your wife about it, naturally?"

"No. Neither her nor anyone else."

"You are positive of that? Did you say anything to anyone which might, even by a remote chance, lead them to suspect that you had the watch?"

"No, I—" Toddy paused doubtfully.

"Did you or not? This is easily as important to you as it is to me, Mr. Kent."

"I talked to the man I sell gold to." Toddy gave him a brief summary of his conversation with Milt. "It couldn't have meant anything to him. Anyway, my wife was killed at just about the time I was talking to him."

"Then he is of no interest to us. It is as I thought. . . ."

"Yes."

Alvarado nodded absently. "Yes, it must be so. . . . But sit down, Mr. Kent. Would you like some coffee?—fine, so would I. Dolores!"

Toddy sat down and lighted a cigarette. Alvarado waited until the kitchen door had closed before he spoke.

"I will tell you something," he said quietly, "and please do not ask me to elaborate at this time. I place no great confidence in Dolores. Do not trust her too far."

"I don't trust anyone very far," said Toddy.

"Excellent. She is an attractive girl and not, I am afraid, above using her attractions. But, to get back to the matter at hand—when you discovered your wife dead and this man Donald fleeing down the fire escape, did you begin your pursuit of him immediately?"

"Of course."

"You made no search of the room?"

"I told—" Toddy interrupted himself with a startled curse. "Hell's bells! The guy could have been there for all I know!"

"Yes. He could still have been there when Dolores looked in. But do not blame yourself too much, Mr. Kent. You acted quite normally."

The kitchen door opened and Dolores came in with the coffee.

"None, thank you." Alvarado waved aside the cup the girl extended. "Pour Mr. Kent's, and then bring me my hat. After that, you may retire."

"I would prefer to remain up," Dolores said.

"It will be bad for your health to do so. Very bad. You will be amazed at the promptness with which the damage will manifest itself."

She gave him a sullen, baffled glare, but she turned and went out. Alvarado snapped his fingers at the dog.

"I will take Perrito with me, Mr. Kent. You will doubtless be able to rest better if you are alone."

Toddy said, "Thanks," and poured more coffee in his cup as man and dog left the house. Setting the enameled pot back on the serving table, he lighted another cigarette. He heard the car pull out of the driveway.

He took a sip of the coffee and let his eyes droop shut. Actually, he supposed, there wasn't much use in thinking. He couldn't be guided by it except to a very limited degree. Until Elaine's murder was cleared up, it was strictly the chinless man's show.

Elaine. . . . He held the word in his mind, turned it over and around; stubbornly, dully terrified, he refused to recognize the emotion which the name conjured. . . . *Hatred, relief, now that she was dead*? Nonsense! He could have got a divorce. He could have let her get one, as she'd wanted to of late. He might feel that she was better off dead, but that didn't mean—And wasn't he doing everything he could to track down her murderer? Wasn't that proof that—proof of how he really felt? He was doing everything he could to lay hands on the guy who killed her. That was his only reason for stringing along with Alvarado. Of course, the latter's offer was unusually attractive, the kind of thing he'd been looking for. . . .

Only one setup could be prettier—to find out who the present supplier was. He'd be loaded, stooped down with dough he wasn't supposed to have.

"*Mr. Kent!*"

Dolores was kneeling beside him, the silken fullness of her breast pressing against his arm. The blue V-necked nightgown cast seductive shadows along the creamy planes of her flesh.

"The coffee—you have been doped. You must leave here at once!"

XIV

TODDY WAS A HAPPY AWAKENER; it was the one characteristic which had maddened Elaine more than any of his others. Shaking with a hangover, sick at her stomach, she would look at him in the morning and profanely demand what the hell there was to grin about.

So he looked at Dolores now, smiling not for her but himself. And then awareness came to him, and with it the chronic suspicion and hardness which life had engendered in him. But the smile still lingered, deceptively trusting and innocent.

"How's that?" he asked. "What do you mean, the coffee's doped?"

"You saw he did not drink of it? Now you must go!"

"Why?"

"You are in great danger. I cannot tell you more than that."

"Sure," said Toddy. "Sure, I'll go. Just as soon as you tell me how to dope black coffee. I've heard of almost everything, but I've never heard of that. There ought to be a fortune in it."

"B-but I—I—"

Her mouth closed helplessly over the words which had seemed so adequate a moment ago. He looked like a different man now. The mold remained the same but the contents had undergone a fearsomely rapid change. The soft crinkles of his smile had assumed the rigid hardness of ice.

"Well?"

"All right," she said, coloring. "I lied about the coffee. But—"

His hand closed suddenly over her arm. With a movement too swift to analyze, she was twirled up and around and smacked down upon his knees.

"You don't mind?" he said. "I like to look at people when I talk to them. Always look at people when you talk to them, and you won't have to wear false teeth."

"I—*let me*—!"

She tried to fling herself forward...and his right foot swung with casual expertness. She fell back into the hollow of his knees, her feet swept from under her. She balanced there foolishly, fury slowly surrendering to a growing fear.

"A little bony, aren't they?" he nodded. "You said I was in danger; I'm willing to be convinced. What danger?"

"It—the danger is not from Alvarado."

"Well, then?"

"That is all I will say."

"Oh, now," Toddy drawled, "we can't leave it there. We just can't do that. You haven't got a twin sister, have you?"

"A twin? I do not understand."

"Uh-huh. Some girl that looked just like you chased me all over hell tonight; hunted me down with a dog the size of a Shetland pony. I had my legs run off. I damned near got killed two or three times. And after the dog had caught me and herded me into her car, she brought me out here—the last place in the world I wanted to go. I tried to bribe her. I tried to argue with her. It was no soap right on down the line. And after all that, she turns pal on me. She's my bosom—no offense, honey— friend. I'm supposed to—"

"Please! If you'll give me a chance..."

"You've got it."

"I had to bring you here. I could not let you escape. Alvarado would have accepted no excuse."

"Why didn't you take it on the lam? Why don't you now—if you really don't like the game? Alvarado's not in any position to make much trouble and neither are you. You'd be even-stephen."

He waited, eyebrows raised, watching the shivering rise and fall of her breast. There were tears in her eyes. She looked pathetically sweet and helpless and baffled, like a child who has had its hands slapped in the act of presenting a gift.

"I'm still here," he said harshly. "Let's have it."

"You!" she snapped, her eyes suddenly tearless, "you are so full of your own image that you can see nothing else! Are you blind? Have you forgotten that I tried to protect you tonight? I could have received much more than a blow. To make my story conform with yours, I—"

"Uh-huh. After it wouldn't do any good. After you'd already told him another one. ... Did you ever get worked over by the cops, honey? It's pretty cute. You're in a soundproof room, see; you're buried where no one can get to you; you're not even booked, maybe. There's not a thing you can do but take it, the slaps, the hose, the kidney kicks; and you've had more than you can take hours ago. And then the door slams open and a nice fatherly guy comes in, and he gives these guys hell. They can't do that to you. He won't stand for it. He's going to get 'em all fired. Cute? Why, you'll fall on his neck—if you haven't been through the routine before."

"Oh," said Dolores, softly. "You think that—yes, you would have to think that. You could not be expected to think otherwise."

"Bingo, gin and blackjack," Toddy said. "Let's see if we can't agree on something else."

"I had better go. There is nothing I can say to you."

"How many times were you in my room tonight?"

"How—Why, once!"

"And the room was in order?"

"Yes! It was in order and I did not move the body—why in the world shoud I?—and you can believe that or disbelieve it and—*and I hate you!*"

"Sit still!" Toddy grabbed her arm and drew her back. "I haven't got much more to say but I want to be sure you hear it. My wife was a tramp. They don't come any lower. But I didn't want her dead. I particularly didn't want her dead that way. . . . No one deserves to die like that, alone, gagged and strangled in a sleazy room in a third-class hotel. If I live long enough, I'll get my hands on the party that did it. When I do. . . ."

"Surely, you cannot think that—"

"Think it?" Toddy shook his head. "I don't even think that you're trying to steer me away from my one chance to find the murderer. I don't even think that I might find myself in trouble if I picked you up on that steer—if I tried to leave. I don't think a thing. All I know is that hell's been popping ever since I came to this house this afternoon, and you've been right in the middle of the fireworks. I don't think a thing, but I don't *not* think anything either. That's the way it is, and as long as it is that way here's a tip for you. Don't toss that pretty little butt toward me again. If you do, I'll kick it for a field goal."

He put a period to the words with a knee jerk. It sent her stumbling to her feet, and she wobbled awkwardly for a moment, startled, furious, fighting to regain her balance.

"*You!*" she flung over her shoulder, and the door banged shut on the word.

She was none too soon. . .if it wasn't an act. For Alvarado had returned; a car was pulling into the driveway. Toddy wondered what line you took in a case like this.

If it was the chinless man's way of testing him, there was only one thing to do. Tell him about it. It wouldn't hurt the girl; it would hurt him, Toddy, if he didn't.

If, on the other hand, she had given him a warning or a threat, the chinless man should still be told. He and Chinless were riding the same boat temporarily. What hurt one was very apt to hurt the other.

So he had every reason to speak of this, the girl's attempt to make him leave. But he couldn't quite make up his mind to do it. He still hadn't when, a moment later, Alvarado and the dog came in.

XV

THE DOG CAME DIRECTLY TO TODDY AND HUNKERED DOWN IN FRONT OF HIM. With the air of one nagged by a worrisome problem, he gazed studiously into Toddy's face.

"Nrrrah?" he said. "Nrrrah...t'ee?" Obviously the song both haunted and tantalized him. He could neither forget it nor recall the melody.

Toddy grinned despite, or, perhaps, because of his own serious situation. It was a relief to encounter something in this house so wholly undevious and understandable. He was humming the refrain of the hymn when a curt command from Alvarado interrupted.

Lugubriously, the dog moved away. Chinless dropped into a chair, rubbing his hands. He was feeling very pleased with himself, Chinless was. His shark's grin stretched from ear to ear.

"You have had some rest? Ah, yes, I can see you have. I see,"—he took an exaggerated sniff of the air—"that you have not been alone either. The girl lost no time in approaching you."

"Maybe." Toddy couldn't smell any perfume and he didn't think Alvarado could. It wouldn't mean anything, anyway, since she'd been in the room all evening. "Maybe," he said casually. "She could have been in while I was asleep."

Alvarado chuckled. "I understand. It has been years since such matters interested me, but I understand well. She is an attractive girl. You have lost your wife—"

"Just," said Toddy, "just a few hours ago."

"My apologies. My remarks were entirely out of order."

"All right," said Toddy.

"In rejoicing one is apt to become tactless, and I have reason to rejoice, Mr. Kent. We both do. The police may not be on your trail yet, but they soon will be. There is no question about it."

Toddy stared at him incredulously. "That's supposed to be good, is it?"

"Oh, very good. It—wait, please. I shall be glad to explain. I could not seriously doubt your story tonight; not after it had been confirmed by two men who obviously hated you. But my believing ws not enough. My principles would demand more than that. So, I got more, much more than I expected."

He chuckled gleefully again, then hurried on at Toddy's frown. "I registered for a room at the hotel in the same wing yours is in. It was my intention to persuade the bellboy to let me look into yours—perhaps on the pretext that I smelled smoke coming from it. I had no way of knowing what I would find, if anything, but I felt certain that—"

"Get on with it," Toddy broke in impatiently. "You did get in. What did you find?"

"But I did *not* get in. Such was not necessary. The door was open and there were men inside. Detectives, beyond a doubt. I could only see one of them, and I could overhear only a snatch of their conversation. But that was sufficient. They were looking for your wife. Patently, they had been informed of her disappearance."

"But"—Toddy frowned—"that means the body *is* gone."

"Yes, it is very strange," murmured Alvarado, lowering one eyelid in a wink. "Very, very strange. Who would have a motive for removing the body? Not the murderer, certainly. To do so would conflict with his reason for committing the murder. So. . . ."

"You're forgetting just one thing," said Toddy. "I didn't know the body was missing. I thought it was still there in my room."

"Did you, Mr. Kent?"

"Yes!" snapped Toddy, and then he shrugged and lowered his voice. "Let it ride. Let's have the rest of it."

"Good," Alvarado nodded sagely. "The point is a delicate one and there is really no point in discussing it. What matters is that your wife was killed—and I know the identity of her murderer. Please!" He held up his hand. "We can have no great amount of time to act. You had best let me explain in my own way.

"When I first missed the watch this afternoon, I notified our gold-supplier immediately. I did so reluctantly. As I have indicated, the man is no friend of mine. I detest him, in fact, and the feeling is reciprocated. Under the circumstances, however, I had no choice. He has many contacts in the gold trade; you might try to dispose of the watch. Such a potentially disastrous attempt had to be stopped at all costs."

"I don't see—"

"You will, Mr. Kent. Not only is this man my enemy, but he has long been anxious to withdraw from this organization. He will not say so, of course. He is afraid to. He knows that when we are willing to dispense with a man's services we also dispense with him—permanently. As long as our organization was functioning, and unless we chose otherwise, he would have to remain part of it.

"So this afternoon, today, he saw his opportunity. We presented it to him, you and I. By killing your wife, he would force you into summary action against me to establish your own innocence. Inevitably the facts of our organization would be brought to light. It would be impossible for us to operate, if ever, for a very long time. . . . That is why your wife was killed, Mr. Kent. So that this man might avenge himself upon me and free himself of an association which has become distasteful to him."

Toddy frowned dubiously. "I don't know," he said, slowly. "It seems to me like he had his own neck out pretty far."

"Not in his opinion. Like many persons who confess to cleverness, he is inclined to overlook the fact that others may be shrewd also. He felt certain, no doubt, that I would never see through his plan."

"Only you and they know who he is, is that right?"

"That is correct." Alvarado smiled sympathetically. "You have a right to know also, and you shall very shortly. I must lay the matter before my superiors and wait for their instructions, but that is a mere formality. The man will pay for his crime. There is not the slightest doubt about it."

"How?"

"Well"—the chinless man pursed his lips—"I imagine he will become conscience-stricken, Mr. Kent. Remorse will compel him to confess to the murder—in writing, of course—after which he will commit suicide."

He grinned mirthlessly. Toddy hesitated.

"I still don't see," he said. "I don't see why your people would go to such trouble to soak the guy. My wife meant nothing to them. He tried to get you, but you were trying to get him, too. He's never said he wanted to pull out of the racket, and—"

"I will tell you why," Alvarado interrupted. "Our work is sponsored by my government. It is a poor government, financially speaking, and an unpopular one; a ragged pariah among the commonwealth of nations. It must have gold to survive. It can get gold in this way. Lately, there have been indications that it might be able to secure loans from this country. There is much sentiment against them here, but there is some cause for hope. Can you imagine what would become of that hope if I, an agent of this already unpopular power, was charged with murder? With specifically the murder of a woman and an American citizen?"

"Yes," Toddy nodded. "I can."

"You Americans are a peculiar people, Mr. Kent. You are undisturbed by what amounts to mass murder, but let one of you be killed—a woman, in particular—and your entire nation is one voice demanding vengeance. . . . That is why this man will be severely and promptly punished. For actually jeopardizing the security of my government for his own purposes."

"Can you prove that he did?"

"I shall be able to. Within the next twenty-four hours, I hope. And please do not ask me how; I cannot tell you. In the meantime . . . "

"I'd better hide out?"

"Yes. It may not be necessary, but we can take no chances. We do not know what the police have been told. It is dangerously futile to guess. Tijuana will be safe. I have contacts there."

With a muttered word of apology, Alvarado took a bus timetable from his pocket and held it up to his eyes. He studied it, squinting, for a moment, then fitted a pair of steel-rimmed spectacles to his nose and peered at it again. Abruptly he thrust it toward Toddy.

"Will you examine this abominable thing? The fine print—even with glasses I cannot read it."

Toddy repressed a smile; the print wasn't particularly fine. "Sure," he said. "What are we looking for ?"

"I thought it would be best to depart from one of the suburban stations. If you will select one, I will drive you there. I would take you all the way to Mexico, but to do so, I am afraid, might endanger both of us."

Toddy's finger traced down the columns of print, and paused. "How about Long Beach?"

"That should do, I think. When does the next southbound bus leave from there?"

"Two o'clock." Toddy glanced at his wristwatch. "About an hour from now."

"Then we had better be going. On the way I will tell you what you must do when you reach Tijuana." Alvarado rose and reached for his hat. "You have money, I believe. Good! . . . Come, Perrito."

XVI

BATHED, shaved and wearing the feshly pressed clothes and the new shirt the bellboy had brought up, Toddy sat on the bed of his San Diego hotel room and poured out the last of his breakfast pot of coffee.

The bus had arrived at six o'clock. It was now almost eight. Except for Elaine's death and his own precarious position, he would have felt pretty good. He actually felt pretty good despite those things. He had a sensation of being at peace with himself, of being able to relax after a lifetime of tension. He was not tired—he felt invigorated, in fact—yet there was a strong desire to sit here and rest. Just rest and nothing else.

And he knew that the quicker he got out of this town, the better off he'd be.

San Diego's unique semi-tropical climate was not the only thing it was noted for. Nor its great aircraft plants, nor Navy and Marine bases. Among the denizens of the world to which Toddy belonged, it was also known as a swell place to steer clear of. Its vagrancy laws were the harshest in the country. To be "without visible means of support"—a surprisingly elastic category in the hands of local cops and judges—was a major crime. In the same month here a vagrant—an unemployed wanderer—and a woman who had murdered her illegitimate baby were given identical prison sentences.

Despite the earliness of the hour, a crowd of holidayers was already waiting for the bus to the Mexican border. Toddy hesitated, thought for a moment of making the seventeen-mile trip in a cab. There'd been nothing about Elaine's death in the morning papers; apparently, there was no alarm out for him. Still—he took his place in the waiting line—he couldn't be sure. It was best to stick with a crowd.

He stood up throughout the thirty-minute ride to the border. The bus unloaded, there, on the American side, and he made himself one with the mass which crowded through the customs station.

He had no trouble in crossing the international boundary. The busy United States guard barely glanced at him as he asked his nationality and birthplace. The Mexican customs officers did not bother to do even that much. They simply stood aside as he and the others filed past.

Toddy climbed into a Mexican taxicab, jolted over a long narrow bridge, and, a minute or two later, stepped out on Tijuana's main thoroughfare. He strolled leisurely down it, a wide dirty street bordered by one-and two-story buildings which were tenanted mainly by bars, restaurants and curio shops.

It was a bullfight day, and the town was unusually crowded. Americans jammed the narrow sidewalks and swarmed in and out of the business establishments. Most signs were in English.

Toddy walked to the end of the street, to the turn which leds off to the oceanside resort of Rosarita. Then he crossed to the other side and walked slowly back. Near the center of town, he turned off onto a side street and strolled along for a few doors. He passed a curio shop, lingeringly, then paused and went back.

He entered.

The shop was stocked to the point of overflowing. Racks of beadwork, leather goods and trinkets jammed the aisles. It was almost impossible to squeeze past them. Once past, it would be impossible to be seen from the street.

A fat Mexican woman was seated on a campstool just inside the door. She beamed at Toddy.

"Yess, please? Nice wallet? Nice bo'l of perfume for lady?"

"What have you got in the way of gold jewelry?" Toddy asked. "Something good and heavy?"

"*Nada!* Such things you could not take across the border, so we do not sell. How 'bout nice belt? Nice silver ring?"

"Oh, I guess not," said Toddy. "Not interested in anything but gold. Real gold."

"You look around," the woman beamed, placing her campstool in front of the door. "I get nice breath of air. You may find something more nice than gold."

Toddy nodded indifferently, and squeezed his way back through the racks. A few feet, and the display suddenly ended; and a Mexican man sat on a stool against the wall, reading a copy of *La Prensa*.

He wore an open-neck sports shirt, sharply creased tan trousers and very pointed, very shiny black shoes. He was no more than five feet tall when he stood up, smiling, ducking his glossy black head in greeting.

"Mr. Kent, please? Very happy to meet you!"

He opened a door, waved Toddy ahead of him, and closed and locked it again. A courteous hand on Toddy's elbow, he guided him down a short areaway and into a small smelly room.

There was an oilstove cluttered with pots and pans, a paint-peeled lopsided icebox, a rumpled gray-looking bed. Toddy sat down at an oilcloth-covered table, smeared and specked with the remains of past repasts. His nostrils twitched automatically.

"The ventilation is bad, eh?" The Mexican showed gleaming white teeth. "But how would you? The windows must be sealed. The disorder is essential. Think of the comment if one in this country should live in comfort and decency!"

"Yeah," said Toddy uncomfortably, "I see what you mean."

The Mexican moved back toward the icebox. "It is nice to meet one so understanding," he murmured. "You will have bo'l of beer, yess? Nice cold bo'l of beer?"

Toddy shook his head; he hoped he wouldn't have to be holed up long in this joint. "I guess not. A little early in the day for—"

"No," said the Mexican. "You will have no beer."

There was not the slightest change in his humbly ironic voice. There was no warning sound or shadow. But in that last split second when escape was too late, Toddy knew what was coming. He could feel the gizmo's swift change from gold to brass.

The blow lifted him from his chair. He collapsed on the table, and the table collapsed under him. There was a muted crash as they struck the floor.

But he did not hear it.

XVII

Tubby Little Milt Vonderheim was not Dutch but German. His right name was Max Von Der Veer. He was an illegal resident of the United States.

The only son of a good but impoverished Hessian family, he had been expelled from school for theft. Another theft landed him in prison for a year and caused his father to disown him. Milt learned the watchmaking trade in prison. He was by no means interested in it, but useful work of some kind was mandatory and it appeared the easiest of the jobs available. He was not sufficiently skilled at the time of his release to follow the trade.

He was not particularly skilled at anything, for that matter. And, after an unsuccessful attempt at burglary, which almost resulted in his rearrest, he became a waiter in a beerhall. He fitted in well there. He was lazy and clumsy, but this very clumsiness, coupled with what seemed to be a beaming, unquenchable good humor, made him an attraction. . . . That waiter, Max, *ach!* Snarling his fingers in the stein handles, stumbling over the feet he is too fat to see. A clown, *ja!* You should hear him when he tries to sing!

Since he could do nothing else, Milt put up with the gibing and jokes. He beamed and exaggerated his clumsiness, and made a fool of himself generally. Inwardly, however, he seethed. He had never been good-natured; he was sensitive about his appearance. He could have toasted every one of the beerhall customers over a slow fire and enjoyed doing it.

Then, one day, the leader of a troupe of vaudevillians noticed Milt, and was impressed by what he saw. This awkward youngster could be valuable; he was a natural for low-comedy situations. He didn't have to pretend (or so the leader thought). He was a born stooge and butt.

Milt joined the troupe. Eventually, early in 1913, he came to America with it.

That was the end of the good-natured business. That was the end of being the clumsy and lovable little brother of his fellow vaudevillians. Cold-eyed and unsmiling, Milt let it be known that he despised and hated them all. One more innocent joke, one more pat on his ridiculously potted belly—and there would be trouble. The funny business was strictly for the stage from now on.

Milt got away with it for four months, during which he extorted three raises in pay. By the time he deliberately forced his dismissal, he had acquired a sizable sum of money and no small knowledge of the country, its language and customs.

He got himself fired in San Francisco. Five days and five hundred dollars later, he had a new name and a number of sworn documents proving his American citizenship. His parents, these documents revealed, had been the proprietors of a San Francisco restaurant. He had been privately tutored by a Dutch schoolmaster. Parents, restaurant, school-master—and the original records of his birth—had been destroyed in the great fire and earthquake. Milt's English was not good—but what of that? Many legal residents of the country talked a poorer brand. For that matter, many legal residents of the country had no legal way of proving their right to be here except by the very method Milt used.

Americans, it seemed, were not as exacting as Germans, and Milt easily found employment as a watchmaker. He pursued it just long enough to discover that his employer's streak of larceny, while latent, was virtually as broad as his own. At Milt's suggestion—for which he took half the profits—the store owner filed hundreds of suits against merchant seamen for articles allegedly bought from him. Since the defendants had shipped out and were unaware of the notices of suit brought in obscure legal papers, judgment was automatic.

Later he opened his own small side-street watch-repair shop. Until a certain day in 1942, he thought he was doomed to remain there, barely making a living, a foolishly cheerful-looking fat man who could not acquire the wherewithal and was rapidly losing the nerve for the gigantic swindles he dreamed of.

One of these last was inspired by his own history. Perhaps there were many persons who had entered and remained in the United States under the same circumstances as his. If one had the means to ferret them out—! Ironically, he was pondering this very scheme on that day in 1942 when, looking up from his workbench, he discovered that others had thought of it also. Thought of it and acted upon it.

Being Milt, he was not, naturally, at all discomfited by the discovery. His words and his expression were actually contemptuous.

"Do not tell me, please!" He narrowed his eyes in mock thoughtful-ness. "Ah, yes, I remember now. Madrid, 1911, was it not? Alvarado and his Animales. There was considerable debate, I remember, as to which was which."

"And, you, I recall you well, also," said the chinless man. "A human swine—there would have been a novelty! Unfortunately, my *pobres perros* rebelled at the thought. But—enough! Listen to me carefully, Herr Von Der Veer, and do not interrupt!"

He spoke rapidly for ten minutes, ending with a sharpsoft, "Well?" that was a statement rather than a question. Milt took a drink from a brandy bottle before replying.

"Let me see if I understand," he said. "You have aligned your cause, unofficially, with that of the Reich where my father is now resident. And unless I accommodate you in this matter, certain unpleasant things will happen to him. He might possibly find himself in prison, that is right?"

"Regrettably, yes."

"Fine," said Milt. "Beat him well while he is there. Starve him also, if you can. He has such a great fat stomach I doubt that it is possible."

Milt smiled pleasantly. The chinless man blanched. "Monster!" he stammered, then recovered himself. "But there is something else, Herr Max. You are in this country illegally. A word to—"

"Any number of people," said Milt, truthfully, "will swear that I was born here. But why do we dispute, Señor Alvarado? That so-foolish man who leads your equally preposterous government—"

"Silence!"

"—may be moved by motives of idealism. You may be also. I am not so stupid. I want money. If you want this thing done, you will pay for it. It is as simple as that, and no simpler."

Thus, Milt, who like everyone else in the jewelry trade had begun dabbling in gold when the price went to thirty-five dollars an ounce— thus, funny-looking little Milt became a large-scale buyer for the Nazi government.

His first move was to build up a group of house to house buyers who worked out of his shop. Their purchases, less perhaps an undetectable third, went directly and regularly to the mint, where he built up and still had a reputation as a man above suspicion. His next move was to rent numerous post-office boxes under different names; small boxes, such as individuals rent. Under those names, he inserted small newspaper ads in as many different sections of the country.

There are thousands of such advertisers; little men, often with little knowledge of a highly exacting business. Because they are little, they feel obliged to place money ahead of good will. They grade and weigh "close"—the doubts which always arise are decided in their own favor. Because they lack the necessary training and wit—and despite their petty and pitiful efforts to do the opposite—they make disastrous buys. It is then obligatory, or so they feel, to be still "sharper" to make up for their losses.

The end result of all this is that the little men acquire a bad or at best "uneven" reputation. They buy less and less gold. Usually, in a few months or a few years, they are out of business.

It would be a physical impossibility to check on all these small mail buyers, and the federal authorities see no need to do so. Before gold can be diverted into the black market, it must first be acquired. And the little men just don't buy it, not a fraction of the quantity needed to pay them for the risk. . . . That is, of course, none of them bought it but Milt's little men. Gold poured in on the little men. They bought pounds of it every day.

Milt had expected to get out of the gold traffic when the Nazis had become unable to buy. But the chinless man gave no sign of ceasing operations, and Milt was far too wise to express a desire to quit. Angrily he realized that, in effect, he was jeopardizing his liberty and perhaps his life for nothing. He could never spend his wealth in the United States. He would never be allowed to leave the United States to spend it. He was getting old. Unless he withdrew from the ring soon, it would be too late. The things money bought would have become meaningless.

Mixed with his anger was a kind of apathy, a dread dead feeling that whatever he did mattered little. Even if he could get away. . .well, what then? How would a man of his age occupy himself in a strange new country? Alone, completely alone, with no one to care whether he lived or died.

He had been unable to deposit his money in a bank and afraid to place it in a safe deposit box; such might attract attention, and what if he should have to leave town in a hurry? So, unobtrusively, he had had a small but excellent safe sunk into the floor beneath his workbench. It could be cracked, of course, as the best of safes can be. But what knob-knocker or juice worker or torch artist would suspect that Milt had anything worth getting?

None did. The idea was laughable. Milt used to laugh, smile a little sadly to himself, as late at night sometimes he examined the stacks upon stacks of large-denomination bills. So much money . . . for what?

So he had gone on, reasonlessly, because there was nothing else to do, and fate in time had brought Toddy and Elaine Kent to him. *Elaine!* There was someone like himself, a woman who thought as he did. With someone like her, with her and the money, life would at last be what it should. And why not have her? It was only a question of ridding her of her fool husband, and if she kept on drinking, making trouble—and if that was not enough, if Toddy would not leave her or permit her to leave . . .

Night after night Milt had brooded over the matter; cursing, thinking in circles, guzzling quart after quart of beer. And, finally, Toddy had stumbled upon the house of the talking dog; and from then on thinking almost ceased to be necessary. Every piece of the puzzle had fallen into place at the touch of Milt's stubby fingers.

True, there had been one slight hitch, a hair-raising moment when all seemed lost. But that was past, now. Nothing remained but the pay-off. There was no longer danger—or very little. Things had not worked out quite as he had planned, but still they had worked out.

The phone rang. Milt answered it, casually, then grinned with malicious pleasure:

"Yes, I did that, *Señor*. Something you should have done yourself. . . . Why? Because he was dangerous, a menace to us. At least that was my honest opinion. I have not acted out of venom—as our superiors will most certainly feel that you have. . . . Eh? Oh, you are mistaken, *mein Herr*. You have but to consult your morning paper—*The News*. The others did not see fit to carry the item. And if that is not enough for you . . .

"If you demand stronger proof"—Milt's voice dropped to a wicked caress—"pay me a visit."

XVIII

A CHILLING, icy, weight enveloped Toddy's head. He tried to move away from it, but couldn't. It kept moving with him. From far away, in a dim fog-muted world, came the sound of voices. . . . A man and a woman, talking, or a woman and two men. . . . The voices came closer, some of them, then lapsed into silence. Something squeezed his left wrist, released it, and regrasped his right arm. The arm moved upward, and a probe dug painfully at the flesh. Then, fire flooded his veins and his heart gave a great bound, and Toddy bounded with it.

Eyes closed, he bounded, staggered, to his feet, and the icy weight clattered from his head. Then, he was pressed back, prone, on the bed; and he opened his eyes.

A dark, neatly dressed man was staring down at him thoughtfully, slapping a hypodermic needle against the palm of his hand. Also gazing down at him, her dark eyes anxious, was the girl Dolores.

"It's all right, Toddy." She gave him a tremulous smile.

Toddy stared at her, unwinking, remembrance returning; then, swung his eyes toward the man with the needle.

"You a doctor?"

"Yes, *Señor.*"

"What's going on here? What happened?"

"I have given you an injection of nicotinic acid. To strengthen the heart. Lie still for another half hour, and keep in place the ice pack. You will be all right."

"I asked you what happened?"

The doctor smiled faintly, shrugged, and spoke rapidly in Spanish to Dolores. Toddy's eyes drooped shut for a moment, and when he reopened them he was alone with Dolores.

"Well?" he said. "Well . . . ?"

"You should not talk, Toddy." She sat down on a chair at the bedside, and laid a hand on his forehead. "There is little I can explain, and—"

Toddy rolled his head from beneath her hand. "That guy tried to kill me?"

"To knock you unconscious. You were to be disposed of later . . . at night."

"Why?"

"I cannot tell you. There is much I do not understand."

"You know, all right. Why did Alvarado want me killed?"

"Alvarado did not want you killed."

"No? Then why—"

"If he had," said the girl, "you would be dead."

Toddy frowned, then grunted as a stab of pain shot through his head. "Yeah," he said. "But—"

"Try not to think for a few minutes. Rest, and I will make you some coffee, and then, if you feel able, we can leave."

"Leave?"

"Rest," said Dolores firmly.

Toddy rested, more willingly than he pretended to. It was almost reluctantly that, some fifteen or twenty minutes later, he sat up to accept the coffee Dolores prepared. She gave him a lighted cigarette, and he puffed and drank alternately. His head still throbbed with pain, but he felt alert again.

"So," he said, setting down the cup, "Alvarado doesn't want me dead?"

"Obviously not."

"He knew this was going to happen?"

"I think—I think he must have."

"What did he stand to gain by it?"

"I cannot say. I mean, I don't know."

"No?"

"No!" snapped the girl; but her voice immediately became soft again. "Believe me, Toddy, I don't know. But you will soon find out. Alvarado himself will tell you."

"Alvarado will!" Toddy started. "What do you mean?"

"That is why I am here, to take you to him. He is in San Diego."

Toddy fumbled for and found his cigarettes. He lighted one, staring at Dolores over the flame of the match. He didn't know whether to laugh or bop her. How stupid, he wondered, did they think he was?

"What's Alvarado doing in San Diego?"

"Again, I do not know."

"But after this pasting I got, I'm still supposed to see him?"

"So I told you."

"What if I refuse to go with you? What happens, then?"

"What happens?" The girl shrugged, tiredly. "Nothing happens. You are free to go your own way. You may leave here now, if you feel able."

Toddy shook his head, incredulously. "You say that like you mean it."

"I do. You will not be harmed. ... Of course," she added, "your situation will not be exactly pleasant. You have little money. You are a fugitive. You are in a foreign country. ..."

"But I'm alive."

"There is no use," said Dolores, "in arguing. I was not ordered to persuade you, only to ask you."

She stood up, walked to the battered dresser, and picked up a flowered scarf. Draping it over her black hair, she knotted it under her chin and took a step toward the areaway.

"Good-bye, Toddy Kent."

"Now, wait a minute. . . ."

"Yes?"

"I didn't say I wouldn't go," said Toddy. "I just—Oh, hell!" He wobbled a little as he lurched to his feet, and she moved swiftly to him. He caught her by the shoulders, his hands sinking into the soft flesh with unconscious firmness.

"Look—" He hesitated. "Give me the lowdown. What had I better do?"

"I am here to take you to Alvarado."

"But should I—?"

"Suppose I said no; that you should remain in Mexico."

"Are you telling me that?"

"Suppose I did so advise you," Dolores continued, looking at him steadily, "and you decided to do the opposite—and repeated my advice to Alvarado?"

"Why would I do that?"

"You have no reason to trust me. In fact, you have made it very plain that you do not trust me. Why shouldn't you tell Alvarado? Particularly, if it appeared that by doing so you would help yourself?"

Toddy reddened uncomfortably and released his grip. The girl stepped away from him.

"I guess," he said, "I can't blame you for thinking that."

"No."

"But you're wrong. If I'd wanted to get you in trouble, I could have told Alvarado about—well—"

"—my warning to you last night? Perhaps you did, after you left the house."

Toddy gave up. She was dead right about one thing. He didn't trust her, even though something had impelled him to for a minute. Perhaps she didn't know what Alvarado wanted. Or perhaps she did. He'd never take her word for it, regardless of the situation. Whatever she advised him to do, he'd be inclined to do the opposite.

"Where's my coat?" he said shortly. "Let's get out of here."

"You are going with me?"

"I don't know. Maybe a drink will help me to make up my mind."

. . . They went out the same way Toddy had come in, squeezing past the crowded racks of trinkets and curios. The little man who had slugged Toddy was nowhere in view. The fat woman was still seated near the doorway on her campstool.

"Nice bo'l of perfume for lady?" she beamed. "Nice wallet for gen'le-man?"

Toddy started to scowl, but something about her expression of bland good-natured innocence made his lips tug upward. He gave her a cynical wink, and followed Dolores out the door.

It seemed like days had passed since he had arrived in Tijuana that morning, but the clock in the bar indicated the hour as five minutes of two. Seated in a rear booth, Toddy drank a double tequila sunrise and ordered another. He took a sip of it and looked across the table at the girl.

"Well," he said, "I've made up my mind."

"I see."

"I'm not going with you. I'll lay low here for a few days. Then I'll beat it back across the border and—" Toddy broke off abruptly, and again raised his glass. Over its rim, he saw the faint gleam of amusement in Dolores' eyes.

"On second thought," she said, "you will head south into Mexico. That is right?"

"Maybe," said Toddy. "Maybe not."

"I understand. It is best to keep your plans to yourself. Now, I must be going."

She slid toward the edge of the booth, hesitated as though on the point of saying something, then stood up. Toddy got up awkwardly, also. On an impulse, as her lips framed a mechanical good-bye, he held out his hand.

"I'm sorry about last night," he said. "I don't know where you fit into this deal, but I think you're playing it as square as you can."

"Thank you." She did not touch his hand. "And I think you also are as—as square—as you can be. Now I would like to tell you something. Something for your own good."

"I'm waiting."

"Wash your face. It is dirty."

She was gone, then, her body very erect, her high heels clicking uncompromisingly across the wooden floor. Toddy stared after her until he saw the bartender watching him. Then he shook his head vaguely, ran a hand over his jaw, and headed for the men's restroom.

It was at the rear end of the room, a partitioned-off enclosure inade-quately ventilated by a small high window opening on the alley: a typical Tijuana bar "gents' room." There was a long yellowish urinal, and two cabinet toilets, flushed by old-fashioned water chambers placed near the ceiling. Adjacent to the two chipped-enamel sinks was a wooden table, supporting a sparse assortment of toilet articles and an elaborate display of pornographic booklets, postal cards, prophylactics and "rubber goods."

"Yessir, mister"—the young Mexican attendant came briskly to attention—"you in right place, mister. We got just what you—"

"What I want," said Toddy, "is some soap." And he helped himself from the table.

He turned on both water taps, scrubbed his hands, then lathered them again and scoured vigorously at his face. He rinsed off the soap and doused his head. Eyes squinted, he turned away from the sink and accepted the towel that was thrust into his hands.

"Thanks, pal." He dried his face and opened his eyes.

"Don't mention it," burbled Shake.

"And keep your hands out o' your pockets," gritted Donald.

XIX

TODDY DID NOT NEED THE LAST BIT OF ADVICE. One swift glance at the hideously scratched mugs of the pair told him they would kill him on the slightest pretext. Kill him and worry about the outcome later. Fury had made them brave.

Shake was holding a blackjack—upswung, ready to strike. Donald had the Mexican attendant backed against the wall, the point of his knife pressing against his throat. The door of the restroom was barred.

"Just don't try nothin'," murmured Shake. "Jus' don't try nothin' at all. You get past us, which you ain't goin' to do, I got two of my *pachucos* outside."

"Someone'll be coming back here." Toddy's voice sounded strange in his ears. "You can't keep that door barred."

"I c'n keep it barred long enough. Turn around."

"You tailed me down here?"

"What does it look like? Turn around!"

The blackjack came down sickeningly on Toddy's shoulder. He turned.

Shake slapped his pockets expertly, located his wallet, and extricated it with a satisfied grunt. There was a moment's silence, another grunt, and another command to, "Turn around."

Toddy turned.

"What you doin' here?" Shake demanded. "What's the deal?"

"Deal?"

Donald ripped out a curse. "Let him have it, Shake. We can't wait here all day."

"No one's tryin' to bust in," Shake pointed out, his eyes fixed on Toddy. "I asked you what the deal was?"

Toddy licked his lips, wordlessly. Helplessly. The blackjack began to descend.

"Wait!" It was the Mexican attendant. "I will tell you, *Señors!*" His teeth gleamed at Toddy in a warm, placating smile, a grin of apology. "I am sorry, *Señor*, but it is best to tell them. These gentlemen mean business."

Donald nodded venomously. "You ain't just woofin', *hombre*. Spill it!"

"But you must know, gentlemen. What else would it be but—but—"

"But what?"

"White stuff," said Toddy, taking the Mexican off the limb. "As my friend says, what else could it be?"

Donald sneered. Shake gave Toddy a look of mock sanctimoniousness. "I might of knowed it," he said. "A man that'll murder his own sweet little wife an' play mean tricks on people that trust him won't stop at nothin'. Dope, tsk, tsk. You smugglin' it across the border?"

"Not at all," said Toddy. "I use it to powder my nose."

He fell back from the blow of the blackjack, and Shake advanced on him. "Okay," he wheezed. "Be smart. Be good an' smart. It's gonna cost you enough. Where you got the stuff hid?"

"I"—Toddy's eyes flicked around the room, settled momentarily on one of the elevated water chambers, and moved back to Shake—"I've got it cached out in the country a few miles."

"The hell you have—" Donald began. But Shake interrupted him.

"You give yourself away, Toddy. You're losin' your grip. Get up there an' get it."

"Up where?"

"You better move!"

"Okay," sighed Toddy. "You win."

With Shake at his heels, he stepped into the first of the toilet enclosures and gripped the top of its two partitions. He gave a jump, swung himself upward, and got a knee over one of the partitions. Grasping the pipe which ran from the flush chamber to the toilet, he pulled himself up until he stood straddling the enclosure.

Donald issued a curt command, and the Mexican hastened to lie down in the adjacent booth. Then the little shiv artist crowded in next to Shake, holding his knife by the blade.

"Don't try nothin'," he warned. "I can't reach you but the knife can."

"Yeah," said Toddy. "I know."

He gripped the ends of the heavy porcelain lid of the water chamber. Grunting, he moved it free and edged backward.

"Have to help me with this," he panted. "It's—"

"Now, wait a—" wheezed Shake. And Donald's knife flashed with the swift action of his hand. But he was too late. They couldn't stop what Toddy had started. They couldn't get out of the way.

"—heavy!" said Toddy. And he hurled the heavy lid downward with all his might.

It caught Shake full in his fat upturned face, one end swinging sickeningly against the bridge of Donald's nose. They sprawled backwards out of the enclosure, and Toddy scrambled down hastily from his perch.

He need not have hurried. The Mexican attendant, apparently, had exactly anticipated his actions. Now he was on his feet, administering one of the most thorough, expert yet dispassionate kickings that Toddy had ever seen. It was a demonstration that would have been envied even by Shake's *pachucos*.

Not a kick was wasted. Each of the two men received two kicks in the guts, by way of obtaining temporary silence. Each received a kick in the temple, by way of making the silence more or less permanent. Each received three kicks in the face as a lasting memento of the kicking.

"*Bien!*" said the Mexican, smiling pleasantly at Toddy. "I think that is enough, eh?" Then he bent over the motionless thugs, stuffed their wallets and Toddy's inside his shirt, and picked up the knife and black-jack.

"I have been put to much trouble," he beamed. "You do not mind the small present?"

"That money," said Toddy, "is all I have."

"So? You want it very much, *Señor?*"

"I guess not," said Toddy. "Not that much. . . . How do I get out of here?"

"The table, *Señor*. Drag it over to the window. . . . You will excuse me if I do not help? It is an easy drop to the alley."

Toddy nodded, dragged the table to the window, and stepped up on it—deliberately destroying as much of the display as he could.

"It is all right, *Señor,*" the Mexican laughed softly. "Everything is paid for."

"Yeah." Toddy grinned unwillingly. "What happens to these characters? And their *pachucos?*"

"People come back here," the Mexican explained, "but no one go out. So, soon, very soon, my father will be alarmed."

"Your father?"

"The bartender, *Señor*. He will summon my brother, the waiter, who will call my two cousins, officers of the police. . . ."

"Never mind." Toddy hoisted himself into the window. "I know the rest. Your uncle, the judge, will give them ninety days in jail. Right?"

"But no, *Señor*"—the Mexican's voice trailed after Toddy as he dropped into the alley—"he will give them at least six months."

Toddy plodded down the alley to the street, lighted the last of his cigarettes, and threw the package away. He thrust a hand into his pocket, drew it out with his sole remaining funds. Sixteen cents. Three nickels and a penny. Not enough to—

A hand closed gently but firmly over his elbow. A blue-uniformed cop looked down at the coins, and up into his face.

"You are broke, *Señor?* A vagrant?"

"Certainly not." Toddy made his voice icy. "I'm a San Diego business-man. Just down here for a little holiday."

"I think not, *Señor*. Businessmen do not take leak in alley."

"But I didn't—" Toddy caught himself.

"For vagrancy *or* leak," said the cop, "the fine is ten dollars. You may pay me."

"I—just give me your name and address," said Toddy. "I'll have to send it to you."

"Let's go," said the cop brusquely, in the manner of cops the world over.

Toddy started to protest. The officer immediately released his grip, unholstered a six-shooter, and leveled it at Toddy's stomach.

"We do not like vagrants here, *Señor*, even as you do not like them in your country. A ver' long time ago I visit your country. I am a wetback, yes, but no one care. The lettuce must be harvest' and I work very cheap. Then I complain I do not get my wages an' I am sick from the food— *cagada*, dung—and everyone care ver' much. I am illegal immigrant. I am vagrant. I go to jail for long time. . . . It is good word, vagrant. I learn it in your country. Now move. *Anda!*"

The gun pointing at his back, Toddy preceded the cop down the side street, across the main thoroughfare, and so on down another side street. Tourists and sightseers stared after him—curiously, haughtily, grinning. Mexican shopkeepers gazed languidly from their doorways, their dark eyes venomous or amused at the plight of the *gringo*.   .

Toddy walked on and on, his jaw set, his eyes fixed on the walk immediately in front of him. He knew something of Mexican jails by reliable hearsay. When you got in down here, brother, you were in. The length of sentence didn't mean a thing. They took weeks and months, sometimes a year, to get around to sentencing you. They just locked you up and left you. And—*and Shake and Donald!* . . . Toddy's step faltered and the cop's gun prodded him. . . . There wasn't a chance that he could persuade the two thugs to play quiet. They'd squeal their heads off about Elaine's death and the supposed dope racket, and—

Somewhere a horn was honking insistently. Then a car door slammed, and Dolores called, "*Un momento!*"

The cop grunted a command to halt, and swept off his cap. "*Si, Señorita?*" he said. "*A servicio de—*"

He didn't get a chance to finish the sentence, or any of the several others he started. After three minutes of Dolores' rapid Spanish, he was reduced to complete silence, answering her torrent of reprimand only with feeble shrugs and apologetic gestures.

At last she snapped open her purse and uttered a contemptuous, "*Cuánto?*—how much?" The cop hesitated, then drew himself erect. "*Por nada*," he said, and walked swiftly away.

Toddy said, "Whew!" and, then, "Thanks."

The girl nodded indifferently. "I must go now. You are going with me?"

Toddy said he was. "Shake and his boys were trailing me. I—"

"I know; I saw them enter the bar. That is why I waited."

"It didn't occur to you," said Toddy, "to do anything besides wait?"

"To call the police, for example? Or to intervene personally?"

"You're right," said Toddy. "Let's go."

As they neared the international border, Dolores took a pair of sun-glasses and a checkered motoring cap from the glove compartment and handed them to him. Toddy put them on, glanced swiftly at himself in the rear-view mirror. The disguise was a good one for a quick change. Even if his mug was out on a pickup circular, he should be able to get past the border guards.

He did get past them, after a harrowing five minutes in which the car was given a perfunctory but thorough examination. He had to get out and unlock the trunk compartment. On the spur of the moment—since he had neglected to do so sooner—he had to invent a spurious name, birthplace and occupation.

He was sweating when the car swung out of the inspection station and onto the road to San Diego. As they sped past San Ysidro, he removed the cap and glasses, mopped at his face and forehead.

"I am sorry," said Dolores, so softly that he almost failed to hear her. She was looking straight ahead, her eyes intent on the road.

"Sorry?" said Toddy vaguely.

"You are right to be angry with me, to be suspicious. What else could you be? Except for me you would not have been involved in this affair."

Well, Toddy thought, she'd called the turn there. But what he said, mildly, was, "Forget it. I was asking for it. A guy like me wouldn't feel right if he wasn't in trouble."

"Wouldn't he?"

Toddy looked at her, looked quickly away again. She couldn't mean what she seemed to, not with Elaine murdered and himself the principal suspect. That, and everything else that was hanging over him. Of course, she wouldn't be any angel herself but ... But he couldn't think the thing through. It was a hell of a poor time to try to.

"I don't know," he said shortly. "Probably not."

"I see." Her voice was flat.

"I"—Toddy hesitated—"maybe. It would depend on a lot of things."

XX

The house was in the Mission Hills section of San Diego, located on a pie-shaped wedge of land overlooking the bay. On one side a street dropped down to Old Town. On the other side another road wound downward toward Pacific Highway. In the front, a multiple intersection separated the house from its nearest neighbor by a block. There were no houses in the rear, of course; only a steep bluff.

Toddy sat in the front room—a room as sparsely furnished as the one in Chinless' Los Angeles dwelling. He had been sitting there alone for some fifteen minutes. As soon as he and the girl had arrived, Alvarado had spoken rapidly to her in Spanish—too rapidly for Toddy's casual understanding of the language—and she had gone down the hallway toward the rear of the house. Alvarado had followed her, after politely excusing himself, and closed the door; and dimly, a moment later, Toddy had heard another door close. Since then there had been silence—almost.

It seemed to Toddy, once, that he heard a faint outcry. A moment later he had thought he heard the dog bark. *Thought.* He wasn't sure. He strained his ears, held his breath, listening, but the sounds were not repeated.

Toddy waited with increasing uneasiness. In the far corner of the room was a desk littered with papers. When he and Dolores had arrived, Alvarado had been working there, and something about the sight had given Toddy an inexplicable feeling of danger. He wanted to get a better look at those papers. He wondered whether he dared risk the few steps across the room and a quick glance or two.

He decided to try it.

Rising cautiously, an eye on the hall door, he tiptoed across the floor and looked swiftly down at the desk. The papers were covered with rows of neatly written figures, interspersed occasionally with what appeared to be abbreviations of certain words. They were meaningless.

"Meaningless, Mr. Kent," said Alvarado, "unless you have the code book."

He came in smiling, closing the door behind him, and crossed to the desk. He picked up a small black book that had been lying face down and riffled its pages of fine, closely printed type.

"This is it. Regrettably, it is much too complex to explain in the brief time we have."

"Better skip it, then," said Toddy, matching the other's irony. And as he resumed his seat on the other side of the room, Alvarado chuckled amiably.

"A man after my own heart," he declared, sitting back down at the desk. "I cannot tell you how disappointed I am that we shall not work together.... For the time being, at least."

"No?" Toddy crossed his legs. The air was heavy with perfume. Alvarado apparently had doused himself with it.

"No. Unfortunately. But we will come to that in a moment. I have had you visit me so that I might explain—explain everything that may be explained. You are entitled to know; and, as I say, I hope we may work together eventually. I did not wish you to be left with an unfavorable opinion of me."

"Go on," said Toddy.

"After I dispatched you to Tijuana, I communicated the fact to our supplier of gold ... the man I suspected of killing your wife. He, reacting as I believed he would, ordered you murdered. To be slugged and disposed of permanently as soon as it was expedient. As soon as the first half of the order was carried out, I intervened. I had the proof I wanted."

"Proof?" Toddy frowned. "I don't get it."

"But it is so simple! He killed your wife—I was certain—merely as a means of disposing of you. He hoped to involve you, and through you me, in a crime which would break up our syndicate and release him from duties which have long been onerous to him. Now you understand?"

"No," said Toddy. "I don't."

"But it is—"

"Huh-uh." Toddy shook his head. "Up to a point, I'll buy it. He killed Elaine. I thought you'd done it. If I played the cards he gave me, I'd have either gone after you myself or hollered to the cops.... But I didn't do that. You and I squared our beef. He didn't have a thing to gain by getting rid of me in Tijuana."

"Hmmm." Alvarado drummed absently on the desk. "I see your point. It was stupid of me not to think of it.... Of course," he added, smoothly, "I was not completely sure of this man's motive. There was a strong possibility that he might have been motivated by revenge."

"Remember me?" said Toddy. "I'm supposed to be the bright boy. So stop kidding me.... This guy tried to get me killed; I'll go along with that. And when he did he proved that he'd killed my wife. Why? I'll tell you. Because he was sure that, given a little time, I'd able to dope out who he was. You were sure I would, too, and, until you got your orders from abroad, you had to protect his identity. You had to pin the rap on him good before I did too much thinking."

"Really, Mr. Kent . . . "

"That's the way it was. That's the way it has to be. Now why beat around the bush about it?"

Alvarado stared at him thoughtfully, a quizzical frown on his pale shark's face. Then, gradually, the frown disappeared and he nodded.

"Very well, Mr. Kent. I suppose there really is no longer need for secrecy. The man you mention has served us well . . . in the opinion of my superiors. He is now closing out his affairs and will soon be out of this country. Possibly—probably—we will find use for him elsewhere. But that is no concern of yours. Long before you can discover his identity and confirm it, he will be beyond your reach."

Amazement choked Toddy for a moment. He could hardly credit himself with hearing the words that Alvarado had spoken. Before he could find his voice, the chinless man was speaking again.

"I can well understand your confusion, Mr. Kent. I share it. But there is nothing I can do about it. Our entire hypothesis was wrong. This man we suspected did not kill your wife."

"You're lying!" Toddy snapped. "Murder or no murder, this guy is valuable to your bosses. They're going to protect him at all costs. That's the whole story, isn't it?"

"It is not. My bosses, as you call them, do not act so whimsically. The man was able to prove, irrefutably, that he did not kill your wife. As an unfortunate result, our superiors retain their original high regard for him while I—for the moment, at least—have been made to appear a clumsy and vindictive fool."

"You're forgetting your lines." Toddy said grimly. "A minute ago you were saying that—"

"I was speaking in theoretical terms. Like you, I was speeding down a trail of theory and I am at a loss when the trail disappears."

"My getting slugged wasn't any theory!"

"Be grateful you were not killed, and dwell no more on the matter. Nothing good will come of it."

Hands shaking, Toddy lighted a cigarette. After an angry puff or two he ground it out beneath his foot. Alvarado nodded sympathetically.

"You are annoyed. I am withholding information which you feel is vital to you. Does it occur to you that I might easily be annoyed with you for much the same reason?"

"I'm not holding back anything."

"Knowingly, no. And I am not doing so willingly."

"I don't," said Toddy, "get you."

"You yourself had the best opportunity to kill your wife. You had ample motive, also. You are not the type to kill with premeditation, but I can readily imagine your doing so in a moment of temporary insanity. And since such a crime is inconsistent with your nature, your conscious mind would refuse to admit it.... All this is conjecture, of course. I know nothing. I want to know nothing."

Toddy laughed shortly. "Tell me why I was slugged. Maybe I'll sign a confession, then."

"You invite the obvious retort, Mr. Kent. Tell me how you disposed of your wife's body and I will tell you why you were slugged."

Toddy stared at him helplessly. "You don't believe that," he said. "You know I didn't kill her. Maybe this guy, the supplier, didn't do it either, but—"

"He didn't."

"Then, what's it all about? What are you trying to steer me away from?"

Alvarado shook his head. Turning back to his desk, he opened the code book. "So that is the way it is," he murmured. "You will excuse me if I work while we talk."

Toddy started to speak; his hand started to knife out in a gesture of angry exasperation. The gesture was unfinished. He remained silent—staring, trying not to stare.

That code book was in unusually fine print. And yet Chinless was studying it without difficulty and without his glasses. He couldn't be— shouldn't be—but he was. What the hell could it mean? Why had he claimed that his eyes were bad right from the moment of their first meeting? Why had he pretended that he couldn't read Milt's card? What reason was there—

"Now," said Alvarado, "let us leave theory to the theorists and take up practical matters. As I indicated, we are ceasing activities in this country indefinitely; but we hope to resume them. When that time comes we can find a profitable place for you. ...."

"Suppose I don't want it?"

"That is up to you. We have no fear of your talking."

"All right," said Toddy, "I'm listening."

"There is a Pullman train leaving here tonight; what you call a through train. I have reserved you a stateroom. It will not be necessary for you to leave that stateroom until you arrive in New York. You will be given a thousand dollars in addition to your passage. That should maintain you in some degree of comfort until I get in touch with you."

"How will you do that?"

"A detail. We will work it out before you leave. Does the idea, generally, please you?"

"It doesn't look like I have much choice," said Toddy. "I want to know why you're jumping the country, though. I'm hot enough without getting any hotter."

"You will not be. I, at this point, am the sole recipient of the heat. The informer in our midst has chosen to make no mention of you to the authorities."

"Informer? Who is he?"

"That need not concern you." Alvarado turned a page of the code book and ran a pencil down the column of symbols. "This informer is one of our unwilling operatives. We were able to obtain his"—Alvarado slurred the pronoun—"co-operation through a brother, a political prisoner in one of my country's excellent labor camps. It was necessary for the brother to die. Our confederate discovered the fact through a relative. He made the very serious mistake of confronting me and charging bad faith."

Toddy nodded, absently. He was staring at the code book, at Alvarado. Something warned him to look away, but he couldn't. "I see," he said. "You knew he'd turn stool pigeon."

"He already had," grimaced Alvarado, "though I was unware of it until yesterday. I had assumed that his tirade against me was immediately subsequent to the news of his brother's death. Then, through a slip of the tongue, he revealed that he had known of it for a month. He had known of it but said nothing, continued the regular course of his affairs, until his sense of outrage overcame his discretion. Obviously, he had done so for only one reason. . . . You followed me, Mr. Kent?"

Toddy didn't speak. Alvarado looked up from the desk.

"I am boring you, perhaps?"

"What?" Toddy started. The answer had come to him at last, at the very moment of Alvarado's question. A beautifully simple yet almost incredible answer. "I don't quite get it," he said, with forced casualness. "This guy has squealed. Why haven't the Feds moved in on you?"

"Because they hope to trap the man who supplies our gold. He is to meet me here—or so I advised our informer—tomorrow night. The efficient T-men will not come near the place, nor do anything else to arouse my suspicions, until then."

Toddy nodded absently, his mind still working on the riddle of Alvarado's "bad eyesight." . . . Let's see, he thought. Let's take it from the beginning. I gave him that frammis about a friend sending me to him, and then I gave him the card. He let me into the house. Then . . . well, I didn't have much to say for a minute or two, and he began to freeze up a little. Asked me my business. Said he couldn't read the card. He must have, but—

Toddy started slightly. *Why, of course! Chinless had thought he'd been sent there to the house. When he discovered the truth, that their meeting was sheer accident, he had pretended that . . .*

The chinless man looked down at the code book. He looked up quickly, and his gaze met and held Toddy's. A frown of regret spread over his dead white face.

"Well?" said Toddy.

"It is not well," said Alvarado, and his hand dipped into his pocket and came out with the automatic. "You have an expressive face. Like our informer, Dolores, it tells too much."

XXI

Toddy forced an irritated laugh. "What the hell's the matter with you anyway? What have I done now?"

"It is not so much what you have done. It is what you surely would do . . . now that you know. I am sorry. I, personally, am sorry you cannot do it. But I have my orders. The man must be protected."

"I still don't know—"

"Please!" Alvarado gestured fretfully. "You know and I know you know. In a little while, a few weeks, it would not have mattered. The man would have vanished. You, I believe, would have grown more philosophical about the matter. Now—"

"About murder?" Toddy dropped his mask of bewilderment. "Why would I stand still for a murder that this guy committed?"

"He did not commit one. At least, he did not kill your wife."

"But—All right," said Toddy. "He didn't. I did. Is that good enough?"

"Not nearly, Mr. Kent. You are certain that he did kill her. You would act accordingly. There would be much talk—many secrets would be aired. It would not do."

"You're forgetting something," said Toddy. "I'm in no position to make trouble for anyone."

"You mean," Alvarado corrected, "you are in no position to make trouble for yourself. And I am sure you would not. You and I both know that the position of this man is a precarious one. He is, as we noted in an earlier conversation, a sitting duck. You would pick him off, Mr. Kent, even though you did not believe he was the murderer of your wife."

Toddy's eyes fell, and his shoulders drooped. He leaned forward a little, disconsolately, his wrists resting on his knees.

"Do not try it, Mr. Kent."

"You won't shoot," said Toddy. "Someone might hear it."

"Someone might," Alvarado nodded, "but I will shoot if necessary."

"I want to ask a question."

"Quickly, then. And lean back!"

"I know this man didn't kill Elaine. He was with me at the time. But he had her killed, didn't he?"

"He did not. It was the last thing he would have wanted."

"Put it this way. He knew the watch was in our room. He sent someone to get it. Elaine put up a fight, and the guy killed her."

Alvarado shook his head. "This man, with more money than he can spend, would go to such lengths for a watch? . . . And that is two questions you have asked."

"All right, then," Toddy persisted, "she'd found out something about him. She tried to work some blackmail and—"

"She did not," interrupted Alvarado. "Let me repeat, he did not want your wife dead. And now, stand up!"

"All right." Toddy got carefully to his feet. "What about giving the departing guest a drink?"

"Of course." Alvarado did not hesitate for so much as an instant. "The cellarette is there . . . and the carafe is heavy. It would be futile to attempt to throw it."

"I don't intend to," said Toddy, honestly.

"And instead of the large drink, which you doubtless desire, take two very small ones. Not enough, to be explicit, to have any effect if thrown."

Toddy sidled along the lounge to the corner cellarette. His eyes watchful, apprehensive, he turned his back on the chinless man and picked up the carafe.

Toddy tipped the carafe and slopped a fraction of an ounce of brandy into a highball glass. He raised it, holding his breath; but Chinless apparently was also holding his. Either that or he hadn't moved: he was still standing by the desk.

Toddy lowered the glass, his thumb pressing with restrained firmness toward the lip. It gave against the pressure; a little more and it would break. But would it break as it had to—and when it had to? There wouldn't be time to turn. The blow would have to be on its way down. If it wasn't, Alvarado would shoot. He'd have to, and he would.

Toddy set the glass down again, rattling the carafe against it as he poured his second drink. He heard it, then: an almost imperceptible squeak of the floor, all but masked by the sound of the glassware.

He lifted the glass, pressing steadily, harder. Suddenly there was no resistance to his thumb, and he heard the swift uprush of air; and he thrust the broken glass up and back, dropping into a crouch in the same split second.

The glass exploded in his hand. His whole arm went numb. There was a wild curse of pain and the clatter of metal against wood. He whirled, awkward in his crouch, and threw himself at the gun. Alvarado kicked him solidly in the solar plexus. He sprawled, paralyzed, and Alvarado kicked him again. He lay fighting for breath, every nerve screaming with shock.

Alvarado picked up the gun. Cursing frightfully as it slipped in his grasp, he shifted it to his left hand. He advanced on Toddy, his right hand scarlet, dripping with blood.

"It is bad, eh, Mr. Kent? But do not worry about it. I will bind it up in a minute. A very few minutes. . . . Actually I am grateful for what you did. What was a painful duty now becomes a pleasure."

He grasped Toddy's ankle with the lacerated hand, grimaced painfully, and dragged him toward the hall door. "Do not resist me, Mr. Kent. Make no overt move. If it should mean my instant death, I would not hesitate. . . ."

Toddy didn't try anything. He couldn't. It was still a desperate struggle to get his breath.

"Now . . . " Alvarado opened the door, tugged him through it, panting, and kicked it shut again. "Now—" Alvarado regrasped his ankle, backed and dragged him down the hallway. His eyes glinted insanely. He was incoherent with fury.

"Now, you will see, Mr. Kent. . . . You will be one of the dogs. *Pobre Perrito's* twin, yes. The one the obliging gentleman from the crematory did not see. . . . Dolores was to have served, but it will be all right. The added weight is excusable. It is the practice, the gentleman tells me, to enclose the pet's belongings . . . the bed . . . the eating and drinking receptacles. . . . So many things and such big dogs. . . . "

He opened a second door, tugged furiously, and slammed it shut. And Toddy knew at last the reason for the chinless man's perfume.

The air was heavy with the odor of chloroform. The room with its tightly closed windows swam with its sickening-sweet stench.

Alvarado released his ankle, and Toddy tried to sit up. He fell back, groaning, and his head banged against the wall. He lay there, not quite prone, staring dully at the two long pine boxes on the floor. Alvarado chuckled.

He had wiped his sweating face, and now it and his hand were both scarlet. He was smeared with blood; his face was a hideous, blood-smeared mask.

The mask crinkled in a mirthless grin, and he picked up a hammer from one of the boxes. He hefted it in his hand, gazing steadily at Toddy, inching a little toward him. And then he burst into another laugh.

"Do not worry, Mr. Kent. There is nothing to worry about yet. I would first have you observe something. . . ."

He inserted the claw of the hammer between one of the boxes and its lid. He pried downward, moved the hammer, reinserted the claw and pried again.

"You do not understand, eh?" he panted. "So much effort—so much more, thanks to you. Why not, simply, since I am leaving, leave the bodies here? It is this way"—he wiped, smeared, his face again—"there is always the chance of some flaw in planning; the possibility of apprehension. And murder is regarded much more seriously than smuggling. But even without that, without error or misfortune, there would be great unpleasantness. Your squeamish countrymen would be outraged, your newspapers vocal. In the end, my government might be faced with demands for my person. ... "

He laid down the hammer and tugged at the lid with his hand. Wincing, he looked carefully at Toddy. He nodded, satisfied with what he saw, and dropped the gun into his pocket. He grasped the lid with both hands, pulled and swung it open on its hinges.

"Now," he said, and started to stoop. "No," he shook his head. "She must lie on the bottom. Otherwise ... "

Picking up the hammer, he turned to the other box and began unsealing its lid. The gun remained in his pocket, but the fact meant nothing to Toddy. He was breathing more easily, but he still felt paralyzed.

"Evidence ... " Alvarado was murmuring. "But there will be none, not a particle; only ashes scattered to the winds. ... Strong suspicions, yes, but no evidence. Nothing to act upon. ... "

The lid swung free. Alvarado lifted out the girl, held her for a moment, then shrugged and tossed her to the bed. "Still alive, like the dog doubtless. It does not matter. I will prepare another sponge, and it has several hours to work."

He started to turn. Then, catching Toddy's eye, he nodded solemnly.

"You are right, of course. They weigh little, but the weight already is overmuch. They will have to come off."

He jerked off her shoes, and dropped them to the floor. Then the stockings. He grasped the dress at its throat, and ripped it off with one furious tug ... The brassiere, then. And then. ...

He glanced down critically at the nude, undulant figure, and grinned spitefully at Toddy. "Tempting," he said. "You are incapacitated, unfortunately, but there is no reason why I ... You could enjoy that, Mr. Kent? You would derive pleasure from mine?"

"Y-you,"—Toddy rasped—"bastard ... "

"I shall kick you some more," Alvarado promised. "As for Dolores, she shall lie with the dog, poor *Perrito*. He deserved it, eh, Mr. Kent? It is small recompense for the death which expedience forces me to inflict. ... If he were smaller, if he could not talk, I might have ... "

Going down on his knees, he looked regretfully at the dog. He got an arm under it, stroked the head absently with his bleeding hand.

"*Pobre Perrito*," he murmured. "I am sorry."

A shudder ran through the dog's body. His tongue lolled out, touched Alvarado's hand. It moved against the hand, licking.

"Cruel," murmured Alvarado. "You are nearly dead, and I let you revive. I let in the air. I kill you twice. ... "

He got up abruptly, brushing at his eyes, and turned to the bed. He lifted the girl and lowered her roughly into the box from which he had taken her.

"Now," he said, bending over the dog again, "it will soon be over."

This time he put both arms under the great black body, and grunting stood erect with it. The animal's eyes slitted open. The huge jaws gaped lazily. Alvarado bent his head—his scarlet face.

The dog's jaws snapped shut on it.

The blood scent ... Like a dream, a nightmare, a scene at the Los Angeles house came back to Toddy. ... *Shake and Donald, their faces spouting blood. And Alvarado holding the lunging dog* ...

Alvarado was bent over, staggering. His fists flailed against the dog and his muffled, smothered shrieks emerged as a horrible humming ... *"Hmmmm? Mmmmmm! MMMMMM!* ..."

Toddy yelled. He got to his hands and knees and lurched forward, tried to grasp the dog by a leg. How this had come about didn't matter now. He only knew that it had to be stopped.

There was a roar in the room and Toddy dropped to his stomach. Alvarado had got out his gun, but he couldn't aim it. He was pivoting in a slow, pain-crazed waltz; doubled over, the automatic sweeping the walls. And the dog waltzed with him, eyes closed, jaws clamped, its hind claws rattling and scratching against the floor.

Suddenly, Alvarado's right arm shot straight out from his body. The dog moved—they moved together—and the gun swerved. It steadied, pointing at the girl.

Toddy could never say how he did it; he could never recall doing it. But somehow he was on his feet, his hands gripping a bony scarlet wrist. He threw his weight forward, and there was a long staccato roar—that and the shattering of glass as the windowpane behind a drawn curtain was blown into bits.

Then, somewhere, in the not too distant distance, a motor raced and an automobile horn tooted angrily.

Toddy staggered backward and sat down on the bed.

Alvarado and the dog lay on the floor, motionless. One paw rested against Alvarado's shoulder, and Alvarado's left hand lay on the dog's black hide. The dog had released his hold at last. What the jaws had clung to was no longer there.

Toddy bent forward suddenly and retched. His dizziness disappeared and he could think again.

He'd have to get out of here—he gripped the edge of the bedstead and pulled himself upright. Those shots had made a hell of a racket; it sounded like they might have grazed a car. It might take the cops a little while to discover their source, but when they did . . . Well, they wouldn't find him here. Alvarado had dough on him. Plenty of it. And the keys to the convertible were in the switch. By the time the cops got a line on him, he'd be through Tijuana, heading for one of the fishing villages below Rosarita Beach. From there, for a price, he could get passage to Central America.

Of course, he'd be on the run for the rest of his life. He'd always have Elaine's murder hanging over him. That couldn't be helped. When you couldn't fight you had to run.

He got up. Eyes averted, he was bending over Alvarado's body, starting to search for the money that must be there, when something made him pause. He straightened, shrugged irritatedly, and stooped again. He stood up again, cursing.

He picked up the girl and laid her on the bed. His tanned face flushed, he pulled one side of the spread over her.

That was all he could do. He wasn't any doctor. Anyway, she'd be all right. She . . .

He pressed his thumb and forefinger against her wrist.

At first there seemed to be no pulse. Then he felt it, faint, stuttering, strengthening for a few beats, then fading again.

His voice trailed off into silence. Angry, desperate. Someone might not be there. Not soon enough. They might—but they might not. She was right on the edge. A little longer and she might be over it.

He dropped her hand—almost flung it from him—and raced into the front room. His shoes grated against the broken glass, as he snatched up the brandy carafe. He let it slide from his fingers, fall gurgling to the floor.

He knew better than that, after all the talks he'd had with Elaine's doctors. Alcohol wasn't a stimulant but a depressant. An anesthetic. Taken on top of the chloroform it would mean certain death.

Running into the kitchen, he yanked open the cupboard doors. No ammonia. Nothing that would act as a restorative.

He glanced at the stove. A coffee pot stood on the back burner. It was half full.

At soon as the coffee began to simmer, he grabbed the pot and a cup and hurried back to the bedroom. He got down on his knees at the bedside, filled a cup and set the pot on the floor, and raised the girl's head.

Her head wobbled and coffee ran from her lips, down over her chin and neck.

He put an arm around her, under her left arm, and rested her head on his shoulder. He poured more coffee in the cup.

This time she swallowed some of the liquid, but a shuddering, strangled gasp made him suddenly jerk the cup away. Too fast—he'd given it to her too fast. She'd smother, drown actually, if he wasn't careful.

He waited a minute—an hour it seemed like—and again placed the cup to her lips. Mentally, he measured out a spoonful, and waited until her throat moved, swallowed. He gave her another spoonful, then waited, and another swallow.

Slowly, a little color was returning to her face. Maybe it would be all right now if he ... He felt her pulse. Sighing, he refilled the cup.

He had almost finished doling it out to her, a spoonful at a time, when her heart began to pound. He could feel it against his hand, skipping a little, still a little irregular, but going stronger with every beat.

He started to remove his hand, but her arm had tightened against her side. Her eyelids fluttered drowsily, and opened.

"You're all—" he began.

"You ... all right ... Toddy ... ?"

"Yeah, sure," he said, somehow shamed. "Now, look, I've got to beat it. Alvarado's dead. The cops'll be here any minute. I—"

"They do not know about ... "

"They'll find out!" Toddy didn't know why he was arguing. He didn't know why the hell he didn't just beat it. "Anyway, there's plenty without that. I'm wanted in half a dozen—half a dozen—"

Her arm had gone around his neck. Her other arm held his hand against her breast. The beat of her heart was very firm now. Firm and fast.

"I tell you, I've got to—"

Her lips shut off the words. She sank back against the pillows, drawing him with her.

... Faintly, then louder and louder, a police siren moaned and whined. Toddy didn't hear it.

XXII

IN THE EARLY AFTERNOON OF HIS THIRD DAY IN JAIL, he sat in semi-isolation in a corner of the bullpen, mulling over his situation.

He knew he was being held at the instance of the federal authorities. Which meant that, since a murder charge would take precedence over others, Elaine's death hadn't been discovered. That seemed impossible; Alvarado himself had seen detectives in his and Elaine's hotel room. But the fact remained. He wasn't—couldn't be—wanted for murder. Yet.

He also knew that Milt Vonderheim was the smuggling ring's gold-supplier, and, more than likely, the man who had had Elaine killed. Why the last, he didn't know; but the first was indisputable. It was no wonder that Milt had wanted him disposed of quickly. Since Toddy's original visit to the house of the talking dog, he had held most of the clues to the little jeweler's real identity.

He had presented Milt's card that day and mentioned being sent by a friend. And Alvarado, not knowing what might be in the air, had admitted him. He had discovered almost immediately, of course, that Toddy knew nothing of Milt's illegal activities—that he had simply stumbled onto the house. But Alvarado had been prepared for that eventuality. . . . His eyes were "bad." He hadn't been able to read the card. In other words, Toddy's entry had not been obtained through Milt.

It was a shrewd subterfuge, but it had one great weakness. It could only be explained, if explanation became necessary, on one basis. Milt was the ring's key man: the gold-supplier. Since he was operating in the open and was confined to his shop, he could handle no other end of the racket.

Toddy's fingers strayed absently to the shirt pocket of his jail khakis, and came away empty. No cigarettes. No dough. And he'd hardly been able to touch the jail chow except for the coffee. The lack of comforts, however, troubled him much less than the reason for the lack. He'd never been able to do time. He couldn't now. And he was going to have to do a lot unless—

They'd have his record by now. They'd know where he was wanted and for how much. Sixty days. Ninety. A hundred and ten. Six months. A year and a . . . And Elaine. Why think about those other raps when they were certain to pin a murder on him?

He tried to accept that fact and salvage what he could from it. He'd

killed her, say, but not with premeditation. She'd slugged him with a
bottle, and he'd blanked out and killed her. Not intentionally. In a fit of
temper. That was manslaughter; second degree manslaughter, if he had
the right lawyer. If he was lucky, he'd get off with five years.

He thought about that, those five years. He thought about Dolores,
then thrust her firmly out of his mind. Jail was hard enough to take
without thinking about her, knowing that she'd come into his life too late,
that never again . . . never again . . .

All day long an oval of men circled the bullpen, moving around and
around in silent restlessness. When one man dropped out, another took
his place in the oval. Its composition changed a hundred times, and yet it
itself never changed.

"Kent!"

The oval stopped moving. Every eye was on the door.

"Todd Kent! Front and center!"

Toddy got up, dusted off the seat of his trousers, and pushed his way
through the other prisoners.

Clint McKinley, bureau chief of investigation for the Treasury Department, was a stocky mild-looking man with thin red hair and a soft,
amiable voice. He wasn't a great deal older than Toddy, and, in his first
brief sizing up, Toddy decided that he wasn't too sharp a character. He
wasn't long in revising that opinion.

McKinley seated him in a chair in front of his desk, tossed him a
package of cigarettes, and even held a match for him. Then he folded his
hands, leaned his elbows on the desk, stared straight at Toddy and began
to talk. About Dolores, or, as he called her, Miss Chavez.

"We have a lot of admiration for her," he said. "She did the right thing
at great personal risk and without hope of reward. We're going to do the
right thing by her. She's in this country on a student's visa. We're going to
pave the way for her to become a citizen. We're going to do everything
else that's in our power to do. That can be quite a lot."

Toddy nodded. "I'm glad for her. She's a nice girl."

"Now we come to you," said McKinley. "We've gone into your record
pretty thoroughly. We find it remarkable. You've preyed on your fellow
citizens with one kind of racket or another ever since you went into
circulation. You get a chance in the Army to redeem yourself, and you
throw it away. You sell out. You help to tear down the prestige of the flag
you swore allegiance to. You've never been any good. You've never done
a single unselfish, honest deed in your whole life."

The soft, amiable voice ceased to speak. Toddy pushed himself up from
his chair. "Thanks for the sermon," he said. "I don't think I'll stay for the
singing."

"Sit down, Kent."

"Huh-uh. You people can't make a charge stick against me. You've had no right to hold me this long."

"We can see that you're held by other authorities."

"Hop to it, then."

"What's the hurry?" said McKinley. "It always gets me to see a man throw himself away. Maybe I said a little too much. If I did, I'll apologize."

Toddy sat back down. He had intended to from the beginning. It had simply seemed bad, psychologically, to let McKinley crack the whip too hard.

"As a matter of fact," McKinley continued, "I think my statement was a little sweeping. If you hadn't tried to help Miss Chavez there in San Diego, you might have escaped. That's something in your favor. Of course, you may have had some selfish motive for staying. But—"

"Try real hard," said Toddy. "You'll think of one."

"Don't coax me." McKinley's eyes glinted. "You want to get along with me or not, Kent? If you don't, just say so. I've got something better to do with my time than argue with two-bit con men."

Toddy swallowed harshly and got a grip on himself. He'd been kidding himself about that psychology business. A little, anyway. He was losing his temper. He was letting a cop get his goat.

"You're trying to do a job," he said, "but you're going about it the wrong way. You're not softening me up. You're getting nowhere fast. Now why don't you drop it and start all over again?"

"Who supplied the gold to this outfit, Kent?"

"I don't know."

"You've got a good idea."

"Maybe."

"Let's have it, then. Come on. Spit it out."

"No," said Toddy.

"You want a deal, huh? All right. You play square with me, and I'll do what I can for you."

"That," said Toddy, "isn't my idea of a deal."

"I'll give you one more chance, Kent. I don't believe you know anything, anyway, but I'm willing to give you a chance. Turn it down and you'll be touring jails for the next three years."

Toddy grinned derisively. *Three years, hell!* McKinley misunderstood the grin. He jabbed a button on his desk, and the deputy jailer came back in.

"Take him out of here," said McKinley. "Lock him up and throw the key away. We won't want him any more."

The jailer took Toddy's elbow. Toddy got up and they started for the door. He was sick inside. He'd played his cards the only way he could, but they just hadn't been good enough. Now it was all over.

"Kent."

The jailer paused, gave Toddy a nudge. Toddy didn't turn around. He didn't say anything. He was afraid to.

"This is your last chance, Kent. You go through that door and you'll never get another one."

Toddy hesitated, shrugged. He took a step toward the door and his hand closed over the knob. He turned it. Behind him he heard McKinley's amiable, unwilling chuckle.

"All right. Come on back. I'll talk to Kent a little longer, Chief."

The jailer went out the door. Toddy, the palms of his hands damp, went back to his chair.

"All right," said McKinley calmly, as though the scene just past had never taken place. "You were saying I was going about my job the wrong way. Could be. I've been in this work for fifteen years, but I learn something new every day. Now tell me where you think I was wrong."

"You want something definite from me," said Toddy. "You haven't offered anything definite in return."

"We can't actually promise anything. Except to use our influence."

"That's good enough for me."

"Call it settled, then. We'll try to wipe the slate clean." McKinley smiled. "You haven't committed any murders anywhere, have you? I don't think we could square those."

Toddy shook his head. "No murders."

"Good," said McKinley. "Now, let's see what we've got. You were buying gold. You accidentally—accidentally on purpose, maybe—picked up a valuable watch—a chunk of bullion—at Alvarado's house. He checked on you, found out you were not, and offered you a job. If you turned it down, he threatened to—"

McKinley broke off and made a deprecating gesture. "Maybe," he said, "Miss Chavez doesn't have her facts straight. Maybe you'd better do the talking."

"She has them straight," said Toddy.

"Why did you go to Tijuana, Kent?"

"Alvarado told me to. I"—Toddy coughed—"I was to go there and wait for him. He didn't say why."

"Cough a little longer," McKinley suggested. "Maybe you can think of a better one."

"No," said Toddy. "I think we'd better let that one stand. There's something in the rules about impeaching your own witnesses. If I *did* take a little gold across the border, it's just as well that you have no knowledge of it."

"Mmmm," drawled McKinley. "You don't know why he wanted you to go there—you weren't in any position to ask questions. So you went, and you got slugged. And if Alvarado hadn't intervened you'd have been killed."

"That's right. It's this way," said Toddy. "After it was all over. Alvarado told me why he'd wanted me to go to Tijuana. He had it in for the gold-supplier. He was trying to wash him up. So Alvarado let him know I was going to this place in Tijuana, hoping that he'd try to kill me."

He paused, conscious of the pitfall he was approaching. How to tell a plausible story without mentioning Elaine.

"Did you ever try telling the truth?" said McKinley. "The complete truth? You might enjoy it."

"I am trying to." Toddy frowned earnestly. "But it's a pretty mixed-up deal. It's hard to explain something when you don't completely understand it yourself. You see, Alvarado wanted to get this guy but he got orders to leave him alone. So he had to back up. He wouldn't tell me anything. I had to guess why I was slugged."

"You knew who the gold-supplier was, in other words?"

"He thought I did—or could find out; it was the only reason he could have for wanting to kill me."

McKinley ran a stubby hand through his thin red hair. He sighed, stood up, and turned to the window. He stared down into the street, hands thrust into his pants pockets, teetering back and forth on his heels.

"It doesn't figure," he said to the window. "It doesn't because you're holding out something. I don't know why, but I'm reasonably sure of one thing. You know who the gold-supplier is."

"I think I know."

"You thought in the beginning. Then you found out. Something Alvarado did or said—something you saw there in the San Diego house— tipped you off." McKinley sat down again and placed his elbows back on the desk.

"Knowing and proving are two different things. Suppose I gave you his name and address. You go there. You don't find anything. He won't talk. . . . "

"That's our problem."

"Is that a promise? Regardless of whether my tip works out, you'll get me that clean slate?"

"Oh, well, now,"—McKinley spread his hands—"you can't expect me to do that. You might give us any old name and address and—and— yeah," said McKinley. "Mmm-hmmm."

He squirmed in his chair, looking down at some papers on his desk. Fumbling with them absently. Abruptly he looked up. "It's Milt Vonderheim! Don't lie! I've got the proof!"

Toddy laughed. After a moment, McKinley grinned.

"It's a good thing you didn't tell me it was Vonderheim. I'd have known you were trying to throw a curve under me."

"I'd pick a better goat than Milt," Toddy said. "Everyone knows that—"

"We know. I don't care about everyone. How would you go about landing this man, Kent?"

"Nothing's been in the papers about Alvarado or—?"

"Nothing yet. I don't know how long we can keep it quiet."

"I'll need a few things. A gun, some money, a car. I'll need a few days. I've got to see some people."

"Why?"

"To make sure," said Toddy, evenly, "that you don't have a tail on me. At the first sign of one, the whole deal's off."

"Why? If you're on the square."

Toddy explained. He was plausible, earnest, the soul of sincerity. If McKinley wouldn't believe this, he thought, he wouldn't believe anything.

"That's the way I'll handle it," he concluded. "He'll have a lot of dough. I'll go through the motions of taking it, highjacking him. Then I'll put him in the car and head for the country. Someplace, supposedly, where I can bump him off and hide his body."

"That part I don't get. Why would you want to bump him off?"

"Because that's the way I'd have to feel about him. When a man's killed"—Toddy caught himself—"when a man's tried to kill you, you want to get back at him. He'll talk. He'll spill everything he knows in attempting to get off the hook."

"Yeah. Maybe," said McKinley.

"But I've got to be left alone. No tails. Nothing that might possibly lead him to think I was working with you. . . . You see that, don't you? It's got a look like I'm giving you the double-cross. Otherwise, he won't talk and you'll never find out how he manages to get pounds of gold every week—you won't be able to prove that he has got it. And if you can't prove that—"

"But suppose," said McKinley. "Suppose you *are* giving us the double-cross?"

Toddy shrugged and leaned back in his chair. McKinley sat blinking, staring at him.

"I'd be crazy to do it," he said, at last. "I give you a car and a gun and a clear field with a man that's loaded with dough. I give a guy like you a setup like that. It doesn't make sense any way you look at it."

He pressed a button on his desk and stood up. Toddy stood up also. It was all over. There was no use arguing.

"Only fifteen years in this game and I've gone crazy," said McKinley. "Chief, take this man back to jail and dress him out. I'll send over an order for his release."

He said one other thing as Toddy headed for the door. Something that made Toddy very glad his back was turned: "We'll spring your wife, too, Kent, as soon as you pull this off. . . . "

XXIII

AFTER VISITING A BARBER SHOP, Toddy went to a pawnshop—where he purchased a secondhand suitcase—a drugstore, a haberdashery, and a newsstand which sold back issues. Then he checked in at a hotel.

With deliberate slowness he unpacked the suitcase, the clean shirts, socks and underwear, the toilet articles, cigarettes and bottle of whiskey. He knew what the back-issue newspapers would tell him. He had seen an evening paper headline, BAIL RACKET PROBE LOOMS, but without that he would have known. Miracles didn't happen. Elaine couldn't be in jail.

Still, he didn't really *know*, and until he read the papers . . . He spread them out at last, a drink in his hand, and read. The foolishly unreasonable hope collapsed.

Only two of the papers carried the story; one gave it a paragraph, the other two. The latter paper also carried her picture, a small, blurred shot, taken several years ago. The former "character actress" had surrendered at a suburban jail. She'd worn sunglasses and was "apparently suffering from a severe cold." Somebody was filling in for Elaine.

Toddy sighed and poured himself another drink. It was about as he'd figured it.

He ordered dinner and put in a call to Airedale. The bondsman arrived just as the waiter was departing.

His derby hat was pulled low over his eyes, and his doggish face was long with anxiety. His first act was to step to the window and draw the shade.

"Can't you smell that stuff, man?" he rasped. "That's gas. It's driftin' all the way down from that little room in Sacramento!"

Toddy poured a glass of milk, handed it to him, and gestured to the bed. Airedale sat down, heavily, fanning himself with the derby.

"Where'd you go," he said. "And why ain't you still goin'?"

"Save it," said Toddy, taking a bite of steak. "Now tell me what happened."

"Me? I tell *you* what happened?"

"They cracked down on your connections. You had to produce Elaine. Take it from there."

"I go to your hotel and get ahold of lardass. We go up to your room. We can't raise no one, so we break in. You ain't there, Elaine ain't there. Period."

394

"Comma," said Toddy. "How'd the room look? I mean was it torn up?"

"You ought to know. . . . No," Airedal added hastily, "it wasn't."

"There weren't any cops around? No detectives?"

"Just me and the house dick, but—"

"What time were you there?"

"Eleven-thirty, maybe twelve."

"Oh," said Toddy, "I get it. You were there when . . . "

"When," Airedale nodded. "When Elaine was going up in smoke. Jesus, Toddy, did you have to draw a picture of it? Couldn't you have done it outside somewheres? You're up there raising hell—everyone in the joint hears her screamin'—and then—"

"That doesn't mean anything. She was always doing that."

"She won't any more," said Airedale. "I honest to Gawd don't get it, Toddy. Getting rid of the corpus delicti won't make you nothing. Not with that incinerator stack running right through your room."

Toddy abruptly pushed aside his steak and poured a cup of coffee. "I didn't kill her, Airedale. Let's get that straight. I didn't kill her."

"Am I a cop?" said Airedale, "I don't care what you did. I ain't even seen you. I ain't even telling you to get away from here as far and as fast as you can before they put the arm on you."

"There hasn't been any rumble yet."

"There will be," Airedale assured him grimly. "It's building up right now. That little hustler, the ringer that's standing in for Elaine, don't like jail."

"So?" Toddy shrugged. "She's in up to her ears. It would be easier for her if she liked it."

"She don't like it," Airedale repeated, "because she's on the dope. She's a heroin mainliner."

Toddy gulped. "But why in the hell did she—"

"Why do they do anything when they're hitting the *H*?" growled Airedale. "She spent so much time in the hay she was starting to moo, but she still couldn't pay for her habit. So she stands in for Elaine, and then she gives me the bad news. I'm over a barrel, see? I've got to take care of her. I got to put in a fix and see that she gets the stuff. Either that or I'm out of business. She'll squawk that she ain't Elaine."

Airedale paused to light a cigar. He took a disconsolate puff or two, and sat staring at the glowing tip.

"Well . . . I've had a doctor in every day. Cold shots, y'know. But that can't go on more'n a few more trips. Even if no one wised up and I was getting those shots for a buck instead of a hundred. I'd have to break it off. I wouldn't play. I've got my own kind of crookedness. It don't drive people crazy. It don't kill 'em."

He paused again, and gave Toddy an apologetic glance. "Not," he said, "that some of 'em don't need killin'. It's just a manner of speaking."

"Skip it," said Toddy. "Will she keep quiet as long as she gets the stuff?"

"Why not? She ain't a bad kid. She doesn't want to cause any trouble. She's beginning to see that I can't keep her fixed, and she ain't kickin'. She'll just go out on her own again."

"She won't be able to do that. They'll stick her on a conspiracy charge."

"Huh-uh." Airedale wagged his head. "She'll get out. She'll get all the stuff she wants. You've read them papers? Well, that little gal's worth her weight in white stuff to certain parties."

The bondsman stubbed out his cigar, sighed, and reached inside the pocket of his coat. He brought out a railroad timetable and proceeded to scan it. After a moment, he looked up.

"What do you think about Florida this time of year?"

"I'm got going anywhere," said Toddy. "Not yet, anyway."

"I am," said Airedale. "I like my fireworks on the Fourth of July. Here's hoping it'll be safe to come back by then."

He waited, as though expecting some comment, but Toddy only nodded. Naturally, Airedale would have to get out of town. The scandal would die down, eventually, be superseded by other and livelier scandals. Meanwhile, Los Angeles would be made extremely uncomfortable for the bondsman and his various political connections.

Airedale rose, looked into the crown of his derby, and emitted a bark of pleasure. "Well, look at that," he said, pulling forth a roll of bills. "And just when you'd changed your mind about leaving!"

"Thanks." Toddy pushed back the roll. "It isn't that. I've got money."

"So? What else do you need?"

"Nothing you can help me with."

"I can help you a little," said Airedale. "I can tell you to forget it if you're figuring on copping a plea. Juries don't like these cases where the body is disposed of. It shows bad faith, see what I mean? You try to cover the crime up and then, maybe, when you see you can't get away with it, you ask for a break. They give you one. Up here."

"But— Yeah," said Toddy, dully, "I suppose you're right."

Airedale slammed on his derby and started to turn away. "I don't get it," he snarled. "What are you hanging around for? Why ain't you on your way?"

"I want to find out who killed Elaine."

"Brother," said Airedale, "that does it!"

"If I run," said Toddy, "I've got to keep running. A few hundred or a few grand won't be enough. I've got to be squared for life."

"You've got something good lined up, huh?" said Airedale. "Why didn't you say so in the first place? What—never mind. Can you pull it off by yourself?"

"It's the only way I can do it. But I'll need more time, Airedale. A couple of days, anyway. I really wanted three, but—"

"Two," said Airedale. "I'd figured on twenty-four hours—enough time for me to clear out. But I'll fix the gal for two; I'll pay for that much. She may not get the stuff if I'm not here, but . . . Oh, hell. I guess it'll be all right."

They shook hands and Airedale left. A drink in his hand, Toddy sat down on the bed and mulled over the situation. Some of his normal fatalism began to assert itself. He grinned philosophically.

He undressed and climbed into bed. Lying back with his eyes open, he stared up into the darkness.

McKinley had promised not to have him tailed. It wouldn't be necessary. Placed at strategic points, a mere handful of men, with the license number and description of a car, could follow its movements even in a city as large as Los Angeles. So there was only one thing to do—rather, two things. Change the license, change the description.

Milt would be stubborn. He'd do nothing unless he was made to—so he'd be made to. There'd be no spot-check, no tails, no T-men to interfere.

XXIV

AT NINE-THIRTY THE NEXT MORNING, Toddy finished a leisurely breakfast in his room and called McKinley. The bureau chief sounded annoyed as he told Toddy where to pick up the car.

"You haven't seen Miss Chavez?" he asked.

"Seen her? Why the hell would I? I don't even know where—"

"Good," said McKinley, in a milder tone. "She's been after us to find out what happened to you. Wanted to see you in jail. Wanted to send you a note. I finally told her we'd turned you loose, and you'd left town."

"That's—that's fine," said Toddy.

"Yeah. You've got a job to do, Kent. You've got a wife. And Miss Chavez is as straight as they come."

"And I'm not."

"You're not," agreed McKinley. "You took the words right out of your mouth."

He hung up the phone. Toddy slammed up his receiver, and finished dressing.

He was irritated by the conversation, but more than that, worried. Dolores knew about Elaine's death. She'd be wondering why, after holding him, Toddy, three days, McKinley had suddenly freed him. She'd be sure that instead of merely leaving town, as McKinley had told her he had, he'd try to leave the country. She'd know that he'd need plenty of money to leave on and that he could only get it in one way.

As long as he was in jail, her deal with the government was safe. They wouldn't care, when the news of the murder broke, whether she'd known about it or not. But if he skipped the country and committed another crime in the process of skipping . . .

No—Toddy shook his head. That wasn't like her. She wouldn't be concerned for herself, but him. She'd want to help him. And that, in a way, was as bad as the other. He couldn't tell her anything. This had to be a one-man show.

Toddy took a final glance around the room, left it, and headed for the elevator.

The car was parked a few blocks away. He almost laughed aloud when he saw it. It was a medium-priced sedan, exactly like thousands of others of the same make to a casual observer. But Toddy was not observing casually, and neither would the T-men.

They'd hardly need to look at the license plates. The gray paint job, the white sidewall tires and the red-glass reflector buttons by which the plates were held would be sufficient identification. They'd be able to spot him two blocks away.

He slid under the wheel, and opened the dashboard compartment. The keys and the gun were there, and—he checked it quickly—the gun was loaded. Everything was as it should be.

He drove north and east, winding back and forth through a maze of side streets, avoiding anything in the nature of an arterial thoroughfare. He didn't think McKinley would have his spot check set up so soon, but he might; and there wasn't any hurry. He had the whole day to kill.

The houses he passed grew shabbier, fewer and farther apart. Many of them stood empty. Most of the streets were unpaved. It was one of those borderline, ambiguous areas common to most cities; an area surrendered to industry but not yet made part of it.

Toddy pulled onto a brick-paved street, and rounded a corner. On the opposite side of the street was an abandoned warehouse. On the right, the side he was on, was an automobile salvage yard, its high board fence set back to allow room for the dingy filling station at the front. A four-wheel truck trailer, all its tires missing, stood between the street and the closed-in grease rack.

Toddy drove into the inside lane of the station. He spoke a few words to a cold-eyed man in greasy coveralls and a skullcap made of an old hat. The man leaned against the gas pump. He looked up and down the street, said "Okay, Mac," and jerked his head. Toddy drove into the greasing tunnel; then, as the rear wall slid up, into the yard beyond.

The job took two men three hours. When it was over Toddy himself, if he had not watched the transformation, would not have believed it was the same car.

A chromium grille disguised the radiator. The white sidewalls were replaced with plain tires. A sunshade sheltered the windshield. The roof and fenders of the car were dark blue; the rest of the body a glossy black. The red reflector buttons were gone, of course, as were the original license plates. The plate holders, with the substitute plates, had been moved to new position.

Toddy paid over one hundred and fifty dollars, adding a five-dollar tip for each of the workmen. That left him with a little less than ten dollars, but that was more than enough for what he had to do. He wouldn't be paying his hotel bill. He wouldn't be going back to pay it.

He took one of the main streets back toward town, stopping once at a restaurant-bar, where he passed the better part of two hours, and again at a drugstore where he bought faintly tinted sunglasses. The glasses were disguise enough; not really necessary, for that matter. They'd be looking for a car, not a man.

It was dusk when Toddy reached the city's business section, and a light drizzling rain was beginning to fall. Driving slowly, Toddy turned north up Spring Street.

Milt wouldn't be buying gold, now. Moreover, he wouldn't be receiving his nightly visit from the driver of the beer truck. He wouldn't because there would be no more scrap gold to go out in the empty bottles.

Toddy swore suddenly and stepped on the gas. Almost immediately, he slowed down again. So what? What difference did it make if he passed by the hotel, the one where he and Elaine had lived? They didn't know anything or want to know anything. All they were interested in was the rent which was paid through tomorrow.

He parked on Main Street, and sat in the growing darkness, smoking, listening to the patter of rain on the roof. For a panic-stricken moment he wondered whether Milt had already skipped; then grinned and shook his head. Milt would see no need to hurry. He'd move cautiously, safely, taking his time.

So that was all right. He wished he had nothing to worry about but that.

It was seven o'clock by the time he had finished his third cigarette. He tossed the butt out the window, transferred the gun from the dash compartment to his pocket, and started the car.

He drove up Main a block, swung over to the next street, drove back three blocks. On a dark side street he turned right and cut the motor. He coasted to a stop a few doors above the entrance to the Los Angeles Watch & Jewelry Co., brokers in precious metals.

Luckily, he waited a moment before reaching for the door of the car. For Milt hadn't stopped buying gold. Doubtless he felt that it was too soon, that he had to go through the motions a little longer. Or perhaps he was waiting for a weekend to beat it. At any rate, the door of the shop opened suddenly and a raincoated fugure carrying the familiar square box dashed toward Main Street. A few minutes later, two other buyers came out together and trotted toward Main.

Crouched low in the seat, hidden by the rain-washed windows, Toddy waited ten minutes more. But no one else emerged from the shop, and, he decided, no one was likely to. It was too late.

He slid over on the seat and rolled down the window. He looked swiftly up and down the street. Then he rolled up the window, opened the door, and got out.

He walked close to the building fronts, pausing as he passed the one next to Milt's shop. He could see in from there—see a scene so familiar, so associated with warmth and friendliness, that what he was about to do seemed suddenly fantastic and hateful.

Milt, seated back in his cage, the bright work light lifting him out of the shadows, draping him in a kind of golden aura. Milt . . . how could he . . . ?

But he had. And his friendliness—his faked friendship—only made matters worse. Toddy reconnoitered the street quickly, strode to the door, and stepped inside. He was halfway down the long dark aisle before Milt could look up.

"Toddy! Iss it you? For days I have been worrying about . . . about . . . "

"Yeah," said Toddy. "I'll bet you have."

He moved swiftly through the wicket of the cage, and brought a hand down on the gooseneck of the lamp. It flattened against the workbench, casting its light upon the floor. No one looking in from the street would see anything.

Milt had started to rise, but Toddy shoved him back in his chair. He seated himself, facing the little jeweler.

"That's right," he nodded grimly. "That's a gun. If you don't think I'll use it, give me a little trouble."

"But I do not understand! Trouble? Have ever I—" He broke off, staring into Toddy's cold set face, and abruptly his mask of bewildered innocence vanished. "Stupid Toddy. Oh, so stupid. At last he awakens."

"Get it out," said Toddy. "Every goddamned nickel. And don't ask me what."

"Ask?" Milt shrugged. "I am not given to foolish chatter. As for *it*, I have anticipated you. It is already out." He started to reach beneath the workbench, then paused abruptly, arm half-extended.

Toddy nodded. "Go ahead. Just don't try anything."

He took the heavy brief case that Milt drew out, laid it on the bench, and slipped the catch. He shook it slightly, his eyes swerving from the jeweler to the bench. There was one packet of scat money—fives, tens and twenties. The rest of the horde was in thousand-dollar bills, dough too hot for the dumbest burglar to touch. Milt couldn't spend it in this country. Abroad, there'd be no trouble. Violation of income tax laws was not an extraditable offense.

"You visit was most inopportune," sighed Milt. "A few hours more and I would have been gone."

"You're still going. You're going out to Venice with me, out to the beach. We're going to have a nice long talk."

"We can do that here. We are alone on this street. No one will come in."

"Someone will tomorrow."

"But ... Oh," said Milt. "Still, is it necessary, Toddy? You have the money. By tomorrow, you can be very far away. In any case, my hands are tied. I dare not complain."

Toddy jerked his head. "I'll be a lot farther away the day after tomorow. And you'd talk, all right. Everyone that's had anything to do with me will get a going-over. I've been in jail, and—"

"Yes. I know."

"Then you probably know how I got myself sprung. You know I can't keep my bargain unless I dig up the guy that killed Elaine."

"Which you cannot do," said Milt, "Not—he added—"that you have any intention of keeping your bargain. Another, perhaps, amlost any other man, but not you." He grinned faintly, his hands clasped over his fat stomach. "You do not want to keep your bargain with the government agents. You cannot keep it. A confession you may extract from me, but it will be worthless. I can prove that I did not kill Elaine or cause her to be killed."

"Maybe." Toddy studied the bland, chubby face. "Maybe," he repeated, "but I'm taking you with me, anyway. No one knows how you worked this setup here. I'm going to find out, just in case I ever get back to this country. If you come clean with me I may just tie you up and dump you somewhere. Some place where you'll be found in a few days. Otherwise ... "

He gestured significantly with the gun. Milt laughed openly.

"Yes? You were thinking of the dunes, doubtless? Oh, excellent! It will be a wonderful place to leave a body ... or should I say two?"

"Two?" Toddy frowned. "What the hell are you talking about?"

"Bodies," said Milt. "Yours and Miss Chavez'."

Toddy's chair grated against the floor. "Damn you! If you've hurt that—"

Behind him the curtains rustled faintly. Something cold and hard pushed through them, pressed into the back of his neck.

Milt nodded to him, solemnly. "That is right, Toddy. Sit still. Sit very, very still. Yes, and I think I shall just take your gun. Miss Chavez"—he glanced at the clock—"should be here at any moment. Your hotel, your former hotel, I should say, was kind enough to refer her to me. I suggested that she return here tonight when you, in your hour of dire emergency, would most certainly come to me for aid. So ... So"—the front door opened and clicked softly shut—"she has come."

She came down the aisle, hesitantly at first, then with quick firm steps as she saw the two men in the dim glow of the lamp. "Toddy! I am so glad I—I—"

"Do not scream," said Milt. "Do not move."

He thrust himself up from his chair, moved around Toddy and out through the wicket. Toddy waited helplessly, his hands carefully held out from his sides. . . . This was the one thing he hadn't foreseen—the fact that Milt might have a confederate. Who the hell could it be, he wondered, and why had Milt behaved as he had? What had he hoped to gain by appearing detfenseless, letting Toddy talk?

Toddy didn't know, and there was no time now to think about it. The person behind him came through the drapes, and the gun barrel dug viciously into his neck.

He got up slowly. He looked into Dolores' pale strained face, and tried to grin reassuringly. He heard Milt's chuckle as he pushed her forward through the wicket.

He turned around.

"Hi-ya, prince," said Elaine.

XXV

THROUGH A BLINDING downpour of rain, the car moved cautiously, steadily westward. Toddy drove, bent over the wheel, staring through the windshield. Dolores was at his side, Milt and Elaine in the rear seat. It was almost an hour before the city proper was left behind them, and silently, except for the humming of the tires and the wet lash of the windshield wipers, they went rolling down Olympic Boulevard. It ran in practically a straight line to the ocean. There was almost no traffic on it now.

Toddy eased up on the gas a little more. He'd outsmarted himself this time. In outwitting McKinley, he'd handed Milt a setup. Now there was nothing to do but stall, postpone the inevitable as long as possible.

The air was thick with the odor of Elaine's cigarettes and whiskey. She coughed, choked, and a fine spray showered Toddy's neck. Milt cleared his throat, apologetically.

"Perhaps, *Liebling*, it might be well to . . . "

"What?" said Elaine. "You trying to tell me when to take a drink?"

Milt hesitated. Toddy felt a faint surge of hope. If she and Milt should start fighting, if she'd only throw one of those wild tantrums of hers . . . But she didn't. Moreover, Toddy knew, she wasn't going to.

"If you put it that way," Milt said, coldly, "yes. Rather, I am telling you when not to drink. And I am telling you that now. There is too much at stake. Later it will be all right; I would be the last to interfere."

There was a moment of silence. Then, "All right, honey," Elaine said meekly. "You just tell li'l Elaine what to do and that's what she'll do."

"Good," said Milt complacently. "We must give our Toddy no advantage, *hein?*"

"Whatever you say, honey."

"He is a very intelligent man," Milt went on. "He tells me in substance how much time the police have given him. He informs me, indirectly, that there is no one following his movements. Finally, by a reverse process, he makes excellent suggestions for disposing of himself. Do you wonder that I fear him, this intellectual gniat?"

Elaine's giggle tapered off to a troubled note. "Yeah, but honey. I don't—"

"Consider," Milt continued, enjoyably. "Everything he is told, yet nothing he sees. He knows that Alvarado has told the annoymous gold-supplier of the theft of the watch. He knows his wife detests him, and he is thoroughly familiar with her talents as an actress. But does he draw any conclusions from these things? Not at all. He is baffled by her strange death and the subsequent disappearance of her body. It does not occur to him that she had simulated death, that she followed him down the fire escape taking the watch with her."

Dolores half-turned in the seat and her eyes flashed. "He is not stupid! He trusted you! It is easy to—"

"Of stupidity," said Milt, "you are hardly a competent judge. You who revealed his release from jail to a stranger. Now if you wish to take full advantage of your remaining minutes of consciousness, you will turn around."

"You are too cowardly! I—"

"Turn around," said Toddy softly. "She called the turn on you, Milt. I trusted you. On top of that, you had a lot of luck. If I hadn't chased off after Donald, I'd have found out that Elaine was pulling a fake."

"There was no element of luck," Milt said. "I telephoned Elaine when you left the shop. There was ample time to locate the watch and prepare for your arrival."

"But if I'd examined Elaine . . . "

"If you had—well, it would be a prank; and later we should have tried again. But we—I—knew you would not do that. So many predicaments has your stupidity placed you in, and always you react in the same manner. You place no faith in the wisdom or mercy of constituted authority. You make no study of the factors behind your contretemps. Tricks you have, not brains; tricks and legs. So, where tricks are futile, you run."

Toddy grunted. "You're a funny guy, Milt. Very funny."

"Oh, there is no doubt about it. Everyone has always said so. There is only one person who did not."

"Me," cooed Elaine, snuggling against him. "I knew better right from the beggining."

"So you did," Milt nodded beignly. "So now, I think, you should have another drink. A very small one."

Ahead and to the right, blurred lights pushed up through the shrouds of rain. Santa Monica. It wouldn't be long now.

A car came towards them, fog-lights burning, moving rapidly. Toddy's hand tightened on the wheel . . . Side-swipe it? . . . Huh-uh. Milt had nothing to lose. An accident, any sign of trouble, would only make him kill more quickly.

Toddy forced a short ugly laugh. Elaine lowered the bottle, squinted suspiciously in the darkness.

"Something funny, prince?"

Toddy shrugged.

"Goddammit, I asked you if—"

"Quiet, my treasure." Milt drew her back against his shoulder. "And, yes, I think I will take charge of the liquor. He is trying to disturb you. Drink makes the task easy."

"But—all right, honey."

"There's one thing I don't understand," said Toddy. "Why was the room straightened up before Elaine skipped out?"

"On the night of her supposed death? Merely a precautionary measure. The police might have been notified if the condition of the room happened to be observed. I felt sure you would hold Alvarado responsible. I wished to make sure you had no interference."

"That part of your plan didn't work out very well, did it?"

"It worked out well enough," said Milt, "as your present situation proves ... But you were laughing a moment ago?"

"I was just thinking." Toddy laughed again. "Wondering about you and Elaine; how long it'll be before she turns on you ... when you least expect it."

"Because she turned, as you put it, on you? But there is no similarity between the two cases. You could give her nothing. I can. She never needed you. She needs me. You tried to hold her against her will. I would never do that. If parting becomes necessary, it will be arranged amicably. We will share and share alike, and each will go his own way."

"That's sound logic," said Toddy, "but you're not dealing with a logical person. Elaine gets her fun out of not getting along. It's the only entertainment, aside from drinking, that she's capable of. She's a degenerate, Milt. She's liable to go in for killing as hard as she does drinking. I wouldn't believe the doctors when—"

Something hit him a painful blow on the head, and the car swerved. He swung it straight again at a sharp command from Milt. In the rear view mirror, he saw the jeweler turn, hand raised, toward Elaine.

"*Dummkopf!*" he snapped. "I have a notion to ... " Then he smiled, and his voice went suddenly gentle. "It seems we both have the temper. It is not a time to give way to it."

"I'm sorry, honey. He just made me so damned sore ... "

"But now you see through his tricks, eh? You see where they might lead to?"

"Uh-huh." Elaine sighed. "You're so smart, darling. You see right through people."

"He doesn't see through you," said Toddy. "If he did he'd take that gun away from you. He'd know what you're thinking—that all of that dough would be better than half."

Elaine made a mocking sound with her lips. Milt chuckled fatly.

"It is useless, Toddy. In the regrettable absence of attraction, there would still be the factor of need. It was I who planned this, and there will be yet more planning, thinking, to be done. Even an Elaine as elemental as the one you portray would not destroy something necessary to survival."

"Anyway," said Elaine, "I don't want the old gun; I wouldn't know how to use it. You take it, honey."

Milt pushed it back at her. "But you must know! It is imperative. Look, I will show you again . . . The safety, here. Then, only a firm, short pull on the trigger. Very short unless you wish to empty it. It is automatic, as I told you previously . . . "

His own gun was in his lap for the moment, and Toddy knew another surge of hope. He couldn't, of course, do anything himself. But Elaine . . .

But Elaine didn't. Milt picked up his gun again.

Toddy turned the car off Olympic and onto Ocean Avenue. They reached Pico Street, and he turned again. Less than a mile ahead was the ocean.

"No more questions, Toddy? Nothing else you would like to inquire about?"

"Nothing."

"After all, the opportunity will not arise again."

"No, it won't," said Toddy. "Look, Milt . . . "

"Yes?"

"Let Miss Chavez go. She won't—"

"I will not go!" said Dolores, calmly.

"You will not," agreed Milt. "I am sorry. It is a terrible penalty to pay for allying oneself with an imbecile."

He rolled down the window of the car and peered out, and the rain sounds mingled with the roar of the ocean, the breakers rolling in and out from shore. Toddy made the last turn.

"You made one mistake, Milt. There's one thing you didn't count on."

"Interesting," murmured Milt, "but not, I am afraid, true . . . This is the place you had in mind, I believe? Yes. You will stop, then, and turn off your lights."

Toddy stopped. The lights went off.

There was a moment of silence, the near-absolute silence which precedes action. Before Milt could break it, Toddy spoke.

This was his last chance, his and Dolores'. And he knew it was wasted, no chance at all, even before he started to speak. What the had to say was incredible. His strained, hollow voice made it preposterous.

"Really, Toddy." Milt sounded almost embarrassed. "You do not expect us to believe that?"

"No," said Toddy. "I don't expect you to believe me. But it is true."

"Only stupidity I charged you with," Milt pointed out. "Not insanity. You did not know Elaine was alive. You were sure you would be accused of her murder. Willing though you might be to pass up a fortune, and I sincerely suspect such a willingness, you would not dare abide by your bargain. In this case, you had no choice but to run."

"I was tired of running." (*Elaine giggled.*) "I knew I hadn't killed her. I was going to fight the case."

"Without money? With all the evidence against you? With a long record of criminality? And if, by some fluke of justice, you cleared yourself, what then? You have no trade but to prey upon others. You—"

"I could get one." The words, the tone seemed ridiculously childish.

"We waste time," said Milt. "You would have me believe you pursued one futility to achieve another. You, risking your liberty—perhaps your life—by keeping a bargain? You, placing your faith, at last, in the courts? You, Toddy Kent, doing these things for a so-called good name, a job, perhaps Miss Chavez—"

"It would not have been perhaps," said Dolores.

"Even so," Milt shrugged. "I know him too well, and he knows himself too well. He does not fit the part . . . Now, I think . . . "

"Let Elaine think," Toddy persisted doggedly. "You can't pull out. You want to get her in as deep as you are. Don't let him do it, Elaine! There's a tape recorder in the car. I—"

"Elaine," Milt interrupted, "is not required to think. And, of course, there is a recorder. How else could you obtain the evidence you were supposed to get? I do not deny the existence of a bargain. Only that you had no intention of keeping it."

"I did intend to keep it! I know it looks like I didn't, but I had to make it look that way! I was supposed to meet them here—I called them just before I went to your shop. Elaine—"

"Tonight?" said Milt. "You were to meet them there tonight, or tomorrow night? Or perhaps even the next? You are transparent, Toddy. Your government men would have given you two days without surveillance as quickly as they would give you two hours. Never would they have agreed to such an arrangement."

"They didn't agree to it, but they had to take it. I'd already ducked out on 'em. It was either play it my way or—"

"Nonsense. You insult my intelligence."

"Now, wait a minute," said Elaine, worriedly. "Let me—"

"It is not necessary," said Milt. "I have already thought. Of everything... You were to meet them here, eh? Bah! Where are they, then?"

Toddy licked dry lips, helplessly. It was no use. The evidence was all against him. He couldn't make them believe something that was incredible to himself.

"I don't know," he said, almost indifferently. "It's a big beach. Maybe they don't recognize the car. I don't know where they are, but—"

Milt's curt, bored laugh cut him off. "They would not recognize the car, certainly. You would see to that. And we both know where they are—anywhere but here. Now, enough!"

"But Milt, honey ... " Elaine began.

"Enough!" sanpped Milt. "Must I explain everything twice? Why do you think I played with him there in the shop, found out exactly where he wished to go? Because it would be safe. It would be the last place his whilom friends would expect to find him."

"All right, honey. I was just—"

"We will proceed! And—*please!*—the bottle will remain here!"

Dolores was shoved over in the seat, squeezed against Toddy. Elaine pushed past her, and got out. She stood back in the sand a few feet, covering the door as Toddy and the girl emerged.

Milt came out last, grunting from the exertion, blinking his eyes against the rain.

"Now," he panted, "we will just ... " He gestured with the gun. Elaine spoke apologetically.

"Milt, baby, are you sure, really sure that ... ?"

"I have said so! It is all finished. Now we have only to—"

He saw, then, heard the childishly delighted laugh—mischievous, filled with the viciousness it could not recognize, signaling triumph in a game without rules. It seemed to paralyze him. The gun hung loose in his fingers.

"*Liebling!*" he gasped. "Darling! There is so much. Why—?"

There was a brief, stuttering blast. "W-why?" Milt said, and crumpled to the sand. And he said no more and heard no more.

Elaine snatched up his gun, and leveled it quickly.

"Huh-uh, prince. You gave me an idea, but I get ideas, too. L'il Elaine's dead. L'il Elaine's in the clear. This is your gun and you shot him, and he shot you and her. And—"

"Elaine!" Toddy's voice shook. "For your own sake, don't! The government men are bound to be near here. They probably missed us in the rain, but those shots are sure to—"

"D—don't make me laugh, prince. D-don't m-make me laugh . . . "

She began to rock with laughter; it pealed out, shrill, delighted, infectious. And suddenly Toddy was laughing with her. Laughing and ridding himself of something, the last, fragile, frazzled tie. "L-like"—she was shrieking—"like Milt said, prince, you d-don't fit the part!"

That was the way he would always remember her—the monkey face twisted with merriment, the scrawny, rain-drenched figure rocking in the abrupt pitiless glow of floodlights, laughing as the guns of the T-men began to chatter.

So he would always remember her, but it was like remembering another person. Someone he had never known.

The gizmo, the golden, deceptive, brass-filled gizmo, was gone at last.

THE END